Rattlesnake Hill

A Berkshire Hilltown Mystery

Rattlesnake Hill
A Berkshire Hilltown Mystery

Leslie Wheeler

Encircle Publications, LLC
Farmington, Maine U.S.A.

Paperback ISBN 13: 978-1-893035-81-2
E-book ISBN 13: 978-1-893035-83-6

Library of Congress Control Number: 2017951090

Editor: Cynthia Brackett-Vincent
Book design: Eddie Vincent
Cover design: Devin McGuire
Cover images: © Shutterstock.com
Author photograph: © Focus Photography

Published by: Encircle Publications, LLC
PO Box 187
Farmington, ME 04938

Visit: http://encirclepub.com

Printed in U.S.A.

Publisher's Cataloging-in-Publication data

Names: Wheeler, Leslie, author.
Title: Rattlesnake hill / Leslie Wheeler.
Series: A Berkshire Hilltown Mystery
Description: Farmington, ME: Encircle Publications, LLC, 2018.
Identifiers: ISBN 978-1-893035-81-2 (pbk.) | 978-1-893035-83-6 (ebook) | LCCN 2017951090
Subjects: LCC Family--Fiction. | Murder--Fiction. | City and town life--Fiction. | Massachusetts--Fiction. | Man-woman relationships--Fiction. | Mystery fiction. | Suspense fiction. | BISAC FICTION / Mystery & Detective / Women Sleuths | FICTION / Thrillers / Suspense
Classification: LCC PS3623.H435 R38 2018 | DDC 813.6--dc23

Dedication

For Nick, a boy when I began this book, and now a man.

Acknowledgements

Every book has a story behind it and *Rattlesnake Hill* has a long one. It began more years ago than I like to admit, as a sequel to the first book in my Miranda Lewis mystery series. But about a hundred pages in, in the midst of a crucial scene, I suddenly realized it wasn't Miranda's story, but someone else's. It took time to determine who this character was, even more time to figure out exactly what her story was. Meanwhile, I wrote two more Miranda Lewis mysteries and numerous short stories, but I kept coming back to *Rattlesnake Hill*, because the story and its setting in the Berkshire Hills of Western Massachusetts remained close to my heart.

As always, I'm grateful to the members of my writers' critique group, past and present—Mark Ammons, Katherine Fast, Virginia Mackey, Cheryl Marceau, and Barbara Ross—for their patience in reading many different drafts, as I struggled to find my way. I also want to thank members of the New England Chapter of Sisters in Crime, whose positive responses to parts of the book I read aloud at meetings, encouraged me to continue. I am further grateful to Ann Collette and John Helfers for their thoughtful reading of the manuscript as a whole and for their suggestions, some of which I initially resisted, that made this a better book. The master class I took from Ramona DeFelice Long helped me over various hurdles during the final, major overhaul of the manuscript. Thanks go also to the New Marlborough Land Trust for showing me places I didn't know existed in my town, including the locale for the book's climax; and to Toby Peltz, for his help in framing the action of that climax. Additional thanks go to Gordon Aalborg and Cynthia Brackett-

Vincent for their careful editing of the manuscript.

Last but not least, I owe a huge debt of gratitude to my family: to my late husband, Robert A. Stein, and to our son, Nicholas L. Stein, for their love and support and for the wonderful times we shared in the Berkshires. For Nick, it was a place where he could enjoy a Huck Finn boyhood, filled with fun and adventure; for Bob, a refuge, where nothing bad ever happened—or so he thought. For me, the Berkshires were and continue to be a source of inspiration. Yet while I appreciate the beauty and peace of the area, as a mystery writer, I'm also drawn to its dark side. And that duality is what I've tried to capture in *Rattlesnake Hill*.

Finally, I want thank my intrepid ancestor, Benjamin Wheeler, for leaving his home in Marlborough, Massachusetts, and pushing through miles of wilderness to found the town where I have a home.

*****

The epigraph that begins this novel was adapted from the hymn, "We Cannot Think of Them as Dead," by Frederick Lucian Hosmer, first published in *The Thought of God*, first series, 1885, second series, 1894. I heard a version of this hymn spoken as part of a "Day of the Dead" service at First Parish, Unitarian/Universalist Church in Cambridge, Massachusetts, sometime in the 1990s.

We cannot think of them as dead who walk with us no more; what they have been to us has left its seal and sign engraven deep within.

—Frederick Lucian Hosmer

Part I: The White Stag

Chapter 1

*Three families lived on Rattlesnake Hill when I was a girl.
At the top of the hill you had the Whittemores. They were
rich folks from New York City. They built a big, brick house
and spent the summers there. That mansion seemed like
paradise to us Judds. We'd look up at it from our farm
and pretend we were just a few rungs below the Pearly
Gates. Beyond the Whittemores, you had the Barkers. They
were a different sort. Backsliders, we called 'em, because
everyone agreed they'd fallen from grace long ago. They
lived on the wild back side of the hill, among the timber
rattlesnakes. They made money off those snakes in the
early days. They'd bring the tails to the town treasurer
for a reward of two pennies a tail. Folks said it was the
rattlesnake venom in their blood gave 'em such violent
tempers.*

—Recollections of Emily Goodale

"Whaddya think?" Brandy Russo asked, as they wrapped up
the tour of the house on Rattlesnake Hill.

"It's nice, but . . ." Kathryn didn't want to sound too eager, lest the
realtor jack up the rent. Also, the house seemed almost too good to be
true. There must be a catch somewhere.

"Look what you're getting," Brandy barged on. "Charming shingle-
style contemporary on eighteen secluded acres. Three bedrooms. One

3

and one-half baths. Large, fully equipped kitchen. Separate dining room. Spacious living room. At $1000 a month this place is a steal."

It was a bargain all right, but Kathryn wasn't quite ready to commit. "I'm surprised no one's snatched it up already."

Brandy coughed. "A family had it for the summer and through the leaf-peeping season. But once the foliage was gone, they split. As for skiers, forget it. Gordon Farley—he's the owner—won't rent to them."

"Why not?"

"Tenants-from-hell. Come in droves, track snow onto lovely hardwood floors like these." Brandy tapped a pegged oak floorboard with the stubbed toe of her high heel. "Party all night and nearly set the house on fire fiddling with that." She jabbed a bitten-down nail at the white enameled Scandinavian wood stove that stood on a slate hearth in the living room. "Leave a ton of trash behind, too. Whereas someone like you," her voice switched to a soft purr, "is an ideal tenant. Single but mature. No kids, no pets."

"I . . . um . . . have a cat."

"One little kitty won't bother Gordon," Brandy backpedaled. "Not with the menagerie he talked about having here. One week it was quail, the next, llamas, then buffalo."

Kathryn smiled. "Sounds like a frustrated zookeeper."

"More like a gentleman farmer with time on his hands and money to burn."

A sour note crept into Brandy's voice. Did it reflect the attitude of a struggling local toward a wealthy outsider? Kathryn had only spent a few hours with Brandy, yet already she sensed a grittiness born of adversity.

Brandy appeared to be several years older than Kathryn; late thirties or early forties. She might have been pretty once, but now her dirty blonde hair hung lank and lusterless, and fault-lines showed in her face despite a heavy coat of make-up. Her breath and clothes reeked of nicotine, the rank odor Kathryn associated with dirty dishes and despair.

"What'd you say you're gonna do while you're here?" Brandy asked.

4

"Research."

"This have to do with your job?"

"Actually not. My ancestors lived in New Nottingham over a hundred years ago, and I want to find out more about them."

"A hundred years ago—wow!" Brandy's glazed expression belied her enthusiasm. "But you've got a paying job, don't you?"

Kathryn nodded. "I'm the curator of prints and photographs at a small private library in Boston. I'm able to take time off, because the building's being renovated, and the collection I oversee is in storage. So there's not much for me to do right now. Still, I plan on keeping in touch with my boss. How's the internet connection here?"

"Fine," Brandy said quickly.

"There's Wi-Fi?"

"The village doesn't have cable yet, but I'm sure it'll happen any day now."

"DSL?"

"Dial-up. There's Wi-Fi in Great Barrington, though, and it's only a twenty-minute drive away."

Hmm. Maybe this was the catch she'd worried about. "What about cell reception?"

Brandy cleared her throat. "You won't get a signal here, but I've heard there are hotspots further up the hill. Besides, convenient as it is, technology can be a huge distraction. I think you'll find that the less of it you have, the more you'll accomplish while you're here. Oh, I almost forgot." Brandy's eyes gleamed like a gambler's about to play her ace-in-the-hole. She swept across the room, heels clicking on the already extolled hardwood floor. With a dramatic flourish, she flung back heavy curtains revealing a panoramic sliding glass door.

The land behind the house sloped down to a pond, fringed by tawny cattails and embedded in the rocky earth like a large shard of antique glass. Beyond the pond, stubbled fields gave way to woods. Deciduous trees, bare of leaves and dun-colored except where bittersweet had caught the branches in an orange stranglehold, formed the front line of the woods' advance. Behind them stood tall sentinel pines. The sky glowed an iridescent red-orange, as if a distant city were on fire. Magnificent.

A loud crack shattered the stillness. Kathryn clutched her heart. "What was that?"

"Probably a car backfiring down the road." Brandy waved a hand dismissively.

The noise repeated: Boom, boom, boom! "Sounds like gunshots."

"Maybe. But don't worry. It's just some guy doing a little target practice."

"Does that happen a lot around here?" Much as she liked the house, she had no intention of putting herself in someone's line of fire. This was a bigger negative than the lack of Wi-Fi and cell reception.

"Oh, no. And never near houses. They always go way off in the woods."

"You're sure?"

Brandy looked Kathryn in the eye. "Would I lie to you?"

Not lie outright—just not tell the whole truth.

"So listen, there are a few more places I could show you, but why waste your time? They're nowhere as nice as this house. How about it?" Brandy thrust her face in Kathryn's.

Resisting the hard sell, Kathryn took a step backward. "Okay if I take another look around by myself?"

"Not at all." Brandy jerked the curtain pull, and the vivid tableau vanished. "I'll wait for you in the car."

Alone, Kathryn relaxed. She roamed the shadowy rooms with their curtained windows. The house was nothing like the Tudor mansion bordering the Beverly Hills Country Club, where she'd lived until her parents' divorce when she was four. Nor was it like her second Eden, her great-aunt's house on Diamond Head, where she'd spent the only happy times of her childhood. Still, she had the odd sense of being back in paradise.

She returned to the red room upstairs Brandy told her had served as a study. She'd wanted a red room when she was young, imagining it would be like waking up in a valentine. Her grandmother had talked her out of it. "You paint your room red, you'll end up loony like your mother." Her great-aunt, on the other hand, would have loved this room and the entire house with its pond and flaming sunset view. A sharp pang sliced through her.

The trip to New Nottingham in the Berkshire Hills of Western Massachusetts had been Aunt Kit's idea. Ever since Kathryn could remember, Aunt Kit had wanted to learn the identity of their family's Dark Lady, a beautiful, nameless woman in an old photograph an ancestor had brought with him to California. Long-distance inquiries proving fruitless, she finally decided a visit to the village was necessary and invited Kathryn to accompany her. "It will be wonderful seeing you after such a long time," she said over the phone. "I'm so happy you're willing to join me on a quest that's always ranked high on my bucket list."

They planned the trip for last summer, but that spring Aunt Kit died suddenly of a heart attack. She bequeathed the photograph, along with relevant correspondence, and the sum of fifty thousand dollars to Kathryn. The photograph sat on Kathryn's dresser, while she debated whether to pursue the quest alone. At first, it seemed quixotic; she'd only accepted the invitation out of a desire to please her beloved aunt. But the more she looked at the photograph, the more she understood Aunt Kit's fascination with it. "There's a story here," her aunt had often said. "A story that's waiting to be told."

She might have added, "A story with special meaning for you," because that's what Kathryn had come to believe. At some point, her aunt's pet project had become hers. Now, standing in the valentine room of this house in the village where her ancestors once lived, she seemed to hover on the brink of discovery. As if she were poised at the tip of a high diving board, waiting to take the plunge, giddy with a mixture of excitement and fear.

Chapter 2

Someone had been here recently.

He—Kathryn guessed it was a man—had sat in the very lounge chair that, tired from the drive and unpacking, she was about to settle into. Sat and popped aluminum rings off drink cans, tossing them onto the patio where they formed an untidy pile. Resisting the urge to scoop up and toss them in the trash inside, she lowered herself into the chair. Might as well enjoy the balmy Indian summer weather while it lasted. She leaned back in the chair and closed her eyes, imagining herself on the lanai of her great-aunt's house on Diamond Head, listening to her speculate about the woman in the photograph. "Who was she, and why did he carry her picture all the way across the continent without ever revealing her name?" Aunt Kit would murmur dreamily.

Who indeed? Opening her eyes, Kathryn reached for her tote. She slipped on the white gloves she wore when handling old prints and photographs. Then she removed the small, rectangular, leather-bound case from a plastic baggie. She opened the case and studied the photograph in its gilded frame. Her curator's eye told her the image was a daguerreotype, a type of early photograph made on a light-sensitive, silver-coated plate. Brown spots marched across the portrait like spreading blight on plant leaves. Still, the young woman was lovely, with large, expressive eyes and a sensuous mouth curved into a wistful smile. Her dark hair was parted in the middle and massed in a loose, old-fashioned coil around her heart-shaped face. She stared back at Kathryn, as beguiling and elusive as ever. Kathryn imagined the young woman slowly changing. Her hair uncoiled,

8

falling upon her shoulders. She sprouted limbs and a torso, and stepped out of the frame, dressed in a loose white gown like those worn by young girls gathered for a May Day dance in a photograph in the Lyceum's collection. The long, red sash tied around her waist trailed after her as she ran down the grassy slope from the patio. At the edge of the woods, the young woman turned and beckoned to her. The vision was so real that Kathryn actually rose to follow her with the same mix of excitement and fear she'd experienced in the valentine room.

She blinked and the apparition vanished. She stared hard at the place where it had been. Nothing like this had ever happened to her. She wasn't one to let her fancy run wild. She shook her head, as if to dislodge any remaining nonsense. She was alone with an old photograph; that was all.

Then not alone. The rumble of a vehicle on the driveway signaled someone's approach. Brandy with an extra set of keys or some other item related to the house? Instead of Brandy's Honda, a pickup came into view. It was a faded red like the walls of the valentine room. There was some lettering on the body, but it was too far away for her to make out.

Wait a minute. The driver must be crazy—he was headed straight for her parked car! She opened her mouth but the cry caught in her throat. The driver swung the vehicle sharply around and headed back down the driveway. That was a close call. The fool ought to pay attention to where he was going. It was probably a local who'd realized belatedly he'd come to the wrong place. Or the right place at the wrong time? Unease rippled through her.

*****

Earl Barker turned the pickup into the Farley driveway. He'd left work early so he could sit on the patio, gaze at the pond, and feel close to her. He visited as often as he could, but this afternoon's visit was special. It was All Souls' Day, the time when the line between the quick and the dead was the thinnest. While other people went to cemeteries, he came here. Her ashes had been scattered on the

9

shimmering green waters he caught sight of as his truck rounded the bend in the driveway.

He saw the pond but something else as well, something that made his heart jump. A figure stood on the grassy slope between house and pond. Even from a distance, he could tell it was a woman. Could it really be her? *Oh, Diana, oh baby.* He leaned forward with yearning. Then fear, as he remembered the harsh words they had spoken the night before her death. What if she had come back, not in love and forgiveness, but in anger? What if she turned away when he held out his arms, defiant in death as in life?

Blue metal flashed before his eyes. Shit! Earl pulled hard on the steering wheel, narrowly missing the car parked in front of the house. The near collision snapped him back to his senses. It wasn't Diana's ghost he was seeing but a living woman. The new tenant?

He'd heard rumors someone might be moving in but had dismissed them. Nobody moved here in this off-season time between the last of the foliage and the first snowfall. He'd counted on the house being empty from now until next summer. He was wrong.

Earl made a sharp U-turn in the parking area and sped back down the driveway. A deep disappointment replaced the anticipation, laced with dread, he'd felt at the outset. Disappointment and annoyance at the new tenant. She was an intruder. He hoped her stay proved as short as those of the previous tenants.

At the end of the driveway, Earl turned right. Might as well go home now—"home" to his tin can. Anger surged through him. He wanted to be out on the patio of the Farley house, dammit, not cooped up in his trailer. But he couldn't while *she* was there. He wouldn't have a chance like this for another year. She had no business moving in today of all days. Had no business moving in at all.

Earl slammed on the brakes and the truck shuddered to a stop. He bounced a fist off the steering wheel. Maybe this time he wouldn't wait for events to take their course. Maybe he'd do something to speed up the process. He cranked the pickup around again. He wouldn't spend the rest of the afternoon sulking in his trailer, no. He'd make his plans over a few beers at the White Stag.

The snake rattle that hung from his rearview mirror whirred as he zoomed downhill. He was so accustomed to its sound that he hardly heard it anymore, but now it almost seemed to be speaking to him.

Chapter 3

The phone rang and rang. Why didn't the old woman pick up? Was she too feeble to get to it? Or even worse, dead? It would be a supreme irony if the one person who had the information she wanted died before Kathryn had a chance speak to her. Finally, a woman's breathless voice came onto the line: "Hello?"

"Mrs. Goodale, this is Kathryn Stinson. I'm calling to confirm our appointment this morning."

"Em's not here. I'm her helper. Heard the phone on the way to my car. If you've got an appointment, she must of forgotten. She left the house a while ago."

"Where did she go?"

"Senior center in Great Barrington like always on Tuesday."

"When do you expect her back?"

"Dinnertime."

"Please leave her a message that I called." Kathryn gave the woman her name and number and hung up.

She was annoyed but not particularly surprised. From past experience with potential donors to the Lyceum's collection, she knew elderly people could be forgetful. But dinnertime? That was a long time to wait. Too long. Although it was only her second day in New Nottingham, she was anxious to get on with the business that had brought her here. She'd drive to Great Barrington and call on Mrs. Goodale at the senior center.

As she was about to leave, Kathryn noticed a few flies buzzing against the living room windowpanes. They must have gotten in during yesterday's move. She'd deal with them when she got back.

Amore, the cat she was taking care of while his owner was abroad, crouched in the living room, tail twitching, fixated on the flies.

*****

The receptionist at the senior center directed Kathryn to the crewel embroidery class. A half-dozen elderly women sat on folding chairs in a circle. Their heads were bent in concentration, while their needles flashed in and out of cloth stretched tight on wooden hoops. Hens scratching the dirt for grain.

"I'm looking for Emily Goodale." Kathryn spoke loudly in case Mrs. Goodale was hard of hearing.

"I'm Emily," a woman said in the cracked voice of an old record. Wisps of cotton-white hair, through which pink scalp was visible, framed features grown blurry with age. But the blue eyes that stared at her were laser-sharp.

"Kathryn Stinson. I'm sorry to bother you here, but your helper said you wouldn't be home until dinnertime."

"Dinner's at noon. You could have waited. What did you say your name is?"

"Kathryn Stinson."

"Kathryn, eh? You're a lot younger than I expected."

"I'm Kathryn Cutter Turner's great-niece. I wrote you I was coming."

Emily's blue eyes clouded briefly then cleared. "So you did. But for a long time now I've been expecting the other Kathryn."

"My great-aunt passed away last spring." This information had also been in Kathryn's letter.

"That's a crying shame. She was supposed to bring the photograph. Now she never will," Emily said plaintively.

"I have it." Again Kathryn repeated information in her letter. She hoped Emily's long-term memory was better than her short-term.

"Let me see it."

Emily snatched the photograph before Kathryn could give her white cotton gloves to put on. The old woman's eyes gleamed triumphantly but her tone was petulant. "The spots make her look diseased."

"Can I have a look, Em?" a woman sitting on Emily's left asked. Twin bull's-eyes of rouge decorated the woman's cheeks. Emily showed the portrait to the bull's-eye woman without letting her touch it.

"Looks diseased, all right," Bull's-eye remarked.

The word "disease" was passed around the circle. Heads turned to Kathryn accusingly, as if she were the epidemic's Typhoid Mary.

"The spots have been there as long as I remember," Kathryn said.

"You staying here in town?" Emily changed the subject.

"I've rented the Farley house in New Nottingham."

"The Farley house." Emily gazed pensively at the photograph. "Lovely girl, Diana," she murmured.

"Lovely . . . Diana." The words were picked up and passed around the circle again.

"Her name's Diana?" Kathryn asked eagerly.

"What?"

"The woman in the photograph."

"No. Diana was Gordon's wife."

"They're divorced?"

"Dead," Emily said in a dirge-like tone.

"Dead," the chorus echoed.

"Like her." Emily stared mournfully at the photograph.

"Who was she?" Kathryn tried again.

"His wife."

"I meant the woman in the photograph." Kathryn tried to keep the exasperation out of her voice. "Do you know who she was?"

Emily's blue eyes fixed on her. "Been to the house yet?"

"I moved in yesterday."

"I meant the Cutter house."

Kathryn stared at Emily, surprised. "My great-aunt told me it burned down years ago."

"Foundation's still there. Ruins of the paper mill your family owned, too. Think you'd want to see those places. When you've visited 'em, come back and we'll talk."

"But—"

"Go now." Emily waved Kathryn away like a queen dismissing an unlucky supplicant.

Kathryn had turned to leave when she remembered the photograph. "I'd like the picture back, please."

Emily held out empty hands. "I already gave it to you. You saw her take it, didn't you?" she appealed to the Greek chorus. Most of the women looked unsure, but Bull's-eye said, "It's right there in your lap, Em."

Emily glared at Bull's-eye. "Must've set it down without realizing it. You don't mind if I keep it just for now, do you?"

She looked at Kathryn so beseechingly that Kathryn was half tempted to let her have the photograph for the time being. But no, best to keep it. Emily hadn't told her anything, and had even set her a task she needed to complete before she would. "I'd like it back," she repeated. Reluctantly, Emily surrendered the photograph. "I'll see you again after I've been to the Cutter house site and mill ruins," Kathryn said in parting.

Emily gazed forlornly at the empty place in her lap. "Be sure to bring the photograph."

Outside, Kathryn collected her thoughts. The meeting hadn't gone as she'd hoped. She hadn't learned the mystery woman's name, and Emily had even tried to hold onto the photograph. Was the old woman genuinely confused, or was it all an act? She knew Emily could be difficult from Aunt Kit's correspondence.

When Aunt Kit had first written to ask if Emily could identify the photograph, she'd included a good-quality copy. Emily had rejected copy after copy, claiming she needed to see the original to make a proper identification. She wanted Aunt Kit to mail her the photograph, but Aunt Kit was unwilling to part with it. Finally, they agreed that Aunt Kit would bring the photograph when she came for a visit.

Why did Emily want the photograph so much? Obviously, she had some personal connection to it, but what was it? Another layer of mystery had been added to the daguerreotype. She'd have to peel away these layers until she arrived at the truth. The next step was to visit the remains of the house and mill. That wouldn't be so hard, would it?

Chapter 4

*My cousins and I were scared to death of Old Man Barker
because we heard he'd murdered someone a long time ago.
When I knew him, he was well into his eighties with matted,
gray hair, cloudy blind eyes, and a face and arms that were
blackened from years of work over a hot forge.*

*The Barkers made their living running a smithy—now an
auto body shop—next to their house. In the fall, there was a
steady stream of traffic to the forge. Farmers brought their
horses to have their shoes sharpened so they'd get through
the snow better. Sometimes we saw Old Man Barker riding
in a wagon beside another member of the clan on their way
to pick up shipments of iron that came by train to Great
Barrington.*

*When Old Man Barker showed up in the village, we
children scampered to the other side of the street. But one
time a group of older boys shouted insults and pelted him
with stones. He shook his cane at them, hollering like a
gored bull.*

—Recollections of Emily Goodale

Emily eased her brittle bones onto the bed. She'd had her dinner
and now it was time for her nap. Through half-closed eyes, she
watched her teenage helper Sis leave the room, belly with its precious
cargo leading the way.

Lordie, she was tired! Young Kathryn had no business barging in on her at the senior center. Girl could have waited till she was home. At least she'd finally gotten a look at the actual photograph instead of those silly copies Old Kathryn kept sending. Almost got to keep it, too, but then Gertie had to tell on her. She'd have more chances, though. Young Kathryn would come again.

Shutting her eyes, she let sleep overtake her. She dreamed she was a slip of a girl frolicking in the fields of the family farm on Rattlesnake Hill. "Betcha can't catch me," she called to Cousin George.

"Bet I can!" he yelled back. Then she was off and running. Too fast for Cousin George, but not for the giant now chasing her. The earth shuddered with his heavy footfalls. She hurled herself forward in a frantic burst of energy, but her foot caught in an animal hole, bringing her down.

Rough hands turned her over. A soot-black face with dead-fish eyes peered down at her. She wanted to scream but no sound came out, even as his fingers clawed at her face.

"Who do you favor? Leonora or . . .?" he asked quietly then more and more loudly until she thought her eardrums would burst.

"Who do you favor? Who do you favor?"

She wanted desperately to answer. But his hands were on her throat, choking back her words, squeezing tighter and tighter.

She woke with a gasp. The hands that scrabbled at her neck were her own. She hadn't had that nightmare for years, not since she'd learned the truth about her childhood bogeyman. She levered herself up, twisting her head so she could see the gold medal in its glass-domed case on the dresser. Poor Clyde.

"Poor Clyde," voices echoed. She glanced around, half expecting to see the Greek Chorus from the senior center. Instead, others emerged from the shadows, insubstantial at first, but gradually assuming distinct shapes. There was her husband Walter, there her mother, there Cousin George, there her great-grandmother Aurelia Judd, there her darling Diana, there Clyde himself. They smiled and held out their arms.

How wonderful to see them again! She smiled back and reached for them. Closer and closer they came until suddenly they were too close: balloon faces pressing against her, sucking up the air, making her dizzy and weak. She tried to push them away, but she had no strength left in her arms. No strength to stop Diana from kissing her cheek with bloated lips. A kiss that numbed the entire left side of her face.

She knew then why they were here, and the knowledge gave her the will to resist. "Go away! I'm not ready yet!" she cried, flinging out her arms. They scattered and grew transparent, dissolving into the air like so many soap bubbles.

The room stopped spinning. She poked her left cheek with a finger and felt the sensation returning. Thank heaven! She wouldn't tell anyone about this. If her daughters ever found out, they'd shut her away in a nursing home. She couldn't allow that. She would die at home, surrounded by familiar faces. But first she had work to do, promises to keep.

Emily opened the nightstand drawer and surveyed the contents. Everything was there, lying in readiness for the last important act of her life.

Chapter 5

Kathryn heard the buzzing before she saw the flies blanketing the living room windows. She attacked them with a flyswatter. Soon bodies smeared the glass and littered the floor. Yet by the time she'd swept the floor and returned with a spray bottle of window cleaner, more live flies had joined the dead ones. There seemed to be no end to them.

In desperation, she drove to the village. Perched on the crest of one of the area's many hills, New Nottingham consisted of a town hall, a general store, a post office, a meetinghouse, and about a dozen houses. She pulled up in front of the general store, where a hand-lettered sign promised "Cold Beer, Cigarettes, Guns, Ammo, Groceries, and Nite Crawlers." A man with a bald, spud-shaped head sat on a bench next to the sign. As if her arrival were a signal for him to depart, he rose and vanished within.

Puzzled, she entered the store. A huge refrigerator case of beer stood front and center. Next to it was a case containing cigarettes. Their odor filled the air, along with the smell of smoked meat that seemed to come from a large man hunkered in front of the deli case in back. He had a thick neck and big hands spilling from the sleeves of his camouflage jacket like slabs of streaky bacon.

The man with the potato-shaped head emerged from a storeroom in back and ambled toward her, smiling. "You must be Miz Stinson, the new tenant at the Farley place." He extended a hand. "Lucas Rogers."

She looked at him, dumbfounded. "How did you know?"

"Word gets around. You're in luck. I just happen to have a box of fly strips left."

Her astonishment grew. "How do you know that's what I came for?"

"Sunny day like this always brings out the flies there. Everybody knows that."

Everybody but her, the outsider. "You mean whenever there's a nice day, I'm going to have a swarm of flies inside?"

"Only in the fall and spring. Come winter they'll die off, and by summer they're happy to be outdoors like the rest of us."

The deli case door slammed shut.

"Hey, Garth, you bagged the white stag yet?" Rogers called.

"Up yours!" the other man growled.

Rogers turned back to Kathryn with a shrug. "As I was saying, the flies are only bad in the fall and spring."

"Isn't there anything I can do besides swatting and putting up fly strips?"

Rogers scratched his head. "Could have an exterminator come. Have to get Gordon's permission, though. Believe he looked into it once and even got an estimate of the cost, but Diana put the kibosh on that."

"Why?"

"Didn't want pesticides killing the birds, poisoning the pond. Knowing her, she probably felt the flies had as much right to live as the rest of us."

Feet shuffled toward her. The door of the refrigerator case rattled. The smokehouse smell was overpowering. She fought back nausea.

". . . raw meat," Rogers said.

"What?"

"Could try raw meat. Put it in a glass jar with a cover and some holes, stick the jar outdoors, and it's supposed to draw the flies out."

The thought of putrefying meat blackened with flies made her even more ill. She'd only try it as a last resort. "Thanks for the tip. What do I owe you?"

Rogers put the fly strip box into a bag. "No charge for this one. Be getting more in a few days."

"Thanks." Kathryn took the bag and turned to go, eager for some fresh air. At the same moment, the smokehouse man also turned. He looked at her with narrowed eyes. The next instant, he rammed her shoulder with a thirty-pack of beer. "Ouch!" Without apologizing, he lumbered from the store. She rubbed her stinging shoulder. "*Who* was that?"

"Garth Barker. Youngest of the boys. Meanest, too. Neighbor of yours on the hill."

Terrific. "Why would he do that? He doesn't even know me."

"Dunno. Could've been the talk about Diana set him off."

Diana again. "I don't understand."

"Bad blood between 'em. Didn't want him hunting on her land and made a fuss about it." Rogers leaned over the counter and lowered his voice. "Was his gun killed her."

Outrage boiled within Kathryn. "If he shot her, why's he on the loose?"

Rogers motioned for her to keep her voice down. "I said his gun, not him. Anyways, could be he was mad at me for ribbing him about the white stag and took it out on you."

"What's the white stag?"

"Big light-colored buck roams the woods around here. Never seen it myself and don't know of anyone who has. But that don't stop Garth from trying to kill it."

"That's crazy."

Rogers held out his hands, palms up. "What can I tell you?"

Chapter 6

Kathryn attached three fly strips to a ceiling beam and watched with satisfaction as flies began to take the bait. Leaving the strips to do their work, she went upstairs. In the hallway a lone fly buzzed near the trapdoor leading to the attic. It was the one place Brandy hadn't showed her. It had never been finished, Brandy explained, so there was no point going up. Could the flies be getting in through the attic? A window could have been left ajar, and there might be a dead critter to attract them.

Unfolding the wooden ladder, she climbed up. Pieces of plywood created a partial flooring over rolls of pink fiberglass insulation. Mouse dung speckled the plywood, and there was an empty tray of poison, but no small, furry body. No open window either. Old suitcases, file drawers, and boxes of papers and magazines lay haphazardly on the plywood. The detritus of the lives lived in this house. Gordon Farley's life and Diana's.

In her work as a curator, Kathryn had spent hours going through people's attics in search of pictorial treasures. But she saw nothing of interest here, unless it was the 10 x 13 color photograph in a tarnished silver frame lying just out of reach on a cushion of insulation. Stepping gingerly onto the plywood, she grasped a corner of the frame and picked it up. Graffiti marred the photograph of a woman. Someone had drawn glasses and a mustache on her face, then, incongruously, huge breasts and a thatch of pubic hair on her body. Devil's horns sprouted from her head. The words "*Fuck you, bitch*" were scrawled across the picture in black marker.

Kathryn's insides knotted. People weren't always kind to family photos. They cut out the heads of detested relatives and sometimes cropped entire groupings, but she'd never seen anything quite as bad as this. It struck her as particularly nasty to deface what looked like a wedding picture, judging from the woman's long white dress. If this was Diana Farley's wedding picture, why had her husband left it here? And who had done this to it? Someone who'd feuded with her like Garth Barker? Or . . .? Brandy had told her a family had rented the house for the summer and through the leaf-peeping season. Maybe one of the kids had come up here and wrecked the photograph as a prank.

She wanted to believe this because the other possibility was too disturbing. The air felt suddenly close. She put down the photograph and fled the attic, then the house in favor of a lounge chair on the patio.

The pond lay serene and still in the late afternoon light. Its peacefulness seeped into her until her body relaxed, her mind cleared, and she was transported back to a rare moment of happiness.

She sat with Aunt Kit on the lanai of the house on Diamond Head, watching the red ball of sun slip into the Pacific. The air was sweet with plumeria and the orchids Aunt Kit raised. Aunt Kit wore a flowery muu-muu which, as she liked to say, "hid a multitude of sins." In her hand was a Mai Tai; in Kathryn's a Shirley Temple with a magenta paper umbrella stuck in the glass.

She twirled the paper umbrella back and forth while Aunt Kit held forth on her favorite topic: the mysterious young woman in the photograph. "Now why would our ancestor, Jared Cutter, take her picture all the way to California if he wasn't crazy about her? Why leave in the first place? He had everything he wanted in New Nottingham: a big house, loads of money, the whole town looking up to him. Why turn his back on all that unless he was running away from a great sadness? I think it had to do with her. Maybe she died before they could marry. Maybe she married someone else. Whatever happened, he was so heartbroken he couldn't bring himself to ever speak her name. So after all these years we don't know a thing about her. But one day I'm going to find out!" For emphasis, Aunt Kit stabbed the harpoon she used as a cane into the pavement of the lanai.

23

Kathryn dropped the leaf she'd been twirling in lieu of a paper umbrella. That wasn't the sound of metal banging into pavement but a gunshot. Then another and another. Dammit! Time to have a straight talk with Brandy.

Chapter 7

"I'm sorry about those flies," Brandy said over drinks, a white wine spritzer for Kathryn, bourbon on the rocks for Brandy, at a Great Barrington watering hole. "I would've mentioned them, but it never occurred to me they'd be a problem. Who would've thought we'd have such hot weather in November? I'm gonna call the exterminator right now." She whipped out her cell phone and frowned.

"What's the matter?"

"The thing is it's kinda expensive. More trouble than you'd think, too. They can't just set off a bomb. They have to drill all these tiny holes in the walls and fill 'em with poison. And I'd have to get Gordon's approval. So if you can just put up with the flies a little longer, I'm sure the weather'll change soon. In the meantime, I'll send a cleaning person to take care of the mess, at no charge to you."

"I guess that will be okay." Kathryn suspected that Brandy was someone who always promised more than she could deliver.

"Fantastic!" Brandy beamed. "Now, about that other little problem you mentioned, I'm gonna find out who's doing that target practice and make sure he does it elsewhere."

"I'd appreciate that."

"I want you to be happy up there on the hill, Kathryn. So . . . met any of your neighbors yet?" Brandy's smile was still pasted on, but Kathryn noticed a wary look in her eyes.

"Only one: Garth Barker."

Brandy swallowed hard. "Nice guy, huh?"

"He rammed my shoulder with a thirty-pack at the general store. I'm pretty sure it was deliberate."

Fault-lines appeared in Brandy's carefully made-up face. "Really? Well, don't take it personally. He was probably having a bad day."

"Lucas Rogers said Garth didn't get on with Diana Farley," Kathryn blurted. "That his gun killed her."

Brandy's features sagged. "His gun, yes," she repeated dully.

"Someone else shot Diana with it?"

Brandy nodded. "It was an accident."

"What happened?"

Brandy gulped down the rest of her bourbon and stood. "I need a refill, what about you?"

"I'm fine."

Brandy returned with her refill and a bowl of peanuts. After taking a swig, she said, "Diana was killed during Deer Week. She was a fool to go into the woods when they were crawling with hunters."

"A hunter shot her?"

Brandy shook her glass, the ice rattling like old bones. "Yeah."

"Why did he have Garth's gun?"

"He . . . uh . . . borrowed it. And like I said, it was an accident. Happened a while ago, before they passed the law."

"What law?"

"The one that says you can't hunt on someone else's property without written permission. It's made things a lot safer." Brandy glanced at her watch. "Gotta run. I'm supposed to meet a friend in Lenox in twenty."

Kathryn reached for her wallet. "I'll take care of it," Brandy said.

They exited the bar into a narrow brick alley that led to Railroad Street. As they proceeded single-file with Brandy in the lead, Brandy said, "I'll let you know when the cleaning person will be coming. Anything else give me a buzz."

"There is something else," Kathryn said. "A family rented the house before me?"

"That's right."

"So there was at least one child in the house?"

"Actually two. A toddler and a four-year-old. Why do you ask?"

Kathryn explained about finding the defaced photograph in the attic.

Brandy staggered, as if struck from behind.

"Are you all right?"

Brandy pressed a hand against the wall to steady herself. "My heel caught in a crack between the bricks. Oughta fix this walkway before someone falls and breaks a leg. But that's awful! I can't imagine who'd do such a thing."

"Does anyone besides you, me, and Gordon Farley have keys to the house?"

"No, though I've sometimes given keys to various handymen when there was repair work to be done. But I don't think any of them—no, it must've been some visiting kid. Gotta dash. Call if you need anything." Her heels clacked on the bricks, sure-footed in flight.

Chapter 8

B randy poured more bourbon into her glass. She stared blearily at the magnetic letters on her refrigerator door. "Be Good to Yourself." "You are Special." "You Are About to Realize Your Full Potential." What a crock!

The sayings came from fortune cookies and the inspirational calendar Millie had given her last Christmas, along with a pot of Paperwhite Narcissus bulbs. She'd been thrilled when the first green shoots pushed through the stones in the pot. Then, without warning, they withered and died.

Like a lot of things in her life. Her husband's early death from cancer. Their son's falling in with the wrong crowd and getting into trouble.

Brandy ground the stub of her Marlboro Lite into the overflowing ashtray, lit another and dragged deeply. She'd been trying to kick the habit for years. But she couldn't quit now. Not with another November to get through.

Someone had once told her April was the cruelest month. He was wrong. It was November.

She'd had such high hopes when she and her son had moved here from Brooklyn. Hopes of making a new start in a place most people thought was idyllic. They didn't know that behind the Berkshires of Tanglewood picnics and The Boston Symphony Orchestra under the stars, of picture-postcard villages with chi-chi shops and restaurants, lay another Berkshires, the Berserkshires, she called it, where people did crazy, violent things. Unless she sold the Farley house she was stuck here.

The current tenant might be her ticket out of Dodge, but already, she felt the downward spiral beginning. It had started the day she showed Kathryn the house with Garth and his goddamn gunshots.

Deer Week isn't until the end of November, she'd complained to him afterward. *Can't you hold off your shooting till then, or do it somewhere else?* The bastard told her to keep her nose out of it. He'd hunt where and when he felt like it. Then he said something that made no sense at all. Told her he wasn't after any old deer but the white stag. And he was gonna bag 'im if it was the last thing he did.

There was a bar by that name, where Garth and his cronies went drinking every night. She'd never heard of any such animal, though. Must have been the booze talking.

Should've known better than to approach him. Hadn't done a bit of good. And it might've have made things worse by turning Garth against Kathryn. That was probably why he'd rammed her with a case of beer.

Then Lucas had to tell Kathryn Garth's gun killed Diana, and Kathryn had found Diana's picture messed up with graffiti. She couldn't pull the wool over Kathryn's eyes forever.

Brandy downed more bourbon, grateful for the buzz. What the hell? What was the worst that could happen? Kathryn would realize the flies were the least of her worries and hightail it back to the city. She'd have to find another buyer then, but she'd been there before; she could deal with it.

As Brandy took another swig, an ice cube hit the exposed nerve of a tooth that had lost the cap put on in better days. The chill snapped her out of her alcoholic haze. Kathryn's leaving wasn't the worst that could happen. There was worse—much worse.

Oh, Brian, oh dear God, no!

Chapter 9

Obadiah Cutter was the first settler of New Nottingham. He built a cabin on the banks of Leech Pond, now called Leech Swamp, and spent the winter of 1737 there. Folks say he nearly starved, because the Indians made him use a bow and arrow instead of his gun.

By the time he died, fifty years later, New Nottingham was a thriving town. The Cutters were the wealthiest family. They built a farmhouse on the site of Obadiah's cabin and established a paper mill nearby. After the last Cutter left the area in the 1850s, the house fell into disrepair. A fire destroyed all but the foundation. The mill fared better. It was bought by another family who ran it into the late 1880s when it finally closed for good. The ruins of the mill are still there. You can see stone entry pillars, high walls, and underground storage rooms. My cousins and I liked to play hide-and-seek in the ruined mill. It was also a popular meeting place for courting couples.

— Recollections of Emily Goodale

Pickups filled the parking area of the general store when Kathryn drove to the village the next morning. She squeezed into a space next to a faded red truck like the one that had pulled into the Farley driveway a few days ago. The lettering on it read: "Earl Barker,

Excavating." She hoped this Barker wouldn't be as unpleasant as the one she'd already met.

Inside, a group of men lounged around the deli counter at the rear, drinking coffee and talking. They fell silent at the sight of her. She gripped her plastic mug, nervous as a kid on the first day of school.

"Hey, Starstruck, have to go to Barrington for your Cap-poo-chee-no," a lean, well-muscled man drawled. He was ruggedly handsome, his blue eyes set off by a deep tan.

The men laughed. A prickly heat grew on her face. She should have known better than to bring a Starstruck Coffee Traders mug in here. Too late now. She marched up to the counter and put down the mug. "Coffee, please." Lucas Rogers poured in black liquid.

"That'll put hair on your chest," the blue-eyed man jeered. "Sure you don't want cream or sugar?" He gestured at an open pint of half and half and a box of sugar.

Sensing this was a test, she shook her head and took a drink. The acrid brew roiled her stomach like battery acid. It was all she could do to keep from clutching her corroded insides.

"That's a first," the man declared. "Nobody, but no-o-body round here drinks Lucas's coffee black. We believe in saving our guts for better things, don't we, boys?"

The "boys" responded with a chorus of agreement.

"Now, Earl, my coffee's not that bad," Rogers grumbled.

So the blue-eyed man was Earl Barker. "It's fine," she fibbed. Handing Rogers a couple of dollar bills, she turned to go.

"See you've got a pussycat," Earl Barker called after her.

She spun around. They faced each other like gunslingers, hands on mugs instead of holsters. "How do you know?"

"Noticed it in the window when I was up there checking the driveway the other day. Heavy rains last summer made a mess of it. Did some patchwork, but the whole driveway needs to be re-graded. Then I'll have to put down several truckloads of gravel. Gordon wants an estimate before I begin."

"You'll be starting soon?" Something else Brandy hadn't mentioned.

"Yup. Gets any worse, you'll have a tough time getting out. Don't think you wanna be stuck up there all by your lonesome."

"No." Which was worse: being stranded, or having Earl Barker around on a daily basis?

Outside, she dumped the coffee into the bushes and headed to the town hall. A girl with cobweb-fine white blonde hair and a pasty complexion sat behind the desk in the town clerk's office, head bent over a sheaf of papers. She looked too young for a town official, so maybe she was filling in for her mother. The nameplate on the desk said "Cheryl Barker."

"I'm looking for Cheryl Barker," Kathryn said.

The girl glanced up and quickly turned her face to one side, though not before Kathryn glimpsed an ugly purplish bruise under her left eye. "I'm Cheryl."

"Of course," Kathryn said quickly, trying to keep her eyes off the bruise. "I'm new here, renting the Farley house. If you're related to Garth, we must be neighbors."

The girl rested her chin in her hand, fingertips covering the bruise. "Garth's my husband."

Poor kid married to that brute. "Kathryn Stinson. Nice to meet you," she said in an effort to put the girl at ease.

"You, too," the girl said shyly. "What can I do for you?"

"I'm trying to locate house and mill sites dating back to the 1850s. Do you perhaps have any town maps from then?"

Cheryl shook her head. "You need to talk to Millie. She's a member of the historical society, works over at the post office."

"Thanks."

The post office was located in a small building next to the general store with a shared parking area. Behind the counter, a petite woman with a pretty face waved a roll of catalogs and shook her head with a swish of her strawberry blonde ponytail. "Not gonna fit," she muttered. Yanking a packing box from under the counter, she tossed in the catalogs.

"Mail boxes must fill up fast with all the junk mail that comes nowadays," Kathryn remarked.

"No kidding!" The petite woman laughed. She wore a tailored blue pants suit that matched her eyes and showed off her hourglass figure. If there was one word that best described her it was "perky." "This particular family won't be back till next summer, so it's gonna take a storage bin to hold all their mail. And most of it will get thrown out, anyway. But that's the breaks," she finished with a good-natured shrug of her shoulders. "How can I help you?"

"I'd like to rent a box."

"Only if you swear to check it regularly."

Kathryn held up her right hand. "I swear."

The woman gave her a form to fill out and wrote the box number and combination on a piece of paper. "I'm Millie, by the way."

"Kathryn Stinson."

Millie's handshake was firm and cordial. Liking her already, Kathryn moved on to the next item of business. "Are there maps of the town dating back to the 1850s? I ask because I'm trying to locate what's left of the house and mill that belonged to my ancestors, the Cutters."

Millie blinked and a shadow crossed her face. The next moment, her expression was as open and friendly as before. "The Registry of Deeds in Great Barrington has the colonial records and proprietary plans for all the towns in Southern Berkshire County. If you want to save yourself some legwork, we've got a copy of the original plan for New Nottingham and other old maps at the historical society room in the basement of the town hall. It's closed now, but if you don't mind waiting till noon when I take my lunch break, I'll be glad to show you what we have."

*****

"Right on time." Millie beamed when Kathryn walked into the post office at noon. As they left the building, Earl Barker hopped from his pickup.

"'Lo, Mill, Starstruck. Better watch out for her, Mill. She drinks Lucas's coffee black!" He grinned.

Millie rolled her eyes. "Grow up, Earl," she said in a voice like the rap of a ruler. "So he pulled the black coffee trick on you," she continued as they walked across the street to the town hall. "Don't take it personally. He tries that with every newcomer. Can't help it his head stayed stuck in high school."

"Really?"

"I should know. I was married to the man for over twenty years."

"You were married to *him*?" Hard to imagine this brisk, self-confident woman tying the knot with that joker.

Millie laughed. "Earl's not so bad. Just doesn't know how to behave sometimes."

"Misbehaving seems to run in the family. Among the men, that is." She told Millie about yesterday's encounter with Garth, including what Lucas Rogers had told her about Garth's feud with Diana Farley.

"It's true Garth and Diana didn't get on, but that was some time ago," Millie said as they approached a side door to the town hall.

"And she's dead now."

Millie took out a bunch of keys. "Yes."

"What about Diana and Earl?" Kathryn asked on an impulse. "Was there bad blood between them, too?"

Millie frowned at a strip of peeling paint on the door. "Earl cleared the land for the Farleys, did the driveway, and dug out the pond. He and Diana got along fine—just fine." She jammed a key into the lock with sudden ferocity. The door opened, and a miasma of cold, mildewed air wafted from below. Kathryn wrinkled her nose.

"Sorry about that," Millie apologized, as they descended the steps. "The boiler burst and flooded the basement several years ago, and we've never been able to get rid of the smell. Still, we're lucky to have this space for our collection."

The room resembled an old curiosity shop. In the center stood an oak schoolteacher's desk, its surface stained with India ink and one side blackened, probably from years of proximity to a wood stove. An assortment of rickety chairs surrounded the desk. The shelves and display cases lining the wall held a hodgepodge of items: an antique sewing machine, part of a plow, a dusty tea set, a handful of arrowheads, and a rusty black top hat.

Millie removed a yellowed map in a glass frame from the wall and laid it on the desktop.

"This is a copy of the original plan of the town, showing the first proprietors."

Examining the plan, Kathryn found a large rectangle with the name "Cutter." Inside the rectangle were two small squares near a kidney shape with a wavy line attached to it. The squares must mark the locations of the house and mill, but what about the kidney shape and the wavy line? Millie told her they represented Leech Pond—or rather Leech Swamp—and the brook that ran into it.

"Do the brook and Leech Swamp show up on contemporary maps?" Kathryn asked.

"Here. See for yourself." Millie handed her a recent relief map of the area.

After Kathryn had located both features she said, "Why are the house and mill so far from the present town?"

"The town moved, but the house and mill stayed put."

"Who owns the property now?"

"Gordon Farley. It's in his woods."

"Then it's right in my backyard. That should make it easy to find."

"You're not planning to go there now, are you?" Millie sounded alarmed.

"Yes. Why not?"

"I wouldn't go into those woods now if you paid me," Millie declared.

"Why? I heard that since the town passed the 'written permission' law, the woods aren't as dangerous as they used to be, even during Deer Week."

"Whoever told you that was wrong. It's one thing to pass a law, another to get people to observe it, particularly around here. Take it from me: you don't want to go in there now." Millie squinted into space, neck craned forward, as if straining for a glimpse of an unseen enemy. Changing the subject, she said, "If you're interested in the early history of New Nottingham, you might like to have a look at this." She rummaged in the drawer of a wooden cabinet and handed Kathryn a file folder.

"What is it?"

"Parts of Emily Goodale's recollections."

"Emily actually wrote down her recollections?" This was exciting news.

"She told them to Diana, who taped and transcribed them. When the Farleys first bought land in New Nottingham, Diana wanted to learn more about the area, especially the old farms on Rattlesnake Hill. She was referred to Emily, because Emily grew up on the Judd farm, where the Farleys built their house. Diana was so fascinated by Emily's stories about the old days she got us started gathering materials for a town history.

"Unfortunately, we lost a lot of those materials when the basement flooded. I don't know what became of the tapes Diana made, but she salvaged some of the typed pages by using a hairdryer on them. That's what's in the folder."

Kathryn flipped through the pages. Many were badly stained, and there were gaps in the sequence of page numbers, but by her rough estimate the folder contained about fifty pages. "Okay if I borrow this?"

"Sure." Millie smiled then her expression darkening, she said, "Remember what I said about not going into the woods this time of year."

Back at the general store, several men lolled on the porch with coffee, sandwiches, and smokes. Lucas Rogers was there, a man in paint-splattered overalls, and Earl Barker, joined by his brother Garth. It was easy to see they were related: same rugged features, blue eyes, and light brown hair. Yet while Earl's features were well spaced, Garth's were compressed, giving him a mean, ugly look.

Her body tensed. It's just a bunch of men, she told herself, but the silent way they watched her was intimidating.

As she approached her car, Garth lobbed his burning cigarette onto the roof of her car. He vanished into the store, the screen door banging behind him. She wanted to go after him and insist he remove the butt. Instead, she reached for it, singeing her fingers. With a cry of pain, she dropped cigarette and file folder. Loose pages scattered every which way. Laughter rang out from the porch. She glared at the men. To her surprise, they turned shame-faced, shuffled off the porch and helped her gather up the pages.

Earl brushed grit off a sheet and handed it to her. "Why did your brother do that?" she demanded.

His cool blue eyes met hers. "Shouldn't have parked in his spot, Starstruck."

"What do you mean?"

He gestured toward a large red-white-and-black Marlboro cigarette sign in the store window. "Always parks opposite that."

"Frigging macho Marlboro man," she fumed.

The skin around Earl's eyes and mouth crinkled. "Yeah," he said in the husky voice of a backwoods crooner. "Yeah."

Chapter 10

Back at the house, Kathryn plopped into a patio lounge chair with Emily Goodale's recollections. She skimmed the pages, looking for mention of the Cutters. The one brief reference told her what she already knew: Obadiah Cutter was the first settler of New Nottingham, and over time the Cutters became the wealthiest family in town. She went back to the beginning and read more carefully in case she'd missed something.

The word "paradise" caught her eye. She smiled. That's how she'd thought of the Farley house. Emily, however, was referring to another location: a mansion further up the hill that had belonged to the Whittemores. She read on—about the Barkers and how people thought the rattlesnake venom in their blood was responsible for their violent tempers. So even then they had a bad reputation.

A few pages were devoted to Old Man Barker, a bogeyman to Emily and the other children in town. Given their fear of him, Kathryn admired the spunk with which young Emily, acting on a dare, approached him.

> *One day when my uncle took a horse to the smithy to be shod, I hid in the straw at the back of the wagon. When the coast was clear, I snuck out. Old Man Barker was in the shop, removing a piece of red-hot iron from the fire with a pair of tongs. I crept up behind him and shouted "Boo!" He let go of the tongs, and the fiery iron dropped onto his boot. He kicked it off and stumbled blindly after me as I dashed back to my uncle.*

"What's going on?" my uncle demanded.

"Keep your boy out of my forge," Old Man Barker growled

"It's my niece Emily who's here," my uncle replied.

"Emily?" Old Man Barker repeated in a less angry voice. "Well then, she should know better than to sneak up on a body."

"It won't happen again," my uncle promised, hoisting me into the wagon.

Here the story took an unexpected turn. The next day, Old Man Barker, scrubbed clean and wearing his Sunday best, showed up at the Judd household and asked to see Emily.

As I stood shaking before him, he put a hand on my head, then moved it downward, tracing my face with his fingers. They were rough and calloused, but his touch was gentle. "Who does she favor?" he asked my great-grandmother, Aurelia Judd, "Leonora or her father?"

"Leonora," my great-grandmother replied softly, tears coming into her eyes.

"'Tis so." He pressed a handful of penny candy into my palm.

After that he visited me once a year. He would touch my face and ask who I favored. Then he would give me candy or a trinket. In spite of the treats, I dreaded these visits. I couldn't forget that the hands touching me had killed someone. I had many nightmares in which he went from feeling my face to strangling me. When I told my great-grandmother, she said, "If you knew the truth, you would understand he is more to be pitied than feared." But it wasn't until after Old Man Barker's death and she was near death herself that she finally told me his story.

Eager for the conclusion, Kathryn turned the page only to discover a gap in the sequence. The narrative shifted to a description of the one-room school Emily had attended as a girl. She thumbed the pages, checking to see if the missing ones were in another place. They weren't. Maybe they had never been retrieved when she dropped the folder. She drove to the village and scoured the general store parking lot without success. She even went inside and asked Lucas Rogers if anyone had found pages and left them with him.

Then she walked over to the post office. Millie sat in the rear, telephone handset wedged between her head and shoulder, her face tight with concentration, while she scribbled furiously onto a pad. Kathryn caught her eye and Millie signaled her to wait. "What can I do for you now?" Millie asked once she was off the phone.

Kathryn explained about the missing pages in Emily's recollections. "They had to do with Old Man Barker. Do you know his story?"

Millie shook her head. "I made up my mind a long time ago that what I didn't know about Earl's family couldn't hurt me."

"You didn't read about him in Emily's recollections?" Kathryn persisted.

"I never gave those pages more than a quick glance. Figured I'd wait until they appeared in print as part of the town history. But why not ask Emily? They're her recollections."

"I'll do that."

Back at the Farley house, Kathryn sat on the patio, thinking about Old Man Barker and the woman in the photograph, and how she had to get their stories from Emily. First, though, she needed to visit the house foundation and mill ruins. Millie's warning came back to her: "I wouldn't go into those woods now if you paid me." Well, she wouldn't go alone. Her boyfriend, Alan, was coming for a visit this weekend, and he could accompany her. Although he worked as an attorney for a large Boston firm, he was from Maine originally and had spent a lot of time outdoors. On one of their first dates, he took her for a long walk in the Concord woods, impressing her with his ability to navigate the confusing maze of trails.

In the meantime, she would do some exploring of her own. She'd drive up the hill and try to find the hot spots Brandy had mentioned. She was also curious to see the Whittemore estate that Emily had described as a "paradise." It had been visible from the Judd farm then, but now it no longer was.

She drove until she came to a long, gravel driveway with imposing stone pillars on either side. The high, wrought-iron gate was padlocked. Disappointed, she turned on her cell phone. No luck there either. A beat-up old car pulled up beside her. A teenage boy, wearing jeans and a black t-shirt with a logo, got out. He was tall, lanky and attractive with light brown hair, blue eyes and a friendly grin. "Looking for hotspots?" He pointed at her phone. She nodded.

"You need to drive a little further up. I can show you the exact spot. I'm Pete Barker, by the way. Earl and Millie's son."

No surprise there. He had his father's good looks, and his mother's pleasant manner. She hardly knew any teenagers, but she liked this one.

"You're the new tenant at the Farley place, right?" Pete Barker said. "From Boston?"

"Yes on both counts."

"Cool." His smile broadened. "Been to any of the clubs there?"

"Clubs?"

"Places like The House of Blues and the Paradise Rock Club."

No fan of rock music, she hadn't gone to either, but she didn't want to appear un-cool. "I've been meaning to, but . . ."

"Well, if you ever have an extra ticket, let me know and I'll be on the next bus. C'mon, I'll show you that hotspot."

She followed Pete's car up the road, stopping when he did to check for reception. Her phone picking up a signal, she gave him a thumbs up, and he drove on. She called Alan at his office to tell him the good news. The call over, she made a U-turn and started down the hill, only to pull over to admire the view. Before her stretched a checkerboard of forest and field, dotted by houses and barns like the colored pieces in a Monopoly set, and pierced by needle-like church steeples. The slumbering giant of a mountain loomed in the distance. The sun was beginning to set. She drank in the fiery beauty until the light faded to gray, and she continued on.

The two girls seemed to pop out of nowhere when she rounded a bend in the road. Kathryn swerved, slammed on the brakes and jumped from the car, heart racing. One girl was sprawled in the middle of the road, while the other tried to pull her up. "Are you all right?" Kathryn asked.

"We're okay," the standing girl said brusquely. It was Cheryl Barker.

"Liar!" the other girl cried. She had the same pasty complexion and cobweb-fine blonde hair as Cheryl, but looked even younger. She was also very pregnant. "Our car broke down a ways back and she expects me to walk all the way up the goddamn hill. I'm seven months' pregnant, for chrissake. But she don't give a shit. Don't want me to have my baby neither. Hopes I'll fall and miscarry."

"That's not true. I take you to your doctor's appointments, don't I? That's more than he ever—" Cheryl bit her lip. The other girl began to bawl.

"I can give you a lift home," Kathryn offered.

"Take it, Sis," Cheryl said. "I'll walk."

"Are you sure? I'm happy to take you."

"Thanks, but I'd rather walk," Cheryl said.

Except for an occasional muffled sob or sniffle, Sis was quiet on the drive up the hill. She merely pointed when they reached her home, a log cabin with a huge satellite dish, a rusted swing set, and various rusted appliances out front. The lights were on inside, and a pickup was parked in the driveway. Sis didn't look happy to be there and shivered even though the evening was balmy.

"Will you be okay?" Kathryn asked.

"Yeah," Sis said in a quavering voice. She got out awkwardly and wobbled toward the cabin, whimpering like a whipped puppy. Kathryn's headlights shone on the rear of the pickup, illuminating two bumper stickers. One read, "How'm I driving? Call 1-800-Fuck-You." The other was even more ominous: "Keep Honking, I'm Reloading."

On the way down, she spotted Cheryl marching determinedly uphill. With her slight figure and wispy, short hair, she might have been a child crusader from long ago. Was she, too, headed into battle against impossible odds? Kathryn slowed in case the girl had changed her mind about a ride. But with a shake of her head, Cheryl strode past.

The Farley house rose up in the shadows like the hull of an ancient ship. Too bad she hadn't thought to leave a light on. She flipped the switch in the front hallway then turned on the living room lights. Everything looked just as she'd left it: fly strips dangling from a beam like streamers from an old celebration, Amore dozing on the couch, her Boston lithography book neatly aligned on the coffee table. Yet something seemed wrong.

She was about to check upstairs when she noticed a long, narrow object that resembled a door warmer draped across the landing, one end wedged between two slats of the railing. It was sewn from a dark, patterned material that looked like snake skin. She stepped closer to examine it. Dear god, it was a snake!

Stifling a scream, she backed away before the snake could spring to life, slither toward her and strike. She held her breath. Nothing happened. Somehow, she found the courage to lob a piece of wadded paper at it.

Again nothing happened. It must be asleep or dead. How had it gotten in? She wanted to get rid of it, but the thought of touching the thing made her skin crawl. She'd have to get help, but who to call? She went into the kitchen, found an emergency number posted on the refrigerator, and dialed. After several rings a gruff male voice answered, "Lapsley, here."

"Is this . . . the police?"

"Yup."

Relief flooded her. "I need your help."

After she explained the problem, the man said, "Get a broom and a sack, laundry bag'll do fine, and—"

"No, you don't understand. I'm not going anywhere near that thing. You need to come and remove it."

"Look, Ma'am, I'm off duty now. And even if I wasn't, I got more important things to do than—"

"Please, you have to help me!" She was becoming hysterical, but she couldn't help it.

"Okay, calm down. Be there in a bit."

A bit? What did that mean? What if the snake woke up before he arrived? She wasn't taking any chances. Abandoning Amore to his fate, she flew out the kitchen door and raced around to the front to wait for Lapsley.

Ten minutes later, a police cruiser pulled up. The car looked official but not the man who got out. Unlike the city cops she was used to, Lapsley wore jeans and a plaid shirt. "So where's the snake?" He removed a sack, a long-forked stick and a shovel from the back seat.

"On the landing, halfway up to the second floor. You can't miss it."

Lapsley disappeared into the house. Kathryn waited tensely outside. If the snake attacked him, what would she do then?

To her relief, Lapsley emerged from the house a few moments later, carrying sack, stick, shovel, and the snake's inert body. He looked as though he were about to have some kind of fit.

"What's the matter?"

"Your snake isn't just dead—it's been that way a long time. It's stuffed!" Lapsley's round, ruddy cheeks quivered with laughter.

"What?"

"Don't believe me, come and touch it."

"No thanks."

"Then I'll take this critter back where he belongs."

Before she could ask him where that was, Lapsley hopped into his cruiser and roared off into the night, leaving her to wonder who had played this nasty trick on her.

Chapter 11

"I want you to send a locksmith out today to change the locks," Kathryn told Brandy over the phone the next morning.

"I'll see what I can do, but are you sure you didn't accidentally leave a door unlocked?"

"Positive."

"At least it was only a stuffed snake, not a real one," Brandy said. "I doubt it'll happen again. Probably just some kid having a little fun."

"That's what you said about the defaced picture. I don't think it's funny that someone can just walk in and—"

"I'll get on it right away."

Twenty minutes later, a locksmith called to say he'd be at the house that afternoon. Relieved, Kathryn went into Great Barrington to run some errands. It was Thursday and she was expecting Alan tomorrow evening. He'd be calling today to confirm. She'd food-shop for the weekend and equip herself for what she thought of as "the expedition" into the woods to find the house and mill sites.

*****

Kathryn had just finished unpacking her shopping bags when the locksmith arrived. He was a talkative man with squinty eyes that made him look as if he spent his time peering through keyholes.

"Way out here all alone, are you?" he said. "You're a lot braver than my wife. Wouldn't last a night in a place like this. Gotta be in the center of town. Even then, she don't like being alone. But to each his own. Might as well start with the front door before I go round to the kitchen."

She looked at him curiously. "You know the house?"

"Been out here a few times before."

"To change the locks?"

"That and other things."

So previous tenants had worried about intruders. Before she could question the locksmith further, the phone rang. She hurried to the kitchen to answer it.

"I'm awfully sorry," Alan said, "but it looks like Sophie and I won't be coming this weekend. She's picked up a bug. I kept her out of school yesterday and today. I just spoke to the housekeeper and she says Sophie's a bit better. But I doubt she'll be up for the trip. And I don't feel right about leaving her."

"Of course not." Metal clattered on wood. Kathryn gave a little gasp. The locksmith must have dropped something.

"Is everything all right?" Alan sounded concerned.

"No, I mean, yes."

"Once again, I'm sorry. I hope our not coming tomorrow doesn't affect any plans you made."

"I didn't make any special plans," she fibbed. "Tell Sophie I hope she's better soon."

While the locksmith worked on kitchen door, Kathryn went upstairs. Alone in the valentine room, she gave in to feelings of disappointment. Unless she went by herself, she'd have to wait a whole week before she visited the foundation and mill ruins. She didn't blame Alan for not coming, though. His devotion to his daughter was one of the things she admired about him. He wasn't about to abandon Sophie like the little girl's mother had, running off to Taos to "find" herself. She had never understood people who did this. She knew herself and didn't need to go to a new place to discover who she was. Alan's ex-wife's behavior was selfish and irresponsible. Like her father, chasing after every new skirt that came his way.

Alan was a nice man, and she was fond of him. She liked it that he was serious and steady, careful in speech and actions. He was also striking-looking: pale, almost translucent skin set off by raven black hair with a white streak running through it like the wake of a boat in a night sea. Maybe this time it would be different. Maybe she'd let him get close in a way she had never let any man before.

"Miz Stinson?" the locksmith called up to her.

"Yes?"

"Just wanted to let you know I'm done. I'll leave the new set of keys on the kitchen counter. You need anything else, give a holler."

"Thanks."

After the locksmith had gone, Kathryn examined the shiny new locks. They ought to do the trick. Or would they? It might not be so easy to keep intruders out here as it was in the city.

Chapter 12

Alan Marquette hated to admit it, but he was seriously lost on his way to Kathryn's. After telling her yesterday he wouldn't come, he'd decided to come today, after all, since Sophie seemed much better. He'd been fine getting to the Berkshires, but as soon as he'd left Route 7, the maze of dark, winding back roads had become confusing despite Kathryn's careful directions. He wished he had a GPS.

It was past eleven. Kathryn would be worried. He'd told her he would probably arrive late, but not this late. After work, he'd had a quick supper with Sophie before tucking her in. When she cried and clung to him, he felt so torn. He wouldn't have left her if she hadn't seemed better. Plus, he hated to disappoint Kathryn.

In the six months they'd been seeing each other, their relationship had become important to him. He felt fortunate to have met her at all. The few times friends had fixed him up hadn't panned out, and he was too busy with work and his daughter to get involved with the singles scene. He'd simply poked his head into the bar that night to see what was out there. The little he observed was a turnoff: the women dressed to the nines with their perfume and pasted-on smiles, laughing while the men sniffed them like dogs. He would have fled if one of those flashy women hadn't caught him by the arm and literally dragged him over to meet her friend.

In that steamy atmosphere, Kathryn seemed like a breath of fresh air. He liked it that she was pretty without trying to be: no makeup, hair pulled back from her face. Also, that she was as shy and uncertain as he. Unlike her friend who had "been there, done that" written all over her, Kathryn had an innocence he found appealing. He knew she'd been involved with other men, but she had somehow emerged from these relationships unscathed. She reminded him of the new notebooks he used to get at the beginning of school, the pages fresh and clean, waiting to be filled with his meticulous script.

She was definitely a keeper. Time to swallow his pride and call. He pulled over and took out his cell phone, but couldn't get a signal. Damn. He'd have to find someone to give him directions. Unfortunately, he'd been driving for at least twenty minutes without seeing a single house. He turned around and retraced his steps, continuing until he came to a crossroads. He turned left. Just when he was beginning to think he should have gone the other way, he rounded a bend, and a squat, one-story building with a sign identifying it as The White Stag magically appeared.

The White Stag—the name tugged him back to his Maine childhood and a story his grandfather had told him. He shook his head. His grandfather had been a great teller of tales, most of them probably untrue.

The lot in front of the roadhouse was filled with pickups and a lone police cruiser. Alan parked and got out. The dim, smoky interior, its walls decorated with frowsy stuffed animal heads and Posted signs, reminded him of bars in Maine. Still, he'd never seen a lighting fixture like the one that hung from the ceiling. A large, rusted animal trap, festooned with Christmas lights, blinked on and off: red, green, yellow, blue.

"You lost?"

A group of men hunkered over beer glasses and bottles at the bar. Dressed in jeans and flannel shirts, they made him feel self-conscious in his dark suit and bow tie. He wished he'd taken time to change before leaving home.

"I seem to have taken a wrong turn somewhere."

"Where you headed?" asked a man with rugged features and a deep tan.

"Rattlesnake Hill Road in the village of New Nottingham."

"Rattlesnake Hill, eh," the man repeated. "Farley house?"

Alan nodded.

"We can tell you how to get *there,* can't we boys?" the man said. The others grinned and bobbed their heads.

"I'd appreciate that."

"Why not join us for a beer first?" the man suggested.

"Thanks, but I really shouldn't."

"C'mon." The man motioned to Alan. "One drink and you're on your way. I'm buying."

Alan hesitated.

"Don't be shy. We won't bite," the man called.

Alan flushed. He didn't want these men to think he was afraid of them, though an inner voice warned about a den of thieves. Alan ignored it.

He strode to the bar. "I'll take you up on that beer."

Chapter 13

At the edge of what was supposed to be a road into the woods, Kathryn paused. Lucas Rogers had told her about it when she said she wanted to visit the old Cutter mill and house foundation. He explained that Gordon Farley had a half-mile-long road put in so he could get firewood. But all she saw was a tangle of wild berry bushes, burdock, and golden rod. Beside her, Alan's pale face had a faint greenish tinge, and there were dark circles under his eyes behind the horn-rimmed glasses. The poor man was still hung over.

Alan had arrived late last night, tipsy and deeply apologetic. He'd been conned into having one too many by a bunch of locals at a backwoods bar, when he stopped to get directions. She wouldn't be surprised if Earl Barker had been among them. It would be just like him to trick Alan into getting drunk the same way he'd tricked her into drinking Lucas Rogers' vile coffee. At least Hank Lapsley had the good sense to realize that Alan might be too far gone to make it to her house in one piece and had delivered him to her doorstep in his cruiser, while another man followed in Alan's Volvo. She was grateful to Lapsley, but mad at the others for leading him astray.

Alan smiled wanly and gestured at the so-called road. "So, my jingling jack-o-lantern, shall we?"

"Okay." Kathryn smiled back. She was, indeed, a "jingling jack-o-lantern" in the bright orange anorak and set of sleigh bells on a leather strap, attached to the daypack she'd purchased in Great Barrington. But thus attired, there was little chance a hunter would mistake her for a deer.

Alan strode gamely into the tangle of brush, holding back branches for her, and helping her over fallen trees. Then, miraculously, the way cleared and they followed a path of burnished leaves, flanked by towering pines, through which patches of blue sky were visible. The road ran parallel to the Farley fields, and she caught glimpses of the house through breaks in the trees. It was reassuring to have this landmark to orient her. But as they moved deeper into the forest, she lost sight of it. Even so, Alan proceeded with the confidence of a born woodsman. And thus far there were no signs of hunters. Aside from the jingle of her bells, the only sounds were the crunch of their feet on the leaves and the occasional creak of a branch in the wind. Maybe Brandy was right about the woods being safer since the passage of the "written permission" law. Or Garth Barker had decided to take a day off from his pursuit of the white stag.

A pile of mossy logs, half-buried beneath leaves, marked the end of the road. Ahead, the land dipped into a gully, where a boulder-strewn stream cut a swath through the leaves, then rose in a hill on the other side. "We do the down, up," Alan said after studying the map.

The leaves were so slippery underfoot she nearly fell on the way down. She was grateful for Alan's outstretched hand, as she hopped from rock to rock crossing the stream. Winded and sweaty by the time they reached the top of the hill, she stopped to catch her breath and take off the orange anorak.

"Too hot inside that pumpkin?" Alan teased.

She picked a burr from the anorak and flicked it playfully at him. "Don't think I need these either." She indicated the bells on her pack.

"Probably not," Alan agreed.

Unfastening the bells, she hung them from a tree branch. When they'd walked a distance, Alan stopped and frowned at the map. "We should have turned awhile ago." They backtracked until they came to Alan's turning point. There was no trail, just the rocky plunge of a dried up streambed. The rough terrain made her glad she'd purchased hiking boots. She started down, using her legs as brakes. Her hamstrings stiffened, and her toes pressed painfully against the hard leather of the boots. She felt blisters forming and knew she'd be sore tonight.

They descended into a level, open area, encircled by pines. In front of them lay a body of water several times the size of the Farley pond. Dead tree trunks rose, gray and spectral, in the middle of the swamp, and interspersed amid its murky waters were little hillocks covered with brown grass and weeds. At one end, a haphazard pile of logs and tree branches, bleached white like bones, marked the remains of an abandoned beaver dam.

The landscape struck her as eerie and primeval, a place where dinosaurs might have roamed. It wasn't beautiful like the view from the Farley house, yet something about it spoke to her. She was almost sorry when Alan broke the silence: "Want to look for the house site?"

They bushwhacked through the woods around the swamp until they came to a hollow in the ground with stones banked along the sides and a scraggly pine sticking out of the leaf-strewn bottom. *This was it?* She'd hoped for something more picturesque. Still, she removed her camera from her pack and took several shots, so she could prove to Emily she'd been here. Alan must have sensed her disappointment. "I'm sure it was a nice house once, with a fine view of the pond. Let's look for what's left of the mill. It sounded like there's more to see."

They found the brook and followed it upstream past a breached dam to a large and impressive collection of moss-covered stone ruins, buried deep in the woods like an ancient castle. Twin stone columns rose up in front of what must have been the main entry. On one side, high walls supported rusted machinery and the remains of the giant wooden waterwheel that had powered the mill. On the other, a set of stone steps led down into a labyrinth of underground rooms—the storerooms mentioned in Emily's recollections. Though the rooms were open to the sky, the walls between them were tall enough that once inside, a person would have a hard time seeing over them. The high walls, combined with numerous nooks and crannies, made for excellent hiding places.

Kathryn could understand why Emily and her cousins had enjoyed playing hide-and-seek at the ruins, also why they appealed to courting couples seeking privacy. She snapped more pictures for Emily, and then turned to Alan only to realize he'd vanished.

"Al-an, where a-are you?" she called in a child's sing-song voice. No answer. "All right, guess I'll just have to find you," she said in the same sing-song voice. She took a step forward. Shots rang out. She froze. *Omigod*. Hunters. Alan jumped out from behind a tree just as a bullet zinged into it. Kathryn's heart seized. "Hey, watch where you're shooting. We're people here!" Alan yelled.

A second bullet bounced off one of the stone pillars, perilously close to Kathryn. "Let's get out of here!" Alan grabbed her and they charged through the woods surrounding the swamp, then up the dried streambed.

Thinking they were out of harm's way, they stopped halfway up the hill to rest. More shots sounded not far behind them.

"He's actually chasing us!" Alan cried.

Kathryn was shocked. It was one thing to accidentally fire into an area where there were people, quite another to deliberately pursue them. She and Alan clambered up the rest of the hill and took off down the leaf-strewn trail that brought them back to the gully where the brook was. When they were safely across and up the other side of the gully, they stopped again to catch their breath and listen. Shots still sounded, but more distantly. Whoever it was must have given up. They proceeded down Gordon's road at a slower pace with Alan in the lead. They'd climbed over the series of fallen logs, and Alan had already plunged into the tangle of brush when branches crackled behind Kathryn. She whipped around, afraid it might be their pursuer.

A large, light-colored buck stood in the road a few yards away. It looked at her with liquid brown eyes. She stared back, awestruck. Being this close to such a magnificent animal made her feel as if she'd been given a wonderful gift. Alan's voice broke the spell. "Coming, Kathryn?"

The buck shook its antlers and stomped the ground. Then it turned and bounded into the woods.

"Kathryn?" Alan burst through the brush. "What is it? What're you looking at?"

Regretfully, she withdrew her gaze from the woods. "I think I just saw the white stag."

Chapter 14

"That was quite an adventure!" Alan collapsed into a patio lounge chair.

Kathryn sank into a chair beside him. "And one I'd rather not repeat anytime soon."

"I can't believe that lunatic actually chased us."

"Me either."

They were silent a few minutes, then Alan said, "That deer you saw—why do you think it was a white stag? How did you even know to call it that?"

"The owner of the general store told me there's supposed to be a white stag in these woods. The deer I saw was light-colored, almost white."

"So there are stories about a white stag in these parts, too. Guess it shouldn't surprise me. The bar last night bore that name."

"How do you know about the white stag?"

Alan cleared his throat, looked slightly embarrassed. "My grandfather back in Maine claimed to have seen one when he was hunting with friends. They shot at it, but it escaped. Another time a bullet found its mark and they saw the buck go down. But when my grandfather and his companions got to the spot where it had fallen, it was gone. They didn't even find a trace of blood. The next year, my grandfather was hunting by himself when the same buck appeared in front of him—close enough for him to touch it. He was so amazed he never thought of shooting. The buck scratched a tree trunk with its antlers then disappeared into the woods."

Alan paused to pick a burr off his pants and lob it into the grass.

"Before I tell you any more, you have to understand that my grandfather, like others of his generation living in a remote, rural area, was very superstitious. To him the stag represented a spirit of nature with magical powers. He believed some of its magic had rubbed off on the tree. He stripped off a piece of bark, put it in a small plastic container, and wore it around his neck as a lucky charm."

Alan chucked another burr. "A few years later, he was on a fishing boat with friends when a bad storm came up. The boat capsized and the other men drowned. My grandfather swore the piece of bark saved him."

"Do you think it did?"

"Probably not. But I keep it with me just in case."

"I've never seen you with any lucky charm."

With a sheepish look, Alan fished his keys from his pants pocket. A small plastic vial dangled from the key chain. The surface was badly scratched, but she made out a sliver of bark inside. She'd seen this object many times without guessing it was a lucky charm. Rational Alan didn't seem like someone who'd have one.

He put the key chain back into his pocket and stood. "Enough of this foolishness. I should check in with Sophie. Back in a few." He bent and kissed her.

He acted like he'd revealed some deep, dark secret and was afraid she would think badly of him. He needn't worry. A silly charm wasn't going to change how she felt about him. But he might feel differently about her if he ever found out her worst secrets.

Chapter 15

"Your hat's on the seat," Kathryn said as they got into Alan's Volvo to drive into Great Barrington for dinner that night.

Alan examined the baseball cap. "This isn't mine. It says 'Earl Barker Excavating.' The guy who drove my car here last night must have left it. I'll have to figure out how to get it back to him."

"We can leave it at the general store tomorrow."

So Earl Barker had been one of the crew who'd gotten Alan drunk. Alan tossed the hat on the back seat and undoubtedly forgot about it. But to her, it remained an unwelcome reminder of its owner.

Distracted, she forgot to watch where they were going. When she did focus on the road, nothing looked familiar. "I don't think this is right."

"Want to turn around?"

"Not yet." They drove a while longer, then rounding a bend, they came upon the bar Alan had told her about. Pulling into the driveway to turn around, he swung past a pickup parked in front of the entrance. He stopped and backed up alongside it.

"What are you doing?"

"This truck belongs to the guy whose hat we've got. Might as well return it now." He grabbed the hat and was out of the car and halfway to the entrance before she could stop him.

"Be right back," he called over his shoulder.

"Right back" stretched on and on. What was keeping him? She left the car and entered the bar.

Mounted on the walls were old rifles, NRA bumper stickers, Posted signs, and a bedraggled assortment of stuffed game birds and animal heads. The main source of light was the strangest chandelier she'd ever seen. A huge, rusted metal trap was attached to the ceiling by tire chains. Colored Christmas lights dangled from the trap's spiked jaws, creating an atmosphere both festive and grim.

Behind the bar, Lucas Rogers dispensed beer from the tap with the same nonchalance he dispensed his wretched coffee. In his daytime incarnation, Rogers seemed benign enough. Yet in the smoky, dimly lit bar he looked almost sinister.

"Sorry, Miz Stinson, but I gotta ask you to leave. Stags only tonight."

"And every night," a man wearing paint-splattered overalls chimed in.

"Kathryn?" Alan turned toward her from where he sat with another man at the far end of the bar.

The other man turned also. "Hey, Starstruck."

Damn! "I thought you were coming right out," she said to Alan.

"Sorry. We got talking and—"

"Miz Stinson," Lucas Rogers said.

"Now, Lucas," Earl drawled, "how about you cut us some slack and let the lady and her friend stay a bit?"

Rogers shrugged, but she was having none of it: "You only want us here, so you can trick my friend into drinking too much again, just like you tricked me into drinking that rotten coffee black."

"You still mad about that?"

Alan shot her a puzzled look.

She tugged on his arm. "Let's go."

Earl rose and stepped in their way. "Can't have you leaving mad. Oughta settle our differences first. You're a lawyer, you can appreciate that," he added with a sly glance at Alan.

"How do you know?"

"Told me yourself last night. Don't you remember? Had ourselves quite a chat." Amusement flickered in his blue eyes.

Alan coughed. "Now I do."

"I'd like to continue the conversation, if Starstruck's willing to let bygones be bygones?" Both men looked expectantly at her.

"All right, we'll stay, but only for a short while."

Earl ushered them to a table. "Pick your poison, the drinks are on me."

Minutes later, he returned with a glass of beer for Kathryn and two bottles, toting them like chickens whose necks he'd just wrung. "Shall we show Starstruck how we open our beer around here?"

Alan looked bewildered.

Earl bit the cap off a bottle, spat it into his hand, and placed it on the table. "Remember? You did a fine job last night."

"Oh . . . right." Before Kathryn could prevent him, Alan followed suit. Blood trickled from his mouth when he finished. How appalling! Alan had never done anything like this in front of her before. While he dabbed his bloody lips, she examined the two bottle caps, then turned angrily to Earl: "You gave him the one with the serrated edge and took the screw top yourself."

"My mistake. Thought they were the same. Can't seem to do right by you, Starstruck. And that's a real shame. I was hoping we could talk more about your grandfather and the white stag," he said to Alan. "My great-great uncle saw him, too, you know."

"Really?" Alan said with interest.

"Yup. Thought he was the only one till you told me about your grandfather."

"Kathryn thinks she saw a white stag today," Alan volunteered.

"Well, I'll be. Tell me all about it."

"There's not much to tell." But she told him anyway.

Earl was silent a long moment, absently moving the bottle caps around the table. Finally he said, "He say anything to you?"

Kathryn exchanged astonished glances with Alan.

"No. Was he supposed to?"

"Just thought he might've. 'Cuz he spoke to my great-great uncle."

A talking deer? This had to be a tall tale. Like Bigfoot or the Loch Ness Monster. She decided to play along. "No kidding. What did he say?"

The lights of the trap-chandelier blinked off and on. Red, green, blue, yellow. In the changing light, Earl appeared sinister, but also strangely seductive. He looked at her through half closed eyes like Amore sometimes did, drowsing in the sunlight. A braying laugh came from the bar then it was quiet again.

"Nothing at first," Earl said. "My great-great uncle saw the stag twice as a young man. Both times he could've shot it, but didn't. The third time the stag appeared to him in a dream. Told my uncle that because he'd let him live, my uncle was gonna have a long life. But he wouldn't see the stag or any other living thing again, except in dreams."

"What did that mean?" Alan asked.

"That my great-great uncle would go blind."

"Your great-great uncle was Old Man Barker?" Kathryn asked eagerly.

"How'd you know?"

"He's mentioned in Emily Goodale's recollections. She and the other children were terrified of him because they heard he killed someone."

Earl's face turned an angry red. "Are you calling my great-great uncle a murderer?"

"That's not—"

"Calm down." Alan jumped to her defense. "Kathryn's only repeating what she read."

"Well, she should know better than to repeat a falsehood," Earl growled.

"What did happen?" she asked. Maybe now she'd finally get the whole story.

Earl rose abruptly. "Hate to break up the party, but I just remembered I'm wanted elsewhere. Gotta lady friend who doesn't like to be kept waiting." He pulled the baseball cap from his jacket pocket and waved it at Alan. "Thanks for returning this, counselor. Drive carefully now. Ciao, Starstruck."

Ciao—was he mocking her again? And Alan, too, calling him counselor and telling him to drive carefully?

"That was fast," Alan said. "You really pushed his buttons when you made that comment about his great-great uncle."

She shrugged. "Let's go."

"I'll use the head then we're on our way." Alan disappeared into the rear of the bar.

Kathryn got up and strolled toward the entrance, thinking she'd wait for him in the car.

The door swung open and Garth Barker burst in. His ugly, squeezed-together features compressed even further when he saw her.

"What the fuck're you doing here?"

"We're just leaving," she said coolly, though she was shaking inside.

Garth glanced around, obviously baffled by the plural pronoun. "You an' who?" he sneered. "Your shadow?"

"I came with a friend."

Garth scanned the room again. "Don't see no friend of yours here."

"He's in the head," Lucas Rogers volunteered.

"Yes, and I'll wait for him outside." Kathryn made a move toward the door, but Garth blocked the way. "I ain't finished. Better stop messing with my womenfolk if you know what's good for you."

Kathryn was stunned. "I give a pregnant woman a ride up the hill and you accuse me of meddling?"

"Damn straight I do!"

"What's going on?" Alan came up behind her.

"Bitch thinks she's a fucking social worker."

"I do not."

"There's obviously been a misunderstanding," Alan said, assuming the role of mediator. "If we can discuss this calmly, I'm sure—"

"Misunderstanding, my arse," Garth interrupted. "Bitch stuck her nose where it don't belong."

Alan's pale face flushed with anger. He looked like he was ready to haul off and hit Garth. Instead, taking her by the arm, he pushed past Garth to the door. She knew she should let it go, but couldn't resist a parting shot. "I'll leave your women alone if you quit planting snakes in my house."

"Snakes?" Alan stared at her with alarm.

"Dunno what the fuck you're talking about," Garth grumbled.

"Oh yes, you do. You put that snake in my house. And I wouldn't be surprised if you also—"

Before she could accuse him of chasing her and Alan from the woods with his shotgun, he interrupted, "How would I do that? Ain't got no key to the Farley place." A crafty expression came over his face. "Was probably Earl. He's the one who's banging Brandy. And Diana before her."

"Come on, Kathryn." Alan guided her out.

*****

"Did he really put a snake in the house?" he asked when they were safely in the car and on the road again.

"I don't know for sure, but he's a likely suspect."

"Why didn't you tell me about this before?"

"I didn't want you to worry, and it was only a stuffed snake."

"It frightened you, though."

"I don't want to talk about it anymore. We've had enough trouble for one day. Let's go to Great Barrington and try to enjoy the rest of the evening."

Alan patted her knee. "We'll do that."

Minutes later, Alan frowned and raised a hand to shield his eyes.

"What's the matter?"

"The truck in back of us has its brights on."

Behind them two yellow orbs gleamed like the eyes of a huge beast. They rounded a bend and the orbs vanished. "That's better." Alan put his hand back on the wheel.

The truck reappeared, blinding Alan again as it bore down on them. "Shit!" He accelerated. The truck did, too. "Idiot!" he cried, flooring the gas pedal. The Volvo rocketed forward. So did their pursuer. Kathryn glanced at the speedometer. Sixty. Sixty-five. Seventy. Way too fast for a winding country road. Heart pounding, she gripped the door handle as the Volvo careened around another bend. It swung wide, landing on the wrong side of the narrow roadway.

"Pull over and let him pass."

"No! I'm going to lose him."

"Alan, please!" she shrieked as they spun into an S-curve. They'd just rounded the second loop when the deer appeared ahead of them, frozen in the light like a creature in amber.

"Hit the brakes!"

62

"I am but—"

The deer loomed before them. Bigger and bigger. Brighter and brighter. Sucking them into its glowing vortex.

"No!" Alan wrenched the steering wheel to the right. The car spun off the road, and they plunged into darkness, bucking and bouncing over rough ground. At last it came to a shuddering halt. Air rasped in Kathryn's lungs. Her heart beat a drum roll. A horn blared nearby.

"Are you all right?" Alan shouted over the blast of the horn.

"Think so. You?"

"Yeah, but I better check on that truck." He fumbled in the glove compartment for a flashlight, left the car and set off in the direction of the noise. She followed on legs wobbly as a newborn colt's.

The truck straddled the roadway, front end smashed in, windshield shattered. Surprisingly, there was no sign of the deer it must have hit. Garth was crushed against the steering wheel. His eyes were shut, his face cut and bloody. Shards of glass embedded in his skin winked like diamonds in the light from Alan's flashlight.

Part II: Snakes

Chapter 16

"Let me do the talking," Alan said, as they waited for the ambulance to arrive. They stood by his Volvo, now moved from the field to the side of the road behind Garth's smashed pickup. "I'm going to say we came upon the accident after it already happened."

"Why not just tell the truth?" Kathryn asked.

"In this kind of situation, it's best to keep the story simple. The police can figure out he hit a deer. They don't need to know we were in any way involved."

"But we didn't do anything wrong. He was the one who came after us."

"Trust me. I know how to handle—" The rest of the sentence was drowned out by the scream of an approaching ambulance. Moments later, the flashing lights of both the ambulance and a police cruiser engulfed them. A grim-faced Hank Lapsley left the cruiser, motioning for them to stay put while he inspected the pickup and the EMTs did their work.

All this seemed to take a long time. When Garth was finally taken away in the shrieking ambulance, Lapsley came over to them.

"Is he—" In her nervousness, Kathryn forgot Alan's advice to let him do the talking.

"Still alive, but . . ." Lapsley shook his head.

"Thank God! I—we were afraid—" She began to shiver uncontrollably.

Alan put an arm around her. "Why don't you wait in the car?"

From the car window, she watched them confer. Lapsley shook

his head a few more times, circled the pickup with Alan and briefly investigated the area on other side of the road before returning to the Volvo. He not only walked around the car but bent to examine the tires and bumpers. Kathryn knew it was irrational, but she couldn't help feeling a twinge of guilt, as if they had caused the accident. Finally, Lapsley left and Alan joined her in the car.

"How did it go?"

Alan ran a hand through his hair, mussing the white streak. "He was a bit suspicious. These country cops usually are when it comes to outsiders. It didn't help that he couldn't find any trace of the deer that idiot hit. Said he'll come back to search for the deer in the daylight, and took my contact information in case he has more questions. But I don't think there'll be a problem."

"I hope not."

"I thought for certain we were going to hit that deer ourselves," Alan said.

Kathryn shuddered as the image of Garth's bloody, glass-studded face rose in her mind. She reached for Alan and they hugged each other.

"So did I. Luckily you yanked hard on the steering wheel, and the deer moved out of the way."

"It did?"

"I think so."

"It probably just looked that way: when the car turned, the deer seemed to move, too." Alan sounded skeptical.

"Maybe, but I think the deer was the same one I saw in the woods today."

"The white stag?"

"Yes. Didn't you see it?"

"I saw a deer but I couldn't swear it was white. It could've been the effect of the light shining on it."

Of course, there were rational explanations for what she'd observed. The key chain with the plastic vial and its sliver of bark jangled when Alan stuck the key into the ignition. "Do you still want to go to Great Barrington?"

"No."

Back at the house, she heated canned soup, and Alan poured glasses of Merlot. They spoke in fits and starts: periods of silence broken by bursts of talk, thoughts exploding into words, as they tried to make sense of the day's events. Around ten, Alan remembered he'd promised to call Sophie to say good-night. He was disappointed but not overly concerned when no one answered. Sophie was probably asleep, and the housekeeper had turned off the ringer to keep the phone from waking her. *At least nothing worse can happen,* Kathryn thought when they finally crawled into bed.

*****

In the middle of the night, the ringing phone wrenched them into consciousness. Alan grabbed the handset. "She's *where*?" he shouted. "I'll get there as soon as I can."

Kathryn shot up in bed and grabbed his arm. "What is it?"

"Sophie—she's in the hospital with meningitis." Alan pulled on clothes, and thudded downstairs, untied bootlaces snapping like whips. Kathryn caught up with him at his car. "Shall I come with you?"

"No, I'll call you." The door slammed and the Volvo roared down the driveway. She stumbled back into the house. Things were happening too fast, spinning out of control. She needed to stay still and get her bearings. She went upstairs and lay on the bed.

When she awoke again, it was nine a.m. She wished Alan would call, but it might be too early. Poor Sophie. She was a quiet, watchful child with a shock of blonde hair thick as lamb's wool, and large, staring blue eyes. Kathryn knew Sophie had been deeply hurt by her mother's desertion, a hurt she understood from her own childhood with only one parent. Still, she wasn't about to offer herself as a replacement mom. She and Sophie were polite but cautious around each other, both afraid to get too close lest things didn't work out between Alan and her.

Kathryn had breakfast, then to occupy herself while waiting for Alan's call, she decided to visit Emily. Now that she'd been to the house and mill sites, surely the old woman would have to answer her questions about the photograph.

69

Chapter 17

No one answered the door at the small, white house with a wraparound porch and gingerbread trim. The cars parked in front of the meeting house next door told Kathryn Emily was probably at church. She sat on a rickety wicker chair on the porch to wait.

After a while, she glimpsed Emily with Millie by her side, threading her way through the crowd of people streaming from the meeting house doors. Emily wore a green wool coat with a spotted fur collar that looked as if mice had nibbled around the edges. On her head was a bright green hat with green feathers. She reminded Kathryn of an exotic bird.

"You're back," Emily said when she saw Kathryn. Millie looked at Kathryn questioningly through dark-circled eyes.

"Emily's been helping me with my research on the Cutter family," Kathryn explained. Emily humphed past them into the house.

"Thank you and your friend for acting quickly and calling the ambulance last night," Millie said. "Garth might've died if you hadn't come on the scene."

"How is he?"

"In critical condition, but the doctors think he'll pull through." Millie pursed her lips. "The strange thing is that although Garth must have hit a deer, Hank Lapsley hasn't been able to find the dead animal or any traces of a wounded one."

"That is strange."

From the house came banging. "I'd better look after her," Millie said. Emily was in the kitchen, opening and shutting cupboard doors. She'd removed her coat but still had her hat on.

"Where's my dinner?" Emily's blue eyes flashed laser-sharp under the green plumage.

"Sis left a casserole in the fridge. I'll microwave it for you," Millie answered.

Sis? That stick of a girl, who carried her pregnancy in a high, round knob like a gall on a branch, actually looked after Emily? Maybe it was the only job she could get.

"Why isn't she here?" Emily grumped.

"She's at the hospital, remember? Garth had a bad car accident."

"Garth Barker, that little hellion. He can't be old enough to drive."

"He's thirty-five, Emily."

Millie helped Emily into a chair at the kitchen table, where a place had been set. She microwaved a piece of tuna noodle casserole and put the plate in front of Emily. "Careful now, it's going to be hot."

Disregarding the warning, Emily stuck a finger into the casserole. "Hot!" she cried like a baby.

"Why don't you start with your Jell-O while it cools?" Millie replaced the casserole plate with a bowl of cubed, lime Jell-O that matched the feathers on Emily's hat. Kathryn marveled at Millie's patience.

Emily spooned a Jell-O cube into her mouth. "Where's Sis?"

"At the hospital," Millie said without a trace of weariness.

"Is she having her baby?"

"Not yet."

"When will I see her?"

"Later this afternoon. I can stay with you a while longer, if you like." Millie stole a glance at her watch, obviously torn between remaining with Emily and returning to the hospital.

"I'll stay," Kathryn volunteered.

"That would be a big help. Is it okay with you, Emily?"

"I suppose so," Emily replied sulkily.

Millie motioned Kathryn to follow her to the door. "I shouldn't be gone more than an hour or so. Will that be a problem?"

Kathryn hesitated, thinking of the anticipated call from Alan. If only there were cell reception, she wouldn't have to worry about missing it. Now, she'd have to wait until she returned to the house to see if he'd left a message on the answering machine.

"If you need to go sooner, Bessie Todd across the street can look in on Emily,"

"All right."

"You're a peach." Millie flashed her a grateful smile.

In the kitchen, Emily held a noodle in front of her open mouth. Her lips made a sucking sound as they closed around it. A fishy odor mingled with the sickly sweet odor of household cleaner. Kathryn's breakfast rose in her gorge. She swallowed hard. "Did you bring the photograph?" Emily asked suddenly.

Kathryn removed the daguerreotype from its bag and set it on the kitchen table, well away from Emily's greasy fingers. "I visited the mill ruins and the foundation of the Cutter house like you told me to. Now will you tell me who she is?"

Emily sucked tuna into her mouth. "Did you really go there?"

"Here's the proof." Kathryn showed her the pictures on her digital camera.

"Haven't changed much," Emily commented.

"When were you last there?"

"Several years ago, with Diana. She was very interested in the past, wanted me to show her all the old places. And once she knew the way—oh dear, I wish I'd never . . ." A troubled look came over Emily's face.

"What's the matter?"

"Why doesn't Sis come?" Emily's voice rose plaintively.

"She'll be with you later. I'm here now."

"You?" Emily stared blankly at Kathryn.

"Kathryn Stinson. The Cutters were my ancestors. I'm trying to find out who she was." Kathryn pointed at the portrait.

"You want to know about Marguerite?"

Marguerite. Finally! And a lovely name for a lovely young woman. Flushed with success, Kathryn pressed on. "Tell me about her."

"I've already told you everything I know," Emily replied crossly. "It's on the tapes."

"You told Diana, not me. And the tapes are missing. Do you know where they are?"

"Don't you have them?"

Kathryn wanted to throw up her hands and scream. Instead, with Millie's forbearance, she began, "Emily—"

"Hush. Finish your dinner, then it's nap time," Emily said in a high, girlish voice like Sis's.

Kathryn made two more attempts to find out about Marguerite. The first time, Emily acted as if she didn't hear Kathryn. The second time, a noodle caught in Emily's throat. She coughed and whitish matter splattered down the front of her dress like droppings from the parrot perched on her head. Kathryn's stomach turned. She'd never be able to look at a tuna noodle casserole again.

Emily stared at the mess, her blue eyes wide with surprise, then stricken with shame. The next moment, shame gave way to feistiness. "You forgot my bib. Over there on the counter."

Kathryn dabbed at the front of Emily's dress with a moist towel then attached the bib, a striped dish towel with safety pins, careful not to stick Emily. She stopped trying to find out about Marguerite and let Emily eat. Emily used a spoon for the Jell-O, her fingers for the casserole, slowly bringing each morsel to her mouth, slowly gumming it. Her tongue clicked against her palate. The ancient electric clock on the wall whirred away the seconds, minutes, hours, days, years, or so Kathryn imagined. She would grow old trying to learn the truth about Marguerite. She was growing old just watching Emily eat.

"All done!" Emily proclaimed with childish pride when her bowl and plate were finally empty.

"Ready for your nap?" Kathryn didn't know about Emily, but she was exhausted from her mealtime vigil. She helped Emily into the bedroom and onto the bed, propping up pillows behind her and spreading a quilt over her legs. Emily still had her hat on, so Kathryn removed it. Stripped of her brilliant plumage with her hair crushed against her skull, Emily looked more shriveled and ancient than ever. Still, life burned in her blue eyes and crackled in her voice. "Where's Marguerite?"

"On the kitchen table."

"Well, bring her in here and put her on the dresser where I can see her."

Kathryn retrieved the photograph and positioned it on the dresser. Emily frowned. "Next to him," she ordered. Seeing Kathryn's look of incomprehension, Emily pointed at a gold medal in a domed glass case.

When Marguerite and the medal were side by side, Emily turned to Kathryn. "I'm so glad you're here," she said in a faint, watery voice. Then her face opened into one of the most beautiful smiles Kathryn had ever seen. It was like a burst of sunshine after days of gray drizzle, a sudden blessing that made her forget her earlier annoyance. She wanted to bask in the warmth of that smile forever. Gradually the light faded from Emily's eyes, her smile lines vanished, and her features became indistinct shapes, over which the flesh was loosely draped like sheets over furniture in a house closed for the season.

Kathryn tiptoed from the room. She washed Emily's dishes and put them in the drainer, wiped off the kitchen table, and swept the crumbs from the floor. It was quiet except for the whir of the electric clock. One-thirty. She hoped Millie wouldn't be gone much longer. She went into the living room and sat in an overstuffed armchair with faded red brocade upholstery and yellowed crocheted coverings— antimacassars, she thought they were called. An old-fashioned word like the room itself, which was more parlor than living room with its drawn curtains and heavy dark furniture.

Framed family photographs covered the table top next to her. One showed a solemn-faced Emily in a wedding dress; another, a man, equally solemn-faced, wearing a suit and bow tie, presumably Emily's husband. There were pictures of two girls at various ages, then grown-up with grandchildren. Finally, there was a color photo of Emily and a much younger woman, who must be Diana, standing in front of the Farley house. Diana was beautiful, with long, raven-black hair, a porcelain complexion, blue eyes, and a radiant smile. She had her arm around Emily, who beamed with pleasure.

After a while, Kathryn got up and wandered into a small adjoining room that served as both sewing nook and study. On one side stood an ancient Singer sewing machine, on the other, a narrow desk with a typewriter under a cloth cover with the embroidered motto: "The pen is mightier than the sword." Slipping off the cover, Kathryn tapped the letter "k" idly. The key still stuck as it had in Emily's letters to her Aunt Kit.

She glanced at her watch. Almost two p.m. Millie should be back soon and then she could leave. First, she'd look in on Emily.

The old woman lay on the bed, a skeleton in a green dress, her skin a grayish white like old wax, her mouth a gaping black hole. The only sign of life was the wheeze-whistle of air passing in and out of her nose. Kathryn wanted to shut the door on this vision of an old woman edging toward death. But something held her there. The afterglow of that beauteous smile bestowed on her like a benediction? Or a fear that if she left, Emily's spirit would slip from her body and drift away, as if her presence were the anchor that kept Emily moored to the world?

"I'm so glad you're here," Emily had said. Had she meant Kathryn personally, or had she momentarily mistaken her for Sis or even Diana? Did it matter? Kathryn couldn't imagine her own grandmother saying she was glad Kathryn was there, as death approached. And her grandmother had certainly never smiled at Kathryn the way Emily just had. Aunt Kit might have done so, if only she had been with her at the end. Regret tore at Kathryn.

On the dresser top Marguerite smiled her wistful smile, almost as if she understood what Kathryn was feeling. Why had Emily wanted the photograph next to the medal? Kathryn was about to return it to her tote when Emily moaned in her sleep. She held her breath, feeling like a thief. Ridiculous; the photograph belonged to her. Still, she waited until she'd counted ten wheeze-whistles before depositing it in her bag.

She settled in a chair by Emily's bedside. Wheeze-whistle. Wheeze-whistle. At first Emily's snoring was an irritant, but gradually, to her surprise, it became a guided meditation, then a lullaby wafting her to sleep.

*****

Voices roused her. "Kathryn?" A doorknob clicked. Millie entered the room, trailed by Sis.

Emily's eyes popped open. "Is that you, Sis?" Millie nudged Sis forward. Emily smiled happily. "Have you had your baby?"

"No." Sis's face contorted; she began to whimper.

"What's the matter, dear?" Emily asked gently.

"Garth's gone blind."

Millie slipped an arm around Sis. "That's not quite true. The doctor said Garth will lose the sight in his right eye, but with surgery he thinks at least some vision in other eye can be restored."

"Yeah, but he ain't making no promises the operation'll work. And who's gonna pay for it? Garth ain't never gonna see his baby."

His baby. That was a surprise, though it explained certain things. Like the tension between Cheryl and Sis when she'd come upon them in the road. Also possibly Garth's angry response to her at The White Stag. He might have been afraid that she, an outsider and therefore suspect, would find out he'd knocked up his sister-in-law and make trouble somehow. Not that she would have. Nevertheless, Millie shot her a cautionary look, as if to deflect an expression of shock on her part. Millie needn't have worried. Kathryn's surprise gave way to sympathy when Sis collapsed, sobbing, onto the bed beside Emily, who offered these strange words of comfort: "Don't worry, child, Aurelia will take care of your baby, too."

*****

No message from Alan awaited Kathryn at the Farley house. She stared disconsolately at the zero on the answering machine. Zero. Zip. Nothing. Nada. The phone rang.

"Alan, thank God! How is she?"

"I'm sorry. I meant to call sooner, but it's been hell here. Sophie was badly dehydrated, almost comatose by the time the housekeeper called an ambulance. I've been afraid to leave. Christ! I can't believe we wasted a week with the doctor telling us it was flu. And now they can't make up their minds if it's bacterial or viral meningitis. They're giving her antibiotics, but if it's the bacterial type it's extremely serious and—she asked me if she was going to die. My own daughter! I didn't know what to say."

"How awful, just awful," Kathryn murmured, aware of how inadequate her words sounded. "Is there anything I can do?"

"Yes, but . . ."

"What?"

"I know this is going to sound crazy, but here goes." Alan cleared his throat and told her.

It did sound crazy, but he was desperate, ready to try anything. "I'll bring it as soon as I can," she promised, though she had no idea how she would get what he wanted.

There was a rush of air on the line, as if Alan had come to the end of a race. "Is it dark there yet?" he asked. As if they stood on the opposite ends of the earth. In a sense, they did: she was in a house of night-blackened windows, while he was in a fluorescent-lit hospital corridor, shut up in a world where night and day were one and the same, and the only distinction that mattered was between life and death.

"Yes, but I've got a flashlight."

"You won't find anything. Wait until daybreak."

"I'll be out at first light."

Chapter 18

When Kathryn's alarm went off at five a.m., she dressed quickly and shouldered her backpack. Inside was a flashlight, a plastic container and a spade she'd found in the garage last night. Amore raised a drowsy, bewhiskered face to look at her then buried his head in the coil of his body.

Outside, mist rose from the pond like steam from a giant cauldron. On the far side, the dim shapes of trees twisted in a devil's dance. Kathryn felt as if she were entering a netherworld with no Hermes to guide her.

The tangle of brush at the beginning of Gordon's road looked even more impassable than before, a no man's land of barbed wire. Steeling herself, she pushed in. Branches snapped back at her; thorns snagged her clothing, pricking the skin underneath and forcing her to stop and disengage herself. The very woods seemed to want to keep her out.

The brush gave way finally to a leaf-strewn path. She trained her flashlight on the ground ahead. The stag had appeared in the area between the last of the fallen logs and the beginning of the tangle of brush. She walked slowly to the first fallen log without finding anything, and then glanced back at the way she'd come. Now her footprints disturbed the leaves. A wave of panic swept over her. She'd never find the stag's prints. If she didn't—what? Alan himself doubted the piece of bark with the white stag's scratch had saved his grandfather from drowning. And did she really believe that because she'd seen a light-colored deer twice in the same day, she and Alan had been spared the crash that had blinded Garth?

She started back toward the tangle of brush. The smell of damp earth and moldering leaves filled her nostrils. Then, to her astonishment, she detected a musky odor. There was a clear patch in the leaves, and in it, a deer track. She knelt to examine it. Alan had explained that buck tracks are larger and more splayed than those of a doe. This one fit that description. She removed the spade from her pack and began to dig.

*****

Alan met her in the lobby of Children's Hospital in Boston. He wore a hospital mask and plastic gloves. "It's bacterial meningitis and highly contagious," he explained, his voice muffled behind the mask. "They've put me on antibiotics, because I've been in close contact with her. The housekeeper, too."

"The poor little thing. I'm so sorry. I hope this helps." She handed him the plastic container of the soil with the white stag's print.

"I hope to God it does!" Alan's eyes glistened, behind horned-rimmed glasses. "Thank you. I'll tell Sophie you came, and that you brought good medicine. There's a chance you may be exposed through me, so if you feel like you're coming down with something, promise me you'll see a doctor immediately."

"I promise."

"Will you stay over in Boston, or go back to the Berkshires?"

"I haven't decided."

"If you do stay over, we can see each other again in a day or two when I've finished with the antibiotics and am no longer contagious. In the meantime, try to get some rest. You must be exhausted."

"You look pretty worn out yourself."

"I can always catch a few winks while I'm with Sophie. I should go back now. See you in a few days, I hope." Alan pressed gloved fingers to the lower part of the mask and blew her an antiseptic kiss. In the elevator, he stood straight and tall, arms at his sides, head tilted upward like an astronaut at the beginning of a dangerous mission. The door shut and he was gone.

Chapter 19

A t last! Kathryn heaved a sigh as she drove up Rattlesnake Hill Road. Making the round trip in one day had been harder than she'd anticipated. Yet in a few minutes, she would be sitting on the patio, gazing at the pond while the peacefulness of the scene flowed into her.

Intent on her goal, she barely noticed the faded red pickup parked by the side of the road. Halfway up the driveway, a pile of gravel brought her to a screeching halt. A front-loader was parked nearby. Apparently, Earl Barker had chosen today to begin work on the driveway. Damn! She'd been looking forward to being alone, and now this man, the last person on earth she wanted to see, was not only here, but had left an obstruction in her path. She slammed out of the car and stormed up the driveway, anger giving her a fresh rush of adrenaline.

What she saw on the patio raised her hackles even more. Earl was stretched out in a chaise longue, drinking beer from a pop-top can and staring at the pond, while Amore stalked a fallen leaf on the grass.

"You sure don't waste any time making yourself at home," she snapped.

His head turned slowly toward her. "Didn't expect you back so soon, Starstruck."

"Obviously not, since you left a load of gravel in the middle of the road."

"I'll move it," he said without budging from the chair.

"Why's the cat out? He's not supposed to leave the house."

"I'm watching him."

"How did you get in? Did Brandy give you a key?"

"You left a sliding door open." He put down his beer can, took another from the cooler by his side, popped the top, and started to toss it on the ground. Instead, catching the top in midair, he shoved it in the pocket of his jeans.

Caught in the act. He was the one who had left the mess of pop-tops on the patio. He'd come here when the house was empty, pretending he was lord of the manor when he was just a hired hand. And now, even though she, the house's legitimate occupant, had returned, he still acted like he was cock of the walk. Her anger boiled over.

"You've got some nerve," she shrilled. To her dismay, she sounded every bit like her grandmother. "It was bad enough your brother nearly ran us off the road. Bad enough my friend's daughter became seriously ill and I had to drive to Boston to bring her some medicine—without you practically moving in the minute I'm gone. I want you to leave and take your trash with you."

She'd expected him to get mad back, or at least make some smart-alecky retort. Instead, he held up a hand to placate her, and also, possibly, to protect himself. As if *she* posed a threat to *him*.

"I'll go," he said evenly, "but first let's get a few things straight. Sit down, please, and have a beer, if you like."

Embarrassed about losing it in front of him, she sank into the other chaise longue and accepted his offer of a beer.

"I'm sorry about your friend's daughter," Earl said. "Is she going to be all right?"

"I don't know. I hope so."

"As for my brother running you off the road, that's not what I heard. Hank said you came on the scene after Garth hit a deer."

She squirmed, wishing Alan had told the truth. "He did hit a deer, but before that he was tailgating us with his high beams on."

Earl frowned. "If you were ahead of him, how did you avoid the deer?"

"We were able to pull off the road in time."

"You saw this deer?"

"Yes. I think it was . . . the white stag."

"No kidding? That could explain why Hank couldn't find a trace of it."

"Do you really think the white stag has magical powers?"

"What about you? You're the one who saw it."

"Seeing doesn't necessarily mean believing."

A leaf crackled on the grass as Amore pounced on it. Losing interest in this inanimate prey, the cat joined them on the patio. Amore rubbed against Earl's leg, and Earl scratched him behind the ears. The cat craned his neck toward Earl's fingers, yellow eyes half-shut with pleasure, purring loudly. Sated at last, he sprawled shamelessly beside Earl's work boot.

Earl smiled then his expression turning serious, he said, "I know you're the tenant here, but I put a lot of work into this place, and sometimes I like to come and look at what I made."

"Millie said you put in the pond."

"That's right."

"Whose idea was it?"

"Gordon's." An edge came into Earl's voice. "He thought it would look very Italian to have a pond by those tall pines. Even made a drawing to show me how he wanted it. Kidney-shaped like a goddamn swimming pool." Earl snorted. "With a deep end and a shallow end. But that's not how you make a pond. You have to hollow out the earth like a bowl, deep in the middle and shallower along the sides. Otherwise, you'll end up stuck like old Mike Mulligan and his steam shovel in the kid's story."

"Gordon must've been pleased with the result."

"He wasn't even around when I finished." Earl paused to take a drink of beer. When he spoke again, his face was rapt with memory. "But Diana was. She'd driven up from the city alone to check on the progress of the house. Saw her car when I pulled up in my pickup. It was late on a Sunday afternoon. Millie was off at one of her meetings, the kids were out with friends, and I had some time to myself. I was sitting in my truck, having a beer like now, staring at the hole, which was just starting to fill, when she came out of the house. Climbed right into the cab beside me." He glanced at Kathryn and seemed surprised to find her there instead of Diana.

His gaze returned to the pond. "Wasn't much to look at then. Just a hole in the ground with some water in it. She couldn't have known how quickly it would fill. Or how the water would change from one season to the next, how it would turn green and murky in the summer, clear out come fall, freeze over in the winter. She didn't know about all the plants and animals this one little pond would draw. How cattails would sink their roots deep into the clay around the sides, how they'd multiply till Gordon was afraid they were taking over and hired my boys to pull 'em out. That's real grunt work, standing knee-deep in muck under a hot sun with leeches sticking to your legs and deer flies biting your back."

She wasn't sure why he was telling her this, unless it was to satisfy some need of his, but she didn't mind listening and actually enjoyed hearing about the pond's evolution. Who would have thought this man of few words, and jibes at that, was capable of such extended and eloquent speech?

"Never could get all the cattails out," he said in his soft baritone. "And those the boys did get were replaced by new ones soon enough. That was fine by Diana. She didn't want them out in the first place, because then the redwing blackbirds wouldn't have a place to build their nests, the muskrat wouldn't have reeds for his house, and there would be no private spaces for the ducks and geese to lay their eggs and raise their young.

"Gordon disagreed. He complained that the cattails were ruining the shape of the pond. Diana didn't care about that. She cared about the redwings, the muskrats, and the ducks and geese. Frogs, too. Couldn't wait for the peepers to start up in the spring, a regular symphony, she said. She loved their long, sweet trills on summer nights with the rumble of the bullfrogs breaking in every now and then. Even loved the mosquitoes, the water snakes, and the snapping turtles.

"That afternoon when the pond was just a hole with a little water in it, she didn't know any of this. Must have seen the possibilities, though, because after we'd sat awhile, she took my hand and said, 'It's beautiful, Earl. You've made something beautiful.'"

Gazing at the pond, its waters tinged a pinkish-orange by the setting sun, Kathryn agreed.

"Diana loved this pond," Earl said. "Her ashes were scattered here. That's why I . . . " His voice trailed off and his face assumed a pensive expression.

So that was it. He'd been in love with Diana, and came to the pond for the same reason others visited the graves of loved ones in cemeteries. She had misjudged him, thinking him crude and unfeeling, as if his vocabulary and emotional range were as limited as his gene pool, when they were not.

The sadness etched in his features reminded her of how Aunt Kit's companion, Kane, had looked when he'd come on his improbable errand, flying all the way from Hawaii to Boston to bring her the photograph after Aunt Kit's death. She'd misjudged Kane, too, by accepting her grandmother's view of him as a houseboy turned gigolo.

Her mind traveled back to that chill March afternoon when they met in the hotel lobby overlooking Boston Common. She'd been surprised to discover that the plump, laughing, steel-guitar-playing young man she remembered from childhood visits had become middle-aged, gray around the temples, his gaunt face riddled with lines. His manner toward her had been stiff and formal, yet when he spoke of Aunt Kit and what she'd meant to him, Kathryn realized that his grief, like his love, was genuine. Impulsively, she reached over and touched his arm. "I'm so sorry, Kane."

He recoiled from her touch like a dog suspicious of strangers. "What did you call me?"

Whoa! This wasn't Kane, but Earl Barker. Still, she owed him an explanation. "Kane. It means 'man' in Hawaiian. I called you that because just now you reminded me of someone with that name."

"Who?"

"He worked for my great-aunt."

"She called him *man*?"

"He had another, longer name but she called him Kane because—" She broke off, unwilling to say more.

"What?" he pressed.

"He was her man."

"Her lover, you mean?" His blue eyes were trained on her with Emily's laser-like intensity.

84

"Yes."

"So your great-aunt had a Hawaiian lover," he chuckled. "Bet that caused a scandal."

"No, it didn't," she lied. Aunt Kit's affair *had* created a scandal with serious consequences for Kathryn. Shocked by her sister's immoral behavior, her grandmother had forbidden her to make any more visits to Hawaii.

"C'mon now. Taking up with a Hawaiian must be almost as bad as taking up with a hillbilly like me."

"You're not a hillbilly. Hillbillies live in Appalachia."

"Hills here, too, and according to some folks, families like mine who've lived in these hills a long time are hillbillies." Earl removed the pop-top from his pocket, tossed it in the air and caught it. "What did *you* think when your great-aunt and this Hawaiian guy got together?"

"I was only twelve at the time."

"Twelve-year-olds have opinions."

"What does it matter what I thought?"

He shrugged. "Just curious."

His probing gaze told her otherwise. "I think it's time you moved that gravel. I'd like to get my car before dark."

"Whatever you say, Starstruck." He stood, crushed the beer can in his hand and tossed it into the cooler. Then he turned and started down the driveway.

Watching Earl walk away, Kathryn regretted the curt way she'd dismissed him. She was half tempted to call after him and let him know she wouldn't mind if he came and sat on the patio occasionally. That's what Aunt Kit would have done, and lately she'd been trying to be more like her beloved great-aunt. But just then an inner voice she'd been struggling for a long time to suppress advised, "Knowledge is power. So keep your cards close to your chest, Missy." It was the voice of her grandmother: small, mean and distrustful, especially towards men. Much as she'd disliked her grandmother, she still found it difficult not to heed her cautionary words, if only because old habits die hard, and her grandmother rather than Aunt Kit had been the dominant figure of her formative years.

Besides, Earl had passed out of sight by now, so if she wanted to speak to him, she'd have to run after him—something she wasn't ready to do. Wasn't it enough that she'd overstepped the boundaries she maintained with most people, including Alan, when she'd told him about Aunt Kit's taking a Hawaiian lover?

Chapter 20

Earl stepped inside the trailer, taking in the Spartan furnishings: Formica table with two metal chairs, army cot, wooden rocker salvaged from the dump, tree stump table with a reading lamp that also came from the dump, rag rug where he put his boots on cold nights to keep them from freezing to the linoleum floor. "You'd live in a cave if it were up to you," Mill had said of him. Probably right. The trailer was his cave. It suited him just fine.

Hard to believe he and Mill had once shared this small, spare space. But they'd been young then, just out of high school, newly married, and excited to be on their own. They hadn't minded roughing it, using the woods as their john and trekking across the road to his parents' house for showers. Besides, he'd promised Mill the trailer would only be a temporary home. They'd move out as soon as he built her the house she wanted. She had that house now. He had moved back here after they'd split, though he still went to the house for showers, the occasional meal, and sports events on TV.

He sniffed, caught a whiff of sweat. Ought to go for that shower now. Except he wasn't ready for the whole domestic scene: the living room with its plush carpet, big, comfy couch with fluffy pillows, flowers, and frills; the bathroom where the scent of potpourri mingled with that of freshly washed towels, still hot from the dryer; the spotless kitchen with its hanging rows of gleaming pots and pans, where Mill would be cooking a delicious meal. No, he wasn't ready for all that. His head was still outdoors on the patio of the Farley house with the new tenant.

She'd surprised him this afternoon, first with her fury, which had reminded him of Diana in her angry moments, then with her gentleness when she'd called him Kane and put her hand on his arm. Earl took off his work shirt and rolled up the sleeve of his t-shirt. Freak her out if she knew that beneath the layers of cotton lay a tattoo of a big, black-and-green, coiled rattler with the words: "Don't Tread on Me." He knew she hated snakes. Hank had told him how she'd flipped out when she found the stuffed snake in the house. They'd had a good laugh over it.

Now he almost wished he hadn't planted the snake. He'd done it to scare her, hoping she would return to the city, leaving him to continue his visits to the pond, undisturbed. Now, he wasn't sure he wanted her to leave.

Earl stroked the place where her hand had rested. *Oh, Kathryn, oh, baby . . .* Wait a minute. What was he thinking? He wasn't ready to open that can of worms again. At forty-one he was too old for that kind of craziness. Too old and too burnt-out by his all-consuming love for Diana.

Sometimes he missed the highs that had come with their love, the dizzy sense of being on top of the world with her. But there were other things he didn't miss, the jealousy that was like a rat gnawing at his heart, the violent way it had ended.

Those were experiences he had no desire to repeat. And yet . . . God, he wished Kathryn hadn't touched him, because he, of all people, knew how little it took to spark love, a few words, a gesture, and before you knew it, you were in over your head. Better quit while he still could.

Earl went over to the small, metal kitchen sink and doused his face with cold water. He would go to the house for his shower, make it a cold one, too. Or maybe he'd take a dip in Lake Clyde. That ought to chill him out. But when he remembered the fireball of passion spawned in those icy depths he changed his mind. He'd shower at Mill's.

Chapter 21

The noise of heavy equipment had long ago faded into silence. She could get her car now. Instead, Kathryn remained on the patio, thinking about the man who, for a brief moment, Earl had reminded her of. His errand completed, Kane had returned to Hawaii and committed suicide by jumping off a cliff. She wished it had been otherwise, but she hadn't known how to ease such fierce grief as his.

Her feelings of regret extended to Aunt Kit as well. The two weeks she had spent with Aunt Kit every summer until she was thirteen had provided her sole escape from the atmosphere of gloom that had overshadowed her childhood. She'd been hurt by her grandmother's ban on further visits to Hawaii, but she had never questioned it. Not then, nor much later when she could, and probably should, have. Free at last from her grandmother's control, she had no excuse not to visit Aunt Kit, unless it was because she was still angry at Aunt Kit for the behavior that had brought on the prohibition. Angry and still a bit shocked by Aunt Kit's taking up with a man who was not only a native Hawaiian, but nearly twenty years younger?

Aunt Kit had sometimes hinted it would be nice if Kathryn visited, but she had never reproached Kathryn for failing to do so. Nor, for that matter, had Kane when he'd come with the photograph. Aunt Kit seemed to understand Kathryn's need to break with her family. She'd made it possible for Kathryn to escape an unbearable situation with her mother and father by giving her the money to attend college in Boston.

Guilt gnawed at her when she thought of Aunt Kit's kindness and generosity to her over the years. It was a long way from Boston to

Hawaii, but she could have made the trip at least once, instead waiting for Aunt Kit to come to her.

The ringing phone pulled her from the patio. "So you're back in the Berkshires," Alan said. "I wasn't sure you'd want to return there so soon—if at all—after that fool tried to run us off the road. How is he, by the way?"

"Not good. The doctors think he'll lose the sight in one eye, and he'll need surgery to restore the vision in the other."

"Well, I'm sorry to hear that, but he had no business doing what he did."

"No. I feel for his family, though."

"Of course. It's not going to be easy for them."

"No . . . As for me returning here, I felt I had to, if I'm ever going to accomplish what I came for. I can't just waltz into town and expect people to give me the information I want right away. It's going to take time and effort on my part. But at least I'm starting to make some progress. Yesterday I visited the old woman my great-aunt was in touch with again, and this time, she told me the first name of the woman in the photograph. Hopefully, I'll learn more soon. But enough about me, how is Sophie?"

"A little bit better, I think. The medicine you brought might be starting to work."

"Oh, I hope so! What did you do with it?"

"Cindy got a potted African violet plant, dumped out most of the soil and replaced it with the other soil. That way, we won't have to worry about anyone accidentally throwing it out."

"Who's Cindy?"

"This nice nurse on Sophie's ward."

"What did you tell her about the dirt?"

"Only that it was special and I wanted it in the room with Sophie . . . Everything else okay on your end?"

"Yup. There's nothing else to report except that Earl Barker's started work on the driveway."

"That must be noisy and inconvenient. Unpleasant for you, too, given how you seemed to dislike him. But it did look like the driveway needed to be repaired."

"Uh-huh." No need to tell him about the sympathy Earl had evoked in her when he had bared his soul. Or that she'd responded by revealing a family scandal.

Chapter 22

The next morning, Earl's loader blocked the way when Kathryn drove down the driveway. He pulled aside to let her pass, and she waved her thanks, glad they were in their separate vehicles, and conversation was unnecessary.

"Would you mind looking in on Emily this afternoon?" Millie asked when Kathryn went to the post office to check her mail. "It'll only be for a couple of hours until Sis is ready to leave the hospital."

Kathryn hesitated, remembering Sunday's mealtime ordeal, but also Emily's beatific smile and her need to get information. "I can do that."

"Thanks. You're a doll."

"How's Garth doing?"

"Better. He's starting physical therapy in a few days, and they think he'll be able to leave the hospital in about a week. But it's going to be tough for him and his family. I'm organizing a benefit in their behalf a week from Friday at the White Stag. There'll be a potluck supper, dancing to the music of a local band, a raffle and a silent auction. I hope you'll be able to come."

"I'll try." *What a good person Millie is,* Kathryn thought as she left.

*****

"Where's Sis?" Emily asked as Kathryn helped her out of the senior center van into the house.

"At the hospital."

92

"Still? I call that a long labor, don't you?"

"She's not having her baby. She's at the hospital because of Garth. He was in a bad accident, remember?" Kathryn hoped they wouldn't have the same conversation every time she visited. She settled Emily at the kitchen table, removed a casserole from the fridge and slid it into the microwave. Thankfully, today's casserole was shepherd's pie instead of tuna noodle.

"Blinded, wasn't he?" Emily said. "Just like his great-great uncle, Old Man Barker."

"He was blinded in an accident, too?"

"No." Emily's expression turned grim.

"What happened?"

"I don't want to talk about it now. What's for lunch?"

Kathryn sighed. Emily was as evasive as ever, but maybe after she'd had something to eat, she would be more forthcoming. When Emily had taken several bites of shepherd's pie, Kathryn said, "The other day when I was here, you told Sis that Aurelia would take care of her baby. What did you mean by that?"

"Just what I said."

"But I read in your recollections that Aurelia was your great-grandmother. How could she care for Sis's baby when she's no longer living?"

Emily was silent, considering this. "I must have meant that if Aurelia were alive, she would have taken care of Sis's baby. It was the kind of thing she did. My great-grandmother was a compassionate woman and a loyal friend."

"I'm sure she was."

Emily glanced at her curiously. "You knew Aurelia?"

"No, but I believe what you say about her."

"If it hadn't been for Aurelia, that poor baby might have—" A look of distress came over Emily's face. After a few moments, it was replaced by something else. "Have you been out to Lake Clyde yet?"

Kathryn sighed again. Emily was one of the most exasperating people she'd ever dealt with. The old woman's brain bounced from one subject to the next like a pinball. "No. Is it someplace I should go?"

Emily sucked meat and potato from her finger. "When I was a girl, I enjoyed trips to the lake. Every summer they held a boat parade. Now, that was a lovely sight with Japanese lanterns lighting the boats on the water and the cottages along the shore. We used to take picnics to Johnson's Grove and go bathing at the beach at Heron Point. From there to Cook's Landing on the opposite shore it was only a half-mile, so swimmers often paddled from one side to the other. I was the first young woman ever to swim the seven-mile length of the lake, however."

"That's impressive," Kathryn said politely.

"I dreamed of swimming the English Channel like what's-her-name," Emily continued with a rueful smile. "Had to settle for Lake Clyde, though. And Walter insisted on following in a rowboat. Afraid I'd get a cramp. We were engaged, and he didn't want to lose me before we got to the altar. He needn't have worried. I'd been swimming since I was a little thing. My great-grandmother made all us children learn. A dear friend of hers nearly drowned. She didn't want that to happen to us."

"Is that what you got the medal for?" Kathryn asked.

"What medal?"

"The one on your dresser. You asked me to put Marguerite's photograph next to it the last time I was here." Maybe she could steer the conversation in that direction.

"Oh dear, no," Emily laughed. "Though they should have presented me with a medal. I did get my picture in the local paper and they ran a story about me, too. I've got the clipping somewhere, if you'd like to see it." She pushed back her chair.

"You can show it to me later. About Marguerite—"

"I thought you wanted to know about the medal."

"I do, but—"

"Then pay attention," Emily snapped. "The medal was awarded to a local man for an act of great heroism. Many years later, he gave it to me."

"That was kind of him."

Emily sniffed. "Old Man Barker always gave me presents when he came to visit."

"Old Man Barker gave you the medal? I thought he killed someone. Surely, they didn't award him a medal for that."

"Of course not."

"Then what did he do to earn it?" Maybe now she'd finally get the rest of Old Man Barker's story.

Emily rooted around in her food for a few moments, as if the answer to Kathryn's question lay there. "Have you met Earl?" she asked finally.

Another question out of the blue. If there was any method to Emily's madness, she had yet to discover it. "Our paths have crossed a few times. Why do you ask?"

"He's the one who should tell you the story."

"Why?"

"Old Man Barker was his great-great uncle."

"I'd love it if *you* told me," Kathryn said in the wheedling tone she used with potential donors to the Lyceum's collection.

Emily pointed a greasy, mashed potato-encrusted finger at her for emphasis. "You get Earl to tell you."

"Emily—"

"The story's about Marguerite, too," Emily added slyly. "And tomorrow when you come, be sure to bring her photograph."

*****

Earl was about to climb into his pickup when Kathryn returned from Emily's. She pulled up alongside and left her car. "Looks like you're finished for the day. Like to join me for a drink on the patio?" Despite her effort to sound casual, she was aware of the stiffness in her voice and wished Emily hadn't put her up to this.

"Thanks, but I've got to be someplace."

She wondered if he felt as uncomfortable about opening up to her yesterday as she did. "How about stopping in for coffee tomorrow morning? I promise you a better cup than you'll get at the general store."

He swung his foot off the runner and planted it on the ground. "What's on your mind, Starstruck?"

95

"I was just over at Emily Goodale's. She's got a medal on her dresser, and when I asked about it, she told me it belonged to your great-great uncle, Old Man Barker. She said you should tell me the story of how he earned it."

"Why didn't she tell you herself?"

"She refused."

Earl put his hands on his hips, elbows jutting outward, coat-hanger style. "How come you're so interested in my great-great uncle?"

"I'm trying to find out about a woman from the past named Marguerite. Emily said the story about your great-great uncle and the medal involves her, too. But if you don't want to tell me, I can always—"

"I didn't say I wouldn't."

"Then you will?"

Earl frowned at a stone embedded in the ground. He dislodged it with the toe of his boot, kicked it out of the way and smoothed over the hole that was left. "Yeah. But it'll have to wait until Thursday."

"Why?"

"I won't be around tomorrow. Gonna rain."

Surprised, she looked at the sky. There wasn't a cloud in sight, and she'd heard no forecast of rain. "Really?"

"See you Thursday after work."

Chapter 23

Earl was right. A hard, driving rain knocked the remaining leaves from the trees, reminding Kathryn how bleak November could be. Bleak like the expression on Emily's face when she'd visited her earlier in the day. "But then she died and that was the end of it," Emily said, as the light went out of her eyes and her face took on the look of an abandoned building.

She'd been speaking of Diana. Every time Kathryn asked a question about Marguerite, Emily changed the subject to Diana. She told Kathryn how Diana had campaigned for the law forbidding hunting on private property without written permission from the landowner, and how she'd fought to get boats with gasoline motors banned from Lake Clyde.

Obviously, Emily had loved and admired Diana, and felt her loss as keenly as Earl. But if Diana had been deeply loved, she'd also been hated by Garth and probably other hunters, as well as by the "power boat people," as Emily called them. The more Kathryn heard about Diana, the more Diana struck her as a force of nature: someone you either loved or hated. She was definitely a person who put herself out there—for better or worse. Unlike Kathryn herself, who preferred to remain on the sidelines. That way, she avoided arousing people's ire, but also winning their affection.

What would it be like to be loved like Diana had been by Earl and Emily, or her great-aunt by Kane? And to feel passionate love in return? But to experience this, she'd have to release emotions long pent-up. Every now and then, she was aware of these emotions straining to get out like wild horses in a pen. In her mind, she was mounted on one of them, without bridle or saddle, gripping the horse's mane, thighs pressing into its flanks, terrified lest the horse escape and thunder off with her. If that happened, she imagined herself screaming just like she had as a child astride the white pony at the fair. The pony had looked so cute that she'd begged her grandmother to let her go for a ride, never dreaming that once she got into the saddle, it would break into a furious gallop and not stop until it had carried her, shrieking her head off and barely holding on, around the ring three times that seemed like an eternity.

"I hope you learned your lesson," her grandmother scolded after Kathryn was lifted, dizzy and shaken, from the pony. "It may have looked like a sweet little pony to you, but horses are unpredictable and dangerous. You're lucky you weren't thrown and killed, or maimed for life."

Her grandmother felt the same way about men: like horses they were unpredictable and dangerous, and to fall too hard for the wrong man, as Kathryn's mother had for her father, was to court disaster.

While there was no danger of her falling for Earl, she, nevertheless, decided it might be best if she kept her distance and didn't meet with him tomorrow. Yet if she didn't, she wouldn't learn how Old Man Barker had earned the medal, and how Marguerite had been involved. Unless she could find the tapes of Emily's recollections. Then she wouldn't have to depend on either Earl or Emily to give her the information she wanted.

She knew that some personal items belonging to Gordon and Diana were stored in the attic. First, though, she'd check the red room upstairs that had been Diana's study.

Aside from a couple of field guides to birds and wildflowers, the bookshelves were empty. The desk drawers yielded stray sheets of stationery, paper clips, a few pencils and pens, a back issue of an Audubon Society magazine, and an old annual report of the town. Buried under these was a cassette.

Eureka! She fished it out with greedy fingers and examined the label. Elvis love songs? Strange. She wouldn't have pegged Diana as an Elvis fan.

Abandoning the study, she climbed into the attic. Rain hammered on the roof, and a musty smell filled her nostrils. Pieces of plywood flooring floated like rafts on a sea of pink fiberglass insulation, laden with castaway baggage—old suitcases, boxes, file cabinet drawers, and Diana's wedding picture. Who had defaced it? Garth, another hunter, or one of the power boat people? There were more candidates now.

The grotesque image on the portrait remained with her, as she searched for the tapes among the various containers. Gobs of ugly, gray dust coating a suitcase flew in her face when she opened it. "Ah-choo!" Covering her nose with her hand, she attacked the remaining suitcases and boxes. Nothing. She might as well go back down where she could breathe, and where the noise of rain wasn't so deafening.

She gave the attic a parting glance. There was a box at the far end, lying next to several gallon-sized plastic containers that looked like they'd been used as solar heating collectors. The box might contain what she was looking for, but the area lacked plywood flooring. A single wooden beam bridged the fiberglass ocean.

She stepped gingerly onto the two by four, holding her arms out to steady herself like a gymnast on a balance beam. A heavy gust of wind rattled the attic windows. She teetered precariously. She was just righting herself when a loud clap of thunder made her lose her balance completely. She fell into pink fluff. Fibers pricked her nostrils and stuck to her skin. A cracking noise sounded beneath her. She hauled herself back onto the beam. She didn't dare stand, but crawled along until she reached the relative security of a plywood strip.

Her legs shook as she climbed down the folding ladder. At the bottom, she took a moment to collect herself then walked down the hall to the master bedroom. There was a gash in the ceiling just short of the bed. Damn! It could have been worse, though. She could have crashed through the sheet rock, landed on the floor, and broken a few bones. She might even have been knocked unconscious, only to wake up later, bleeding and disoriented, as had happened to her father in the advanced stages of his illness.

Pushing these disturbing memories aside, she called Brandy to report the damage. Brandy wasn't at the office, so she left a message.

From the bedroom window, she noticed that the surface of the pond was still. The rain had stopped. Eager to flee the scene of the crime, or rather accident, she hopped in her car and set out without any particular destination. After ten minutes of driving around, she came to the town cemetery, situated on a grassy knoll just before the fork that led into the valley below. A familiar Honda was parked near the entrance. She'd barely left her car when a figure rose from the middle of a row of headstones and started toward her.

"Hi, I thought I recognized your car," Kathryn called. With a stricken look, Brandy ran to the Honda and drove off, spraying her with brown water.

Chapter 24

Dark splatters covered Kathryn's jeans and jacket like leopard spots. What had caused Brandy's sudden flight? Mist rose from the headstones like ascending spirits, and the wet ground gave off an earthy smell like a freshly dug grave. The base of her spine tingled. She shook herself. Silly to imagine there were ghosts here. Yet something had spooked Brandy.

Kathryn slipped inside the gate and went to the row of stones where she'd first glimpsed the realtor. She walked along, scanning the names on the stones until one stopped her short: Brian Russo. His dates showed that he had died six years ago, at the age of sixteen. Not only that: he'd died in November. The anniversary of his death was only a few weeks away. Poor Brandy! No wonder she was distraught.

To lose a child . . . She hadn't thought about what that would be like until Alan had almost lost Sophie. "*She asked me if she was going to die. My own daughter! I didn't know what to say.*" She could still hear the anguish in his voice. And knew it was his worst nightmare.

A nightmare that had come true for Brandy. She walked slowly back to her car, saddened by the thought of Brandy's loss.

The phone was ringing when she stepped inside the house.

"Sorry about running out on you just now," Brandy said. "I was having a tough time back there, and I didn't deal with it very well."

"It's all right, I understand. I'm sorry about your son."

"Yeah. Thanks."

In the silence that followed, Kathryn wondered if she ought to mention the damage to the ceiling, or save it for another time.

"Feel like joining me for a drink in Barrington?" Brandy surprised her by asking.

"Well, okay, I just need to change."

"Jeez, did I spray you when I left? Sorry 'bout that. I'll pay for the cleaning, of course."

"It's not necessary."

"No, I want to. And 'bout that drink, how 'bout coming to my place? Save us a trip into town, 'cuz I'm home now."

*****

Brandy lived in a cottage behind a big white colonial on the New Nottingham/Great Barrington Road. The side entrance she told Kathryn to use opened into the kitchen. Brandy sat at a small, round table, cigarette in one hand, glass of bourbon in the other. The room reeked of smoke and something else: a demoralization bordering on despair. It was in the air with its hint of moldering garbage, in the overflowing ashtray, the dirty dishes in the sink, the pile of unopened mail on the counter, and the dead plant on the table.

Her mother's room had looked and smelled this way after several days of neglect, when her grandmother was too tired to go in and open the windows, change the sheets, empty the ashtrays, and remove the collection of dirty glasses and food wrappers. Unlike Kathryn's mother, Brandy appeared to be trying to lift her sagging spirits, judging from the upbeat tenor of the magnetized sayings on the refrigerator door. Also, unlike her mother, who usually hadn't bothered to get up from bed when she came into the room, Brandy rose and greeted her.

"Have a seat while I fix you a drink." Brandy pulled out the other chair from the table, saw it was filled with newspapers and dumped the pile on the floor. "Sorry 'bout that. I've been so busy at the office lately I haven't had time to do much picking up here. What can I get you, a white wine spritzer like the other night?"

In short order, Brandy discovered she was out of "spritz," then white wine, and the only bottle of red in the house contained vinegary dregs. Kathryn settled for beer from a can Brandy scrounged from the back of a cupboard.

"It must be nice and quiet up there on the hill now," Brandy said, plunking ice cubes into Kathryn's glass. "With Garth in the hospital and—" She clamped a hand over her mouth.

"He was the shooter, wasn't he? The one you told me was doing target practice, but who was actually hunting deer."

Brandy pulled a face. "I tried to get him to stop, but he wouldn't listen. At least now you can enjoy some peace."

"Yes, though I had a bit of an accident today."

Brandy ground her cigarette into the ashtray with such force that used butts spilled onto the table. "What happened?"

"I was in the attic looking for something in the part where there's no flooring and—"

"Don't tell me you fell through?"

"I stopped myself in time. But there's a crack in the ceiling of the master bedroom now."

"That's all?" Brandy lit another cigarette and took a drag. Her look of relief told Kathryn she'd been expecting something much worse. "Don't worry. I'll send a repair person over tomorrow."

"I'll pay, of course."

"Gordon can afford it. He doesn't need to know you were responsible. I can say there was a leak or squirrels got into the attic and messed things up. What were you looking for?"

"Tapes Diana Farley made of Emily Goodale's recollections. I'm hoping they'll contain information about my ancestors."

"That's right, you've got local roots. It must give you a wonderful sense of belonging. Did I mention that if you're interested in buying the Farley house, your rent can be applied toward the purchase price?"

"No, but it's too soon to think about buying. I've only been here a little more than a week."

"Of course. I didn't mean to put you on the spot. It's just something to think about for the future. And you've got plenty of time. I won't start actively showing the house again until the spring. But having roots here—just imagine. I'm a newbie myself."

"You're from New York?"

"How'd you know? My accent gave me away?"

Kathryn shrugged.

"Anyway, you're right. Moved here with my kid after his dad died. Brian had fallen in with the wrong crowd in the city, and I thought that here in the country, it would be different but—" The ringing phone interrupted her. "Excuse me a sec." Brandy disappeared into the next room.

"Hi there," she said in a sultry voice then silence punctuated by a series of uh-huhs, each more annoyed than the last. "Well, screw it, if you can't get your shit together enough to . . . aw right, aw right, see ya tomorrow night."

Who was Brandy talking to? Garth had mentioned she was involved with Earl, though he'd put it more crudely. Maybe it was him.

Brandy returned to the kitchen. "Where were we?"

"You were talking about your son and why you moved here."

Brandy gnawed on a bitten-down nail. "Yeah, well, what I didn't realize until it was too late is that if you're looking for bad like Brian was, you're gonna find it wherever you go."

"He got in with the wrong crowd here, too?"

"One bad kid. That's all it takes sometimes. And once they started hanging out together, wasn't much I could do. If Brian's dad had lived, he might've set him straight." Brandy shook her head and threw back more bourbon. "Hid the booze, smashed the bong I found in his drawer, and warned 'im I was gonna call the cops if I ever caught 'im doing that again. Joey's dad told 'im the same thing. Didn't do a bit of good, though. Joey was local, so he knew of this place in the woods, where they could go and do their thing without being bothered. And that's where—" She broke off, squeezed her eyes shut, and gritted her teeth, as if a spasm of pain had just shot through her.

She asked me if she was going to die. My own daughter!

Kathryn patted Brandy's arm. "I'm sorry, really sorry." Again, she was aware of how inadequate those words sounded.

"Thanks," Brandy murmured. Opening her eyes, she gulped down more bourbon and lit another cigarette. She pointed it at the dead plant on the table. "I really oughta throw this out, but the bowl's nice. Maybe I could get something else to grow in it. You like to garden?"

"Not really." The abrupt change of subject surprised her. Obviously,

Brandy didn't want to talk about her son anymore.

"You might get into it if you stay here. Lots of people have gardens, grow flowers, their own vegetables. It's something to think about. If you're hungry, I could fix us a bite. Got some pasta in there somewhere." She gazed blearily at the kitchen cabinets.

Kathryn stood. "Thanks, but I should be going."

Brandy rose unsteadily. "We should do this again. Have dinner, go to a movie, make it a real girls' night out."

"Yes, another time. Good night now," Kathryn murmured, giving Brandy's shoulder a comforting squeeze.

Chapter 25

"How's the research going?" Millie asked when she went to the post office the next day. "Has Emily been helpful?"

"Somewhat, but her mind wanders a lot, so it's hard to keep her on track."

"Welcome to the world of the elderly. You gonna visit her today?"

"Thought I would."

"Good. With Garth in the hospital, we're stretched pretty thin at the moment."

Kathryn nodded. She was about to leave when she remembered there was something she wanted to ask Millie. They were alone in the post office. Still, she leaned in and lowered her voice. "I was over at Brandy's last night, and she was in a bad way."

Millie grimaced. "Too much to drink?"

"Yes. She started talking about why she moved here and the troubles she had with her son. Said he and another kid she didn't like hung out at a place in the woods. She got too upset to say anymore. I sensed it had to do with her son's death. Can you tell me what happened?"

Millie's face turned pale. She was silent a long moment. Finally, she said, "I guess you might as well know." She motioned for Kathryn to come behind the counter and follow her to the rear of the office.

"Brian did hang out with this kid, Joey Fletcher," Millie said. "They were a lot alike—both messed up. They got into fights at school and were suspended a couple of times. Outside of school, they'd get drunk and stoned and may have been into harder drugs, too. Brandy couldn't control Brian and the Fletchers had a hard time with Joey.

The parents tried to keep the boys apart, but whenever their backs were turned, Brian and Joey would sneak off to their hideout in the woods to drink, smoke dope and play their music."

"This hideout in the woods—where was it?"

Millie looked away, her face paling even more. "I hoped you wouldn't ask . . . it was the ruins of your ancestors' mill."

The very place where she and Alan had been shot at a few days ago. Kathryn's chest tightened. "That's not where Brian died, is it?"

"Yes." Millie's voice was barely above a whisper.

"Was he . . . killed by a hunter like Diana Farley?"

Millie's face registered surprise. "Who told you Diana was killed by a hunter?"

"Brandy."

Millie heaved a sigh. "I guess that was easier for her than telling the truth."

Kathryn stared at her, perplexed. "What *is* the truth?"

Millie frowned. "Actually, it's kind of complicated. There are different theories about what happened that night, but—" She broke off, her eyes flitting around the room like a bird seeking a perch.

"What are these theories?"

Millie's gaze returned to Kathryn. Reaching for her ponytail, she tugged on it—so hard it came undone. Strawberry blonde hair flopped around her face, giving her a disheveled, almost wild look. "Shit," she muttered, as she bent over to retrieve the scrunchie that had fallen to the floor. The profanity surprised Kathryn; it didn't fit Millie's wholesome image. But then she figured Millie was entitled to an occasional lapse, especially when speaking about what must be a difficult subject.

And the lapse was short-lived: Her ponytail restored, Millie became herself again: perky and put-together. "Before I answer that question, I better backtrack a bit. As you know, the mill ruins are in the Farley woods. One time when Joey and Brian got really drunk and stoned, they played their music so loud it could be heard all over the hill. Diana went in there and ordered them out. She said if she ever caught them in her woods again she'd call the cops. I think they stayed away for awhile. Or if they came back, they must have kept their music down or not on at all. But that night Joey left before Brian, and once he was by himself, Brian either forgot or was too drunk and stoned to care and blasted the woods with music. When Diana heard it, she must have gone ballistic. Instead of calling the police she stormed in there, confronted Brian, and ended up getting shot to death."

"Brian had a gun?" Kathryn asked, incredulous.

Millie nodded. "Garth's gun."

Of course. Lucas Rogers had told her that Diana had been shot by Garth's gun, but not by Garth himself. "How did Brian get his hands on that gun?"

"Stole it from his cabin. Everyone knew Garth didn't lock it up, so it was there for the taking."

Kathryn shuddered imagining the scene: the blare of rock music drowned out by the deadly boom of a shotgun. Or rather two booms, because Brian had also died that night. "So Brian shot Diana and then . . . ?"

"That's where things get fuzzy," Millie said. "The police think that either Brian turned the gun on himself in a fit of remorse, or was killed in a struggle over it."

The horror of this so overwhelmed Kathryn that it was a few moments before she found her voice. "That's awful, just awful. No wonder it's been hard for Brandy."

"Yes. I found a grief group for her and when she started hitting the bottle, I got her going to AA for a while. November's always a tough month for her, though. It doesn't surprise me she's fallen off the wagon . . . You look like you could use a stiff one yourself."

"I'll be okay," Kathryn said, though she felt far from it.

"I hope so. And I hope what I've told you won't spoil that place for you. It's a nice spot and—"

"You've been to the mill ruins?"

"Yes, but not for a long time. Earl and I used to go there when we were courting."

That's right, the ruins had been a place where lovers went. Now they were associated with death. A murder and a possible suicide. Could anyone who knew this ever visit there without thinking of that?

A package thumped on the counter in front. With a resigned sigh,

Millie left to deal with the customer. Kathryn stumbled from the post office and drove home.

Maybe she should follow Millie's suggestion about a stiff drink, she thought. Instead, she went out onto the patio. Earl hadn't resumed work on the driveway yet, so it was quiet. He was probably waiting for the ground to dry after yesterday's rain. She wiped a lounge chair with a towel and sat. The water level of the pond had risen, and the color had changed from azure to a dark green, speckled with fallen leaves.

This was one of many changes Diana would have observed during the years she'd lived here. Had Diana derived the same peace from the beauty of the scene that she did? Peace broken by hunters' gunshots and loud rock music? The latter noise must have really infuriated Diana for her to march into the woods for a fatal encounter with the teenager responsible. If only Diana had called the police. That's what she would have done. Called the police and let them deal with it. But that wasn't Diana's way; she was someone who took matters into her own hands, however great the risk.

The rumble of heavy equipment sounded on the road. She checked her watch. It was a few minutes past noon. She was due at Emily's.

*****

"Earl's going to tell me the story of how his great-great uncle earned the medal," she told the old woman.

Emily's hand stopped midway to her mouth with a morsel of taco pie. "What's this about Earl?"

Kathryn resisted the urge to roll her eyes heavenward. "You said I should get the story from him."

"I did?" Emily's blue eyes clouded.

"Don't you remember?"

"No, but I suppose I might have." Emily brought the morsel to her mouth and ate it noisily. "You mustn't be afraid of him, dear."

"Who—Earl?" Kathryn asked, startled.

"No. It's the other one you need to beware of."

"What other one?"

"Your husband."

"I'm not married."

"Aren't you?" Emily stared wonderingly at her.

"No." Obviously, Emily had confused her with someone else. Diana?

"Really? I could have sworn you were." Emily looked past her toward the doorway. "Where's Sis? Has she had her baby yet?"

Kathryn groaned inwardly. *Here we go again.*

Chapter 26

Earl's truck was gone when she returned to the Farley house. He'd either forgotten his promise to tell her the story, or something had come up.

Amore met her at the door. "Looks like I've been stood up," she groused, following the cat into the kitchen, where she opened a can of food and started to spoon it into a bowl. A loud knock made her drop the spoon with a clatter. Finishing the task, she went to the door. It was Earl, dressed in clean jeans and a work shirt that matched his faded blue eyes. His light-brown hair was slick from the shower, and he smelled of aftershave. "Ready, Starstruck?"

"Sure." Too bad she hadn't had time to freshen up herself. "I'll get some beer from the fridge, and we can go into the living room."

"I've got beer in the truck. Thought we'd go for a drive."

"Where?"

"Lake Clyde, where the story I'm going to tell you took place."

Uh-uh. She hated surprises. He should have mentioned Lake Clyde beforehand. Alan would have. He always consulted her about plans for their get-togethers, and they often had lengthy discussions about which movie to see, which restaurant to eat at. Yet here was Earl, a man she barely knew, expecting her to go with him to a place she'd never been. "Why can't you tell me the story here?"

"Better there."

"Look, I—"

"C'mon. Please."

At least he had some manners, knew to say "please." And it was a "pretty" please, spoken in the same gentle but firm voice he'd used to get her to sit on the patio the other day when she was so mad. After a moment's hesitation, she followed him to the truck and climbed in. The next instant, she gasped with horror and nearly hopped out.

"What's wrong?"

She pointed at the snake rattle dangling from the rearview mirror.

"Take it down if it bothers you."

"It's okay, I guess." She didn't want him to think she was a complete wuss. "Did your family really kill rattlesnakes and bring their tails to the town treasurer for a reward?"

Earl chuckled. "Yes, but we don't do that anymore. The timber rattlers we have in this state are an endangered species. Now I go with Norm to the den sites in the fall and help him do a count."

"Who's Norm?"

"The naturalist down at Barthlomew's Cobble in Ashley Falls."

"You actually count snakes?" The idea horrified her.

"Sure. They're so gentle lying there in the sun you could almost pick 'em up."

"I wouldn't want to get within ten feet of a rattler."

"Didn't bother Diana." Earl tapped the rattle so that it made a faint noise. "But there wasn't much frightened her."

"Maybe she should've been more cautious."

"What d'you mean?" he asked with an edge in his voice.

"Then she wouldn't have gone into the woods to have it out with Brian Russo."

His expression turned stony. "That *was* a big mistake."

He started the engine, and the truck lurched forward, snake rattle whirring ominously. "Is it true a rattler will always warn you before it attacks?" she asked as they rumbled down the hill.

"Usually, but if you take him by surprise, he might strike without warning." They continued on in silence until, squinting at the rearview mirror, Earl muttered, "What the hell?"

Kathryn had an uncomfortable sense of déjà vu. Was someone tailgating them? She glanced over her shoulder, relieved to see faint headlights in the distance instead of huge, gleaming orbs. Moments later, the headlights disappeared.

After they'd driven a while longer, Earl turned off the road onto a strip of pavement. The truck beams shone on asphalt that had buckled and cracked in places. Weeds grew in the cracks. On one side, a rusty metal structure resembling a giant tiller reared into the air. Beyond lay an expanse of black water. The dark, lonely spot with its derelict equipment gave her the creeps. "This is it?"

"Yup. The lakeshore's all privately owned now except for this ramp. People launch their boats here during the day, and at night, well, couples come."

A parking spot. A place where teenagers came to neck, grope, and even go all the way. There were places like this in California where she'd grown up, in the hills or at the beach. But she'd never been to any of them. Her grandmother had seen to that. Parking in the driveway of their tract home hadn't been possible either, because her grandmother would be watching for them, ready to come out and shine her flashlight into the window if she and her date lingered in the car.

Without firsthand experience, she could only guess at the heady mix of excitement and fear that accompanied those furtive encounters. But she knew what the consequences could be from the whispered innuendo and finger-pointing when a girl lost her reputation or, even worse, became pregnant. She'd been spared this fate, thanks to her grandmother. And yet she sometimes wondered if it would have been better if she hadn't been quite so sheltered.

Earl shifted in his seat and reached for something on the floor, his fingers brushing against her leg. She moved out of the way, surprised to feel a spark of electricity at his touch. He removed a beer can from the cooler and popped the top. "Like one?"

"Thanks."

He got his own beer, took a drink and gazed out at the water. "Before I begin, try to imagine what the lake looked like more than a hundred years ago. There were no powerboats then, only rowboats, canoes, and a steamer that made trips from one end of the lake to the other. People came in their wagons and buggies to picnic on the grounds at Johnson's Grove and go swimming at the beach at Heron Point. And every year on the first Saturday night in August, they held a boat parade.

"It was a beautiful sight with the boats on the water and the cottages on the shore lit up with Japanese lanterns. The boat parade was the second biggest social event of the summer after the Fourth of July. There was dancing and supper at Johnson's Grove for a charge of $1.50. Or you could pay 15 cents just to watch."

She could easily picture the scene from old photographs of similar events in the Lyceum's collection.

"My great-great uncle couldn't afford to pay $1.50, but he was able to scrape together 15 cents from working at the family forge and selling rattlesnake tails. He was eighteen then, a big, strapping fellow, and when he was cleaned up, handsome enough to turn the heads of the village girls despite being a Barker."

Earl might have been describing himself at eighteen. He'd undoubtedly been handsome then and was handsome still. Handsome and well-spoken, his normally laconic speech having assumed the rolling cadences of a storyteller.

"My great-great uncle never paid much attention to the girls, though. Until he saw her."

"*She* was Marguerite?" Kathryn guessed.

"Yes. He first noticed her when she and her party were having supper. He was struck not just by how pretty she was, but by the dainty way she held her glass. Later he watched her dance, and she floated past him like a cloud in her white dress."

Marguerite must have looked much as Kathryn had imagined her the day she'd moved into the Farley house: hair loose on her shoulders, red sash trailing after her as she ran. Without thinking, she removed the clip that held back her own hair so that it fell to her shoulders.

Earl murmured something she didn't hear. She glanced at him and realized he was looking at her. "What?"

He shook his head, withdrew his gaze and continued: "When it was dark, he watched her step into a boat. She lifted her skirts and petticoats, revealing one slippered foot he would have given anything to kiss. But he didn't dare approach her because she was so much above him, a dollar-fifty lady while he was only a nickel-and-dime man. So he just watched as the boat moved out on the water with

Marguerite's dance partner at the oars, another couple seated at the stern, and Marguerite at the prow, a vision in white. As more and more boats went out onto the water, their lanterns lit up the lake like fireflies. Like this." Earl switched off the truck beams and flicked on a lighter.

The sudden movement startled her. Light from the flame played on his face, giving it a sinister cast.

"He managed to keep her boat in sight so that when the accident occurred he was ready."

"What accident?"

"I'm getting to that. There was a bunch of rowdies among the onlookers. They whooped and hollered and passed around a whiskey bottle. As the evening wore on, they grew wilder and wilder. Finally, they decided to set off a couple of sticks of dynamite as the lighted boats went past. The explosion blew out the candles on the boats and threw the passengers into a panic. Their frantic motion rocked the boats until some of them tipped over, including the one she was in." He waved the lighter wildly in the air, then capped it, plunging them into total darkness.

Kathryn gasped. She couldn't see him but knew he'd moved closer because the scent of his aftershave filled her nostrils. His breath tickled her earlobe.

"It's okay," he said softly. "Your eyes will adjust like his did. He dove into the lake, and somehow in all the confusion, he found her. Her skirts and petticoats swirled around her like an unfurling sail, dragging her down. But he felt the flesh and fine bones inside the wet cloth, slipped an arm around her and towed her to shore."

Calmed both by what he said and how he said it, she relaxed and turned toward him to catch his next words, intimate and compelling like a confession whispered in the shadows.

"He laid her on the ground in her white shroud. Then he put his mouth on hers and drank until he had drained her dry of all the water and little fishes and weeds she'd swallowed. She opened her eyes and looked at him. Drops from his face fell on her. She caught them with her tongue and lapped them up, as if she were thirsty and hadn't already drunk several gallons of lake water. But before she could ask who he was, he dove back into the lake to rescue others."

Kathryn's mouth felt dry. She might have been doing the talking instead of him. She took a drink of beer, licking her lips afterward. Beside her, she heard Earl swallow and knew he'd taken a drink also. Then his voice, beguiling as ever, "Although she was ill for some time afterward, she made it her business to learn his name and where he lived. When she was well, she rode in her buggy up Rattlesnake Hill and found him working at the smithy, his face and arms black as a chimneysweep's. 'Are you Mr. Clyde Barker?' she asked. When he answered 'yes,' she took his sooty hand in her white-gloved one and said, 'Then, I thank you for saving my life.'

"Later she and some other important people in town saw that he was awarded a medal for his heroism that night. She wanted the lake renamed in his honor, also. That didn't sit well with the town fathers. They couldn't imagine naming anything after a Barker. But she kept after them until finally they gave in and changed it from Seven-Mile Pond to Lake Clyde."

Clyde. The word hung in the darkness like the lingering note of an old ballad, "The Ballad of Marguerite and Clyde." An unfinished ballad. She wanted to hear the other verses. "What happened to Marguerite and Clyde?"

Earl switched on the headlights and reached across her to get a flashlight from the glove compartment. "What's the matter?"

"Think I heard something just now. Gonna check it out."

He left the truck and beamed his flashlight into the woods on either side of the boat ramp.

"Must have been the wind," he said when he returned. If that was all, why did he look grim as he put the truck in gear and backed off the ramp?

"What about Clyde and Marguerite?" she prodded. "Aren't you going to tell me what happened next?"

"That's another story. Get Em to tell you." The snake rattle whirred menacingly as the truck sped along the road.

"What if she won't?"

"Why wouldn't she?"

"I don't know. Sometimes I think she's forgotten what happened, other times that she knows but refuses to tell me out of sheer

116

contrariness."

"Maybe she doesn't think you're ready yet."

"What's that supposed to mean?"

"Just what I said."

She was bursting with questions. Sensing his resistance, she tried another tack. "Who told you the story?"

"I heard bits when I was a kid. They were like loose pieces of a puzzle. I didn't put them together until Diana told me the whole story. She got it from Em and passed it on to me, because she wanted me to know something good about my family."

"Emily's the original source?"

"Yup, but if you ever played telephone, you know the message can get changed from one person to the next. There may be things that weren't in Em's version, but were added by Diana, or by me just now."

Which were his embellishments? Clyde draining water and little fishes from Marguerite? Marguerite lapping up the drops of water that fell on her from Clyde? Clyde's story was his in certain respects. Like Clyde, he was a nickel-and-dime man who'd fallen for a dollar-fifty lady. And in both cases a body of water had brought the lovers together. Clyde had come to Marguerite's attention when he'd rescued her from drowning. Earl had been noticed by Diana when he'd created the pond. Were there other similarities? She knew how Earl and Diana's story ended, but not how Clyde and Marguerite's had.

In the driveway of the Farley house, she made a final attempt: "You can't just leave me hanging. I want to know what happened to them."

"Ciao, Starstruck." He shooed her unceremoniously from the truck and drove away.

Off to pick up Brandy? In spite of herself, she felt a prick of jealousy. On the other hand, his abrupt departure could be related to whatever he had seen at the boat ramp. He'd seemed different afterward, spooked almost.

Amore was waiting for her at the door just like her grandmother when she'd been out on a date. "You didn't have to worry about me tonight," she told the cat. "He didn't lay a hand on me, unless you count the time he accidentally brushed my leg."

She made herself a sandwich and ate mechanically, her mind on Earl and what he'd told her about Marguerite and Clyde. When Alan called ten minutes later, she was still preoccupied.

"Where have you been? I've been trying to reach you for the past hour and a half."

"Sorry. I went out for a while." No need to tell him where she'd gone or with whom. "Is everything all right?"

"That's why I'm calling. Sophie's so much better the doctor thinks she can come home by the end of next week. I'm planning a small party in honor of her recovery. I hope you'll come."

"That's wonderful news! I'll definitely be there."

"Good. I've missed you, Kathryn."

"I've missed you, too. I know this is going to seem like a strange question but—" She broke off, embarrassed.

"What?"

"If I were drowning, would you rescue me?"

Alan was silent a long moment. Then clearing his throat, he said, "I think so. But first, I would like to know the circumstances surrounding this hypothetical drowning?"

"Circumstances?"

"For example, are other people in danger—children or elderly people, who would be in greater need of rescue than a healthy, young woman like you?"

Her cheeks burned with shame. "I didn't think of that."

"I would also want to know a little more about the situation. Did you develop a sudden cramp in a swimming pool, or were you swept overboard in thirty-foot waves?"

"Why does that matter?"

"If it was the latter, I'd have to think twice. I'm a single parent with a young daughter. It would be irresponsible for me to attempt a rescue when there was a strong possibility I would be killed."

"Of course. It was a stupid question. I shouldn't have asked."

Alan sighed. "No, no, I'm the one who ought to apologize. I've given you a long-winded response when a simple 'yes' would have sufficed. It's my legal training."

"I'm so glad Sophie's better." She changed the subject.

"Thanks in part to you."

"Me?"

"You brought the special soil."

Although the conversation ended on a positive note, Kathryn felt bad afterward. Sophie's near fatal illness had given Alan enough to worry about without foolish questions from her. His devotion to his daughter—so unlike her own father's complete disregard of her and her mother in pursuit of his various amours—was one of the things that had attracted her to him in the first place. That and the fact he was eminently rational and responsible, and not given to reckless, extravagant gestures.

*****

That night, she dreamed she was floating on the pond. A gentle rain began to fall, and she opened her mouth to catch the drops. In the distance thunder rumbled. She knew she should leave the water before the storm approached, but she went right on lapping up the rain.

Chapter 27

"Please tell me the rest of the story," Kathryn begged Emily the next day. "What happened between Marguerite and Clyde Barker? And what was her connection with my ancestor, Jared Cutter?"

Emily was silent a long time, her expression unreadable. "You ought to visit her grave," she said finally.

*****

Finding Marguerite's grave would be difficult but not impossible, Kathryn thought as she drove to the town cemetery later that afternoon. With only a first name to go on, she'd have to look for Marguerites in the various family plots, but at least she only had to check the older ones. She'd start with the Barker and Cutter plots, in case Marguerite had married either man.

It was almost four. In this dark season, the light would soon be gone. She climbed the hill to the older section and began scanning the names on stones. She had to stoop often to make them out. Her eyes hurt from squinting at the shadowy letters and her back ached from bending, but the sense she was on the verge of an important discovery drove her on.

She was unable to find any Barker graves, but eventually she located a cluster of Cutter graves. Her ancestors lay there. She should pay her respects, adopt an appropriately reverential attitude, but she felt only disappointment she hadn't yet found Marguerite's grave.

She was about to move on when an inscription caught her eye: "Marguerite, beloved. . . " Moss covered the rest of the words except for the dates at the bottom: "Born December 3, 1834; Died June 25, 1855." The dates fit: This Marguerite had died in the same year Jared Cutter left for California. Perhaps Aunt Kit had been right to believe his departure was related to something that happened between them. Had she been his beloved then? Beloved sister or wife?

She knelt on the damp ground and scraped the moss away. Where the words should have been, there was a rough, hollowed-out space. It looked as if someone had taken a chisel and deliberately destroyed the carving. Who? And why? Cold seeped into her bent legs and traveled up her spine. Her fingers were numb. She felt a sense of defilement deeper than any surface damage, as if Marguerite's very grave had been desecrated. Maybe it had.

Joints stiff from kneeling, she rose and made her way down the hill. In her car with the heater turned on full blast, she felt better. Yet when she saw the Farley house, looming out of the shadows with its blank, blind-eye windows, she knew she didn't want to be alone. After the graveyard, she needed to be among the living.

*****

The bar in Great Barrington was noisy and crowded with people waiting for tables. Brandy sat in a booth with a man. Earl? Kathryn was about to leave when Brandy spotted her and waved. Reluctantly, she approached, relieved to discover that Brandy's companion wasn't Earl, but a burly, bear-like man. Black hair bristled on his head, chin, forearms, and through the v-neck of his shirt. Brandy introduced him as Norm St. Clair.

"I'm the naturalist at Barthlomew's Cobble," he said after Kathryn joined them. "You been there?"

"No."

"It's the place to go if you like flowers or ferns. We've got nearly five hundred species of wildflowers and fifty-three kinds of ferns.

People come from all over the world to see them. The Cobble's rich in plant life because of the marble and quartzite. Marble releases lime, an important plant food, while quartzite . . ."

He went on explaining the unique features of the Cobble during drinks and dinner. Brandy looked bored and Kathryn's thoughts kept drifting back to Marguerite's defaced gravestone.

"Only buy fiddleheads at the supermarket," Norm St. Clair's voice broke her reverie.

"Pardon?"

"Only buy fiddleheads at the market because the ones you pick yourself might contain liver toxin which can kill you."

"I'll remember that. Earl Barker said you two count rattlesnakes in the fall."

"That's right. We were just at the ledges last month."

"Yuck." Brandy made a face. "You wouldn't catch me up there with all those rattlers."

"They're not so bad," Norm said. "Didn't bother Diana. But then she was something else," he added with an appreciative chuckle. "She and Earl went to the ledges a lot. I think they even—"

"Norm," Brandy said sharply.

He shrugged. "Anyway, as I was saying, I used to envy Earl having a woman who'd—"

A scuffle under the table told her Brandy had kicked him.

"Who'd go all those places with him," Norm finished sheepishly.

"Where else did they go?" Kathryn asked.

"The boat ramp, an old ruined mill, the—"

"What old ruined mill?" she interrupted.

"In the woods near a swamp."

The news gave her a queasy feeling in the pit of her stomach. Diana and Earl had visited the ruins for the same reason he and Millie and other couples had. They'd kissed and perhaps even made love at the very place where she was later killed.

"You okay?" Brandy asked. "You look kinda pale."

Kathryn took a deep breath and let it out slowly. "I'm all right."

"We're going to a movie. Want to join us?"

"No thanks."

As they were leaving, Norm St. Clair turned to her. "You see Earl again, tell him I've got a bone to pick with him. It's about the—"

"C'mon, Norm." Brandy took him by the arm, "We don't get a move on we'll be late."

Chapter 28

"I visited Marguerite's grave in the village cemetery," Kathryn reported to Emily the next day. "But someone scraped away part of the inscription, so I didn't learn much except her dates."

"You went to the wrong grave."

"There's more than one?" she asked, dumbfounded.

Emily separated a macaroni noodle from its cheesy crust with her fingers and nodded. "The grave you found was her first resting place. She's somewhere else now."

"You mean she was moved?" This was beyond bizarre.

"Yup."

"By whom?"

"Clyde."

"Why?"

"He wanted her up on the hill with his folks."

"He had permission to do that?"

"He just did it."

"Nobody tried to stop him?"

"He moved her at night when everyone was asleep."

"But afterward people must've noticed her grave had been tampered with."

"If they did, they didn't make a fuss. The only person who might've cared was Jared Cutter, and he'd already left for California."

"Then she was Jared Cutter's beloved? Beloved what?"

"Wife," Emily said softly.

"Why didn't you tell me in the first place?" Kathryn cried, exasperated.

"I believe I did."

Had she missed something? "When?"

"The morning you came to the senior center with the photograph. You asked who she was and I said his wife."

"I thought you were talking about Diana."

"Goodness, no. She was Gordon Farley's wife, not Jared Cutter's."

"If Marguerite was Jared Cutter's wife, why did Clyde move her to the hillside?"

"Barkers have always buried their own," Emily replied cryptically.

"She wasn't his wife."

"He loved her. Earl told you the story about how he rescued her from drowning, didn't he?"

"Yes, but—"

Emily placed a gnarled, greasy hand on her arm. "You visit her real grave then maybe you'll understand."

"Where is it?"

"On the ledges behind the Barker place." Emily stabbed a finger at her plate. "You better zap this again. My dinner's cold."

*****

Later that afternoon, Kathryn drove up Rattlesnake Hill past the gated driveway of the old Whittemore mansion, then Garth's crude cabin. Beyond the cabin, the road climbed, then dipped and leveled out again. Ahead on the right, she spotted a freshly painted white house with green shutters and a green door, flanked by twin barrels of mums. The house sat on a square of manicured grass. House and lawn looked as if they'd been lifted from a suburban neighborhood and plopped down on the wild backside of the hill. She doubted any Barkers lived there.

More likely, the collection of ramshackle, dark-timbered buildings a little further on belonged to the family. Nearby was a jumble of rusted appliances, old farm equipment, several trucks and a couple of early-model cars that looked like leftovers from a demolition derby. She parked opposite the compound. A steep, rock-strewn hill rose behind it. The family burying ground must be there, though she saw no path leading upward, no cluster of gravestones at the top, which was covered with stunted pines, interspersed with boulders.

Before she could get out for a closer look, a pack of snarling black and tan mongrels surrounded the car. They reared up on their hind legs, claws scratching the metal sides, teeth snapping at the windows, tongues smearing them with slobber. She shut her eyes in sheer terror. When she opened them again, the dogs were still there. Surely, someone would come and call them off. No one did, but eventually they grew tired. After several face-saving barks, they straggled back to the buildings. All but one mangy beast. He clung to the car so closely that when she made a U-turn and drove back down the road, she worried she'd run over him.

The dog followed her all the way to the Farley house. She was afraid to open the car door lest he leap inside. Luckily, he discovered the pond. While he plunged in, she made a dash for the house. Amore hissed at the dog when he appeared on the patio and shook himself, splattering the glass door. The cat gave her a severe look, as if she were to blame for bringing such a loathsome creature home.

The dog hung around the rest of the afternoon and evening like a hound from hell. He clawed at the door, barked and howled, and pressed his black nose against the window. Finally she closed the curtains, putting him out of sight, if not out of mind.

Chapter 29

By mid-Sunday morning, the dog was still there, and Kathryn felt like a prisoner in the house. Desperate, she telephoned Hank Lapsley. The phone rang and rang. When he finally answered, she could tell from his groggy, annoyed voice she'd woken him. She apologized then explained about the dog.

"What d'you expect me to do?"

"Take him away."

"Barkers' dog, they should get 'im. And please, Miz Stinson, don't call me again 'less it's a real emergency."

"But—"

The drone of the dial tone filled her ears. Hauling out the phone book, she found four Barkers listed on Rattlesnake Hill: Earl, Garth, Roy, and Wayne. Garth was in the hospital and she didn't know the other two, so Earl was the logical one to try. Yet for reasons she didn't want to examine too closely, she was reluctant to call him. She wished there was someone else in town she could turn to. Still, as Hank had pointed out, it *was* the Barkers' dog.

"Is this about the driveway?" Earl sounded surprised to hear from her.

"One of your dogs followed me home yesterday and he won't leave."

"You want me to get him?"

"Please."

Ten minutes later, she heard his truck on the driveway, then his voice calling the dog, followed by a knock on the door. Earl stood on the stone landing, the dog sitting obediently beside him. She stepped back warily in case the dog changed its mind and lunged at her.

"He won't bite," Earl assured her. "Hold out your hand and let him sniff you."

She extended her hand gingerly, feeling the dog's warm breath on her fingers, then his wet nose and tongue.

"See, he just wants to be friends."

"He acted vicious earlier. All your dogs did."

"What were you doing up at our place?" His blue eyes bore into her.

"I'm trying to find out more about Marguerite. Emily told me I should visit her grave in your family's burial ground. I would have asked your permission, but I never got a chance because of the dogs."

Earl studied the large rock that formed the doorstep. He seemed to find its surface very interesting. Finally, he said, "I'll take you to the cemetery, but you better put on hiking boots if you got 'em."

*****

Again, the day was unseasonably warm. Even with both windows wide open, the truck felt like an oven. The heat, combined with the whirring of the snake rattle, made her nervous. "I hope there aren't any snakes where we're going."

"Matter of fact, there are. But don't worry, they won't be out this late in the year."

"Sure?"

"I'd be awfully surprised if they were."

"Whose little bit of suburbia is that?" she asked when the white house with green shutters came into view.

"Mill's. And our youngest son, Pete. The other two are out on their own."

"Where do you live?"

"I've got a trailer in the woods that we used when we were building the house."

He pulled off the road onto a stretch of grass, flattened by tire marks, just short of the collection of tumbledown buildings. The dog leaped from the truck bed and joined the swarm of black and tan mongrels that bounded over, barking excitedly. They fell silent and bowed their heads when Earl got out. Clearly, he was boss. He scratched their ears and shooed them away.

The coast clear, she left the truck and followed Earl along the tire tracks to the back of the compound. A white-haired man in overalls appeared in a doorway. "That you, Earl?"

"Yeah. Grand-dad, this is Kathryn Stinson. Kathryn, grand-dad."

"Where're you going?"

"I'm taking her to the cemetery to look at graves."

"You behave yourselves up there, you hear?" grand-dad advised.

"What did he mean by that?" she asked after the old man had gone back into the building. Earl shrugged and looked away. She flushed. The ledges were one of the places he'd gone with Diana.

"This way." He strode briskly toward a rocky slope several hundred yards away.

She trotted after him. "That's the first time you've called me by my real name."

"He's my grand-dad," Earl replied, as if this were explanation enough. At the foot of the hill, he stopped. "There's not much of a trail, so follow me."

They found the occasional foothold between the rocks, but mostly they had to scramble over boulders, slippery with moss and lichen. She climbed slowly, keeping an eye out for snakes. When the going was especially rough, Earl gave her a hand. By the time they reached the top, she was winded and sweaty. "Why on earth did they put the graveyard up here?"

"High ground's always better."

"They must have had a terrible time getting the coffins up."

"They used ropes and pulleys and once the coffins were there, nobody could mess with them."

"I still don't understand why they couldn't have just used the town cemetery."

"Barkers have always buried their own." He repeated Emily's words. "I'll show you Marguerite's grave now."

He led her to a jumble of headstones in a clearing amid the brush and stunted trees. Many of the headstones were overgrown with weeds and tilted at odd angles. A few looked well-tended, though. "That's hers." He pointed at a well-tended stone. A blue glass bottle filled with faded asters stood on the ground beside it. The stone was old and weathered, but the inscription appeared newly minted. Kathryn squatted to read it.

Marguerite
Beloved of Clyde Barker
Born December 3, 1834, Died June 25, 1855
Parted in this life, yet shall we be joined
Forever in the next.

Below was a pair of entwined hearts. A shadow fell on the stone. Earl stood behind her. "They say Clyde used to spend hours here. Although he couldn't see the stone on account of his blindness, he touched it over and over again. That's why the sides are smooth and the inscription looks like it was cut yesterday. Feel it and you'll see what I mean."

She ran a finger along a polished edge, moved by Clyde's devotion. "Where's he buried?"

"Next to her." Earl gestured at a headstone to the left of Marguerite's. Again she had to squat to read the inscription:

Clyde Barker
Born March 5, 1836, Died May19, 1938
He dwelt in darkness,
Ever yearning for the light of
Her smile.

Her vision blurred. Drops of sweat or tears? Wiping her eyes, she stared at the dates. "He lived to be one hundred and two?"

"That's right. He survived her by more than eighty years. He never married and those who knew him said not a day passed when he didn't speak her name with longing. He used to come up here every day when he was younger. Toward the end, he could only come every few months. They had to carry him in a litter. He died trying to reach her. They found his body halfway up the ledges."

More salty drops filled her eyes. This time she knew they were tears. *Don't get all weepy. Remember how he desecrated the other grave.* Something else bothered her, something she couldn't identify. A hard knot of anger began to form. "Who tends these graves now?"

"I do. And while we're here, I might as well replace the asters." He moved away.

Kathryn stared at Marguerite's headstone, then at the bottle with its withered blooms. Before her eyes, the bottle became a small bowl filled with dried rose petals. It sat on her mother's dresser beside a framed photograph and a votive candle. "Your father's picture needs to be dusted," her mother called from bed. Kathryn started to reach for the photograph but stopped short.

"Do it," her mother ordered.

Her heart was beating very fast. The knot of anger grew until it burst apart. Her arm swung outward, sweeping the dresser top clean. China and glass shattered against the floor. Her mother screamed.

"What the hell?" Earl's voice jolted her back to the present.

She blinked. Flowers and shards of glass littered the ground in front of Marguerite's grave. Dazed, she rose and faced him. "I don't know what came over me just now. I thought. . ." She trailed off, ashamed.

Earl stared at the wreckage, then at her. "The bottle you destroyed was special. Clyde himself put it there. What's wrong with you, anyway?" He took a step toward her.

"Nothing," she snapped, shock giving way to a fresh burst of anger. "Clyde had no business digging up Marguerite's coffin and moving it here. He should have left her where she belonged, in the grave her husband made for her. He loved her, too, and after she died he kept her portrait with him the rest of his life."

"Big deal." Earl's face turned as red as the berries on the branch in his hand. "He hightailed it out of town the minute she was in the ground, and never came back to visit her grave."

"So? He realized it was time to move on. That's what normal people do. Move on and start a new life. It's only the crazy ones who stay stuck in their stupid grief. Like Clyde making her grave into a goddamn shrine. And you mooning over Diana by the pond."

Earl's fists clenched and his features compressed until she caught a glimpse of his brother's mean, ugly mug. She half expected him to haul off and hit her as Garth might have. "I'm sorry I brought you here." His voice was tight as a steel trap.

"I'm sorry I came."

"Then go! Get out of here!" He jabbed the branch at her like a spear. She darted past him and began the descent, gravity propelling her downward, reckless in her fury. What a fool he was to keep up the family tradition of crazy love, endless mourning! Her boot slipped on a loose stone and she nearly fell. Regaining her balance, she continued her headlong plunge. She heard the clomp of his boots behind her and quickened her pace, even though getting down was harder than getting up. Then, she'd only gotten winded. Now, her leg muscles ached from braking. How absurd to put a cemetery on this steep hill without a proper path. The Barkers were insane.

"Watch out!" Earl's voice came from behind. Probably just trying to frighten her. Her gaze fell on a rope-like shape sprawled on the rock below. Too late—one foot was already in the air when the rope came alive. It spun around to face her, long neck rearing up from the coil of its body. She saw the flicker of a forked tongue, heard a telltale rattle. She wanted to scream, but her throat had gone completely dry. The snake craned its head toward her, its fangs only inches away. She shut her eyes, steeling herself against the pain that would come any second. An arm hooked around her middle, jerking her away.

She landed hard on her left side, with Earl piled on top. He eased himself off and stood. "That was close. Let's go."

She shook her head, pointed wordlessly at the rock below. The snake was still there, body raised in attack mode, rattle whirring ominously.

"We steer clear of him, he won't bother us." Earl held out a hand.

She didn't move, her body rigid with fear.

"C'mon." He tugged on her hand.

"No."

He squatted beside her. "You won't walk, I'll have to carry you." He slid an arm around her and lifted her. His legs buckled under her weight. She clung to his neck, terrified he'd drop her. "Gotcha," he said, steadying himself.

Giving the snake a wide berth, he started down. One arm encircled her shoulders, the other cradled her thighs, his muscles flexed and hard beneath her. She felt the jog of his every step, the rapid rise and fall of his breath, the sticky dampness of his sweat. He stopped once or twice to reposition her, but gave no other sign she was a burden. She began to relax and even enjoy the downhill trip. Closing her eyes, she rested her head against his chest.

She knew they'd reached level ground from the change in his gait and was almost disappointed when he stopped and said, "You can walk now." Yet he held her a moment longer. When he did release her, he sighed deeply. With relief or . . . ? She slid down, scraping against his belt buckle, her hair snagging on something. She tried to stand and pull free, but her legs wobbled, and she was all tangled up with him.

"Hold still a sec." His fingers sifted through her hair, unsnapping the clip that held her hair back, which had caught on a chain he wore around his neck. When he'd separated them, he gazed at her hair, hanging loose around her face.

"What's that?" she asked to get him to stop staring at her. She pointed at a small blue medallion at the end of his chain.

"My St. Christopher medal."

"The saint who protects travelers?"

He nodded, his eyes still on her hair.

"Maybe he protected us today."

"I thought you didn't believe in that kind of thing."

She shrugged. He stared at her a moment longer before looking away. A dog barked in the distance then it was quiet again.

"Never seen a rattler out this late in the season before," he said. "Usually they have a last big meal, spend some time digesting it, and disappear into their dens for the winter. The hot weather must've confused him. Heat's starting to get to me, too." He swiped a hand across his forehead. "I'm awfully thirsty. How about you?"

"I'd love a glass of water."

"C'mon, then."

He turned away, the corners of his mouth curling upward in a smile.

Chapter 30

As they crossed the road to the white house, she noticed a blue station wagon parked in the driveway. Earl frowned but said nothing. He led her to a clearing behind the house, where a dark green trailer blended in with the surrounding woods. Two barrels of mums stood on either side of the door, just as they did at the house. Millie's touch? If so, there was no sign of her or any other woman's influence inside. Judging from the minimal furnishings, Earl was a man who required few comforts. Snowshoes, animal traps, a fishing rod and a gun case were attached to the otherwise bare walls. The trailer was cool as an animal's den.

Earl motioned her to a chair at the Formica table, filled two glasses at the sink, and gave her one. "Better?" he asked after they'd each taken a long drink.

"Yes."

He ran a hand through his light brown hair, studying her until the scrutiny made her uncomfortable. "What?"

He stared into his glass, then at her again. "Want to tell me what was going on at the cemetery?"

She'd hoped he wouldn't bring that up. "What do you mean?"

"You got pretty upset."

"I said some things I shouldn't have. I'm sorry. I still think Clyde was wrong to move Marguerite from the village cemetery, though."

"You're entitled to your opinion." He paused to take a drink of water. "But what happened at the ledges wasn't only about Clyde and Marguerite." He leaned forward, staring at her intently.

She squirmed, her back pressing into the hard metal of the chair.

"I don't know what you're talking about."

"After you broke the bottle, you looked dazed. Like you'd been somewhere else and just returned."

"Can we drop it? I said I was sorry."

He looked at her with his infernal blue eyes. Waiting for her to spill the beans like she had about Aunt Kit's scandalous affair with Kane. *Not on your life*. She rose and headed for the door. "Thanks for the water. And for taking me up to the cemetery and seeing me safely down."

"Whatever happened in that other place must've really hurt you."

The observation stopped her. How could he possibly know? Unless he saw the well-concealed wound others hadn't. She spun around to face him. The wound ripped open and fresh blood spurted out.

"Yes! My mother kept a photograph of my father on her dresser next to a bowl with dried flowers and a votive candle. Like it was a shrine. He didn't deserve to be worshiped. He left when I was four. Married four more times and would have married a sixth if—"

She bit her lip. Why was she telling him this? She'd better stop while she still could. Silence stretched between them. Silence she felt compelled to fill. "He would have married again if he hadn't become ill with Parkinson's. Imagine: an orthopedic surgeon and a celebrity doctor who'd treated big-name athletes with hands that shook too much for him to operate. He lost his practice. And once the money was gone, his fifth wife walked out on him. But my mother, she, she—"

Even now, she stumbled over the sheer improbability of her mother's action. She half-expected Earl to urge her to continue. If he had, she might have come to her senses and left without another word. Instead, his silence goaded her to speak.

"She took him in, goddammit! She'd spent the years since he left, holed up in her room, too depressed to get out of bed. She was never there for me. My grandmother had to look after her and raise me at the same time. Yet when she found out my father was ill, couldn't work, and had been abandoned by his wife, she invited him to come and live with us."

She paused to give him a chance to show his disbelief and

disapproval, but he merely gazed at her.

"Incredible, isn't it?" she said. "The whole thing was like some twisted fairytale with my mother as Sleeping Beauty. A Sleeping Beauty, who wasn't awakened by the kiss of a handsome prince, but by this sick old man who'd dumped her years ago. He could hardly dress himself, hardly get through a meal without spilling his food. He had to wear diapers and couldn't walk without a cane. Even then, someone had to be with him in case he fell and wound up on the ground, bleeding and unconscious. This was the man my mother roused herself from her long sleep for—the man she expected my grandmother and me to help her care for."

She paused, hands on her hips, features twisted with rage. Again she hoped for a reaction and got nothing. He seemed to be waiting for her to finish before he passed judgment. She plunged on.

"My grandmother was so furious she moved out and went to live with a woman she knew from work. I was stuck there with this awful man and my crazy mother. How could she take him back after what he did to her?" The question was rhetorical: she didn't expect a response. This time she got one.

"Sounds like your mother never stopped loving your father," he said quietly.

"Love!" she exploded. "What she did was sick, perverse. He'd already ruined her life once, and she let him do it all over again. My life, too! I was seventeen, in my last year of high school, working after school and on weekends so I could be free of them. She made me quit my job and stay home to help out with him. I hated every minute of it. I wanted him to die. If I hadn't left when I did, I might have killed him."

There. She'd said it. Her worst secret was out in the open. His gaze held steady and sympathetic. His disgust she could have handled, but not his sympathy. It was like a current flowing from his eyes into her, loosening something deep within. She began to sob, her whole body shaking, hot tears streaming down her cheeks. Through the blur of her tears, she was aware of him walking over to her. His very nearness made her feel better. He was there in case she needed him while she rode out the emotional storm.

When she was calmer, he removed a red bandanna from the pocket of his jeans and gave it to her. She wiped her face and blew her nose. Embarrassed, she stuffed the bandanna into her pocket. "I'll return this after I've washed it."

"Okay."

It wasn't okay. She wished she hadn't exposed her innermost self to him. Still, it was good to get the poison out of her system, if only for a while. She felt empty, purged, then apprehensive. "What I told you just now, you must think . . ."

He shook his head, as if to forestall further words. "C'mon. I'll take you home."

Walking out of the trailer was like leaving a darkened movie theater after a matinee: the light too bright, the heat oppressive. She felt disoriented and tripped on the last cinder block step. She grabbed his arm to steady herself, letting go as soon as she was on solid ground. The sense of disorientation continued. The scene in the trailer, the trip to the hilltop cemetery, the rattler and her miraculous rescue—had any of that really happened? Or had she dreamed the whole thing? If so, it was the most vivid dream she'd ever had. Vivid and unsettling.

Shaking her head to clear it, she followed Earl out of the woods to the road. As they were about to cross to his truck, he suddenly broke away. He loped over to a utility pole with a rusted metal hoop, dribbling an imaginary basketball as he went. He leaped into the air, grabbed the rim of the hoop, and slam-dunked the ball through. His t-shirt sleeve hiked up on his arm, and she caught a glimpse of a dark blot on his skin. A birthmark? A tattoo? He smiled when he landed, and so did she. As if he were a basketball star, and she his biggest fan.

When they arrived at the Farley house and she saw the white BMW with the rental sticker parked in the driveway, it, too, seemed part of the dream.

Chapter 31

A man walked slowly toward them from behind the house. He was about Earl's height, but heavier with a round face and the beginning of a paunch protruding from the pink polo shirt he wore with khaki cargo pants.

"Didn't expect to see you here, Gordon," Earl said tightly.

So this was Gordon Farley. He had yellow-flecked hazel eyes and longish, curly dark blonde hair that framed his face like a lion's mane. He reminded her of a big fat cat.

"A gallery in the city wants to exhibit my work," he said.

"Still taking pictures of door knockers?" Earl scoffed.

"Actually, I've switched to window sashes. How about you? Still fooling around with snakes and . . .?" He glanced at her curiously.

"I'm Kathryn Stinson, the new tenant."

"Pleased to meet you." He extended a pigskin-gloved hand. "Brandy was supposed to let you know I'd be stopping by. I guess she forgot."

"I'll be going," Earl said.

"You need to fill in this low spot with more gravel first." Gordon pointed to a place that looked perfectly level to Kathryn.

Earl strode to his truck. "Fix it when I'm back on the job. It's Sunday."

"Trash," Gordon muttered as Earl drove off.

Kathryn bristled. Although she'd found Earl annoying on first meeting, she never would have described him as "trash." And she certainly wouldn't do so now when she knew that behind the jokey exterior lay a man capable of deep feelings and eloquent speech.

Catching her frown, Gordon said, "I apologize for using that word in front of you, Miss Kath—Miss Stinson. But that's what he is. He and the rest of his tribe. I'm from the South, I know about these hill people."

"If you dislike him so much, why did you hire him?"

"You live in this town, you have to do business with the Barkers. They're a local institution. Besides, Earl's one of the best excavators around." Gordon smoothed a patch of gravel with the toe of his tasseled loafer. "I hope he hasn't been bothering you."

"Why would you think that?" She looked at him with a mixture of surprise and irritation.

Gordon's toe burrowed into the gravel. "It's none of my business, but you look like you've been crying."

"I'm fine," she snapped. "He hasn't bothered me a bit."

"Consider yourself lucky. I know of one woman he bothered to death."

If he meant what she thought, he'd gone too far. "Are you implying that—"

Gordon seemed to realize this, too. He held up a placating hand. "Enough said. I have to go through some boxes in the attic. That won't disturb you, will it?" His voice was soft, almost silken, but there was a cold anger in his gaze.

"Well . . ."

Without waiting for her to finish, Gordon barged on, "Good. I'm staying with friends in the area, but I'll probably need to come to the house from time to time. If I see your car in the driveway, I'll knock before entering. Now if you'll excuse me."

While Gordon rummaged in the attic, Kathryn went and sat on the patio. So much had happened today. It would take her a long time to get everything sorted out. Even then, she doubted she could arrange the various events into neat, orderly files the way she did the Lyceum's collection of prints and photographs. Right now, she wasn't sure how she felt about anything except that Gordon was one of the most disagreeable people she'd ever met. Especially after his comment about Earl bothering a woman to death. He must mean Diana, but did he have a reason for believing Earl had been somehow involved in her death, or was it simply Gordon's jealousy talking? Clearly, no love was lost between them.

A rap on the window ended her reverie. Gordon stood on the other side, holding a file drawer. She opened the sliding glass door and joined him in the living room.

"There's a crack in the ceiling of the master bedroom," he said. "Did you make it?"

She explained what had happened.

"What were you doing in the attic? Didn't Brandy tell you there's no proper flooring?" Gordon set the file drawer down on the coffee table with a thud.

"I was looking for the tapes your wife made of Emily Goodale's recollections."

Gordon frowned. "What do you want with them?"

"I'm trying to find out about my ancestors. They lived in New Nottingham a long time ago. I hope the tapes will give me more information."

"Have you tried Emily?"

"Yes, but she hasn't been that helpful."

"I'm not surprised. The old bat's as ornery as the rest of the tribe."

Old bat!? Gordon didn't seem to have a nice word to say about anyone here. Still, the last part of his remark intrigued her. "What tribe?"

"The Barkers."

If Gordon had suddenly lobbed a grenade at her, she couldn't have been more surprised. "Emily's a Barker? How do you know?"

"My wife told me. She and Emily were great friends."

"I thought Emily was a Judd. That's what it says in her recollections."

"She's related to the Barkers somehow. Most of the old families are related to one another. It's a very inbred population. Surely, you've noticed these people aren't the brightest—"

Before he could finish the slur, she cut him off. "If you come across those tapes in the attic, would you let me know?"

"I've got enough to do without searching for a bunch of stupid tapes," Gordon retorted. As he bent to pick up the file drawer, he noticed a gray prison-stripe of dust across his polo shirt. "Sh—sugar!

Now I'll have to take this to the cleaner's. I didn't realize how filthy that drawer is. Get me a damp cloth."

"There's a bag full of rags in the cabinet under the kitchen sink."

Let him take care of it himself. She wasn't his maid. If he'd been a real lion, Gordon might have growled at her. Instead, he stalked to the kitchen with an irritated switch of his imaginary tail.

*****

"Have you seen him? Has he been to the house yet?" Emily asked excitedly, when Kathryn helped her into her chair at the kitchen table the following afternoon. She told Emily Gordon had come to get some things from the attic.

"What things? Did you see what he took?"

"Just some boxes of slides."

"Nothing else?"

"Not that I noticed."

"If he comes again, keep an eye out and tell me what he takes."

"Why are you so interested?"

Ignoring the question, Emily asked, "Did he say why he's come back?"

"He mentioned that a gallery in the city wants to have an exhibit of his work."

"A likely story!" Emily's blue eyes blazed.

"He is a professional photographer, so wouldn't a gallery want to exhibit his work?"

"Gordon's not a professional anything. He's a playboy with expensive hobbies. Did he tell you anything else about his plans while he's here?"

"Only that he's staying with friends in the area and will need to come to the house from time to time."

"Did he mention anyone in town?"

Kathryn hesitated, reluctant to reveal how Gordon had badmouthed both Earl and Emily herself. The old woman's eyes drilled into her. "Earl was there so . . ."

"He called Earl 'trash' behind his back, didn't he? Gordon's always

142

hated Earl. And not just because Earl took up with Diana. No. Gordon hates Earl because for all his talk about Earl being trash, he knows Earl's a thousand times the man he is. Earl's worked hard to support Millie and the kids, while Gordon's nothing but a parasite living off his dead wife's money."

"Emily!"

"I believe in calling a spade a spade," Emily said primly. "Did Gordon say anything about me?"

"Just that you and Diana were good friends," she fibbed.

"Sure he didn't call me an 'old bat'?"

"Why ask questions when you already know the answers? Gordon did say something that surprised me, though."

"What?"

"He said you were a Barker."

"So?"

"It doesn't say that in your recollections."

"Not in the beginning, but later on it does."

"The beginning's all I have. The later pages were ruined when the basement of the historical society flooded."

"Listen to the tapes then."

"Emily, as I've told you many times, I don't have the tapes."

"Misplaced them, eh? Well, they'll turn up."

"Can't you just explain to me how you're a Barker?"

"It's a long story. I'll never finish my dinner if I tell you now. Besides, you haven't told me if you've been to Marguerite's other grave yet."

Kathryn described the visit to the grave, including Earl's rescue of her from the rattler.

"Didn't I say you'd be safe with him? It's the other one you've got to watch out for."

"Who?"

"Gordon. You keep your eyes and ears wide open when he's around. I want to know everything he says and does while he's at the house."

Kathryn stared at Emily, amazed. "You want me to spy on him?"

"That's right."

"Why? Do you think he's up to something?"

143

"Just do it."

Kathryn sighed. Emily was as exasperating as ever. Still, she'd never dream of calling her an old bat. To her surprise, she realized she'd actually grown fond of the old woman. So why not humor her? "I guess I can do that while I'm still here."

"You're not going away, are you?"

"Only for a few days." Alan's welcome-home party for Sophie was on Friday, and she figured she'd stay the weekend.

"When?"

"Friday through Sunday."

"You can't leave while Gordon's here. And Friday's when we're having the benefit for Garth. You should come. That poor, blind boy needs all the support he can get."

"Sorry, I have another commitment."

"Fiddlesticks! You stay here and come to the benefit."

Kathryn rolled her eyes. Fond as she now was of Emily, there were limits to what she was willing to do for her, especially when she'd already told Alan she'd come to Sophie's party.

Chapter 32

At the post office that same afternoon, Kathryn was surprised to find her mail torn and covered with dirt. She showed Millie the damaged mail. "What's with this?"

Millie shrugged. "Must've fallen off the truck. It happens sometimes."

She didn't seem particularly concerned, and Kathryn noticed Millie didn't give her a friendly smile as usual. She decided not to take it personally. Perhaps Millie was having a bad day. "Well, I hope it doesn't happen again. I'm expecting an important package, and I'd hate to have it ruined."

"Oh?" Millie looked at her inquiringly.

Kathryn told her about the old-fashioned doll with a porcelain head and real hair she'd special-ordered as a gift for Sophie. She hoped it would arrive in time for the little girl's welcome home party on Friday.

"If you're going to Boston for a party, then you won't be coming to the benefit?"

"No. I'm planning to donate an item to the auction, though. Okay if I leave it with you?"

"Fine." Millie's face broke into a smile. "I'll speak to the driver who delivers the mail and tell him to be more careful. Want me to telephone when your package arrives?"

"I'd appreciate that."

*****

On her way back to the Farley house, Kathryn had to swerve aside to avoid Gordon as he roared past. *Just like him to hog the road,* she thought with a flash of annoyance. Yet when she noticed the red truck parked next to the house, her heart leaped. Earl was back. When he hadn't shown up to finish the work on the driveway this morning, she'd wondered if he were staying away to spite Gordon, or to avoid her. Maybe she was being paranoid, but she couldn't help feeling that after the ugly disclosures about her past, he'd want to keep his distance.

On closer inspection, she realized the truck wasn't his. It belonged to the man who had come to repair the crack in the bedroom ceiling. The repairman was just folding up his ladder when she went into the bedroom. "Won't have to worry about the ceiling falling on you now." He indicated strips of plaster-coated tape in the place where the crack had been.

"Thanks for fixing it. You must have seen Gordon Farley while you were here."

"Yup. Said he needed to get some things from the attic and promised to be careful. Didn't want him crashing down on me."

Remembering her promise to Emily, Kathryn asked, "Did you happen to notice what he took from there?"

"Too busy, but I sure heard 'im rummaging around up there."

Rummaging for what: more slides or something else? After the repairman had gone, she went up to have a look. From the top of the ladder, she surveyed the boxes and file drawers. They had obviously been rifled since her previous visit. Without an inventory of the attic's contents, she couldn't tell what had been taken, however. She did notice that Diana's defaced wedding picture wasn't where she'd left it. Maybe Gordon had removed it. He must have seen it when he'd first gone up to the attic, yet he hadn't mentioned it. Strange.

Although the ceiling was fixed, she had the uncomfortable feeling, lying in bed that night, that something was about to come crashing down.

*****

146

Millie telephoned on Thursday to say Kathryn's package had arrived in good condition. "Have a nice trip," she said when Kathryn went in to get it.

"Thanks. I hope you raise lots of money at the benefit." Kathryn gave Millie her contribution to the raffle, a lavishly illustrated coffee-table-book catalog of an exhibit of Civil War photographs and prints she'd curated for the Lyceum.

Now that she had Sophie's present, she could leave for Boston today instead of tomorrow, and arrive in time to help Alan with the preparations for the party. Yet, as she packed her bag, she discovered she was in no hurry. Earl's absence gnawed at her. He knew things about her no one else did, and intimacy seemed to have bred contempt. Or had it? She hated not knowing how things stood between them.

The light had begun to fade when she heard a rumble on the road. She raced to the front window in time to see Earl's truck pull into the parking area, turn around, and head back out the driveway, just like it had the day she moved in. Then, his arrival and immediate departure had worried her. Now, it hurt her more than she cared to admit.

Listening intently, she heard no further sounds of the departing truck, only silence. Maybe he hadn't left. She went out to investigate.

Rounding a bend in the driveway, she saw Earl spreading gravel from a small mound with a shovel. He stopped and looked at her, his face shadowy in the dim light.

"I didn't think you'd come," she blurted.

"Why not? I've got a job to finish."

"Yes, but I thought . . ."

"What?"

"That you'd wait until I was gone."

"Why?"

"Because of Sunday." What an effort those three words cost her.

He looked away, worrying a piece of gravel with the toe of his boot.

Finally, he said, "Sunday was pretty damn intense. First with you, then with Gordon showing up out of the blue. It stirred up a lot of stuff. I needed time to let things settle, get them sorted out."

"You stayed away on purpose, then?"

147

"Yes. But why should my comings and goings matter to you? You're going back to Boston, aren't you?"

News traveled fast on the village grapevine. "Only for a few days. My friend Alan's having a welcome-home-from-the-hospital party for his daughter."

He worried the gravel more. "So, tell me, is Alan your *kane*?"

"What?"

"Your *kane*, your man."

The question caught her off guard. "Well, I—I don't know."

"You don't *know*?" he repeated incredulously.

"We've only been seeing each other a few months. That's not long enough to—" She broke off. How could she expect him to understand her relationship with Alan when he'd plunged willy-nilly into a wild love affair?

"No?" he challenged.

His presumption irked her. "Speak for yourself."

"Huh?"

"Is Brandy your *wahine*?" She couldn't believe her boldness.

The shovel he was holding clattered to the ground. "My *what*?"

"Your *wahine*, your woman. Your brother said you and Brandy were an item."

"He did, eh? That was a long time ago. Right after Diana died. I went kind of crazy. Brandy, too, with grief for her son. We both realized pretty fast it was a mistake, and we quit. Since then I've been solo."

"There's no lady friend who doesn't like to be kept waiting?" Again, her boldness astonished her.

"That was just talk." He picked up the shovel. "I'd better finish while it's still light."

She started back toward the house. She hadn't gone far when she heard him murmur, "Star."

She scanned the sky for the evening star without seeing it. "Where?"

"I meant you."

"Me? I thought it was Starstruck."

"Star suits you better."

"Star," she repeated, surprised to find that she, who usually hated nicknames, actually liked this one.

He took out a small object from the pocket of his jeans. "I almost forgot to give you this. Catch!"

He lobbed the object into the air. It rose with the long, slow arc of a fly ball. A last, slanting ray of sunlight caught the metallic underside, making it shine briefly, before it began its descent into her outstretched hands. Her fingers closed around the hair clip he'd removed after it had gotten tangled in the chain of his St. Christopher medal. The clip was warm from being in his pocket, lodged against his hipbone, moving when he moved.

"Thanks. I washed your bandanna. Do you want it now?"

"No rush. You can give it to me another time."

Back at the house, she placed the red square on the dresser top in readiness for that time.

Chapter 33

On Friday afternoon, when Kathryn arrived at Alan's home in Lexington, Massachusetts, the house was filled with friends and neighbors, including a tall redhead she'd never met.

"I'm Cindy Lockhart." The woman extended her free hand. In the other, she held a pot with an African violet.

"Kathryn Stinson."

"Ah. You're the lady who brought the dirt."

"Dirt?"

"The dirt from the country that Alan—Mr. Marquette—wanted in Sophie's hospital room."

That dirt. With the white stag's hoof print. Even now, the soil seemed to give off a faintly musky smell.

"You must be the person who put it in a pot."

"That's right." Cindy beamed. "Sophie's one of my favorite patients. I had to swap shifts with another nurse to come. I wouldn't miss her homecoming party for anything. I think they're here now." She put the pot on a table in the hall and hurried to the front door just as Alan walked in with Sophie in his arms. With her pale, drawn face and wide, staring eyes, the little girl looked even more like a lost lamb, except now she was returning to the fold, safe in her father's arms. The way she'd felt in Earl's arms when he carried her down the mountain. But why think about *that* now?

Alan put down Sophie and Nurse Cindy gave her a big hug. "I'm so glad you're well and back home again," Kathryn said, patting the top of Sophie's curly head.

"Thank you, Kathryn." The girl smiled wanly up at her.

The guests gathered in the living room, where Sophie sat on the couch with Alan and Kathryn on either side and opened her presents. Afterward, they adjourned to the dining room. Alan switched off the light and his housekeeper emerged from the kitchen with a big chocolate "welcome home" cake for Sophie, lit with a single candle. He hoisted Sophie up so she was level with the cake. "I know it's not your birthday, sweetie, but I thought you should have a candle to blow out and make a wish on."

Make a wish. That was what people did when they blew out candles. Or glimpsed the first star in the evening sky. But yesterday, Earl hadn't been talking about a real star. *Star suits you better.*

A popping noise, and something came flying at her. She caught it, half disappointed to discover it wasn't her hair clip, but the champagne cork. Alan poured bubbly for the grown-ups while his housekeeper poured juice and soda for the children. "I'm glad you're here," Alan said as he handed her a glass. Then, moving closer, he whispered, "And I'm looking forward to later when we can be alone."

"Sophie's waiting for you to cut her cake," the housekeeper told Alan. "She wants the piece with that big red rose and her name on it."

"I'll be right back." Kathryn barely heard Alan. Her mind drifted to the Berkshires where preparations for another party were underway: the benefit for Garth Emily had insisted she attend. *That poor, blind boy needs all the support he can get.* She had no doubt Millie would see to it that Garth got plenty of support. Still, if she hadn't had a prior commitment, she probably would have gone to the benefit. In the short time she'd lived in the village, she'd begun to feel less of an outsider and more a part of the community. Attending the benefit would have been a way of showing she wasn't just there to take but to give back as well. Pity she couldn't be two places at once.

"Aren't you going to take a bite?" Alan's voice broke into her reverie.

Only then did she realize she was holding a plate with a piece of cake.

"Delicious," she said after tasting it.

Alan looked at her strangely. "Are you all right? You seem distracted."

"I'm fine, just a bit tired from the drive and not sleeping very well last night."

"Maybe you'd like to go upstairs and lie down? I'm going to take Sophie up to her room soon, anyway. "

"I'm okay."

A half hour later, Alan carried Sophie upstairs and the guests began to disperse. Eventually only Kathryn and Nurse Cindy remained. They stood in the front hall with Alan. Kathryn glanced at her watch. Five-thirty. If she left now . . .

". . . such a brave little girl," Cindy was saying.

"She was lucky to have you as a nurse," Alan said. Cindy smiled, and bidding them both good-bye, she left.

"I should be going, too," Kathryn said abruptly.

Alan stared at her, aghast. "I thought you were staying for the weekend."

"I know and I'm sorry about the last-minute change in plans. But I need to return to New Nottingham tonight." She got her coat from the hall closet.

"Whatever for?"

"They're holding a benefit for Garth Barker."

"The guy who tried to run us off the road?" Alan's face registered anger and surprise. Even so, he held her coat for her. As she was slipping her arms into the sleeves, one elbow banged into the hall table. The pot with the African violet Cindy had placed there teetered and almost fell. She caught it just in time.

"Yes. It's to raise money for an operation to restore the sight in one eye, and I . . . well, I just feel I ought to at least make an appearance. I'll call you." Giving him a quick kiss, she hurried from the house.

As she was about to open the car door, she realized she was still holding the pot. Should she return it? Glancing over her shoulder, she saw Alan standing in the doorway with a stunned expression. If she went back now, she'd have to do more explaining and he might try to persuade her to stay. Better just to leave. She got in the car and drove away before she could change her mind.

Chapter 34

Cars and pickups jammed the parking lot of The White Stag and formed long lines on either side of the road when Kathryn arrived later that evening. Inside, the Christmas lights on the trap chandelier blinked on a crush of people, turning their heads blue, green, yellow and red. She stood in the doorway, feeling out of place and almost wishing she hadn't come.

People pressed behind her, pushing her into the room and up against a long table where the auction items were on display, along with bidding sheets. She glanced at a sheet. Gordon had donated a week at his house in Provence, valued at $10,000. The wonder was that he'd contributed anything at all, though perhaps it was his way of keeping on the good side of the locals, none of whom had bid on the house, anyway.

There were lots of bids on Millie's offer of a week of home-cooked dinners for a family of four. And on Earl's offer of a week's excavating work. She wondered if her donation, the book of Civil War photographs and prints, had generated any interest. To her amazement, she saw that Earl had bid seventy-five dollars. She picked up the sheet and squinted at it, just to be sure.

A man walked out of the restroom, just beyond the table. Head bent, he was checking his fly. Earl. The sheet fluttered from her hand, landing at his feet. He picked it up, saw her, and did an immediate double-take.

"I didn't know you were interested in the Civil War," she blurted.

"Oh, that." He colored beneath his tan. "I didn't expect to see you here. Thought you had a party in Boston."

"I did, but it ended early, so I decided to come back for the benefit."

"I'm glad." A smile spread over his face, as he gave her the once-over, his gaze taking in the mauve silk blouse and brown suede mini skirt she'd worn to Alan's and then her legs in their black-patterned stockings.

"You look nice . . . Star," he added, lowering his voice and moving closer.

"Thank you."

A band began to play. Earl said something, but the noise drowned out his words.

"What?"

"I said, 'Would you like to dance?' " He held out his hands.

"Well, I . . ."

Just then, a man who looked very much like Earl, but was neither as tall nor as handsome, came up and spoke in his ear. "My brother Wayne reminded me I promised Em the first dance. Looks like she's going to hold me to it, too." He pointed across the room to where Emily sat.

In her green dress and green-feathered hat, one hand waving emphatically at Earl, she resembled an impatient parrot. Beside Emily, Sis looked sullen, holding her pregnancy in her lap like a beach ball. On the other side, Garth slouched in his seat, dark glasses hiding his sightless eyes and a beer can concealing all but the corners of his mouth. If he'd been a different sort of person, she might have pitied him. Instead, she felt relief that, blinded, he couldn't harm her or his wife, Cheryl, who sat next to him, staring stoically into the press of people. Again, she reminded Kathryn of a child crusader girding for battle.

"Don't go away now," Earl said as he started toward Emily.

Couples swirled past. Millie was dancing with Norm St. Clair, Gordon with Brandy. Millie laughed and shook her head at something Norm said. Seeing Kathryn, she flashed her a puzzled look. Gordon and Brandy were having a serious conversation. Perhaps it had to do with the prospects of selling the house.

Earl and Emily came into view and Kathryn stopped noticing the others. Emily was much older than Earl, but she seemed a mere slip of a girl beside him. He bent over her, one arm crooked around her waist, the other extended like a tree branch into the vine-curl of her fingers. He guided her carefully around the floor, shortening his strides to match hers and keeping a distance from the other couples, as if he feared the slightest jolt would break her brittle bones. She beamed up at him and he smiled down at her. They had the same faded blue eyes, were related in some way. But the how of it no longer mattered. All that mattered was watching them dance.

When the band switched to a fast dance, Earl brought Emily back to her seat and rejoined Kathryn. "I liked how you danced with Emily," she said.

He grinned. "Ready for a turn yourself?"

Before she could answer, he took her in his arms. The dance was a swing number. She knew the steps but had never mastered the twirl part. When he swung her away from him, she bumped into another couple. When he tried to spin her back, she got them hopelessly tangled. "I can't do this."

"Sure, you can. We'll go where there aren't so many people, and I'll take you slowly through it." He led her to a corner of the room and walked her patiently through a successful twirl. But when he tried to speed up the pace, she became flustered and crashed into a table behind them.

"Watch it!" A man at the table barked. "Spilled my beer."

She apologized then turned back to Earl. "This isn't going to work. You'll have to find another partner."

"No. Wait here." He walked over to the band and said something to the lead electric guitarist. The music changed to an Elvis song, "Can't Help Falling in Love." Earl guided her away from the corner, stopping under the trap chandelier. The lights flashed on his rugged features: blue, green, yellow, red. One hand rested lightly on the small of her back, the other clasped her fingers, their arms outstretched as if they held the neck of a large stringed instrument between them. Then, with a slow deliberateness, he drew her close, folding her arm against his chest and pressing her hand to his heart. She nestled her head in the curve of his neck and shoulder, closing her eyes while he crooned in her ear.

155

They swayed to the music like willows in the wind. He slid his arm out from between them and hugged her to him. Her arms encircled him. Each time he squeezed her, she squeezed back. They were pressed so close she could feel the buttons in his shirt, his belt buckle and the hardness below. She'd never been in a clinch like this before. She could have swooned with pure joy.

Someone tapped on her shoulder, gently at first, then more firmly. Reluctantly, she opened her eyes. Millie stood beside her. Smiling but with a hint of something else in her expression. "You don't mind if I dance with my ex, do you?"

"Of course not." She released her hold on Earl with a stab of regret. He opened his eyes and stared at her, confused, until he saw Millie.

"Sorry to interrupt, but you promised me a dance also," she said.

"I did?" Earl looked dazed, as if he, too, was coming out of a near swoon.

"Yup." Millie took him by the arm and assumed dance position. After some hesitation on Earl's part, they began to move with the music. Kathryn stumbled to the sidelines where Norm St. Clair stood laughing and shaking his head.

"What's so funny?" she asked irritably.

"Millie." He chuckled. "Married to Earl for over twenty years, divorced for six, and you'd think she'd be over him by now. But when she saw the two of you dancing, she couldn't get there fast enough to break it up. Know what she reminds me of?"

"What?"

"A hummingbird."

"*A hummingbird?*"

"Uh-huh. Got 'em at the Cobble. Come for the columbine. In June, the hillside's covered with 'em. Everyone thinks they're such pretty little things, but when they're competing for nectar from those blossoms, things can get downright nasty."

"That doesn't sound like Millie. All she did was claim a dance Earl promised her."

Norm shrugged. "Speaking of critters, did you tell Earl I have a bone to pick with him?"

"No, you never said what it was."

"He borrowed the stuffed rattler we got in the visitor center at the Cobble a while ago, and still hasn't returned it. I want it back."

So Earl had put the stuffed rattler on the stairs. She might have known, given his family's history of snake handling. He'd wanted to scare her away. But that was then. Things were different now. Or were they? A door creaked open in her mind. A door she'd tried to keep shut. It was barely cracked, but that was enough for the smallest of doubts to creep in. And once inside, the doubts multiplied.

I warned you, she imagined her grandmother saying. *But you didn't listen. He's played you for a fool. He knew the rattlesnakes would be out when he took you to that hilltop cemetery.*

He rescued me.

He only did that to gain your trust, get you to confide in him. And it worked. You revealed your worst secret. And just now on the dance floor—

No!

"Earth to Kathryn," Norm's voice replaced the one in her head. "Listen up." He leaned in and leered at her. "You get tired of Earl, come to me. I can give it to you as good as he does—better!"

She was appalled. "What makes you think . . . ?"

"I got eyes. I saw how you two were dancing."

"That was—"

"Didn't believe him at first when he said you were hot. But now—"

"When did he say that?"

"Ever hear of the locker room? Men talk about these things, you know. And Earl's a great one for bragging about his conquests."

She opened her mouth to protest, but no words came out, and she wasn't sure Norm would have believed her, anyway. "Better round up Brandy now," he said. "Been with that Farley fellow too long. Don't forget what I said about you and me getting it on."

He ambled off, leaving her caught in a whirlwind of emotions. Shame. Humiliation. But most of all, fury at Earl. If Norm was a sleaze, Earl was a hundred times worse. Twisting what was still tentative and awkward into a tawdry affair. And tricking her into making a fool of herself on the dance floor, so anyone watching them would believe they really were lovers.

Anger built within her to a dangerous degree. She knew she should control herself, cool off somehow. But when Earl caught her eye and grinned, as he glided past with Millie, it was more than she could take. She scowled back. Earl left Millie and hurried over. "Why the dirty look, Star?"

"Don't call me that."

"I thought you liked it."

"I don't like it—any of it!" She gestured at the dance floor.

He looked bewildered. "But just a moment ago, you—"

"Norm told me what you've been saying about me in the locker room."

"*The locker room?*"

"You know perfectly well what I'm talking about."

"No, I don't."

Around them, couples had stopped dancing to stare. She hated scenes and now she was in the midst of one, making an even bigger fool of herself.

"It's not worth repeating." She turned to go.

Earl caught her by the arm. "Star, please. If I don't know what I'm being accused of, how can I defend myself?"

She twisted in his grasp, but he held firm. "Leave her alone." Gordon loomed blimp-like beside them.

"Keep out of this," Earl shot back.

"She doesn't want your attentions," Gordon sneered. "Or is your hillbilly head too thick to realize that? Just because you screwed my wife doesn't mean you can screw every woman who lives in my house."

Earl flushed a deep scarlet. His eyes were like ice. He reached behind him as if to get something. The blow caught Gordon on the jaw and sent him crashing to the floor. "Earl!" Millie shrieked. Wayne and Lucas Rogers grabbed and held him. Millie knelt beside Gordon. "Are you all right?"

Gordon started to get up, groaned and collapsed like a prizefighter down for the count. Hank Lapsley hurried over and together he and Millie helped Gordon lever himself up. Gordon swiped at his bleeding lip and spat, leaving a small red pool just short of Earl's boots. Earl strained in his brother and Rogers' grip. Emily pushed through the crowd. "Hit 'im again, Earl, hit 'im again!" she cried, shadowboxing the air with tiny, liver-spotted fists.

"Stop it, Emily!" Millie commanded. Emily went on punching the air until Lapsley thrust himself between her and Gordon. "Now, Em, this ain't the time for more fighting. We're supposed to be raising money to help Garth. 'Member, everyone?" His gaze swept the room.

Brandy stepped forward with a towel and a plastic bag filled with ice. "I'll help you get cleaned up," she told Gordon. He let her guide him to the restroom.

Wayne and Rogers released Earl. For an instant, he looked like he'd go after Gordon. Apparently thinking better of it, he turned to Kathryn. "Star?"

The hurt and confusion in his voice made her wonder if she'd been wrong to listen to her grandmother. Her grandmother who always believed the worst of people. Men especially. Wrong also to listen to Norm. He could have lied to her about Earl for reasons of his own. At the very least, she should have given Earl a chance to defend himself before rushing to judgment.

"Earl, I—" she began.

"What the fuck's going on? Where is everybody?" Garth roared. He blundered across the room, clawing the air.

Earl sighed and went over to him. "Just a little trouble in the school yard," he said. "But everything's okay now." He steered Garth to the bar, where Rogers was again tending to thirsty customers.

Kathryn wavered. She could still go to him. Go and apologize for letting her temper get the better of her. But seeing Earl surrounded by the crowd at the bar, she decided the moment for this had passed. For the second time that day, she left before she could change her mind.

Chapter 35

Garth waited until he heard Cheryl and Derek leave the cabin and Sis close the bathroom door. Now was his chance. He rose from the chair and started groping his way toward the shelf where his gun case was. He tripped on a hard object and nearly fell, arms flailing as he steadied himself. Little fucker Derek must've left one of his toy trucks lying around. He hoped Sis didn't hear the noise.

Sneaking around in his own house—how could he have sunk so low? He inched forward, hands reaching out until his fingers closed on the metal edge of the gun case. He scrabbled in his pants pocket for the key. Had a moment's panic when he couldn't find it. But it was there, lodged in a deep fold.

Was a time he hadn't bothered with locks and keys, kept his gun where he could grab it in an instant. Asking for trouble, his dad and brothers said. But why have a weapon if it wasn't handy? Then the bitch Diana got herself killed with it. "You don't put that under lock and key, I'm gonna use it on you," Earl warned.

He'd learned the hard way not to argue when Earl got that look in his eyes. The snake-about-to-strike look, their mother called it. Pain in the arse, having to unlock the case every time he wanted his gun. He'd taken to wearing the key on a chain around his neck. But while he was in the hospital, key and chain disappeared. Put it away in a safe place, his bitch-wife told him in a snotty voice she wouldn't have dared use before the accident. Lost his sight but not his balls. Little piss-ant Derek got the key fast when Daddy threatened to beat the shit out of him.

Garth scraped the key along the metal surface of the case, searching for the lock. He found it, but in his excitement, the key slipped from his fingers and clinked to the ground. Godammit to hell! He felt like pounding his head against the wall like when he was a youngster having one of his fits. They'd had to restrain him to keep him from hurting himself. He wrapped his arms around himself, digging his nails into his shirtsleeves, until the urge passed.

He got down on his hands and knees and pawed the ground. Weak and helpless. Like when he was a kid scouring the playground for his lunch money after the bullies at school called him a retard and knocked him down. Then, he couldn't see because of his tears, now because he was blind. And now, no one came to his aid. No big brother found his money for him, helped him up, and went after the bullies. Earl had quit defending him long ago, when Garth became a bully himself. Or so Earl said.

But what did he know? He'd never been called ugly and retarded, never been beaten up. He'd always been the favorite, the best-looking and the smartest, the one with good grades, the one chosen captain of the basketball team, the one all the girls wanted.

Their other brother, Wayne, was content to stay in Earl's shadow, but not him. He'd hoped to show them he was better than Earl by shooting the white stag. Ever since he was little, he'd heard stories about the buck that had appeared to his great-great uncle, Clyde, and spoken to him in a dream. He'd wanted them to see that for all his legendary power, the white stag could be hunted and killed like any other deer.

Said he was crazy to even try. And called him a damn fool each time he failed. Let them. He wouldn't have to put up with their mockery much longer. Their pity either. He wasn't going to live out his life in darkness like Clyde.

He patted another part of the floor, and this time, found the key. Was so happy he felt like hollering. But he couldn't risk anyone hearing him.

He rose and stood listening. From the bathroom came the sound of running water. Sis was still in the shower. Lazy bitch took her time, but this once he was glad of it. Outside, he heard the creak of the rusty swing set as Cheryl pushed Derek back and forth. They wouldn't stay out all morning. The brat would whine for lunch soon.

He opened the case without a hitch. A mixture of burnt powder, oiled metal, wood, and forest pine. God, he loved that smell! Loved holding the gun even more. Garth gave a small moan of pleasure, they fit together so well. Better than him and any woman.

A door opened. He heard a gasp, then footsteps hurrying toward him.

Then his head exploded.

Chapter 36

The ringing phone roused Kathryn from troubled sleep. She half hoped it was Earl, because she wanted to clear the air between them. Still, as the person responsible for the rift, she wasn't looking forward to explaining why she'd suddenly lit into him, starting a fight that led to his backhanding Gordon. It was a relief to hear Millie's voice on the other end: "Sorry if I woke you, but we need to talk. Can you meet me at the historical society room at noon?"

"Sure . . . This is about last night?"

"Yes. Gotta go. See you at noon."

Kathryn hung up, curious about what Millie had to say. She considered calling Earl herself, but decided to wait until she'd spoken with Millie.

*****

Millie was waiting for her at the side door of the town hall. Kathryn searched her face for signs of what to expect, but Millie's expression was as open and friendly as before. She unlocked the door, and they descended into the damp, mildewed basement. Millie perched on the oak school teacher's desk, while Kathryn settled in a rickety chair. Teacher and pupil. Except that Millie was on top of the desk instead of behind it, her upper body erect, hands neatly laced in her lap, legs crossed at the ankle.

"Well," Millie began with a wry smile, "last night was full of surprises."

Kathryn shifted uneasily in her chair. The floor must have been uneven, or one of the chair legs was shorter than the other, because the chair rocked from side to side, banging when it landed.

Millie frowned slightly. "For starters, I didn't expect to see you at the benefit. Thought you had a party for your boyfriend's daughter in Boston."

"It ended early."

"Fine." Millie re-crossed her legs. "But what was going on between you and Earl on the dance floor? You were all over each other."

Kathryn flushed. "I guess we both got a bit carried away."

"Sure did," Millie said. "To the point where it was getting embarrassing. That's why I cut in: to save you from embarrassment." She re-crossed her legs again. "I hate to ask, but were you on something?"

Kathryn felt her flush deepen. "No, why would do you think that?"

"Because your behavior seemed so . . . unlike you. Earl's an attractive man, but you're the last person I'd expect to fall for him. I didn't think you even liked him."

There was another bang as Kathryn rocked in her chair. "I didn't in the beginning. But as I've gotten to know him, I've realized he's not just a jerk who likes to play stupid pranks on people. You already know that, of course. You were married to him all those years."

"I do know him well," Millie said. "His good side and his bad one. And by his bad side, I don't simply mean the pranks. He's got this wild streak. All the Barker men do. People say it's the rattlesnake venom in their blood. My parents didn't want me to marry him for that reason. But I was stubborn. And very much in love." A fond smile came over her face. "I told them I'd die an old maid if I couldn't have Earl, so finally they gave in. It was the best thing Earl and I could have done. When we married and had a family, he became a settled man. For a long time he was a good husband and father to the boys. Until Diana came along and the craziness started." Millie's smile faded, and her face assumed a grim cast.

"Crazy how?"

"Diana was beautiful, passionate, and strong-willed. An activist always campaigning for one cause or another. An outsider, too. She'd grown up in the city, attended private school and a prestigious university, and traveled abroad. Earl had never met anyone like her, and he fell hard. But he was never sure of her like he was of me or any of the other local girls who wanted him. And that drove him crazy. Crazy-jealous."

"I'm not—" Kathryn began.

Unlacing her fingers, Millie held up a restraining hand. "Let me finish. I know you're not like Diana, but you're still an outsider. And last night when you and Earl danced, quarreled, and he got into a fight with Gordon, I felt like the craziness was starting all over again."

Kathryn started to reply, but Millie cut her off again, this time with a shake of her index finger. "It doesn't have to continue. If you quit now, you'll save yourself a lot of trouble down the road. Earl doesn't know how to behave with outsider women. And you're best off with someone from your own world. Like your lawyer boyfriend."

Wood hit wood, as Kathryn teetered in her chair. "I'll fix that." Millie slid off the desk. Rummaging in a drawer, she withdrew a dusty journal and wedged it underneath one foot of the chair.

"Better?" she asked, resuming her former position on the desk, legs crossed at the ankles and fingers laced.

"Much."

"I like you, Kathryn, and I want things to go well for you. So I hope you'll take my advice in the spirit it's intended." Millie leaned forward, bending at the waist so that her back remained straight, and regarded Kathryn with raised eyebrows, head slightly cocked, a silent appeal in her eyes.

Kathryn stared back, and saw a strong woman who was supremely confident in her physical and emotional being. Millie wouldn't have crashed into a table at the benefit, or nearly fallen through the attic at the Farley house. Rather she possessed the natural grace of a born athlete. She was sure of herself and of her place in the village. At some point she must have decided her role was to help people, because that's what she did. She arranged care for Emily, found a grief group for Brandy, got her going to A.A., and organized the benefit for Garth. When Earl knocked Gordon down, it was Millie who extended a hand. She was the glue that held things together, the one who fixed things when they were out of whack. Like Kathryn's wobbly chair. And her relationship with Earl.

Millie didn't speak to her with the anger and bitterness of her grandmother, or the sometimes reckless abandon of her great-aunt Kit, but as a friend. And the advice she offered was sensible and well-thought-out. Millie knew she'd drifted into potentially dangerous waters, and like a skilled mariner was trying to steer her back on course.

"I'll think about what you've said and—" Kathryn broke off at the sound of someone pounding on the door.

"Millie, come quick!" Lucas Rogers cried. "There's been trouble up at Garth's. He's dead, Sis's fainted an' bleeding something fierce."

Millie rushed from the basement. Kathryn followed. "What happened?" She caught Rogers by the arm.

"Shot himself, according to Cheryl. She was outside with their kid, an' when she opened the door to come back in, there he was with his gun. Next thing she knew, he blew his head off. Gotta go." He pulled free of her and raced toward his car.

Kathryn staggered into the sunlight. The whole thing seemed unreal. Another nightmare. In broad daylight. But the ambulance shrieking past told her it was no bad dream.

She didn't know how she got back to the house. Once there, she couldn't stop shaking. This was the second time an ambulance had been summoned for Garth: first, he'd been blinded, now he was dead by his own hand. Alan had been there to calm her the first time. Now, there was no one. She longed to hear Alan's voice, to connect with the world of sanity and reason he represented. Taking a deep breath, she dialed his number.

"Kathryn? I wasn't sure I'd hear from you again."

His wounded tone pushed her over the brink. "Oh, Alan, I'm sorry I ran out on you last night. I thought it was important for me to attend the benefit for Garth Barker, but it was all for nothing, because he— he shot himself!" She began to cry.

"When did this happen?"

The concern in his voice made her cry all the harder. She didn't deserve his sympathy but craved it all the same. "Just now."

"That's awful. No wonder you're upset. Hold on a minute, Sophie's calling me."

She clung to the handset as if to a lifeline. "Is Sophie all right?" she asked when he returned to the phone.

"She will be when she's more rested. I'm afraid yesterday's party was too much for her. I was about to say you could come here, if you want."

"It's probably not a good idea with Sophie still recovering."

"You could always stay with a friend."

"I'll be okay. It's just that this whole thing has been such a shock."

"Of course. I wish I were there to hold you. But call whenever you want. Maybe in a few days when Sophie's better, we can see each other. I was hoping we could all spend Thanksgiving with my family in Maine. I mentioned that, didn't I?"

"A while ago, yes."

"I meant to bring it up again the weekend I came to the Berkshires, but with everything that happened, I forgot. Anyway, I'm thinking that if Sophie's up for it and it's something you'd like, you could come here on Tuesday and we could all drive to Maine the following day."

"I'd love that."

"Good because I—I don't want to lose you, Kathryn."

His words caught her off balance. "There's no danger of that," she said with a nervous laugh. Nervous because it wasn't like Alan to express his feelings so openly, and because her own feelings were confused.

She was relieved he still wanted her, but at the same time, she felt guilty. Alan would be hurt if he found out how she'd carried on with Earl at the benefit. And she hadn't told him the whole truth about why she was so upset. Garth's violent end was disturbing in itself, but coming on the heels of what Millie had said about Earl, it was even more so.

He's got this wild streak. All the Barker men do.

Kathryn went to the kitchen sink and splashed cold water on her face. She was done with the foolishness that had drawn her to Earl.

She would lie low for the next few days, stay in close touch with Alan by phone, then on Tuesday drive to Boston and on to Maine with him. When she returned, things would be different. Earl would realize she had a serious relationship with Alan, and that her behavior on the dance floor was an aberration and not to be repeated.

Everything would be all right again.

Chapter 37

Kathryn's resolve to lie low lasted until the next day, Sunday. Only a week ago, Earl had taken her up to the family cemetery. Now, he would be going there for his brother's burial. Tragedy had struck his family again. It was only right that she should—what? Write a condolence note? Surely, there was no harm in that. She got paper and a pen but after several attempts gave up. Silly to send a note when he lived just up the hill. Yet she didn't want to go to his trailer and say she was sorry in person. She'd telephone. That would be safe.

Safe but nervous-making, dialing his number and waiting while the phone rang and rang. When a machine finally picked up, she wasn't sure whether she felt relief or disappointment. Maybe a bit of both. She left a message. "I'm really sorry about your brother. Also for the way I lit into you on the dance floor. I'll explain another time. Please give my condolences to your family." The words came out haltingly, and her voice sounded high-pitched and awkward, but at least it was done.

******

Tuesday morning, Kathryn was fortifying herself with a second cup of coffee in readiness for the drive to Boston when Gordon strolled into the kitchen.

She was so startled she almost spilled her coffee. She put her mug on the counter. "Why didn't you knock? You must have seen my car in the driveway."

He shrugged. "I forgot. And no harm was done. It's not like I caught you and Earl going at it like he and my wife did in this very room."

"If you think I—"

"Oh, don't sound so shocked. I saw how you two danced at the benefit."

The benefit again. Would she ever live that down?

Gordon settled his bulk onto a bar stool at the kitchen counter. "Have a cup of that myself." He gestured at her mug.

"The pot's almost empty, and I'm about to leave for a few days." He had his nerve: barging in unannounced, insulting her and then expecting her to wait on him.

"I'm going away myself," Gordon volunteered. "To spend Thanksgiving with my family in North Carolina. But first I need to go through the attic again, and before I do, I'd like a cup of coffee."

"There's a can in the refrigerator."

"You mean you don't grind your own beans?" He sounded incredulous.

"Too much trouble."

"I'll switch to tea then."

She pointed at a cupboard. "Bags okay?"

"In that case, I'll have water."

She put a glass on the counter. "Help yourself." She expected him to request mineral water, which she didn't have either. Instead, Gordon got up reluctantly, filled the glass at the tap and took a long drink. "Almost as good as the water in Les Baux."

"That's where your house is?"

"Yes. It's a lovely old town that dates back to the Romans. Do you know Provence?"

"Only from books."

"You've read Peter Mayle then? He doesn't do the place justice. You really ought to see it yourself." When she didn't respond, Gordon went on, "Getting back to the benefit—"

"Please," Kathryn protested, "Enough's been said about that already."

"Au contraire," Gordon said. "When I saw you and Earl dancing,

170

it brought back painful memories of my wife and him. That's why I intervened." He paused to brush a piece of lint from his pants. "It was like a sickness with Diana. A sexual addiction. I tried to get her into a treatment program. She wouldn't hear of it, of course. Went right on carrying on with Earl."

"Did you consider divorce?"

"No. Despite all the pain she caused me, I loved Diana. She needed me, too. I was her anchor, her support, the person she came back to when she'd alienated everyone else."

Kathryn found it hard to imagine this big, lazy man being anyone's anchor and support. But maybe he possessed reserves of strength she wasn't aware of.

"My wife made many enemies here," Gordon continued. "That made things extremely difficult while she was alive. Even now, six years after her death . . ." He left the sentence unfinished.

"You found her defaced wedding picture?"

"Yes. Awful thing to do. Really upset me."

If the wedding picture was so important to you, why did you leave it behind?

"That's not all." Gordon studied the tassels on his loafers, as if trying to decide whether they needed re-tying.

"What?"

Gordon's gaze returned to her. "My wife had so many enemies that any one of them could have wrecked her wedding picture, just as any one of them could have killed her."

His words sent shock waves through her. She gripped the edge of the kitchen counter to steady herself. "You don't think Brian Russo shot her?"

"I don't know. I've often wondered if that boy was in the wrong place at the wrong time, if he got in someone else's way."

Her grip tightened on the counter. "Who do you think it could have been?"

"Well, Garth was mad at her for refusing to let him hunt on her land, and Earl was her lover. And a jealous lover at that, I might add."

She might have known he'd single out Garth and Earl. Earl especially. Yet his calling Earl a jealous lover troubled her. Millie had said the same thing. *Crazy-jealous* was how she'd put it. Still, Earl's being a jealous lover didn't make him a murderer. Not when he seemed devastated by Diana's death.

"So? I've never heard anyone around here mention them as suspects."

"They were at the time, though," Gordon said. "The only reason the police settled on the theory that Brian shot Diana, and either turned the gun on himself or died in a struggle, was that Earl and Garth both had alibis. They claimed they were at The White Stag when the killings occurred."

"Well, then."

"Ah, but consider the source: their brother and their drinking buddies. Hillbillies protect their own. They've got a code of silence so tight that even the $50,000 reward I offered after Diana's death couldn't crack it. But now it looks like someone's finally decided to come forward."

"What're you talking about?"

Gordon removed a piece of paper from his wallet. "I know who killed your wife" the typed message read. Kathryn noticed the *k* had been typed over several times.

"I received four of these over the past several months," Gordon said. "That's another reason I came back to New Nottingham. But it's been frustrating because the writer of the notes hasn't contacted me again. I'm hoping he will, unless this is a hoax." He put the note back into his wallet. "I'll mosey up to the attic now. I suppose you heard about the violence at the Barkers the other day?" he said over his shoulder.

"I heard Garth shot himself."

Gordon turned back to her, his yellow-flecked eyes intent as a cat on its prey. "If you believe he was the shooter, you're a bigger fool than I thought. He was blind for heaven's sake, and his wife Cheryl had the key to his gun case. His wife whom he'd been beating up on for years. Diana tried to get her to go to this place in Great Barrington where they provide counseling to battered women. I think Cheryl did go a few times, till Garth found out and threatened to kill her. Then he went and knocked up her sister. At least that's taken care of now, too."

"What do you mean?"

"She lost the baby."

"That's awful. She must be very upset."

Gordon shrugged. "As far as I'm concerned Sis did the world a big favor. Now there's one less Barker bastard to worry about."

If she'd disliked Gordon before, now she hated him. "That's a terrible thing to say!"

"You don't know these people the way I do. They're the worst kind of trash, and the sooner you understand that, the better."

"Let me know when you'll be coming to the house again," she said icily. "I don't want to be around."

"Suit yourself."

Kathryn waited until Gordon had disappeared into the attic before going upstairs herself. In the bedroom she examined the file containing Emily's typed correspondence with her great-aunt just to be sure.

*****

Halfway up the steps to Emily's porch, Kathryn heard raised voices within.

"I won't go!" Emily cried.

"Please," Millie said. "Your daughters are expecting you."

Kathryn started back down. She'd return another time.

"Quit pussyfooting around, and come on in," Emily hollered. Reluctantly, Kathryn entered the house.

"She wants me to go all the way to Springfield just to have Thanksgiving dinner at a restaurant," Emily told Kathryn.

Millie sighed and caught Kathryn's eye, obviously hoping to enlist her support. "The arrangements have already been made. Earl will take you to the bus stop in Lenox tomorrow, and your daughters will meet you on the other end."

"I'm not going. My daughters and their families want to see me so much, they can come here and we can have a home-cooked dinner with you all on the hill."

"That's not possible," Millie said. "I mean, we'd love to have you and your family join us, but this year we're keeping things small and quiet. Nobody's much in the mood for a celebration."

"Why not?" Emily demanded.

Millie bit her lip and looked away.

"Oh, you mean . . ." The light went out of Emily's face. She looked like someone who's fallen to the bottom of a deep well with no hope of rescue. "That baby didn't have to die," she said in a voice heavy with sorrow. "Aurelia would have taken care of it."

"I'm sure she would have," Millie said, "but your daughters—"

"I'm staying right here." A cunning look came over Emily's face. "With Kathryn."

Kathryn exchanged startled glances with Millie. "Actually, I'm spending Thanksgiving in Maine, with my boyfriend and his family."

"But you can't leave now. You've got to stay and—" Emily broke off.

"What?" Millie asked.

"None of your business," Emily snapped.

"Gordon's going to North Carolina for Thanksgiving," Kathryn volunteered.

"How do you know? Did he—"

"What's Gordon got to do with it?" Millie interrupted.

"Nothing," Emily said.

"How are you getting to Maine?" Millie asked Kathryn.

"I'm driving to Boston in a little while to meet my boyfriend. Then we'll head up to Maine tomorrow."

In the silence that followed, Kathryn could almost hear the wheels spinning in Millie's brain. "If Kathryn's driving to Boston, she could drop you off in Springfield," she said to Emily. "That way, you can avoid a tedious bus ride, spend some time with your friend here, and see your daughters for Thanksgiving. It's the perfect solution!" She clapped her hands and looked at them hopefully.

"I guess so," Kathryn said.

Millie didn't wait for Emily's response. "Then it's settled. I'll help you pack."

Chapter 38

Emily was waiting on the porch when Kathryn returned later that day. In her green dress with the matching coat and hat and an overnight bag by her side, she looked like a small, worried child being sent off to stay with relatives she didn't like.

"Are you sure Gordon's going to North Carolina for Thanksgiving?" she asked in the car.

"That's what he said when he came to the house this morning."

"Why didn't you say he was at the house? How long was he there? Did he take anything?"

"We spoke briefly in the kitchen, he went to the attic, and I came to you."

"You left him alone!" Emily sputtered. "Why didn't you stay and keep an eye on him?"

"He said something that bothered me. That's why I came to you."

"Still badmouthing Earl and Diana, is he?" Emily said. "Calling 'em sex addicts and all that other nonsense. You best believe Gordon didn't talk that way about him and his chippy in the city."

"Gordon had a lover?"

"I said chippy. Diana and Earl were lovers, but the only person Gordon's ever loved is himself. He only took up with his chippy because she worked at a gallery in New York, and he wanted an exhibit of his photographs. He didn't get it, but she did give him an alibi for the night Diana was murdered."

So Gordon had an alibi, too. That meant he'd been a "person of interest" also. Kathryn tightened her grip on the wheel, forcing herself to keep her eyes on the road. It was hard to drive and have this conversation at the same time. But she was determined to get to the bottom of things. When they were stalled behind a line of cars at the entrance to the Massachusetts Turnpike, she asked the question that had been on her mind since Gordon's visit that morning.

"Gordon showed me a note from someone claiming to know who killed his wife. It was typed on an old machine with a stuck letter 'k' like the one you used for your letters to my great-aunt. You wrote that note, Emily. Why?"

Emily's blue eyes blazed. "I promised myself I'd bring Diana's killer to justice before I died."

"If you know who the killer is, why not go to the police?"

"I don't have enough evidence yet."

"How will you get it?"

"Gordon'll show his hand eventually."

Kathryn stared at Emily, astonished. "You wrote those notes to—"

Loud honking from behind interrupted her. The way to the toll booth was now clear. Once they were on the Pike, Kathryn repeated her question.

"Flush 'im out, bring him back to the scene of the crime, at the time of year it was committed. He took the bait, so he's guilty."

"If he killed her, why would he offer a $50,000 reward for information?"

"Same reason as what's-his-name, that other crook who offered a big reward for information about his wife's killing, when everyone knew he did it."

"But what was Gordon's motive—jealousy?"

"Not by a long shot. He didn't give a hoot about Diana and Earl as long as she stayed married to him and he had the use of her money. It was when she was going to leave him that he decided to kill her."

"How do you know she was going to leave him?"

"She told me. Said she was gonna have a second will drawn up. She'd been told that under Massachusetts law she couldn't cut Gordon out of her will while they were still married. But she wanted to be sure he got as little as possible in case something happened to her before the divorce."

"She was afraid of that?"

"You bet she was!" Emily cried.

Kathryn was silent a moment, while she considered this. "What happened to this second will?"

"Her lawyer claimed he didn't know anything about it, that if there was one, she must have made it herself and put it away somewhere. You can do that, you know, and still have it be legal."

"Yes, but . . ."

She must have looked skeptical, because Emily lit into her. "I'm telling you there is a second will, and now Gordon's scouring the attic for it—if he hasn't already found and destroyed it. He knows someone's on to him, and he wants to get rid of the evidence."

"I didn't come across any will when I was in the attic."

"What were you doing up there?"

"Looking for the tapes of your recollections. I searched all the boxes and file drawers, although there was one box I couldn't reach. It's in a corner of the attic where there's no flooring. When I tried to get to it, I almost fell through the ceiling."

"Damnation! That box is probably in Gordon's hands now."

"I'm not so sure. If I couldn't get to the box, it'll be even harder for him. He's not in the best physical shape."

"He's a fatty, all right," Emily agreed. "Diana used to be after him to exercise, but all he ever wanted to do was lounge around and dream about being a famous something-or-other."

"Aside from this second will, is there anything else that suggests Gordon might've killed Diana for her money?"

"She says so on one of the tapes of my recollections."

Kathryn looked at Emily, dumbfounded. "Why would she bring up Gordon there?"

"You listen to it, you'll see."

"I'd love to, Emily, but, as I've told you many times, I don't have those tapes."

"They may turn up yet."

"What if they don't? Couldn't you just tell me what's on them? I want to know about Marguerite, Clyde and Jared Cutter. I've done everything you wanted, visited the house foundation, the mill ruins and the hilltop cemetery where Marguerite and Clyde are both buried, but I still don't know the whole story."

"You'll hear it in good time. But not now. You've worn me out with all this talk about Gordon." Emily yawned. A few moments later, her eyes closed and her head drooped onto her chest. Emily looked so tiny and vulnerable that Kathryn half wished she'd made Emily sit in the back as children do for safety reasons. She sighed. So much for getting Emily to tell her about Marguerite, Clyde and her ancestor, at least on this leg of the trip.

What to make of Emily's suspicions about Gordon, though? Could he really have followed his wife into the woods and shot both her and Brian Russo? She had a hard time imagining him exerting himself that much, though he could have hired someone to do the job. And the whole business of a second will as evidence against him seemed farfetched. Kathryn wished Emily would wake up so she could question her more.

The old woman didn't stir until they reached the Springfield exit. "Are we there yet?" she asked, rubbing her eyes with her fists.

"Almost."

"Good. It's been a long trip."

"Emily," Kathryn said, voicing a worry that had been knocking at the back door of her brain since their conversation earlier. "If Gordon did kill Diana and he finds out you sent those notes, I'm afraid he'll try to harm you."

Emily's eyes narrowed to gimlets. "Don't worry. I'll be ready for him."

*****

Emily's older daughter, Irene, a middle-aged woman who had her father's features and who towered over her mother, greeted them at the door. "I'm so glad you're here, Mother," she said, then to Kathryn, "Thank you for bringing her. Won't you stop for coffee before continuing on to Boston?"

"Thanks, I'd like that."

Irene ushered them into the living room, returning a few minutes later with a pot of coffee, mugs, and a plate of cookies. Emily snatched a cookie and bit into it. "Store-bought," she said with a frown, putting it back.

"I didn't have time to bake," Irene apologized.

"Is that why we're having Thanksgiving at a restaurant, because you don't have time to make the dinner?" Emily demanded.

"No. It's just easier at a restaurant where they can accommodate different people's food preferences. Sarah's allergic to turkey, and Ruth's new boyfriend will only eat gluten-free meals and—"

"When my great-grandmother Aurelia was alive, we always had Thanksgiving at home, and we ate what was put on our plate and were glad of it," Emily retorted.

"Yes, Mother, but that was then, and this is now." Irene's weary look told Kathryn she and her mother had been over this ground many times before. Brightening, Irene said, "Mary and Jack's daughter, Cynthia, is due in March, so you'll be getting another great grandchild. Won't that be nice?"

"Really?" Emily appeared surprised. "I thought she lost the baby. I'm sure that's what you told me. I remember thinking what a shame it was because Aurelia would have helped take care of it."

"Cynthia has not lost her baby," Irene said firmly. "I think you've confused her with that girl in New Nottingham who had the miscarriage. One of the Barkers, wasn't it?"

"Sis," Emily murmured. "Her baby didn't have to die. Aurelia would have taken care of it."

"Yes, Mother," Irene soothed, putting a hand on Emily's arm.

"I want to lie down," Emily declared irritably.

"I'll take you upstairs."

When Irene returned to the living room, Kathryn stood. "I should be going. Thanks for the coffee."

"You're welcome." Irene followed her to the door. "My sister and I really appreciate your bringing Mother here. The shooting and that girl's losing her baby have taken their toll on her. It's good for her to get away for a few days."

"Yes." Kathryn lingered on the threshold. "There's something I don't understand. Why does your mother keep saying her great-grandmother would have taken care of Sis's baby?"

Irene glanced warily toward the stairs, as if she expected to see Emily's childlike figure crouched there, eavesdropping. Lowering her voice, she said, "Mother gets things mixed up sometimes. She's confused that girl's baby with another baby Aurelia Judd took care of a long time ago."

"Whose baby was that?"

Irene stole another glance at the stairs. "Why don't we step outside?" When Irene had closed the door behind them, she said, "I don't know how much you know about Mother's family background."

"I read in her recollections that she's a Judd and grew up on the family farm on Rattlesnake Hill."

"She was raised by the Judds, but she's not one of them," Irene said.

"I don't understand."

Irene looked at her watch, then at the shadows creeping toward them across the patch of lawn in front of the house. "It's a long story, and I don't want you to get stuck in rush hour traffic."

"I'm in no hurry."

Irene sighed heavily. "All right. I'll try to keep it short. You see, Aurelia Judd had a good friend named Marguerite Soule."

Kathryn's pulse quickened. Maybe now, she'd finally find out what had really happened all those years ago.

"They were classmates at a female seminary in Connecticut and kept in touch afterward. During a visit with Aurelia, Marguerite met a man named Jared Cutter at a ball at his house. He was smitten with her, and they soon married."

So that was how they'd met. She could almost picture the scene: the ballroom filled with local girls, each vying for the attention of the town's most eligible bachelor and, as the evening wore on, becoming more and more disappointed and envious when they realized he only had eyes for the beautiful stranger.

"A few years later," Irene continued, "Marguerite fell in love with another man, Clyde Barker, after he rescued her from drowning. They used to meet secretly in the woods." Irene hesitated, as if reluctant to say more. Even in the dimness Kathryn could see her frown.

"What?" she probed.

"There was . . . well . . . a child," Irene said in a hushed voice.

"Clyde was the father?" Kathryn guessed.

"He thought so. Marguerite, too. But in those days it wasn't so easy to establish paternity. Anyway, after the baby was born, Clyde begged Marguerite to run away with him. Finally she agreed. On the eve of their departure, Marguerite left the baby girl in Aurelia Judd's care, planning to send for her later. She and Clyde set off through the woods."

A gust of wind rattled the pile of leaves at one of end of the lawn, scattering them every which way. Irene's frown deepened. Kathryn hugged herself against the chill. "And?"

"Nobody knows for certain what happened that night. The next day they found the blinded Clyde weeping beside her dead body in the woods near the Cutter mill. They figured he'd shot her, then tried to kill himself, but blinded himself instead. They were going to hang him, but Aurelia made such an eloquent plea in his behalf that they let him go."

"Where was Jared Cutter while all this was going on?"

"Away on business. He came back the following day to find his wife murdered. He stayed in town long enough to bury her and settle his affairs. Then he left for the West, and that was the last anyone heard of him."

A car turned onto the quiet residential street and drove slowly toward them. "That'll be my husband coming back from the airport with my sister and her family." Waving eagerly, Irene headed for the curb.

"What about the baby?" Kathryn trotted after her.

"Baby?" Irene's puzzled tone told Kathryn her focus had shifted to the present.

"Clyde and Marguerite's baby."

"Oh, *that* baby. She was brought up believing she was a Judd. Given the scandal surrounding her parents, Aurelia and Clyde felt it was for the best. He used to visit her, though. And later on her daughter, my grandmother, and finally Mother herself. He was an old man by then, and he especially doted on Mother. But it wasn't until after he died and Aurelia was close to death herself that Mother learned the secret of her background."

"So your mother really is a Barker," Kathryn said softly.

"If Clyde was the baby's father, she is. But my sister and I prefer to think of Mother's family as the Judds. If you've met any of the Barkers, you can understand why," Irene finished with a wry look.

The car pulled into the driveway and Irene rushed over to greet the arrivals. "Have a nice Thanksgiving," Kathryn called, as she walked to her car. She got in and immediately became aware of a pungent, earthy smell she hadn't noticed while Emily was with her. A pot with a tired-looking African violet plant lay overturned on the floor of the passenger side. She'd forgotten all about it after taking it from Alan's. Now, she was tempted to toss it, but something stopped her.

The pot rode with her the rest of the way to Boston, its scent pulling her back to the woods where the white stag still roamed, impervious to hunters' bullets, and where two women had died more than a hundred years apart, under mysterious circumstances.

Chapter 39

Kathryn left Alan's on Friday afternoon, filled with a sense of well-being. It had done her a world of good to be with him and his family. They were pleasant, ordinary people with none of the craziness or propensity toward violence of the Barkers. Even the woods, where she and Alan took a long walk after Thanksgiving dinner, seemed less menacing than the New Nottingham woods.

But as she approached Springfield, her mood darkened. This time, both Emily's daughters met her at the door. The younger Mary was shorter and bore a strong resemblance to her mother. "Mother's upstairs getting ready," Irene said. "Could we speak with you a minute?" The sisters ushered Kathryn into a small room off the living room that served as a study.

"Mother's getting on," Irene said after they sat down. "She needs round-the-clock care, which is difficult to arrange in a small village like New Nottingham. Millie and the others do their best, and I know you've been a help, too. But Mother really should move into an assisted living place either here or in Florida, close to Mary. She won't listen to us. We thought maybe you could speak to her, even get her to look at some of these brochures." She handed Kathryn a stack from the desk.

"I'll try, but I can't guarantee anything will come of it."

"Thank you, Kathryn," Mary said, "we appreciate your help. We'd like to get Mother moved before she gets any worse. That girl's losing her baby has really upset her."

Emily came downstairs and they left almost immediately. Kathryn had barely driven a block when Emily told her to pull over next to a trash barrel. "You can toss those brochures now."

"How do you know about them?"

"Figured my daughters would give 'em to you. Always trying to get whoever they can to gang up on me."

"Won't you at least look at a brochure? I promised your daughters."

"I've looked at 'em and you've talked to me. Get rid of 'em."

Kathryn obeyed. "How was your Thanksgiving?" she asked after a moment.

"Too many people," Emily groused. "Can't keep 'em all straight. Same with the food at the restaurant. Tastes all the same, so I can't tell what I'm eating half the time. I'll be glad to get home. Did Gordon say when he's coming back?"

"No, but I assume it won't be until Saturday or Sunday."

"You keep an eye out for him."

"I will, but do you really think he killed Diana? You don't have much of a case against him."

"We'll see about that." Emily scowled at the dusky highway, as if the proof of Gordon's guilt lay around the next bend in the road.

Changing the subject, Kathryn said, "I understand now why you keep saying your great-grandmother would have taken care of Sis's baby. You're thinking of another baby she cared for a long time ago, the baby that was left motherless when Clyde Barker shot Marguerite and blinded himself."

Emily turned on her in a fury. "He did nothing of the kind! Whoever told you that is a damn liar."

"That's the story I got from your daughter Irene. If it's not true, why did they almost hang him?"

"He was a Barker. People in town have always believed the worst of that family. You want the true story of what happened, you listen to the tapes of my recollections."

"I'd like to, but I don't have them."

"I thought you told me you found 'em in the attic."

Kathryn sighed inwardly. Was Emily genuinely confused, or had she deliberately distorted what Kathryn had said? "I looked for the tapes in the attic, but I never found them."

184

"If I'd known that . . . " Emily rummaged in her handbag. "I would've given them to you."

"What!" Kathryn couldn't believe it when Emily produced a batch of cassettes. "I thought you didn't have them."

"I didn't know I did," Emily replied innocently. "A few days ago, I was looking for something, and lo and behold, there they were. Figured I'd bring 'em along on account of the grandchildren always pestering me for stories about the old days."

Kathryn glared at Emily. The old woman had had those tapes all along.

"You don't want them, I'll . . ." Emily started to put the cassettes back into her bag.

"I want them all right," Kathryn cried. "I want to listen to them now." She grabbed a tape and was about to jam it into a slot when she remembered her newer model car was equipped with a CD player instead of a cassette player.

"Guess you'll have to wait until you get home," Emily said. "I think there's a cassette player on the stereo, unless Gordon's made off with that, too."

Kathryn wondered if the old woman had planned it this way.

*****

Millie was waiting for them at Emily's. "I'll help her get settled for the night," she said to Kathryn. "How was Thanksgiving with your boyfriend and his family?"

"Great. How was yours? Did you cook?"

"I have to," Millie said with a resigned smile. "Earl and the boys won't eat anyone's turkey but mine."

Back at the Farley house, she called Alan, as he'd asked her to.

"Glad you made it okay," he said. "It was a lot of driving for one day."

"You did the Maine to Boston stretch," she reminded him.

"It was still a lot of traveling. I hope that old woman and her family appreciated what you did."

"Her daughters thanked me. And driving her there and back paid

185

off, because she gave me tapes of her recollections. I'm hoping they'll contain information about my ancestors."

"I hope so, too. I know how important that is to you."

"I'm going to start listening to them tonight."

"I'll let you go then. And, Kathryn," he added, lowering his voice, "I miss you already. Maybe you could come to Lexington next weekend? Or Sophie and I could visit you in the Berkshires?"

Kathryn barely heard him. Her attention had shifted to the tapes lying on kitchen counter near the phone. "Mmm," she murmured.

"You'd like us to come to the Berkshires, then?" Alan asked.

"What?"

"Sorry. You must be exhausted. We can decide about next weekend when I call tomorrow."

Kathryn made herself a turkey sandwich with the leftovers Alan's mother had insisted she take. She carried the tapes into the living room, where there was indeed a stereo with a cassette player. She slid the tape marked number one into the slot. Might as well begin at the beginning.

This is Diana Farley recording the recollections of Emily Goodale on Saturday morning July 23, at ten a.m. What was it like growing up on Rattlesnake Hill?

Diana's high, girlish tones surprised Kathryn. Given what she'd heard about Diana's ability to rub people the wrong way, she would have expected a harsher, more strident voice.

Emily sounded exactly like herself, though. *Three families lived on Rattlesnake Hill when I was a girl,* she began.

Kathryn fast-forwarded the tape, hoping to find the place where Emily told the story of Marguerite and Clyde. After several attempts, she gave up. That part didn't seem to be on this tape. She had five more to go and was too tired to listen to them all tonight. Tomorrow, when she was fresh, she'd continue.

Chapter 40

By Saturday afternoon, Kathryn had yet to locate the part on the tape with Emily's version of the end of the love triangle. Or, for that matter, where Diana said she thought Gordon might kill her. Listening to the tapes was more of a chore than she'd anticipated. Emily had a tendency to natter on and, still tired from yesterday's trip, she had trouble concentrating. She snapped to attention, however, when Emily suddenly launched into the story of how Clyde rescued Marguerite from drowning.

It was essentially the same story Earl had told, but devoid of the poetry that made his version so evocative. There was nothing about Marguerite floating past Clyde like a cloud on a summer afternoon, nothing about the Japanese lanterns lighting up the lake like fireflies, nothing about Marguerite lapping up the water dripping from Clyde after he carried her from the lake.

As Kathryn filled in the missing words in her mind, a strange yearning came over her. She wanted to be back in the dark cab of Earl's truck, smelling his aftershave, and listening to his voice growing richer and more vibrant the further he got into the story. God, she missed that! She shut off the machine. Better take a break before the longing became unbearable.

Outdoors, wind blew in her face and whipped at her clothes, hindering her progress up the hill. In the yard at the cabin she'd shared with Garth, Cheryl struggled to remove wildly flapping sheets from a clothesline. Moved by her lonely battle, Kathryn caught the end of a twisting sheet and helped Cheryl collapse it into the basket. When they had wrestled down the remaining laundry, Cheryl invited her in.

"I'm awfully sorry about your husband's death and the loss of your sister's baby," Kathryn said after they'd sat. "It must be hard for you both."

"Sis moved out," Cheryl replied. "She's living with our parents now. Except for Derek, I'm alone."

"Derek's your son?"

"Yes. His uncle Earl took him for the afternoon."

Kathryn felt a fluttering in her chest. Just the person she wanted to avoid. Yet she *had* set out in the direction of the Barker compound and Earl's trailer. Now she was here with his sister-in-law. What if he came back early with Derek? She ought to leave, but she didn't. "It must be hard for Derek, too," she said.

Cheryl didn't reply. Her silence said it all. They'd lived in fear of Garth and were probably relieved to have him gone.

"You ever find the remains of the old house and mill you were looking for?" Cheryl surprised Kathryn by asking.

"Yes, as a matter of fact."

"Sorry I wasn't more help, but I knew Millie would get you on the right track. Thanks for your help with the laundry just now," she added shyly. "And for the offer of a lift."

Kathryn looked at her, confused. "If you need a ride someplace, I'm happy to take you."

"I meant the afternoon our car broke down. It was good of you to stop and offer Sis and me a ride. I know I must have seemed ungrateful, but I was too ashamed to accept on account of the fight we were having."

"It's okay."

"No, it's not," Cheryl protested. "Millie's always saying I need to learn to accept help when it's offered instead of trying to make it on my own. Ellen used to tell me the same thing."

"Ellen's a friend?"

"The counselor I saw for awhile. She gave me lots of good advice. It wasn't her fault things turned out . . . well, the way they have." Her young face assumed such a grim cast that Kathryn felt sorry for her.

"If there's anything I can do, please feel free to call on me."

Cheryl's features softened. "Thank you, Kathryn. You've shown real Christian charity toward me and my family."

"I've hardly—" Kathryn began, embarrassed.

"Oh, but you have," Cheryl declared. "In church they tell us to turn the other cheek, and that's what you did. You came to the benefit for Garth even though he tried to run you and your friend off the road."

"How do you know about that?"

"Earl told me. He gave Garth quite a tongue-lashing when he found out."

Again Kathryn felt a fluttering in her chest. She really should leave before Earl returned with Derek. She stood. "I need to go now, but please let me know if there's anything I can do."

Cheryl rose and took Kathryn's hand in hers. "Thank you, Kathryn."

As she walked back down the hill, Kathryn heard the noise of a vehicle behind her. Her heart lifted, then sank when she saw it wasn't Earl's truck, but Pete's beat-up car. She moved to the side of the road to let him pass, but instead of driving on, he pulled up alongside her. "Hey, Boston, heard you went home for Thanksgiving. You didn't happen to get to any clubs while you were there, did you?"

She shook her head. "There wasn't time. I was in Maine mostly."

He shrugged good-naturedly. "Too bad. Let me know when you do go to a club, though. I'd love to know what band you heard and what you thought of it."

"I will."

Chapter 41

The slide caught Kathryn's eye, as she climbed onto the large flat rock that formed a stepping stone into the Farley house. Lying on the ground just below the rock, it must have fallen out of a file drawer that Gordon had removed from the attic during his last visit. She held it up to the light. It was a picture of Diana with a slightly pensive expression.

The slide reminded her of Emily's suspicions about Gordon. This, in turn, made her wonder if the box in the far corner of the attic was still there, and if so, it contained Diana's second will. It couldn't hurt to have a look.

Opening the trap door, Kathryn saw that Gordon had done what she had not: built a plywood bridge to where the box had been. He must have wanted it very badly to make such an effort. Did that mean Emily was right about his need to destroy incriminating evidence? If only she'd thought to create a path herself. But after her first attempt ended in disaster, she hadn't wanted to risk another.

Yet the will—if in fact it existed— might still be hidden elsewhere in the house. In Diana's study perhaps? She'd searched there earlier, but she'd been looking for the tapes.

This time, Kathryn shook out the pages of the few magazines and annual reports that remained in Diana's desk. No document fell out. Kathryn's gaze settled on the tape of Elvis love songs she'd noticed before. She and Earl had danced to an Elvis song, and it had been so—*Don't go there! You know in your bones, he's trouble.* She shut the drawer with a bang.

Downstairs, she made herself listen to Emily's meandering

monologues, every now and then punctuated by a question from Diana. Eventually, though, Emily wandered to the very place Kathryn wanted to avoid:

When I was a young girl, I enjoyed dancing. They used to have dances at the town hall every Friday night. In my great-grandmother Aurelia's day, people had dance parties in their homes. These parties were often held in the kitchen because it was the largest room in the house. A few of the houses had their own ballrooms, though. According to my great-grandmother, the grandest ballroom was in the Cutter house. It occupied the entire second floor and even had a balcony for musicians and built-in benches along the walls under the windows. At a ball there, Jared Cutter, the young heir to the family fortune, met and fell in love with Marguerite Soule, who later became his wife.

Kathryn hit the "stop" button. Too late. Marguerite and Jared Cutter had already become she and Earl, gliding around the dance floor, pressed as close as two people could be. She couldn't control herself any longer. She ran upstairs, got the Elvis tape, and brought it back to the living room, where she replaced Emily with Elvis. She fast-forwarded the tape until she found the right song. *Their* song.

The opening bars of "Can't Help Falling in Love" sent a tremor of excitement through her. Clasping a couch cushion to her chest, she rose and swayed to the music, imagining Earl was the singer rather than Elvis. She thrilled to the sound of his crooner's voice and the feel of his hard, muscular body against hers. Millie didn't cut in this time, but when the song ended, she was left alone in the middle of the room, hugging a cushion instead of a sexy man.

You listen to that trashy music, you'll wind up like your Aunt Kit, taking up with a Hawaiian half your age. Turn it off this instant! Kathryn heard her grandmother cry, as she banged on the locked door of Kathryn's room. Her grandmother hated it when she played the Alfred Apaka records Aunt Kit gave her that last summer in Hawaii before she was forbidden to visit. She'd wept when Apaka sang

"Aloha Oi." Wept because she couldn't return to the one place where she'd been happy and might never see Aunt Kit and Kane again. One day when she was at school, her grandmother threw out the records.

There was no one to stop her now, though. She rewound the tape and danced to the song again and again. But it was over too quickly, and rewinding broke the spell. She decided to dance to *all* the songs on the tape. To her surprise, she discovered that three of them could have been written just for her. Yes, she was lonesome tonight. Yes, she wanted to surrender. Yes, it was now or never.

Halfway through "Now or Never," the phone rang. She dashed into the kitchen and grabbed the handset. "Is this a good time to talk?" Alan asked. "You sound out of breath, and I hear music in the background. Have you got company?"

Her cheeks flamed. She dropped the cushion she'd been clutching. Thank heaven Alan couldn't see her now! "No, I'm alone. Hold on while I turn off the music."

"That was . . . Elvis?" Alan asked when she returned.

"I found a tape of his songs in the house and put it on as a goof."

"Ah, I thought you were going to listen to the tapes of that old woman's recollections."

"I have been. All day practically."

"Have you found what you were looking for?"

"Not yet."

"I wish I were there to help you. If you could wait until next weekend, we could listen to them together."

"No! I mean, that won't be necessary. I'm sure I'll be finished by then."

"About next weekend, have you given any thought to whether you'd like to come here or have Sophie and me come there?"

"I'd probably like to come to you, but can I let you know at the beginning of the week?"

"Of course."

That was a much-needed wake-up call. *Wake up and die right*, her grandmother would have said. Returning to the living room, Kathryn caught a glimpse of herself in one of the glass sliding doors. Her face was flushed, strands of hair had escaped from her clip, and her blouse was wrinkled and hiked up. What a mess! She was glad there were no Peeping Toms around. She closed the curtains, anyway, and went into the bathroom, where she washed her face, combed her hair and straightened her blouse.

In the living room, she replaced Elvis with the final tape of Emily's recollections. This time, she would listen till the end if it killed her. But after a few minutes, she started to nod off. Maybe she was still worn out from the trip. Or coming down with a bug. She did feel a bit feverish.

Emily's voice droned on. She'd take a short nap and wake up, refreshed.

Wake up and die right.

Chapter 42

Voices penetrated the dimness. Somewhere nearby, people were talking.

At least he did it for love, a woman with a soft, girlish voice murmured.

More like jealous rage, an older woman said.

That wouldn't be the case with my husband, the young woman said bitterly.

What do you mean? the old woman asked.

He'd never kill me for love. The only thing he cares about is my money, which he'll lose when I divorce him. But if something happens to me before that, he'll get a big chunk. That's why I'm having my lawyer draw up a new will.

Kathryn opened her eyes and fumbled for the cassette player. This must be the part Emily had wanted her to hear, where Diana spoke about why Gordon might kill her. She pressed "stop," rewound to the beginning, and listened again. Of course, Emily, who already hated Gordon, would believe him guilty of his wife's murder based on what Diana said here. Disliking him herself, she was almost willing to believe he was the culprit. But aside from Diana's words, there was no other evidence against him. Kathryn kicked herself again for not getting to the box at the far corner of the attic before Gordon.

At least he did it for love. Kathryn returned to Diana's earlier remark. Who was the "he" in question? It dawned on her that Diana and Emily must have been talking about Marguerite's murder, the very story she was eager to get. She started to push "rewind," then hesitated, fingers hovering over the button. Did she really want to do this? She could simply accept the version Emily's daughter had given her, in which Clyde shot Marguerite and blinded himself. But there were two sides to every story. And so much depended on the teller. Irene was prejudiced against the Barkers. She'd revealed as much when she said she preferred to think of her mother's family as the Judds. Emily, Kathryn suspected, was prejudiced in the opposite direction. She'd have to take that into account when she listened to Emily's version. Taking a deep breath, she pressed "rewind," "stop," then "play."

My great-grandmother always said Clyde Barker was a man more sinned against than sinning. But she didn't explain why until after his death and she was close to dying herself. You already know how Clyde and Marguerite met and fell in love at the lake that bears his name. Now I'll tell you about the sad end of their romance. They'd been lovers for several months, meeting secretly in the woods, when Marguerite discovered she was pregnant by him.

How did she know the baby was his?

Women just know these things. The baby was probably conceived while Jared Cutter was away on business. When she told Clyde the news, he urged her to run away with him. But Marguerite was afraid of traveling into the unknown while she was with child. She wanted to have the baby at home, where she knew she would get good care. Reluctantly Clyde agreed. Months later, Marguerite gave birth to a healthy baby girl. It was named Leonora after Jared Cutter's mother, because he assumed the baby was his.

Again, Clyde urged her to run away with him. But she still wasn't ready. Finally, when the baby was about six months old, she agreed. They planned their flight for a time when Marguerite knew her husband would be away. She arranged with her dear friend, Aurelia Judd, to care for the baby until they could send for it.

You'll hear all kinds of nonsense about what happened

that night, but the true story is the one my great-grandmother got from Clyde. He and Marguerite hadn't gone far when they heard someone coming after them. They ran, but Marguerite fell and twisted her ankle. "Shoot me, if you will, but spare her," Clyde pleaded. But Cutter showed no mercy. Before Clyde's horrified eyes, he shot Marguerite then turned the gun on Clyde. Sometime later, Clyde came to. His head hurt and when he opened his eyes, he couldn't see a thing—only darkness.

The next morning a mill worker discovered him weeping over her body. Clyde told the man what had happened. Since Clyde came from a disreputable family, and Cutter from a prominent one, most people believed Cutter's story—that he'd been away and only returned home that morning. Clyde was found guilty of Marguerite's murder and would have been hanged if my great-grandmother hadn't appealed on his behalf.

What happened to Cutter?

He left for California soon afterward. Eventually, people in town learned that he'd remarried and begun a new life. But I think he remained a troubled man. Why else would he have kept Marguerite's photograph with him until his dying day? Seems he never spoke of her or revealed her name, because his descendants are still trying to find out who she was. I like to think he spent the rest of his life tormented by guilt—that even now he's rotting in hell.

You're terrible, Emily.

Nope. Man like that doesn't deserve happiness, in this life or the next.

At least he did it for love.

Kathryn hit "stop." She'd guessed Emily would try to pin Marguerite's murder on Jared Cutter, but hearing her actually say so made it worse. And more damning. Could the dignified, silver-haired old gentleman in the photographs Aunt Kit had showed her, the man her great-aunt had always spoken of with such reverence, really have been the merciless killer that Emily described? Was this the awful truth she'd gone to such lengths to discover?

Be careful what you wish for: the cautionary words echoed in her brain, followed by noise from overhead. It wasn't Amore. The cat crouched beside her, ears pricked, suddenly alert. Someone was in the house. She heard the scrape of metal against wood, then footsteps. Her blood froze. "Who's there?" she called in a voice that barely masked her fear.

"Me." The next instant Gordon's big shape loomed at the top of the stairs. He lumbered down, carrying a file drawer that he dumped on the coffee table in front of her.

"I can't believe you just walked in without letting me know," Kathryn flared.

Gordon shrugged. "It's my house, and I'm used to coming and going as I please. But this time, I did knock, and when you didn't answer, I let myself in. You were asleep so I went upstairs."

"I asked you to telephone beforehand."

"I didn't think you'd be back yet."

"I didn't think you would either. Why did you come back early?"

"Let's just say the family scene in North Carolina got old fast."

"Or was it because you wanted to search the house when you thought I wouldn't be here?"

"Why would I want to do that?"

"You tell me."

"There's stuff I need in the attic, and you don't seem to like my coming here."

"Something up there must be pretty important to you, because you've sure spent a lot of time rummaging around."

"My art is very important to me," Gordon puffed.

"Your art?" she mocked.

"I'm having an exhibit and I need to prepare for it."

"That's *all* you've been doing up there?"

"I don't have to explain myself to you. This conversation is over." He reached for the file drawer.

"Wait." Kathryn put a hand on his arm. "You took that box, didn't you?"

197

"What box?"

"The one in the far corner where there's no flooring."

"What if I did?"

"Then you . . ." She backed off, unwilling to accuse him outright of taking a box that might or might not contain incriminating evidence.

"I don't know what you're getting at, and frankly I've no desire to find out. Now, if you'll remove your hand, I'll take my file drawer and go." His gaze fell on the Elvis tape she'd left on the coffee table. "What's this? Elvis love songs, well, I'll be! Where did you find it?"

"Diana's study."

"You were going through *her* things?"

"I was looking for the tapes of Emily's recollections."

"You obviously found them, because that's what was playing when I came in. Put you to sleep, didn't they? Would've put me to sleep, too, the old bat's so incredibly dull."

"She's actually quite interesting. I was tired."

Gordon picked up the Elvis tape and scowled. "Earl gave this to Diana, and got her listening to this trashy music."

Kathryn hadn't been an Elvis fan until recently, but she decided not to let the slight to the King go unchallenged. "Lots of people wouldn't agree with you."

Gordon's yellow-flecked eyes narrowed. "Including you? You and Earl danced to an Elvis song at the benefit, though 'danced' hardly describes what you did."

Kathryn's face burst into flames. "Shut up!"

Gordon shook his head pityingly. "Kathryn, Kathryn, you poor thing. Don't tell me you've let that hillbilly hunk cast a spell on you like he did Diana?"

His condescension infuriated her. "He really loved her, but all you ever cared about was her money."

"Is that what Emily told you? Has the old bat poisoned your mind, too?"

"Diana says so herself on—" She broke off but not before Gordon guessed her meaning. He reached for the cassette player and jabbed "play" with a speed Kathryn hadn't expected from such a large, languid man.

More like jealous rage.
  That wouldn't be the case with my husband.
  What do you mean?
  He'd never kill me for love. The only thing he cares about is my money, which he'll lose when I divorce him. But if something happens to me before that—

Gordon stabbed "stop." "So Emily's at the bottom of this. She's the one who wrote those notes, who's trying to—I'll fix her good!" His fat body quivering with anger, he hurled himself toward the door. Kathryn sprang from the couch and ran after him. On the walkway leading from the house, she got close enough to grab at his sweater. The soft wool slipped through her fingers, but then she found purchase and yanked hard, pulling Gordon backward. He whirled around, twisted free, and gave her a shove. She skidded on the leaf-strewn path, lost her balance and landed hard on her rear, dazed and hurting.

The engine noise of his departure brought her to her feet. She had to stop him.

She raced to her car and sped out the driveway onto Rattlesnake Hill Road. The narrow roadway was level for a short stretch before curving to begin the steep descent to the bottom. Around the bend, the lights of an oncoming car barreled at her. She slammed on the brakes, felt them lock, and the car go into a slow, sickening spin. It slid across the roadway, ground to a halt off the pavement, and then tipped precariously, throwing her against the driver's side door. She shut her eyes and clung to the door handle, bracing herself for the inevitable fall through the trees, down the hill, into the swamp below.

Nothing happened. The car remained tilted at an angle. Something had stopped its downward hurtle. She opened her eyes. A tree trunk filled the window, holding the car in place like a bookend. Thank god! She had to get out of here, had to reach Emily before Gordon harmed her. She fumbled with the buckle of her seatbelt. It wouldn't unsnap. Terror had drained the strength from her fingers. She heaved herself toward the passenger side. The belt stretched but didn't break. She was stuck like her car. Tears of frustration spilled down her face. She tried the buckle again. This time, it came undone. As she scrambled across the seat, the door suddenly opened and strong arms pulled her out.

"Jesus! Are you all right?" Earl exclaimed.

"I . . . Emily—Gordon's gone after her."

"What?"

"I'll explain later. We've got to hurry."

He helped her into the pickup and jumped into the driver's seat. They careened down the hill, the snake rattle swinging like a pendulum gone wild. She wanted to believe Emily would be all right. Surely, Gordon wouldn't dare harm a woman over ninety. But, despite being old and frail, Emily was feisty. She might say something to provoke Gordon even more. And then who knew what he might do? Kathryn pictured Emily growing smaller and smaller until she disappeared altogether, swallowed up by the giant, spreading blob of Gordon.

"Faster!" she cried.

Earl floored the gas pedal. The speedometer needle jumped from sixty to seventy. They shot up the hill to the village. Kathryn leaped from the truck before it came to a full stop behind Gordon's vehicle at Emily's house. She fairly flew up the porch steps, not even looking to be sure Earl was behind her.

Inside, nothing was as she'd imagined it. Wearing a blue, quilted robe, Emily perched on a wing chair at one end of the parlor. She held her head high and sat so straight she might have been a child-queen. Gordon sprawled at her feet like a supplicant. An unlucky one. Blood leaked from his body onto the carpet. An acrid odor filled the air. A revolver lay on the table beside Emily.

Kathryn opened her mouth, but no sound came out. "God Almighty, Em!" Earl exploded behind her.

"Gordon is dead," Emily said. "You'd better call Hank."

Part III: The Woods

Chapter 43

"My life was in danger, I had no choice," Emily told Hank Lapsley.

Lapsley raked a hand through his graying hair. "Still gotta do things by the book. Take pictures, get statements. Don't anyone touch anything." He shooed them to the sidelines while he went about securing and photographing the scene. After the EMTs had removed Gordon's body, Lapsley told Earl and Kathryn to wait in the bedroom while he questioned Emily in the kitchen.

Kathryn sat on Emily's bed, still too stunned to speak. She glanced at Earl, seated on a nearby chair. He looked at her with a mixture of sympathy and something she couldn't name. "Why did Gordon go after Em just now?" he asked.

She explained about the anonymous notes Emily had written to bring Gordon back to town, and how Emily hoped he'd betray himself as Diana's killer. "When he came to the house to get more stuff from the attic, I was listening to a tape of Emily's recollections. There's a part where Diana tells Emily she thinks Gordon would kill her for her money. When Gordon heard that, he realized Emily had written the notes. He got really mad and said he'd fix her. I tried to stop him, but . . . well . . . you know the rest."

"Except how you ended up on the other side of the road with your car leaning against a tree."

"I'd just rounded the bend when I saw another car speeding toward me in the middle of the road. My brakes locked and I went into a skid."

"A car passed me going like a bat from hell," Earl said. "Bastard didn't even stop to see if you were all right." His features compressed with anger.

"Did you have any idea what Emily was up to?" she asked.

He shook his head. "If I had, I would've done something about it."

Lapsley entered the room with Emily. "You're next, Cousin." He nodded at Earl.

Cousin—they were related? Kathryn rose from the bed and asked Emily if she'd like to lie down and rest.

"I'm all right, but you look awful." Emily settled into the chair Earl had vacated. For someone whose life had been threatened and who'd shot a man dead, Emily seemed remarkably calm. Calm and almost content.

Minutes later, Lapsley returned with Earl. "Your turn, Miss Stinson."

Walking past Earl, Kathryn caught a whiff of aftershave. He wouldn't have put it on if he hadn't been out someplace, with a woman probably, even though he'd told her he wasn't involved with anyone. She felt a sudden, absurd flash of jealousy as she followed Lapsley into the kitchen. She sat across from him at the table where she'd spent long hours watching Emily eat. He raked a hand through his hair again and looked at her with a kindly but bewildered expression.

"Why would someone would want to hurt a woman over ninety and so frail the slightest breeze could knock her down?"

Kathryn told him what she'd told Earl.

"Well, I'll be damned!" Lapsley exclaimed. "Looks like Em was trying to do my job for me."

"Do you think Gordon killed his wife and Brian Russo?"

Lapsley leaned thoughtfully back in his chair. "He was a suspect—husband usually is. But he had an alibi, and we never could prove anything against him. Now that he's dead, I don't know if we'll ever find out. I'm gonna need that tape, along with your testimony, as evidence of Gordon's state of mind if this thing comes to trial."

"Do you think it will?"

"As far as I'm concerned, Em acted in self-defense. Most folks around here will probably agree that Gordon had no business scaring the daylights out of a poor old lady. But he's got family and friends who may make a stink. Still, I don't see Em going to jail for shooting a man who was trying to hurt her." He stood. "That'll be all for now."

They returned to the bedroom and Lapsley said to Emily, "I don't think it's a good idea for you to remain here tonight. Is there a neighbor you can stay with?"

"I want to sleep in my own bed," Emily protested.

"Now, Em, you come along with me," Earl said. "Mill will put you up for the night."

"Oh, all right," she replied crossly. Turning to Lapsley, she asked, "Am I gonna get my gun back? It was Walter's service revolver."

"Yes, but I gotta hold onto it awhile. Evidence, you know. And when I do give it back, you better get yourself a license to carry."

"Don't let her skip town now," Lapsley called after Earl and Kathryn as they left with Emily.

"We'll put her under house arrest," Earl said.

Emily punched his arm. In the truck, she snuggled against him like an affectionate child.

He eased her gently off when they reached the Farley house. "I'll see Kathryn to the door then I'll be right back."

Kathryn opened the front door and stepped into the lighted hallway. Earl stayed in the shadows. "If you don't feel right about being here by yourself, I could come back and stay with you. Sleep on the couch, of course."

She didn't trust herself alone with him. Not after the state she'd worked herself into earlier that night. "I'll be okay."

"'Night then." He turned to go.

"Earl?"

"Yes, Star?" He moved out of the shadows.

Why did he have to call her that? Didn't he know how the name made her want to rush into his arms? She took a step backward. "Where were you tonight before you found me?"

"I had a few beers at the Stag."

"You put on aftershave to go to the Stag?"

"No, I—" He broke off with a guilty expression. "Tell you about it sometime. I need to get Emily to Mill's. Try and get some sleep."

He *had* been with another woman, dammit! But what was the

matter with her? She'd been shoved to the ground by Gordon and run off the road by a reckless driver. She'd discovered Gordon shot dead by Emily, and she was upset because a man who wasn't her lover had been with another woman. Crazy but she couldn't help herself. The suspicion that Earl had found a new love tormented her.

Too wound up to even think of sleep, she prowled the empty rooms. Amore followed. When he howled to be let out, she went with him.

They stood on the patio, gazing at the pond, its dark surface glittering with reflected stars. The lake must have looked like this on the night Clyde rescued Marguerite from drowning, except the lights had come from Japanese lanterns on the boats instead of the stars.

"Why can't I stop thinking about him?" she cried aloud. Amore cocked his head at her. He was no help. He'd fallen for Earl himself, letting Earl stroke him into a state of bliss. He scampered off after a leaf.

She couldn't look at the pond anymore. It reminded her too much of its maker. On the other side of the house, she forced herself to gaze at the stars until their cold remoteness calmed her enough to go back inside. Amore didn't respond to her repeated calls, so she left him outdoors to pursue whatever the wind and chance brought his way. She turned off the lights and lay on the couch, where Earl would have slept if she'd let him. She imagined the dark ceiling overhead lit with late autumn constellations, whose names she didn't know but would one day learn.

Eventually she fell asleep. In her dreams, she returned to the pond, floating on her back, her lips parted to catch the falling raindrops, heedless of the distant thunder.

Chapter 44

The file drawer was the first thing Kathryn saw when she awoke the next morning. In her wound-up state last night, she'd barely noticed it. The drawer lay on the coffee table, gray, hard-edged, inert. Gordon had meant to take it with him. Now he never would. She felt a strong urge to cover it with a cloth, just as Gordon's body had been shrouded. But she was curious about its contents. Could it contain the draft of the will, or other incriminating evidence? The drawer appeared to be filled with orange slide boxes, but something could be buried underneath.

She scooped out the boxes and piled them on the floor. The bottom was empty. Still, she ran her hand over it, searching for a secret compartment. There was none. She glanced at the slide boxes. Some were labeled, others not. She picked up a box labeled "Door knockers, NYC." *Door knockers?* She held up several slides to the light and saw they were indeed door knockers. Perhaps, after all, Gordon had wanted them for an exhibit of his photographs. Then, Emily's suspicions about him were unfounded. The possibility disturbed her. Because if the killer was someone other than Gordon or Brian Russo, then—she didn't want to even think about who it might be.

The other labeled boxes contained door knocker slides as well, but she found one marked, "St. Barts." The first slide showed a smiling Diana and Gordon with their arms around each other on a tropical beach. The image of the apparently happy couple went against Emily's version of their marriage. Kathryn knew people often put on smiley faces for the camera. Even so, she wished Diana had looked just a little pensive. She'd started to examine another slide when she heard a loud knocking at the front door.

"Sorry to bother you," Hank Lapsley said. "Probably should've called first, but figured I'd stop by and get that tape on the way to church."

Kathryn was about to remove the tape from the player, but Lapsley stopped her. "Might as well have a listen now." She played him the part that had enraged Gordon. He was silent a moment, then he said, "Don't see why this made him so mad, unless he had a guilty conscience." He ejected the tape and deposited it in a plastic baggie.

"Do you think he did have a guilty conscience?"

Lapsley loosened the tie that went with his brown, church-going suit. "As I said last night, we never could prove anything against Gordon. And now that he's dead, well . . . " He shook his head.

"Were you on duty the night it happened?"

"Sort of. I mean, I was at the Stag when the call came."

"Why were you at the Stag?"

Lapsley shifted uncomfortably. "The chief of police job is supposed to be part-time, but I get calls at all hours wherever I am. And that night I was at the Stag."

"With Earl and his brothers?"

"They were there. How'd we get started on this?" Lapsley's face wore the look of someone who's taken a wrong turn and realizes too late it's brought him to a place he never intended to go.

Before she could remind him, the phone rang. "Excuse me." She hurried into the kitchen.

"Just called to see how you're doing," Earl said.

The sound of his voice gave her a fluttery feeling. "I'm okay. Hank Lapsley's here."

"Hank—how come?"

"He wanted to get the tape with the part that made Gordon so mad."

"I won't keep you then. Something I wanted to ask, though."

"Yes?" The fluttering grew.

"What're you planning to do about your car?"

"My car?" She drew a momentary blank then remembered her car was leaning against a tree by the roadside. "Have it towed, I guess."

208

"My brother Wayne could do that for you. Repair work, too, if it needs it."

"That's very kind of him but—"

"Don't worry, it's not gonna cost you an arm and a leg like it would in the city."

Earl had gone to a lot of trouble on her behalf. Was more than neighborliness involved?

Back in the living room, Lapsley peered at the contents of the file drawer. "This yours?"

"Gordon's. He brought it down from the attic last night. He went up there every time he came to the house. Emily thought he was looking for Diana's second will. She said Diana was planning to divorce Gordon and had another will drawn up so he'd get less of her estate if something happened to her beforehand."

"Hmm. I don't remember anything about a second will. If there was one, seems like somebody would've brought it up and challenged the first will."

"It's possible there isn't one. Emily herself admitted that Diana's lawyer didn't know anything about it. But she still believed another will existed, and that Diana made it herself and hid it somewhere."

Lapsley shook his head. "If there ever was a second will, it's not going to make much difference now. Better get a move on, or I'll miss the whole sermon." Tape in hand, he started for the door.

Kathryn followed. "What happens next?"

"There'll be an inquiry, of course. And his family is flying in. They'll probably want to come to the house. I'll keep you posted."

After Lapsley had gone, Kathryn considered what to do. He hadn't seemed interested in pursuing the matter of the second will. But she was. Before Gordon's family arrived and had his belongings removed, she'd make a final search.

She had breakfast or rather lunch, as it was nearly noon. Then she headed to the attic, where she started with the accumulated papers, which included old magazines and tax returns. She fanned the pages of the magazines to be sure no loose papers were hidden inside and checked the bottoms of the various boxes. She spent more time on the tax returns. A scrutiny of several years' worth corroborated what she'd been told: the couple had lived on Diana's money.

She turned to the more tedious task of checking the file drawers filled with slide boxes. There were more shots of door knockers. Gordon seemed obsessed with them. He had also meticulously recorded every stage of the house's construction from the clearing of the land to the finish carpentry of the interior. She found herself lingering over the shots of Earl and his bulldozer; the others she merely glanced at.

A flash of color in another box caught her eye. She pulled out a large, rectangular, unopened package. The card, dated the year Diana died, read: "To Diana, Merry Christmas, Love, Gordon." The realization she was holding a gift the dead woman had never received sent chills down Kathryn's spine. Should she open it? None of your business, she told herself. On the other hand, she'd already spent several hours poking into Gordon and Diana's private affairs, so why not poke more? What would a man like Gordon give his wife for Christmas? The package felt like a framed picture: an enlarged photograph of a door knocker, or a studio portrait of Gordon? Either would be in keeping with his egotistical nature.

Inside was a collage of pictures Gordon had taken of the pond. They captured its many moods by showing it at different times of day, in different seasons, and in different years. Often stunning, the photographs reminded her of Claude Monet's lily pad series. She was also struck by the care Gordon had taken in selecting and arranging the photographs. This didn't seem like the work of a man who was planning to kill his wife. The uneasiness she'd felt returned in full force. Emily had given her one view of Diana and Gordon's marriage, but these photographs told a different story.

There were also two stories about what had happened between Clyde, Marguerite, and Jared Cutter. Would she ever know the truth in either case? Once, she thought she heard the phone ringing in the distance. But she didn't feel like hurrying from the attic to answer. Whoever it was could always leave a message.

A while later she became aware of someone calling her name. With the trapdoor closed, the sound was muffled. Opening the trapdoor, she called out, "Who is it?"

Footsteps thudded up the stairs. Earl appeared in the hallway.

Chapter 45

"What're you doing up here?" Earl joined her in the attic. "Just looking at some stuff."

"How come?"

Before she could answer, his gaze fell on the collage. He picked it up and glared at the photographs like a bull seeing red. Then he saw the wrapping paper with the attached card. He put down the collage while he read the card. His scowl deepening, he crumpled the paper into a ball and tossed it across the room. He reached for the collage.

"Don't," she said, afraid he was about to wreck it. "They're beautiful pictures of something you made."

"But Gordon . . ." he muttered, shaking his head.

"Is dead," she said softly.

"Why're you going through their things?"

"I was hoping to find a copy of a second will Emily told me Diana had drawn up."

"A second will?" He seemed surprised.

"You didn't know about it?"

"No— yes, come to think of it, Diana did mention something about another will. But I don't believe she ever got around to doing anything about it."

"So there probably isn't one?"

"That's right." Earl stared into space, his expression grim and abstracted.

Kathryn put the collage back in its wrapping. "Did you telephone a while ago?"

Earl blinked and looked at her. "Yes. I wanted to let you know your car's ready. Give you a ride to the shop if you like."

In the truck, he appeared more relaxed. Kathryn would have relaxed herself if she hadn't become aware of his aftershave. Surely, he hadn't put it on just to give her a lift to the garage. He must have plans for later. With the other woman? Her suspicions of the night before rushed back.

Wayne was waiting at the shop, and again Kathryn was struck by the resemblance between the two brothers. They might have been twins except that Wayne was shorter and heavier and not as good-looking. "Thanks for taking the time on a Sunday to fix my car," she said.

Wayne smiled and handed her the keys. "Wasn't much to do, just a loose hose. The dents will have to be fixed later, but for now you can drive it."

"Don't thank him till you've seen what kind of a job he did," Earl teased.

"Get on with you!" Wayne laughed.

"What do I owe you?" Kathryn asked.

"Nothing now. I won't bill you until I've fixed the dents."

"Seriously now," Earl said, "I better ride down the hill with you to make sure your car's running properly." Earl winked at Wayne as he slid into the passenger seat. Kathryn's heart leaped. Perhaps, after all, the cologne was for her.

They hadn't gone far when Earl said, "You know you've got a plant down here." He pointed at the pot with the African violet.

"Oh, *that*. It's been riding around with me for days. I keep meaning to do something about it, but I keep forgetting."

"Looks dead, but with some water, it might come back." He cradled the pot between his legs, its pungent, earthy smell mingling with the scent of his cologne.

Waiting at the house was something else she'd neglected. Amore sat patiently by the front door.

"Thought you didn't let your cat out." Earl left the car, carrying the plant.

"I don't usually. But last night I was in such a state. When he made a fuss, I opened the door and he vanished." No need to tell him she'd gone out with Amore, too. Gone out and nearly driven herself crazy with thoughts about him. "I can't believe he's been out all night and most of the day."

"He doesn't look too much the worse for wear." Earl reached down and scratched Amore's ears. "Left you a present, too." He pointed at a dead mouse on the ground next to the cat. The mouse's front paws were curled as if begging for mercy. Kathryn looked away while Earl disposed of it in the bushes.

"Would you . . . um . . . like to come in for a beer?" she asked.

"Sure."

Amore dashed ahead of them and streaked up the stairs. "I'd think he would be hungry," she said.

Earl shook his head. "He's had a big night and now he just wants to sleep it off."

He knew about these things. Knew what it was like to spend a night on the wild side. Knowledge she lacked.

"How about that beer?" Earl said. "Your plant could use a drink, too." He stepped past her into the kitchen, and for the second time she caught a whiff of his musky smell, mixed with the pot's earthy one.

He took the pot to the sink while she rummaged in the refrigerator. When she turned around, he'd finished watering the plant and was splashing water on his face. The sight filled her with a sudden, overwhelming longing. He was just reaching for a paper towel when she went to him. She pressed her lips against his cheek and began kissing him—on his face, on his neck, wherever it was wet—like Marguerite drinking the drops that fell from the handsome stranger who saved her from drowning.

Earl stood perfectly still, neither stopping her nor responding. Finally he put his hands on her shoulders and gave her a little push backward, holding her at arm's length. "You know what you're doing, Star?" He fixed his faded blue eyes on her.

"What do you mean?"

"Things got pretty hot at the benefit, but then Mill cut in, you got scared, and ran back to your boyfriend in the city."

"Speak for yourself."

"What?"

"Last night's aftershave. You didn't put that on just to have a few beers at the Stag."

"You think I—" He broke off, shaking his head. "I put it on to pay you a visit."

"You did?" It was her turn to be amazed.

"I knew you were back. Cheryl said you'd been at the cabin. When I got to the house, you had the music on so loud, you didn't hear me. I went around to the rear and watched you a while," he finished sheepishly.

"You spied on me!" She turned red. He'd seen her sway to the music, clutching a pillow, pretending she was dancing with him.

"I was going to let you know I was there, but the phone rang. It was Alan. I heard you making plans. I left and went to the Stag. I love you, Star, but every time we start to get close, you pull away. I don't want an on-and-off thing. You go with me, you stay with me." He gripped her shoulders tightly, looking deep into her eyes.

You go with me, you stay with me. His demand frightened her, but she desired him more than she'd ever desired anyone.

As if sensing her turmoil, he said, "I don't expect you to decide on the spot. I'm going back up the hill. When you've made up your mind, you know where to find me." Removing his hands from her shoulders, he turned to go.

She couldn't just let him walk away. Not while she could smell his scent, taste him on her tongue. It was now or never. She grabbed his arm. "Yes!"

He let out such a joyful whoop he might have won the lottery. Scooping her off the ground, he swung her in the air like the winning ticket. As he brought her down, he covered her with kisses. Their coming together was like an explosion ripping the clothes from their bodies and landing them on the floor in a tangle of arms and legs. He lifted her up again, carrying her into a realm of sensual delight she had not known existed. She couldn't believe the sensations erupting within her. The more pleasure he gave her, the more she craved. More, more, more.

At last, a hazy bliss settled over her. Through it she was dimly aware of a chain being slipped around her neck. Opening her eyes, she saw the small blue round of his St. Christopher medal dangling between her breasts. "You're mine now," he said. "And you're gonna stay mine."

Chapter 46

The commotion jolted Kathryn from sleep. Outside, men were shouting and hooting. Earl stirred and cursed softly next to her. "What is it?" she asked, as he got up and began pulling on clothes.

"The start of Deer Week. I'm supposed to go hunting with Wayne and the other guys. But if you don't want me to, I won't."

"It's okay. When will you be back?"

"Dusk at the latest, sooner if I'm lucky and get a deer."

She smiled drowsily at him. "I hope you're lucky then."

"Me, too. But if I'm not, it won't matter because I'll be coming home to you." He bent and kissed her.

"You coming, brother?" Wayne called from below.

"In a minute," Earl yelled back. He kissed her again before leaving. Outside, she heard more shouts and hoots. They were probably ribbing Earl about where he'd spent the night. Let them, she didn't care. A truck rumbled away and the noise faded into silence. She yawned and stretched, sleek and satisfied as a well-groomed cat. Like Amore after Earl had stroked him. She snuggled into the place where his body had been, feeling his warmth, inhaling his scent. And drifted back to sleep.

When she woke, light was streaming in through a crack in the curtains. At first she missed Earl. Then she was glad he wasn't there. What had happened last night was still so new and strange she needed time to get used to it. She'd never given herself so completely to a man. Always before, part of her had held back. There was no holding back with Earl. She had let him be intimate in ways she hadn't thought possible.

She wandered through the empty house like a silent sleuth, seeking traces of him and surprised to find how precious each was. She felt tender toward the sheets where he had lain, the loose change that had fallen from his pants pocket, a button torn from his shirt in her eagerness.

She put the change and the button in a box for safekeeping. She imagined sewing the button on his shirt. Then she had to laugh. When buttons needed replacing, she got the cleaners to do it. But after a single night with Earl, she was ready to perform this and countless other domestic tasks. She wanted to cook him breakfast, wash and fold his laundry, iron his shirts. She was so busy imagining all the things she'd do for him it took an angry meow from Amore to remind her that he, too, needed care.

She fed him and made a meal for herself out of what remained of the bread and wedge of cheddar she and Earl had feasted on during a break in their lovemaking. He must be hungry now himself. She hoped Wayne had thought to bring him a sandwich. If he went hunting tomorrow, she'd see to it. She started to make a shopping list then realized it was almost eleven a.m. and she was still in her bathrobe. She went back upstairs. If Earl returned early, she wanted to be ready.

In the hallway, she noticed the attic trapdoor was ajar. She must have forgotten to close it when she and Earl had left the attic. Standing on tiptoe, she gave the door a shove. Dust motes rained down. The cord swung wildly like a hangman's noose. Distracted by Earl's arrival, she hadn't finished yesterday's search for the second will. Should she continue now? No. She didn't want to mar her current bliss with more discoveries like the pond collage, which hinted at Gordon's innocence. And neither Hank Lapsley nor Earl seemed to think a second will existed.

She went into the shower. The hot water washed away the dust, but also, regrettably, the smell of him. Showered and dressed, she returned to the shopping list. To her dismay, she realized she didn't know Earl's food preferences. How could she have been so intimate with him and not even know if he liked peanut butter and jelly sandwiches? She should have paid closer attention to what he'd had for lunch while he was working on the driveway. But how could she have foreseen how important this information would be? Millie knew, but she was the last person Kathryn wanted to talk to right now. Not Millie and . . . certainly not Alan.

She was supposed to be seeing Alan next weekend. She'd have to call him and break things off. She had chosen Earl, and she didn't regret that choice. But she did regret having to tell Alan. He was a good man, and had meant more to her than any of the other men she'd been involved with. She hated the thought of hurting him, but what else could she do? Last night had changed everything. She was a different person now. She could no more go back to Alan than return to being her old self. She decided to put off telephoning him, though.

Kathryn floated through the rest of the day, alternately making lists of things she wanted to ask Earl about himself and reliving each exquisite moment of their intimacy. Gunshots sounded at intervals. Looking out the window, she saw a truck parked down the driveway near where Gordon's road led into the woods. Earl and his companions might be nearby. She went out onto the patio, where she had a view of the spot where they would come out, and sat down to wait.

After what seemed like a long time, two figures emerged from the woods, dragging a deer. A third figure trailed behind them. She ran toward the men. By the time she reached them, Earl, Wayne and Pete had hefted the deer carcass onto the cab of the pickup. Earl turned and hugged her. Dressed in camouflage and blaze orange, he was unfamiliar and even a little intimidating. He smelled of damp earth, sweat, and gore. Her stomach twisted. Over his shoulder, she saw Pete watching them. He broke eye contact immediately. "Have a look at the buck Pete shot," Earl said.

She glanced at the dead animal then back at Pete, who was already getting into the truck. "Congratulations," she called after him.

"Thanks," he mumbled.

"You coming back with us?" Wayne asked Earl.

"Nope. I'll catch you later." He tossed his gear into the back of the truck.

"Are you disappointed you didn't get a deer, too?" she asked, as they walked arm in arm up the driveway.

"No, because I've got you." He gave her a squeeze.

When they reached the house, she said, "You must be starving. Have you eaten anything since last night?"

"Wayne brought me a sandwich."

"If you go out again tomorrow, I'll make the sandwiches."

"You don't have to."

"I want to. I want to do for you," she finished awkwardly.

Earl kissed her. "Sure, Star. But right now I need to shower and change."

He rejoined her in the living room where she'd put out beers and a bowl of chips and some dip. He settled on the couch beside her and took a long drink. "This really hits the spot."

The phone rang. "Aren't you going to answer that?" he said.

"The machine can do it." She nuzzled his cheek, but he pulled away at the sound of Alan's voice. "Hi, Kathryn. Thought I would have heard from you by now. Hope everything's okay. Give me a call when you have a chance, so we can finalize our plans for next weekend."

Earl gave her a long look, his eyes the icy blue of a glacial tarn. Finally, he said, "You need to talk to him, Star, tell him it's over between you."

"I know. I'm going to. But it's hard. I don't want to hurt him."

Earl said nothing, merely looked at her. She felt naked and vulnerable under his gaze, as if she'd shed her defenses along with her clothes last night. "I know what you're thinking," she said. "You think I won't break things off, but I will, I really will! I'm not going to run back to Alan like I did before. I promise I'll never—"

"Stop it, Star!" He gripped her by the shoulders. "There's no need to get all upset. You'll call him and everything will be fine." He tipped her head gently back and smiled at her. "Okay?"

Chapter 47

Kathryn's fingernails beat a rat-a-tat-tat on the kitchen counter. She frowned at the phone on the opposite wall. How to break it to Alan? In the past, her relationships had ended with a whimper rather than a bang. Maybe she should write a letter instead of calling. But her letter wouldn't reach him for a few days. It wasn't fair to keep him in the dark. And she'd promised Earl she would call.

She'd put it off all morning. Now, she couldn't wait any longer. It was already past two p.m., and the Spitzers, Gordon's mother and stepfather, were due to arrive at three. Reluctantly, she dialed Alan's office number. She would have preferred to call him at home, but that meant waiting until evening when Earl would be here.

"Mr. Marquette's office," the secretary said crisply.

Kathryn's throat went dry; she could barely get the words out. "I'd like to speak with him, it's Kathryn Stinson."

"Just a minute."

Kathryn hoped the secretary would tell her Alan was in a meeting. Instead, he came onto the line. "Kathryn, thank God! I was starting to worry about you. Is everything okay?"

"Yes—no, I mean, there's been another shooting," she blurted.

"That's terrible. What happened?"

She gave him an abbreviated version of Saturday night's events.

"You must be very upset. If it weren't for Sophie, I'd drive there tonight. Maybe you could come here."

His concern was touching, but it made what she had to say all the harder.

"Look . . . um . . . it's not a good idea for me to go there, or for you to come here. I—I'm involved with someone else now."

"I beg your pardon?"

"I'm involved with another man."

"But we just spent Thanksgiving with my parents. We were making plans for this weekend."

"I know it's sudden."

"That's the understatement of the year! Who is this other man?"

"Earl Barker."

"The guy who suckered me into getting drunk at the bar, whose brother tried to run us off the road. Is this some kind of joke?"

"No, I'm perfectly serious." Kathryn heard a rapping noise. "Someone's here. Hold on a minute." She hurried to the front door. No one. She returned to the kitchen. "False alarm. As I was saying, I really am involved with Earl Barker."

"But that night at the bar, you seemed repelled by him."

"I know, but since then, I—" Kathryn gasped, as a woman's face appeared at the kitchen window. The woman waved and mouthed something at her. Then she stepped into the kitchen. Tall and robustly built with a heavily made-up face and perfectly styled silver hair, the woman looked to be in her late sixties or early seventies.

"What's going on?" Alan demanded.

The woman reached for Kathryn's free hand and shook it. "Yvonne Spitzer. And this is my husband, Jerry," she said in a loud voice, gesturing toward a short, dark, reedy man who had followed her into the kitchen. "Go ahead with your call. We'll wait for you in the living room. But first I need a little sustenance." Yvonne Spitzer opened the refrigerator and peered inside.

"Kathryn?" Alan said.

"I'll have to call you back. The Spitzers are here."

"Who?"

"The Spit—"

"What kind of ham is this?" Yvonne Spitzer held up several slices in plastic wrap.

"Deli ham," Kathryn said.

"What's this about ham?" Alan's voice filled the room.

"You don't have the healthy kind?" Yvonne Spitzer asked.

Kathryn shook her head.

"Well, I guess I'll just have to make do." Yvonne Spitzer took out bread, lettuce, and mayonnaise, and proceeded to make herself a sandwich.

"Kathryn, talk to me," Alan pleaded. "Who are these people, and what are they doing?"

"Mrs. Spitzer is having a sandwich." Mrs. Spitzer could have had a sandwich in Great Barrington or at the New Nottingham General Store instead of waiting until now. But apparently she shared her son's sense of entitlement.

"Why? Did you invite her for lunch?" Alan sputtered.

"No, she just—"

Yvonne Spitzer grabbed the handset and spoke to Alan, "I'm hypoglycemic. If my blood sugar drops too low, I'm in trouble. All the stress I've been under lately has made my condition worse."

Alan must have made a dismissive comment, because Yvonne Spitzer said, "You don't have to be nasty. It's a serious condition."

"Was he rude to you, Vonnie?" Jerry Spitzer jumped in.

When Yvonne Spitzer nodded, her husband seized the phone. "How dare you insult my wife! This is our house, and we're here on important business. You'll just have to wait your turn!" He slammed the handset into its cradle.

Kathryn didn't know whether to laugh or cry, the situation was so awful and absurd. She'd been spared the continuation of a painful conversation with Alan, but the Spitzers' overbearing manners were too much. She opened her mouth to protest. Jerry Spitzer beat her to the draw. "Sorry, but I can't stand it when people are mean to Vonnie. Especially at a time like this. And we do have important business. We need to inspect the house before we put it on the market. We also need to have a look at whatever personal belongings my stepson left."

"Most of his stuff's in the attic," Kathryn said. "You could start there and work your way down."

"We'll do that," Jerry Spitzer said. "But first we'd like to ask you a few questions about the night Gordon was killed."

Kathryn tensed. "I already made a statement to the police."

"Let's go into the living room," Jerry Spitzer said, leading the way.

He and his wife sat on the couch, while Kathryn took a seat opposite. Even seated, Yvonne Spitzer possessed the erect carriage of someone accustomed to balancing a book on her head. In contrast, her husband had the darting eyes of a ferret and restless hands which he kept clasping and unclasping, as he spoke: "In your statement, you refer to a place on the tapes of Mrs. Goodale's recollections, where Diana says she thinks Gordon might kill her for her money, right?"

Before Kathryn could reply, Yvonne Spitzer said, "But that's ridiculous! Gordon didn't kill Diana. It was that boy they found in the woods with her. Or someone else from around here. Gordon told us she'd been having an affair with a local man—a trashy sort of person. There was that hunter she'd been feuding with, too." Yvonne Spitzer shuddered and glanced anxiously around, as if she expected Diana's killer to appear at a window.

One of Jerry Spitzer's restless hands closed over his wife's. "It's all right, Vonnie. Of course, Gordon didn't kill Diana. But Mrs. Goodale believed he did. That's why she set him up."

"What?" Yvonne Spitzer looked surprised.

"Don't you see, Vonnie? Mrs. Goodale wrote anonymous notes to lure Gordon back to the Berkshires. She figured he would find out she'd written the notes eventually. Then, when he confronted her, she used it as an excuse to shoot him."

"But that's so twisted and evil!" Yvonne Spitzer cried. "This is an awful place with awful people. I never understood why Gordon and Diana moved here. If only they'd stayed in New York, she'd be alive and so would he!"

Her voice shook and her upper body wobbled dangerously. Spitzer reached out a hand to steady her. Kathryn leaned forward also.

Pulling herself together, Yvonne Spitzer asked in a calmer voice, "Did you have much contact with my son before he was killed, Miss Stinson?"

"We only met a few times when he came to the house to get things."

"That's a pity because if you'd gotten to know Gordon, you would have seen what a kind, gentle man he was. Not a mover and shaker perhaps, but an artist and a dreamer who was just starting to come into his own. He seemed so happy when we saw him at Thanksgiving. He

223

loved living in France, his photography was going well and a gallery in New York was planning an exhibit of his work. This never should have happened. Something went wrong, dreadfully wrong!"

This time Yvonne Spitzer didn't regain her composure, but collapsed inward onto herself in a paroxysm of emotion. Kathryn's heart went out to her. However disagreeable Yvonne Spitzer might be as a person, right now she was first and foremost a mother who'd lost her child.

"I'm sorry about your son." She probably should have said this when the Spitzers first arrived, but had forgotten in the press of the moment. "And if there's anything I can . . ."

Jerry Spitzer, who had his arms around his wife, trying to comfort her, replied with a curt headshake. He held her until she seemed calmer, then he rose and held out his hand. "Come Vonnie, let's have a look at the rest of the house."

"No!" Yvonne Spitzer batted his hand away and stood. "I don't want to stay here another minute!"

"All right then, we'll go," her husband said. "Brandy Russo will be in touch with you about arrangements for the house," he told Kathryn. "Our lawyer may want to take a deposition from you at some point, so make sure Ms. Russo has your address when you move out."

The Spitzers' words remained with Kathryn long after they'd gone. She kept hearing Jerry Spitzer's comment about Emily setting up Gordon. A set-up in which she had played a part, albeit unwittingly. And what Yvonne Spitzer had said about Earl. Like her son, she'd called him trash, and also like Gordon, she'd suggested that either Earl or his brother could have killed Diana.

When Earl emerged from the woods at dusk, she ran to meet him. "What's the matter, Star?" he asked, noticing the tears in her eyes.

"The Spitzers, Gordon's family, came to the house this afternoon. They aren't nice people, and I disliked them for same reasons I disliked Gordon. But when Mrs. Spitzer broke down over her son's death, I felt bad for her."

Earl slipped an arm around her and drew her close. "God knows I hated Gordon, and I probably wouldn't have liked his parents either. But to lose a child is just about the worst thing that can happen to anyone. I know how *I'd* feel if one of my boys were killed . . . But try to put it behind you." His fingers brushed her cheek. "I thought we'd go up the hill for dinner. The rest of my family's eager to meet you."

Chapter 48

"I want you all to meet Kathryn," Earl said to the group gathered in the kitchen of the main house. "This is my mother, June." He indicated a large, placid-looking woman with gray-blonde hair standing by the stove. "My sister-in-law, Suzy." He pointed at a slim, young woman with flaming hair who stood by the stove with his mother. "And my dad, Roy." He gestured at a big, handsome man with a florid face, who sat drinking beer at the kitchen table with Wayne and an elderly man Kathryn recognized as Earl's grandfather. Black and tan dogs sprawled on the floor, creating an obstacle course for two young boys racing trucks around and occasionally over them.

"Well, well, what have we got here?" Roy Barker drawled. "I thought Pete was the only one who had any luck the other day, but I see you've bagged yourself a nice little doe, Son. And don't she just look good enough to eat?"

Kathryn squirmed inwardly. She'd sensed the meeting would be awkward, but this was worse than she'd expected.

"Saw 'em going up the ledges together," the grandfather volunteered.

"Is that right?" Roy leered at her.

"I wanted to see one of the graves," Kathryn explained.

"Sure, that's all you were doing up there?" Roy asked.

"Yes, Dad," Earl said firmly.

Roy chuckled. "I'm surprised at you, Son." Turning back to Kathryn, he said, "How come you're interested in those old graves?"

"One of them belongs to a woman who was married to my ancestor, Jared Cutter."

226

"The bastard who blinded poor Clyde?" Roy said.

Blood rose into Kathryn's face. She opened her mouth to protest, but Earl beat her to it. "Nobody knows exactly what happened that night. And it was a long time ago."

"Maybe so, but—" Roy began.

"I'm glad you could join us, Kathryn," June Barker interrupted. "Why don't you have a seat? Dinner's almost ready."

At dinner the conversation was mostly about hunting; Kathryn was glad to have the attention off her. The men swapped stories of previous hunts and argued the merits of stand-hunting versus stalking, deer calling, and the use of scent trails and fake scrapes.

"Know what a scrape is, Kathryn?" Roy asked suddenly.

No, but I have an awful feeling you're going to tell me. She shook her head.

"It's what a buck does to attract the ladies during rutting season. He scratches the ground with his hoof, then he urinates on the spot."

Charming. Hunters all, Alan and his family could have told her what a scrape was, but they were much too polite to mention such things in her presence. Not Roy. He wasn't just earthy, he was downright crude.

"Do you like venison?" June asked Kathryn, perhaps sensing her discomfort.

"I've never tried it."

"Then you're in for a real treat," Suzy said. "The only question is how to cook it. I clipped a stir-fry recipe from the newspaper I'd like to try. But that venison sauerbraten you made a few years ago was awfully good, too," she told June.

The women continued their talk, the men theirs. During a lull, Roy turned to Kathryn. "Bet I know how you and Earl got together. My boy's got pheromones something fierce and if he was to—"

"Dad," Earl interrupted warily.

"Let me finish," Roy insisted. "As I was saying, if my boy made a full-sized scrape like a buck in rut, he'd attract every doe in creation. But he only wanted one doe. You, Kathryn. So he made a teeny scrape, just enough to draw you to the spot."

Kathryn couldn't believe her ears. This was turning out to be a dinner from hell.

"Jesus!" Earl exploded.

"Now, Son," Roy said sternly, "you know I don't allow swearing at the table."

Kathryn stared at Roy, dumbfounded. Evidently cursing was prohibited, but coarse remarks were acceptable.

Earl stood angrily. "We're leaving. C'mon, Kathryn."

Suzy and Wayne exchanged glances, but stayed out of it. Kathryn was about to rise when June held out a restraining hand. "Sit down and finish your dinner," she ordered Earl in a voice she'd probably used with him as a child. After a moment's hesitation, he obeyed. "Suzy and I worked hard on this meal," June continued. "And I won't have it spoiled with silly talk about bucks and does." She glared at her husband, who shrugged, and lowered his gaze to his plate. Kathryn felt as if she'd witnessed a long-established family dynamic in which father and son sparred and mom played peacemaker.

To her relief, the rest of the meal passed without incident. When it was over Earl told her to wait in the truck while he had a word with his father. "I'm sorry about Dad's behavior tonight," he said after he rejoined her. "He's always had this thing about comparing women in the family to the female of one animal or another. Millie was a filly and Suzy was a heifer. Or maybe it was the other way around. Cheryl was definitely a bunny, though. We put up with it because after awhile he quits. But tonight he went too far and I let him know that."

"It was a bit much," Kathryn agreed. "But I hope, as you say, he'll quit of his own accord."

"He'll quit because I told him to. I'm not going to let Dad or anyone else come between us." He took her hand and squeezed it so tightly she winced with pain.

Chapter 49

Millie was occupied with a customer when Kathryn slipped into the post office the next morning.

Convinced that Millie knew about her and Earl, she'd avoided the post office for the past several days. Now, she expected to find her box full. Instead, there was a yellow slip with instructions to pick up her mail at the window. No avoiding Millie now.

"I hope you didn't stay away, because of . . . you know," Millie said with her usual friendly smile, as she handed Kathryn her mail.

"I'm afraid I did. I thought you'd be angry I went against your advice."

"Well, as you can see, I'm not. Disappointed, yes but—" Millie broke off as a customer entered the post office. Lowering her voice, she said, "Let's talk more later."

"Want to meet at the historical society room at noon?"

"I know a better place. Come to my house around twelve-fifteen. You know where I live, right?"

*****

Even before Millie opened the front door of the white house, Kathryn was aware of a wonderful cooking aroma emanating from within. "I hope you didn't go to any trouble on my account," she said.

"No trouble," Millie assured her. "I made the soup yesterday, so I just needed to heat it up. Didn't seem right having you over without giving you lunch. Would you like a grilled cheese sandwich with the soup? I'm going to make one for myself."

"Sounds great."

"Good. While I finish getting lunch together, have a seat and make yourself at home." Millie gestured toward a large, flowered couch in the living room before disappearing into the kitchen.

Kathryn did as she was told. Glancing around, she found herself thinking how different the living room with its plush carpet, comfortable couch with fluffy pillows, and lacy curtains on the windows was from Earl's Spartan trailer. A couple of glossy home decorating magazines were neatly arranged on the coffee table in front of her, but what especially attracted her attention was the array of family photos on the mantel above the fireplace. She went over to examine them. There was a formal wedding portrait of Millie and Earl. They looked solemn and every bit the teenagers they'd been. The rest of the photos were candid shots, showing the couple and their three boys from babyhood to young adulthood and beyond, for the two older boys. They made an attractive family. She noticed a candid half hidden by one of the family shots. She picked it up to get a better look. It was a wedding photo; Millie's mouth was wide open, as if she were whooping with joy. Instead, she was about to receive the piece of wedding cake a grinning Earl held out to her. "Almost ready!" Millie called from the kitchen.

Kathryn put back the photo and joined her in the kitchen. "Can I give you a hand?"

"Sure."

Millie ladled steaming tomato soup into bowls then flipped golden brown sandwiches dripping with cheese from the hot griddle onto plates beside the soup bowls. "I forgot to ask what you'd like to drink. Coffee, tea, water?"

"Water's fine."

Millie filled two glasses and handed them to Kathryn. "You take these and I'll bring the plates."

The soup smelled so good Kathryn could hardly wait to have a taste. It was rich and tangy. "This is the best tomato bisque I've ever had."

"Thanks, but it's simple fare. The sandwich too, though the bread is homemade. I'm sure you've had much fancier meals eating out in Boston."

Kathryn shook her head. "For lunch, I usually just grab something to eat at my desk, and dinner's often Chinese take-out."

"I'd probably do the same if I were single in the city, but as the mother of a hungry teenager, I can't afford to. Your boyfriend must have taken you out to some nice places, though."

"Oh, he did, but . . ." Kathryn looked at Millie inquiringly, wondering why she'd brought up Alan.

"He's a lawyer, right?"

"Yes."

"What's his name?"

"Why do you ask?"

"I just thought he might be someone I've read about in the papers. There's this Boston lawyer who's in the news a lot."

"You mean Alan Madden?"

"That's him."

"Well, my boyfriend's name is Alan, but Marquette, not Madden. And he's not my boyfriend anymore."

Millie's soup spoon stopped in mid-hair. "You've really broken off with him?"

"I had to, didn't I? Now that I'm with Earl."

Millie brought the spoon to her mouth and swallowed. "Of course . . . How's the research going?" she asked, changing the subject.

"I think I've found out all I ever will."

"Then you'll be returning to your job in the city?"

"Not right away. When I first came here, I wasn't sure how long I'd stay. Now that's changed. I want to remain as long as I can. Fortunately, when I asked my boss if she needed me back, she reminded me that the weeks from Thanksgiving until New Year's are always a slow time. So it's fine for me to stay until the beginning of the year. After that, I'll only be able to come for weekends."

"Nice . . . but haven't you missed your job? It must be fun being a curator. There aren't opportunities like that around here."

"Maybe not, but this place has its advantages."

"You'll rent the Farley house until you return to Boston?"

"I'd like to, but I need to talk to Brandy. I don't know what Gordon's parents will want to do with the house now. I don't have a formal lease, and they . . . might want to sell it quickly."

"Well, I hope you can stay there, because I don't think you'd be very comfortable in Earl's trailer. We lived there when we were first married. But we were young and didn't mind roughing it—using the woods for a john and taking showers at his parents' place. After he moved back to the trailer, he added an outhouse, but he still comes here for showers, the occasional meal, and to watch sports events on TV."

"He does?" This was news. But then she hadn't given much thought to what Earl did when he wasn't with her.

Millie nodded. "But enough about that. When you're as smitten as you obviously are, you don't want to be worrying about such mundane matters."

Then why did you bring them up in the first place?

"Earl's and my romantic relationship ended some time ago," Millie went on. "Now we're just friends. And as a friend to you both, I hope things work out."

"You're not concerned about 'trouble down the road' anymore?"

"Trouble?" Millie repeated. She took a bite of her sandwich and chewed thoughtfully. "No, not particularly." She glanced at her watch. "Goodness! I've got to get back to the post office. Time sure flies." She jumped up and cleared the table in a blur of motion that reminded Kathryn of the videocassettes of her childhood, after she'd hit fast-forward.

As they were leaving, Millie suddenly turned to her and said, "Just don't do anything to make him jealous."

Chapter 50

"This'll have to be repainted." Brandy pointed at the ceiling in the master bedroom, through which Kathryn had nearly fallen. "But the rest of upstairs rooms look all right." Brandy had arrived later that day to inspect the house for things that needed to be done before she started showing it.

"Do the Spitzers want me to move out?" Kathryn asked, remembering her lunchtime conversation with Millie.

Brandy looked up from her note pad. "Actually, they told me it was okay for you to stay. They'd just as soon collect rent until the house is sold."

"Any idea when that will be?"

"I'll start showing it as soon as the painting and other minor repairs are finished, but I doubt there'll be any action until spring when the serious house hunters start coming. Sure you're not interested? They've lowered the price, you know."

Kathryn shook her head. "It's a nice house in a beautiful setting, but not for me."

"Too bad. But you'll stay until I find a buyer?"

"Yes, though I'll only be able to use it on weekends after the first of the year when I go back to work."

"Good, because I'd rather have the house occupied when I show it. There's nothing more off-putting to prospective buyers than a cold, empty place, especially when both owners have died. Lived-in is better for sales, provided the occupant isn't a total slob. Which you obviously aren't."

"The furniture will stay then?"

"Yup, it'll be the last to go."

"What about all the stuff in the attic?"

"The Spitzers didn't mention it, so I suppose it can wait, too."

Kathryn wasn't sure whether to be glad or sorry. The stuff's staying meant she could continue going through it, if she wanted, but it also meant the house would hold troublesome reminders of its ghosts.

They went downstairs, and Brandy headed for the door. Halfway there, she stopped and gazed out the window at the pond and the woods beyond. "Poor Gordon," she said with a sigh. "First Diana, now him. Never dreamed he'd be killed, too. And by Emily of all people." She shook her head. "But speaking of that, if anyone asks, I'm going to say they died in a car accident, miles from here. Otherwise, prospective buyers might think the place is jinxed. I'm telling you this now, so you won't be surprised if you happen to be around when I'm showing the house. Okay?"

Kathryn nodded. Brandy had lied when she'd shown her the house, so it didn't surprise her that Brandy was planning to lie again. Now, though, she understood why Brandy hadn't told her the truth. She'd wanted to spare herself the pain of revealing and perhaps even reliving what could well have been the worst night of her life. The night her son had shot Diana and died himself.

But was that really what had happened? Gordon's words came back to her: "*My wife had so many enemies that any one of them could have wrecked her wedding picture, just as any one of them could have killed her.*"

"Brandy, have you ever . . .?" She left the question unfinished, reluctant to re-open the wound.

"What?" Brandy prodded.

"I know it's hard for you to talk about this and I probably shouldn't ask, but have you ever wondered if someone other than Brian did the shooting that night?"

Brandy bit her lip and looked away. Then, meeting Kathryn's eyes, she said in a voice choked with emotion, "'Course I have! I didn't want to believe Brian was capable of what the cops think he did. I still have trouble accepting it. Sure, he had issues, lots of teenagers do, but it's hard for me to imagine him shooting Diana in cold blood then killing himself. And I gotta tell you, my life's been hell since that night. The way people around here sometimes look at me, I might as well be wearing a sign, 'Mom of the Murderer.'"

Kathryn's heart went out to her. "I'm sorry," she said softly.

"Thanks . . . But what's behind your question?"

"A remark Gordon made. He said he wondered if Brian was in the wrong place at the wrong time, if he got in someone else's way."

"Did he say who he thought this 'someone' was?"

"Garth or Earl."

"He *would*. No love lost between him and either of them. Earl especially. You were there when a fight broke out between those two."

"Yes, but aside from what you've just told me, is there anything else that makes you think the shooter could have been another person?"

"Actually, there is. Joey Babcock, the kid who was with Brian in the beginning, insisted they didn't swipe Garth's gun, that Brian was unarmed when Joey left him."

The news gave Kathryn a jolt. "Really? What did the police make of that?"

"Nothing. They decided Joey was lying to protect his ass, so he wouldn't be accused of gun theft or of being involved in the murder in any way. And as a kid who'd had his share of run-ins with the authorities, Joey didn't have a whole lot of credibility with them."

"Whose prints were on the gun?"

"Garth's and Brian's. But Garth had an alibi and so did his brother. Gordon, too. Still, if I was gonna put money on one of them, alibi notwithstanding, it would be Garth. He was mean enough to shoot both Diana and Brian. But he's dead and so are they. And dead people can't tell tales."

Hank Lapsley had said much the same thing about Gordon. Yet there was one suspect left standing. He loomed before them like the proverbial elephant in the room. She and Brandy had each mentioned his name, but then they'd let it drop. Brandy because she knew he and Kathryn were lovers and didn't want to upset her by suggesting he could have been the shooter? Or as a woman who'd had an affair with him herself, maybe Brandy didn't think Earl was the kind of man who could make love to her after killing her son. Kathryn wasn't ready to believe that of him either, but at the same time, she wanted to know more.

"What else can you tell me about that night?"

Brandy looked stricken, started to shake her head. "If I'm gonna talk about it, I need a drink. You wouldn't happen to have any bourbon in the house, would you?"

"Only wine. Will that do?"

"I guess."

Kathryn got the wine and brought it into the living room, where they both sat down. Brandy took a long drink and began, "I got home from work between five-thirty and six. Brian wasn't there, but that wasn't unusual. He and Joey often hung out together after school. I didn't like it, but there wasn't much I could do. We had this deal that if he made it home by seven, I wouldn't give him a hard time. He stuck to it for awhile, but that night, he didn't." She paused to gulp wine, finishing the glass. "Sure, you don't have any bourbon?"

"No, but how about another glass of wine?"

"Thanks. Mind if I smoke?"

Normally Kathryn did mind, but she sensed Brandy needed the crutch of a cigarette. She refilled Brandy's wine glass, found an ashtray, and put it on a table next to the realtor.

"Where were we?" Brandy asked after she'd taken a deep drag.

"Your son didn't come home when he was supposed to."

"Right. When eight p.m. rolled around, I started getting worried. I called the Babcocks. Mrs. Babcock said Joey was at home, that he'd returned around seven, in time for dinner, but that he'd been with Brian beforehand. Of course, I wanted to know where. Mrs. Babcock went to ask Joey. I heard arguing in the background. Apparently, Joey didn't want to rat on his friend, because both parents had to twist his arm to get an answer. Mr. Babcock got on the phone and said the boys had gone back to their old hideout in the woods, and that Joey had left by himself, because Brian wanted to stay awhile longer. He tried to reassure me that Brian had probably lost track of time or fallen asleep, and would come home soon. But I was worried. As the minutes ticked away with no sign of Brian, I got even more worried. I'd never been in those woods, but I knew they were big enough for someone to get lost."

Brandy made a sweeping motion with her cigarette as if to indicate the extent of the forest. Ash landed on her lap. Brushing it off, she continued, "I also figured it was a place where someone could get hurt. Especially if that person were drunk or stoned, as I suspected Brian was. When I couldn't take it anymore, I called Diana."

"Diana? Wouldn't she be angry to learn Brian was in her woods despite her orders to keep out?"

"Maybe it wasn't my best idea. But I was reluctant to involve the police, and I thought if I reached out to her as a frantic mom with a missing son, she'd help me find him. Besides, she knew those woods like the back of her hand."

"So you were the one who alerted her to Brian's presence there?"

"Uh-uh. When I called the house, Cheryl Barker answered the phone."

"What was she doing there?"

"Beats me. Anyway, Cheryl told me Diana wasn't home, but must have gone out for a walk because her car was parked in the driveway. She promised to let Diana know I'd called when she returned. I waited some more, and when I didn't hear from Diana, I broke down and called the police. I reached Hank Lapsley at the White Stag. He told me not to worry, that Brian would show up eventually. I must've sounded pretty desperate, because he finally agreed to organize a search party. I heard him ask the men at the bar if anyone wanted to go with him. Earl was the only one who volunteered. 'Earl knows those woods better 'n anyone,' he said, 'so if your boy's in there, we'll find 'im.'

"I waited by the phone for over an hour. I hated sitting there, not knowing what was going on. I got in my car and drove up Rattlesnake Hill. When I turned in the Farley driveway, I saw flashing lights. There was an ambulance and a couple of cop cars. A trooper got out of one. He said two people had been killed in the woods, and they were bringing the bodies out. He ordered me not to go any farther, but I had to see for myself. One of those bodies could be my son, for chrissake! I started running. He grabbed and held me until we saw them coming out."

Kathryn's mind flashed to another scene of men emerging from the woods. They were hunters, not police. They lugged a buck instead of two human bodies. One of the men was her lover.

"I broke away from the trooper and ran toward them." Brandy's voice was ragged with emotion. "Earl caught me in his arms. I hardly recognized him, he looked so wild, like a crazy person. He told me how sorry he was about Brian, that he'd lost a loved one, too: Diana. I asked what happened. He said the police weren't sure yet, just that they'd probably been shot by the same gun. I cried so hard, I was shaking all over, thought I'd never stop. He held me until I was calmer. Then he drove me home and stayed the night."

Yes, that was something Earl would do. He'd offered to spend the night with her after Gordon had been killed.

Brandy's face assumed a dreamy expression, like someone in a trance. When she spoke again, the agitation was gone from her voice. "Came back the next night and the night after that for about a week. We made love a few times, but mostly we just held each other."

Just held each other. She knew what that was like, too. Except that afternoon when she'd broken down in his trailer, he hadn't held her, but had managed to comfort her merely with his nearness.

"She came, too, but separate from him," Brandy said.

"Who?"

"Millie. Brought me meals and sat with me while I ate."

How like Millie to bring food.

"Don't know what I would've done without 'em," Brandy said. "Then one night he told me he wouldn't be coming back, that it was time for us to grieve and, he hoped, heal on our own. But if I needed anything to let him know. She brought meals awhile longer, until she found this grief group for me, and I went to it and . . ." Brandy's voice trailed off. She shook herself, as if rousing herself from a trance. "I've told you more than you asked for. Time for me to go anyway 'cuz you've got company." She motioned to the picture window with the view of the driveway, where Earl's red truck had just become visible. "I'll be in touch about the painters."

Chapter 51

When the phone rang the next morning, Kathryn tensed. What if it was Alan? They'd spoken a few times since that awful, aborted call the day of the Spitzers' visit. He was wounded, angry and unwilling to let go without a plausible explanation of what had made her dump him for Earl on such short notice. But how could she put into words the powerful feelings that had drawn her, against all reason, to Earl. She let the machine pick up.

"Kathryn, are you there?" Emily demanded in her scratchy-record voice. "Why haven't you been to see me lately?"

Reluctantly, Kathryn picked up the handset. "I've been busy," she fibbed. The truth was she'd stayed away on purpose. Whenever she thought of Emily these days, she saw Gordon's dead body sprawled at the old woman's feet, heard Jerry Spitzer's charge, "She set him up," and felt a stab of guilt at her own role in the possible set-up.

"Fiddlesticks! You get over here this afternoon. I've got something for you."

"Oh? Did you find more tapes of your recollections?"

"You'll see when you come."

Kathryn felt mystified and more than a little apprehensive. The last time Emily had given her something it had led to trouble. Big trouble.

*****

Emily sat in the wing chair in the parlor, eyes closed, head drooped on her chest, apparently napping. Kathryn noticed that the braided rug where Gordon had lain only a week ago had been replaced by another, smaller rug from the bedroom. Instead of a smoking gun, a small red box rested on the table. She tiptoed to Emily, wondering whether to wake her.

Emily's head jerked up and her eyes popped open. "Leonora?"

"It's Kathryn."

Emily squinted at her. "Oh, so it is."

"Who's Leonora?"

"Marguerite's daughter. Don't you remember anything?"

Kathryn sighed. "I guess not. You said you had something for me?"

"Yes. It was supposed to be Leonora's. But Aurelia never—oh, why won't she leave me alone?" Emily's voice shook with distress.

"What's the matter?"

"Here, take it!" Emily thrust the small red box at her. "Well, open it, for heaven's sake!" Emily snapped when Kathryn hesitated.

She obeyed. Inside was one of the most beautiful rings she'd ever seen—rose-cut diamonds and rubies on a delicate gold band. "Why are you giving me this?"

"It was her engagement ring. Now it's your ring."

"Whose?"

"Marguerite's."

"How did you get it?"

"Quit pestering me with questions and put it on."

Kathryn removed the ring from the box and examined it. "The band's too small. It's not going to fit."

"You don't know until you've tried." Emily seized the ring and tried to force it onto her left finger. It wouldn't clear the knuckle. Emily pushed harder.

"Ouch!"

"Stop being such a ninny," Emily scolded. "Go into the bathroom and put soap on your finger."

"But—"

"Do it!"

Again, Kathryn obeyed. Emily seemed so agitated she felt she had to humor the old woman. Even with soap easing the way, Emily still had to yank hard before the ring made it over her knuckle.

"A perfect fit!" Emily crowed, holding up Kathryn's red, swollen finger with triumph.

Hardly. Kathryn doubted she'd get the ring off without a similar struggle.

"Aren't you going to thank me?" Emily demanded.

"Thank you, it's a beautiful ring. But I'd still like to know how you got it, and why you're giving it to be me."

"Aurelia told me to."

Aurelia? Kathryn was about to ask how Emily's long-dead great-grandmother could have told her to do anything, but stopped. She knew all too well how people from the past could become so ingrained in your memory that you actually heard their voices speaking to you, telling you what to do, or *not* do, like her grandmother. Still, she didn't understand why Emily thought Aurelia wanted her to have the ring.

Yet when she asked, Emily gave her the brush-off: "Go now. I need to take a nap. Between Aurelia and you, I haven't been getting any rest."

Chapter 52

After the door shut behind Kathryn, Emily smiled and sank back in her chair. She closed her eyes. She was ready for them to come for her now. She waited and waited, but no one appeared. What was the matter? Didn't they know her time had come? "Aurelia," she called finally, "I did what you wanted. Now will you let me die in peace?"

Silence, then Aurelia slowly swam into view. "You must give her the letters," she said.

"Letters?"

"The ones he wrote me. I gave them to you before I died, along with the ring."

"But there were no letters with the ring."

"Then you must have put them somewhere else."

"I don't remember where. Isn't it enough that she has the ring?"

"No. She needs to see the letters."

"What if I can't find them?"

"You must."

"I'm too worn-out. I just want to die now."

"Not until you've done this."

"Please, I'm begging you!"

Aurelia's shadowy figure did not smile or hold out her hands to Emily, as she had earlier. Instead, her arms barricaded her chest, and her expression was stern and implacable.

Emily glanced wildly around. Perhaps one of the other spirits who'd come with Aurelia before could be persuaded to intercede with her great-grandmother. But no one else was there.

"Diana?" Emily called.

"I'm here," Diana replied in her girlish voice. A moment later, Diana's lovely face materialized before Emily's eyes.

"Talk to Aurelia. Tell her that when I killed Gordon and gave Kathryn the ring, my work on earth was finished. She'll listen to you. It was your death I avenged."

"Avenged my death? No, Emily, you did no such thing." Diana shook her head sadly and drifted away, vanishing into the ether. Emily turned back to her great-grandmother only to discover that Aurelia, too, had vanished, leaving her frightened and alone.

Chapter 53

Back at the Farley house, Kathryn debated what to do about the ring. Her first impulse was to remove it. She wasn't accustomed to wearing jewelry, and the ring felt uncomfortable. But her finger was still red and swollen. She'd best wait until the swelling went down. In the meantime, the ring was lovely to look at. She spread her fingers out in the lamplight. The diamonds and rubies winked at her. She gazed at them, mesmerized.

"Star?" Earl walked into the living room. Kathryn whisked her hand behind her back. "How come you're not ready?" he asked.

"Ready?"

"We're going to a family party, remember? Uncle Fred and Aunt Marsha, Hank's parents, are celebrating their fortieth anniversary."

"Oh right, sorry. I'll just be a minute." She went upstairs to change.

In the pickup on the way to the Grange Hall, Earl spoke about Hank's parents and other relatives Kathryn would be meeting for the first time. Distracted by the ring, she barely listened. She turned it around and around on her finger, imagining she was turning back time, that each revolution was bringing her closer to the moment when Jared Cutter had placed this very ring on Marguerite's finger. It must have been a happy moment for both of them. Yet tragedy had followed. A tremor of fear shot through her. She shook it off. Silly to imagine that just because she was wearing the ring of a murdered woman, she was in danger. But how had Emily gotten it and why did she want Kathryn to have it?

"You gonna get out?" Earl stood outside the pickup, holding the door open for her.

"Sorry."

He gave her a look, as if to say, "What's with you tonight?"

"Hey, Cousin. Kathryn, glad you could make it," Hank greeted them inside the Grange Hall. He patted Earl on the back, and was about to shake hands with Kathryn when his gaze settled on the ring. He took her hand and held it up to the light. "Well, well, ain't that a beaut! You didn't tell me you two were getting hitched."

"We're not," Kathryn said quickly. She glanced at Earl. He frowned at the ring. Before she could explain, he brushed past her and disappeared into the crowd.

Hank stared after him. "Did I say the wrong thing?"

"Looks that way. You see, Earl didn't give me this ring. Emily did. It belonged to someone a long time ago."

"So why's he mad?"

"I don't know, but I'm going to find out."

Kathryn made a move to leave, but Hank caught her by the elbow. "Speaking of Em," he said, lowering his voice, "you heard any more from the Spitzers or their lawyer?"

His tone was casual but he seemed intent on her reply. "Not since they came to the house after Gordon was killed. How about you?"

"No, and I think that's a good sign."

"Why?"

"Could mean they've realized they don't have a case against her. Gordon had no business going over there and scaring the daylights outta her. He brought it on himself. That's what I believe and that's what most folks are gonna believe no matter what the Spitzers and their hotshot lawyer say."

He looked Kathryn in the eye, as if he expected her to agree. But she balked at giving the nod to this overly pat version of Gordon's killing. "Do you think Diana Farley brought it on herself, too?" Whoa! Now where had *that* come from?

"What's Diana got to do with it?" He lowered his voice even more.

"She confronted Brian Russo like Gordon confronted Emily, and both of them were killed. Of course, neither Gordon nor Diana knew the people they were going after would be armed. If Brian was armed."

"Who said he wasn't?"

"Joey Babcock."

"Well, Joey . . ." Hank shook his head dismissively. "This isn't the time to talk about that. Now if you'll 'scuse me, I see someone I need to have a word with." He walked over to a man Kathryn didn't recognize.

Talking about the night of the killings clearly made Hank uncomfortable. Because he was related to two of the suspects? She doubted she'd get an answer to that question tonight. What she could do, though, was locate Earl and find out why the ring bothered him. She scanned the crowd. Not seeing him in the hall, she poked her head into the kitchen. Millie stood at a table with her back to Kathryn, slicing a loaf of bread into perfectly even pieces with a large knife. She marveled at Millie's speed and dexterity. "Have you seen Earl?" she asked.

Millie turned, knife in hand. "He passed through here on his way outside a few minutes ago. Looked grim. Is something the matter?"

Kathryn explained about the ring.

"He probably thought some other guy gave it to you. That's so Earl to shoot first and ask questions later."

An alarm went off inside Kathryn. "Really?"

"Just a manner of speaking. But he does have a way of jumping to the wrong conclusion. Good luck getting it sorted out." Millie went back to her slicing.

Kathryn walked out the back door. A small knot of men were gathered around kegs behind the Grange. She spotted Lucas Rogers, but no Earl. She started walking around the building. A shadowy figure stood relieving himself in the bushes. "Earl?" she called. He zipped up and stepped into the light. "It's me, Wayne."

"Oh, for a moment there, I thought you were Earl."

"People often mistake us. It's only when they get close, they see the difference." He smiled shyly, a man most at home, she suspected, stretched out beneath the body of a car or truck. In social situations, he seemed content to remain in the shadow of his wife Suzy and his older brother.

"Thanks again for fixing my car a couple of weeks ago."

"Glad to oblige."

She continued around to the front of the building. People were still arriving but she saw no sign of Earl, so maybe he'd gone back inside. Before going in herself, she decided to complete the circuit.

On the far side, two men stood at a distance from the hall, their backs to her, facing a clump of trees. At first, they kept their voices low, but then she heard Roy exclaim, "Snap out of it, Son! This one's a keeper. Not like the other one."

"I thought you liked Diana," Earl said.

"Did in the beginning. Thought she was one helluva foxy lady. But when I saw how she drove you crazy, swinging back and forth between you and her husband, I changed my mind. She was a vixen, that one."

Vixen. So that had been Roy's nickname for Diana.

"I'm glad you've got a nice little doe this time. So don't you be doubting her. Anyone can see she's wild about you. But if you think it would help, I could . . ."

She didn't catch what followed. The next thing she knew, Roy took Earl by the arm and guided him toward the hall. Not wanting to be caught eavesdropping, she turned and slipped quickly through the front entrance.

Inside, she stood at the edge of the crowd. Earl and Roy spotted her and moved in her direction. The DJ put a CD on and people began to dance. Millie approached Earl and said something in his ear. He glanced at Kathryn, then back at Millie. After a moment's hesitation, he took Millie in his arms and they started dancing.

It was a fast dance with the twirls Kathryn had never mastered. Millie, however, was expert at them. Her cheeks turned pink and her face broke into a smile as Earl spun her away from him, then reeled her back toward him—so close their bodies blended. In, out, in, out. Around and around they went, making ever wider circles and claiming more and more of the floor until the other dancers retreated to the sidelines. Their dancing was both flamboyant and perfectly controlled. Kathryn was sure they'd won their share of contests in high school and afterward. The chemistry that had brought them together still clearly existed.

In, out, in, out. They were so well attuned to each other that when Earl removed his jacket, the gesture was choreographed into the dance. Millie helped him slip his arms from the sleeves when she was near, then cast the jacket aside on her next spin-out. Earl, meanwhile, used his free hand to undo the top buttons of his shirt. His face and neck glistened with sweat and his eyes shone.

Kathryn felt a stab of envy; she'd love to be able to dance with him the way Millie did.

"Why don't you cut in on her?" Roy stood by her side.

"I can't."

"You love my boy, don't you?"

"Yes, but—"

"The 'but' have to do with this?" Roy took her hand and examined the ring.

"What do you mean?"

"He thinks the guy you were with before him gave you the ring."

"That's crazy. Why would I wear another man's ring when I'm with him?"

"Told 'im it didn't make sense. Pretty ring, though. Where'd you get it?"

"Emily. It was Marguerite's engagement ring. Emily insisted I take it."

"You tell Earl that?"

"I was going to, but he stalked off before I could."

Roy shook his head. "That's my boy. Let's get this straightened out."

On previous occasions, Kathryn had noticed that while Roy enjoyed an easy camaraderie with men, around women he behaved like a hyperactive herd dog, nudging and nuzzling, poking and prodding, patting and even pinching the fanny of any female within range. Now he used his poking, prodding moves to steer her over to Earl and Millie.

The dance ended with a burst of applause, as Earl brought Millie twirling back to him. He dropped to the ground, and she did a graceful back bend over his knee.

"That was quite a show," Roy remarked when the dancers resumed upright positions. "But now it's Kathryn's turn. You seen the ring Em gave her?" he asked Millie.

"Um, yes, it's lovely," Millie replied, her face still aglow. To Kathryn, she said, "I didn't mean to steal your man, but when the music started, I couldn't resist."

Roy did a herding maneuver that brought Earl and Kathryn together, then cutting Millie from the pack, he led her away. For a long moment neither Kathryn nor Earl spoke. He stared doggedly at the ground. She glanced around the room. "Did Em really give you that ring?" he asked finally.

"Yes. You don't believe me, ask her."

"No, no, I believe you. But where'd she get it? And why'd she give it to you?'

Kathryn explained as best as she could.

"If that's so, why'd you hide your hand when I came to house? And later in the truck, you weren't paying attention to a word I said, just kept fussing with that ring and staring into space."

"I'm sorry, I should have told you sooner. But the business with Emily was so strange. It didn't occur to me you'd think the ring came from Alan."

"Who else could've given it to you? Not me for sure. I couldn't afford to buy you something that special. Made me crazy knowing he could and I couldn't."

"But now you know the truth." She stroked the snake tattoo on his arm, where he liked to be touched, and felt him relax. He took her hand and kissed it.

"Hey, lovebirds," Roy called. "Finish kissing n' making up 'cuz Marsha and Fred are about to cut their anniversary cake."

Even as Roy spoke, people moved to one side of the room, where a table with the anniversary cake stood. The cake was a three-tiered extravaganza, frosted white with a fat pastry-tube-fed swirl of aquamarine around the circumference of each layer. Pink rosettes and faux pearls decorated the swirls. On the top layer, spokes of rainbow-colored sprinkles, M & M's, and Reese's Pieces led inward to the center, where the plastic figures of a bride and groom stood under a canopy.

The figures struck Kathryn as hokey, but also touching in the hopefulness they projected. They perched atop the snowy eminence like climbers on a mountain summit, winded but exuberant, reveling in the vista their endurance had won them. As well they should: it was no mean feat to stay married forty years like Marsha and Fred Lapsley. Her own parents' marriage had only lasted a few years. She wondered how many other married couples in the room would reach the forty-year mark. Roy and June were probably almost there. Wayne and Suzy had a solid marriage, so they seemed likely candidates.

Earl handed her a glass of champagne and she raised it mechanically. What about those who'd tried and failed at marriage? Earl and Millie, for example. And Cheryl, still in her teens and already a widow. Then there were those who'd never married. Hank was a bachelor, and she remained single. Should she take Marsha and Fred's success as a hopeful sign? Her gaze settled on the plastic bride and groom figures. Had the person who'd designed the cake put them there to affirm her own belief in the possibility of happiness within marriage? Or had she simply thought they looked cute?

The guests cheered and applauded when Marsha and Fred, careful not to disturb the figures perched on top, cut the cake and shared a piece. Then slivers of the aquamarine-and-white confection were distributed among the crowd. When a rosette-and-faux-pearl-studded slice reached Kathryn and Earl, he scooped it from the plate and held it for her to take a bite. A light flashed as Suzy Barker caught the moment on her digital camera. "There's a sight for sore eyes!" Roy bellowed. "Gotta get a copy of that one."

Kathryn peered at the image on the screen. Her head was bent and her jaw hung open like a trap about to shut on the morsel of cake Earl held. She looked foolish but also happy. The expression on her face reminded her of Millie's in the wedding candid. She glanced around, wondering if Millie had seen this. But Millie had vanished. Instead, her eyes met Pete's. He held her gaze a moment, his expression unreadable. Then, turning on his heel, he left the hall.

Chapter 54

Kathryn had checked in with Gertrude Braithwaite, her boss at the Lyceum, on a weekly basis since the beginning of her stay in the Berkshires, and each time Mrs. B. had assured her everything was under control. Today, though, Mrs. B's voice had a note of urgency. "Do you remember Mrs. Winship?"

"The woman with the collection of early nineteenth-century lithographs she was trying to decide whether to donate to us or to Harvard?"

"Correct. Mrs. Winship is still trying to make up her mind, but she seems to be leaning toward us now. She's requested another meeting. I would like you to be there, Kathryn. You know our collection better than anyone, and you can explain to her how her lithographs would complement those we already have. You inspire confidence, Kathryn, and you know how to make the right impression, whereas your assistant . . ." Mrs. B's voice dropped to a conspiratorial whisper. "Let's just say she lacks both your expertise and social skills. The acquisition of the Winship collection would be a real coup for us. We must be careful not to do anything that might jeopardize the proceedings. Mrs. Winship needs to feel complete confidence in the Lyceum as the best repository for her precious lithographs."

"Of course. When is the meeting?"

"Tomorrow, actually. I know it's short notice, but Mrs. Winship just called today. You know how she is: Things need to happen when she wants them to, or she gets upset. And in this instance, I don't want to upset her. Please tell me you can make it."

Kathryn hesitated. "All right," she said finally.

Now all she had to do was to let Earl know she was going to Boston. That shouldn't be difficult, but she knew in her heart it would be, because to Earl, Boston meant Alan. Alan who could afford to give things he could not—like the ruby and diamond ring that had come from Emily.

*****

"My boss at the Lyceum called today," Kathryn told Earl that evening after he'd had a few beers and begun to unwind.

He stiffened. "And?"

"She wants me to come to a meeting in Boston, so I can convince an old lady to give her collection of lithographs to the Lyceum instead of Harvard."

"When's the meeting?"

"Tomorrow afternoon."

"You're kidding."

"I wish I were. But that's when the prospective donor wants it, and her collection's important enough to us that we let her call the shots.

"Then I guess you've got to go."

She could tell he wasn't pleased, even though he said nothing more about it the rest of the evening. But waking toward morning, she found him propped on an elbow staring at her with a gloomy expression. She sensed he'd been watching her for some time, and it made her uncomfortable. "Something wrong?"

With his free hand, he stroked her cheek then feathered his fingers down the side of her face and onto her breastbone. He tugged gently on the chain of the St. Christopher medal he'd slipped around her neck the first night they'd made love.

"When you're in Boston, you won't forget you've got a man back here?"

"Of course not. How can you even think that?"

"Guess I just needed to be reassured." He paused, fingers continuing to pull on the chain. "Because I'd hate it if you did, Star," he said softly.

Chapter 55

"Well done, Kathryn!" Mrs. Braithwaite said, as they left the restaurant where they'd taken Mrs. Winship for a lunch that had lasted into the late afternoon. "I knew that together we could pull this off."

"The martinis helped," Kathryn said.

"Perhaps. I wanted to be sure Mrs. Winship felt completely at ease."

Two sheets to the wind was more like it. But she couldn't deny she'd made a convincing case for Mrs. Winship's donating her collection to the Lyceum. So convincing that Mrs. Winship had promised to have her attorney draw up the appropriate papers the next day.

Mrs. Braithwaite spotted a cab and hailed it. "Good-bye now. Have a safe trip back." Kathryn hurried to the parking garage to get her car, hoping to avoid the worst of rush hour traffic.

She had no such luck. Rush hour traffic, combined with an accident on the Massachusetts Turnpike, added an extra hour to the trip from Boston to the Berkshires. It was eight-thirty by the time she reached Stockbridge, a half hour away from her final destination. Main Street was decked out with boughs of holly, pine wreaths and Christmas lights in readiness for another holiday a la Norman Rockwell. The picture-postcard perfection of the scene made her smile. This was the image of the Berkshires that drew tourists by the thousands. Even on a weeknight in December, visitors strolled along the sidewalks or sat, bundled in fur and down, on the porch of the Red Lion Inn, sipping hot chocolate and hot buttered rum.

But it was the other Berkshires she was traveling to—the Berkshires of lonely towns perched high on hills, of narrow back roads whose winding darkness come nightfall never ceased to amaze an urban dweller like her. She'd been away less than a day, but already she'd half forgotten what it was like to turn off the main thoroughfare and plunge into a world of blackness, broken only by the lights of an occasional house, or if the sky was clear like this evening, a crescent moon and a pinprick pattern of stars. Past experience had taught her to drive these roads with care, because you never knew when a deer might dart out, or when rounding a bend, you might find yourself on a collision course with a wrong-sided vehicle.

Even if she made it back safely, what kind of reception would she get? Earl hadn't wanted her to make this trip, and now she was late.

When she arrived at the Farley house, she was surprised to see that no welcoming lights illuminated the path to the front door, nor shone from within. Dark and deserted, the house might have been returned to its ghosts: to Diana and now Gordon. She imagined his ghost hovering blimp-like and baleful within the shadowy interior. Yet perhaps his ghost had already left this "awful place with awful people," as his mother called it. Perhaps it had sought the more hospitable clime of Provence, because in death as in life, Gordon liked his comforts.

But where was Earl? Had he grown tired of waiting and gone back to the trailer? She hurried inside, turned on the lights, and fed Amore. She was just about to telephone Earl when she heard the sound of his truck in the driveway. Thank heaven! She ran out to meet him, straight into his outstretched arms. "Sorry I'm so late," she said breathlessly. "Did you give up on me and go home?"

"Nope. I just arrived. Let's go in and I'll explain."

"I don't know about you, but I'm starving," Kathryn said, heading for the kitchen. "How about I make us an omelet or heat up some soup?"

"Thanks, but I've already eaten."

"Oh?"

"Mill called me at work and asked if I could stop by afterward. Pete's been having some problems at school and she wanted to talk about it. When we were finished, she invited me to stay for dinner.

254

She'd gone to a lot of trouble making a pot roast for her and Pete only to have him call at the last minute and say he was eating at a friend's. I called the house to see if you were back. When you didn't answer, I figured you were still on the road and would pick up a bite on the way. I accepted."

"Why didn't you call me on my cell?"

"I don't have that number."

Of course not. She was so used to being off the grid here that it had never occurred to her to give it to him. Still, she felt a prick of annoyance that he'd had dinner with Millie instead of waiting for her. "Okay, I'll just fix something for myself." Opening the refrigerator, she pulled out bread and sandwich makings. Moments later, they sat down opposite each other, Kathryn wolfing down a turkey sandwich with lettuce, tomato, and mayonnaise, while Earl popped the tops of two beer cans and poured the foamy brew into glasses. He took a long drink and studied her. "So what made you so late? Was it just rush hour traffic or . . .?"

"There was an accident on the Pike."

"Must've been a bad one to hold you up for this amount of time."

"It was. I left messages on the landline here and at your trailer that I'd be late. I didn't think to try the white house."

"Mmm . . . what kind of an accident was it?"

She started to tell him about the tractor-trailer that had turned over, but stopped when she realized he was no longer looking at her, but staring moodily into space. "Earl?"

"What?"

"Are you listening to me?"

"Course I am. You were telling me about the accident."

"What did I say about it?"

"Something about a three-car pile-up?"

"No."

He flashed her a rueful smile. "Guess you better repeat what you said."

She did and this time he not only paid attention, but asked detailed questions about the accident. He went over her account so many times it almost seemed like he didn't believe her and was trying to trip her up. Which could mean he suspected she'd been with Alan instead of stuck in traffic.

Chapter 56

After the trip to Boston, Kathryn had hoped for a quiet day, but her hopes evaporated when Cheryl called to say she needed help with Emily. The old woman had her searching all over for some old letters Cheryl couldn't locate for the life of her. Kathryn arrived to find Emily's house cluttered with dusty boxes, suitcases, and trunks. Cheryl was going through a collection of yellowed papers at the kitchen table, while Emily hovered. "Have you found them? Have you found them?" Emily repeated herself in a monotone like a stubborn parrot.

Kathryn took Cheryl's place at the table, and for the next two hours went through everything again. She came up empty-handed. "Could you have put them in a safe deposit box?" she asked Emily.

"Don't have one."

"Did you live anywhere else before here?"

"We lived at the Whittemore estate while Walter was the caretaker," Emily said. "But that was some time ago, and since then the house has changed hands a couple of times."

"Do you know who the current owner is?"

"Some family from Florida, or maybe it's Arizona? They're only here in the summer."

"Is anyone looking after the place while they're away?"

"Could be. There's a fellow named Gene Herrick who does house watching. But if I left the letters there, I'm sure they're long gone . . . Oh dear, Aurelia's never going to give me any peace," Emily wailed.

Kathryn exchanged glances with Cheryl. "Still, it's worth checking," she said. She called Herrick, got an answering machine and left a message. "That's the best I can do for now. Need some help putting all this stuff away?" she asked Cheryl.

"Thanks, but I can manage. You had a long day yesterday."

Kathryn was about to ask how Cheryl knew when she realized Cheryl probably heard it on the village grapevine, and stopped. Still, there was something else she'd meant to ask Cheryl. It wasn't a question she wanted to raise in front of Emily, however. "Can you stop by the house when you're finished here?" she asked Cheryl.

"Sure, but . . .?" Cheryl looked at her inquiringly. A sidelong glance at Emily and a quick headshake on Kathryn's part were enough to discourage the girl from pursuing the matter.

*****

It was starting to get dark when Kathryn returned from her errands in Great Barrington, which had included a massage. She'd no sooner pulled into the driveway than she spotted Cheryl's car. Damn. Relaxed by the massage, she'd completely forgotten about asking Cheryl to stop by. She hoped she hadn't kept the young woman waiting too long.

Cheryl was curled up on the couch in the shadowy living room, apparently asleep.

"Diana?" she said in a groggy voice, as Kathryn walked over to her.

The dead woman's name jarred Kathryn. "No, it's me, Kathryn," she said, trying to keep her voice steady.

"Sorry. I must've dozed off." Cheryl sat up and brushed cobweb fine hair out of her face "Must've been dreaming, too."

"About Diana? Is that why you mistook me for her?"

"No, but I was thinking about her before I dozed off."

"What were you thinking?"

Cheryl shrugged. "Stuff."

Kathryn came to the point. "You were here the night she died."

Cheryl stiffened and a wary look came into her eyes. "How d'you know?"

"Brandy said you answered the phone when she called the house."

"Yeah, well, Diana and I were friends so we visited back and forth."

"Were you surprised to find her car parked outside, but no sign of her?"

"No, I knew she sometimes went for walks at night."

"Where did you think she'd gone?"

"I dunno. Down the road. Into the woods."

"Did she often go into the woods after dark?"

"Occasionally."

"To meet Earl?"

"They might've met there a few times." Cheryl's eyes skittered away. When her gaze returned to Kathryn, her face had a set, determined cast. "But *not* that night. Earl was at the Stag that night. Diana went into the woods to find Brian Russo after his mom called."

Kathryn frowned. "But Brandy didn't call until after Diana left."

Cheryl appeared flustered. "That's right. I got confused. Diana must have found out he was there some other way."

Obviously, but how? Kathryn thought back to what she'd been told about that night, first by Millie, then Brandy. Brandy hadn't shed any light on this, but Millie had. "Did you hear music?" she asked.

"Music?" Cheryl gave her a blank look.

"According to Millie, Brian blasted the woods with rock music that night."

"Oh, *that* music."

"You heard it?"

"I . . . um . . . think so. If Millie said there was music, I must of; heard it loud and clear the first time." Cheryl shifted position on the couch, as if the place where she'd been sitting had suddenly become uncomfortable.

Her uncertainty gave Kathryn pause. Of course, there were reasons having to do with timing why she might not have heard the music. Still, the fact that Cheryl wasn't sure bothered her. So did something else about Cheryl's account. "Getting back to Earl, how did you know he was at the Stag that night?"

"He and the other men said so."

"Afterwards. But at the time how did you know he was at the

Stag?"

"I figured he'd go there after—" Cheryl broke off, worrying a strand of hair.

"After what?" Kathryn asked quietly.

Cheryl stood. "I have to go. Suzy's watching Derek, but I need to get home and give him dinner."

Kathryn rose, too. "Please. You figured Earl would go to the Stag because?"

The hair twisting became more pronounced. "All right," Cheryl said finally, "I'll tell you: him and Diana had a bit of a spat the night before."

Kathryn's spine prickled. No wonder Cheryl had been reluctant to tell her. "How do you know?"

"Millie heard some of it."

"What was this spat about?"

"I dunno, some silly thing."

Although Cheryl tried to downplay the seriousness of it, Kathryn sensed that more than a minor squabble had been involved. Why else would Earl have chosen to spend the night at the Stag rather than with his lover?

Cheryl looked her squarely in the eye. "Just because they had a spat doesn't mean—"

"Of course not." She wanted desperately to believe this, and even hoped Cheryl could tell her something that would point the finger elsewhere. "Anything else happen while you were at the house?"

"Gordon called."

"What did he want?"

"He said he was spending the night in the city on account of his business taking longer than expected. Told me to write down the message in case I left before Diana came back."

"Did you?"

"No. I fell asleep. The next thing I knew Earl and Hank were calling my name and shaking me."

"You must have been really zonked."

Cheryl's eyes shied away from Kathryn's. "I took some pills I found in the medicine cabinet. I didn't realize how strong they were."

Or you did realize and decided it would be a painless way out of an abusive marriage.

As if she guessed Kathryn's thoughts, Cheryl said, "Things were bad between me n' Garth. We had a fight. He was mad because somebody'd swiped his gun. I told 'im he should've kept his gun locked up like his dad and his brothers were always telling 'im. Said to keep my nose out of it and yelled at me for not getting home sooner to fire up the stove and fix dinner. Threw things and hit me. Then he stormed out. I knew he'd go to the Stag and come home drunk and meaner than ever. I'd had enough. I came here."

"The Stag seems to be a favorite cooling-off place for guys after they've—"

"No!" Cheryl turned on her with sudden fury. "It wasn't like that with Earl. Sure, he and Diana had their differences, but he never laid a hand on her like Garth did me. And they always made up afterward. They would've done so if she hadn't been killed. He's a good man, Kathryn. And if anyone tells you otherwise, don't believe 'em."

She spoke with such fervor that Kathryn didn't have the heart to disagree. Earl might not be the paragon Cheryl thought, but compared to Garth, he probably looked pretty good. "I won't."

Cheryl smiled for the first time since Kathryn's arrival. Changing the subject, she asked, "Have you heard back from Gene Herrick yet?"

Kathryn shook her head.

"Well, I hope you do. Also hope he can find those letters at the old Whittemore house. Because Em's not going to give us any peace until she gets them."

"You can say that again." Kathryn gave Cheryl a wry smile.

*****

That evening Gene Herrick returned her call. He said he checked the Whittemore house once a week, and since he'd just come from there, he wasn't eager to go back right away. But after Kathryn explained about Emily's giving her and Cheryl a hard time until certain letters she might have left there were found, he promised to have a look the next morning.

Chapter 57

True to his word, Herrick searched the former caretaker's house, now used as a guest house. He found a metal box containing some old letters stashed in the back of a closet, and delivered it to Kathryn a little before noon the following day.

When Kathryn arrived at Emily's, the old woman was sitting in the kitchen eating her lunch while Cheryl looked on. Kathryn deposited the metal box on the table. "Here are the letters you wanted, I think."

Emily gasped and pushed her chair back with a horrified expression. She acted as if Kathryn had placed a ticking bomb in front of her. "Get that away from me!" she cried. "I never wanted those letters. Aurelia was the one who said I had to give 'em to you. And now that you've got 'em, take 'em and go."

"Don't you at least want to have a look?" Kathryn asked.

"No!" Emily pounded a gnarled fist on the table for emphasis. "I already know what's in 'em."

Kathryn exchanged puzzled glances with Cheryl, then picked up the box. "All right, have it your way."

Back at the Farley house, Kathryn settled on the living room couch and opened the box. Inside was a stack of blue envelopes tied with a faded yellow ribbon. The envelope on top was addressed to Mrs. Aurelia Judd on Rattlesnake Hill Road in New Nottingham. The return address identified the sender as Kathryn's ancestor, Jared Cutter, writing from a boarding house in Los Angeles. So he hadn't broken off with everyone from his past life, after all. He'd kept in touch with Aurelia, his dead wife's close friend. Kathryn's fingers quivered with excitement as she opened the first letter, dated October 24, 1855.

Dear Aurelia,

I have been in the City of Angels long enough to make me wonder if I made a serious error in leaving New Nottingham and coming here. Had I remained there, I could at least have visited poor Marguerite's grave and looked upon dear Leonora's face. I continue to think of her as my daughter, although you assure me that in all likelihood that awful Barker man is her father. Yet in those first weeks after Marguerite was so cruelly murdered by him, I could not bear to stay in a place where at every turn I would be reminded of all I had lost with Marguerite's death.

Reading these lines, Kathryn imagined the silver-haired gentleman she knew from old photographs speaking to her, a deep sadness in his voice. He didn't sound like the merciless killer Emily described. Emily, who based her account on what Aurelia told her, which had come from Clyde. Here, at last, was Jared Cutter's side of story. As she re-read the last sentence, an alternate scenario took shape in her mind. Perhaps Marguerite had second thoughts about running away with Clyde and tried to go back. They quarreled, he shot her, then turned the gun on himself, blinding rather than killing himself.

She read on:

I am strongly tempted to return at once, but better judgment tells me to at least get a foothold here. When I am settled and in such a position to provide a suitable home for Leonora, I will journey east to claim her. In the meantime, I am comforted by the knowledge that the dear little girl is safe in your care. I enclose a bank draft for the amount of fifteen dollars to help you provide for said care.

The letters that followed spanned a period of five years. Kathryn was struck by Cutter's concern for the child who might not be his daughter, as well as his oft expressed desire to return for her. She was also struck by Aurelia's apparent efforts to persuade him to postpone this.

> *In your last letter, you propose that I wait until she is older before coming to fetch her—that were I to come now, it would be like pushing a baby bird from the nest before it is ready to fly, that if I, a total stranger to her, removed her from the only home and family she has ever known, it would cause her great distress. Now, I do not claim to know children as well as you, but what I have observed suggests they are more adaptable than some believe. However, I am willing to wait yet awhile longer if you deem it in her best interests.*

Finally, however, he decided he could wait no longer.

> *Perhaps you will say I am selfish, but I have come to the conclusion I have missed too much of my darling's growing up, and can never be happy until she is by my side. I have therefore booked passage on the Arabella, which is due to arrive in Boston on the 20th of next month. To help prepare her for my arrival, I am sending by a private carrier, which is fully insured, the ring I gave Marguerite when we became engaged. I want her to have something of value from her father.*

Kathryn stared at the ring on her finger. That strange afternoon when Emily had given it to her, the old woman had never explained how she'd gotten it. Now Kathryn knew her ancestor had sent the ring to Aurelia to give to Leonora. Leonora, in turn, must have passed it down to her daughter, Emily's mother, who gave it to Emily. In that case, Leonora must have remained in New Nottingham. Did that mean Jared Cutter hadn't come for her after all? Or perhaps he'd come and Leonora had refused to leave with him. She opened the final letter with anticipation, but also a certain dread.

Dear Aurelia,

Your letter with the news of Leonora's death has brought me such deep sorrow I hardly know what to say. To think she should be taken away by a cursed fever, just as I was about to come for her! I blame myself for not coming sooner, for ever leaving in the first place . . .

Stunned, Kathryn dropped the letter. Leonora hadn't died at a young age, but had lived to marry and have a daughter of her own. Aurelia had lied to Cutter to prevent him from coming. He'd spent the rest of his life, believing the daughter he hoped was his was dead. Leonora, meanwhile, had grown up thinking she was a Judd, when, in fact, she was the daughter of Marguerite and either Jared Cutter or Clyde Barker. Aurelia hadn't given Leonora the ring, because then she would have had to explain about the love triangle. She'd held onto it until, on the verge of death herself, she finally told Emily the truth—or rather Clyde's version of it. For some reason—a need to make long-overdue amends to Cutter?—she'd also given Emily the ring and Cutter's letters. Aurelia hadn't wanted to die with a guilty conscience. Emily probably didn't either.

Damn Aurelia! Kathryn wished the woman were still alive so she could tell her off to her face. She'd have to settle for Emily. Emily who had evidence that Cutter was more victim than villain, but had, nevertheless, perpetuated the lies about him.

She grabbed the box of letters and hurried toward the door. She'd confront Emily with the awful wrong that had been done to her ancestor.

Chapter 58

Emily sat queen-like on the wing chair in the parlor. When she saw the box, she scowled. "I told you I didn't want anything to do with that."

Kathryn's heart hammered, but she managed to keep her voice calm. "So you did, but now that I've read the letters, we need to talk."

"There's nothing to talk about."

"Yes, there is. If you really do know what's in these letters, why did you say you hoped my ancestor was rotting in hell?" She hadn't meant to come on quite so strong, but her anger got the better of her.

"I never said that," Emily shot back.

"To Diana you did. It's on a tape of your recollections."

"So?"

"He didn't deserve that from you."

Emily wrinkled her nose and sniffed, as if a bad odor had entered the room. "Why not? Killed his wife and blinded her lover, didn't he?"

"In the very first letter, he claims Clyde killed Marguerite."

"'Course he'd deny he was the killer. But him hightailing it to California right afterward shows he was guilty."

"He was planning to come back for Leonora."

"He may have said that, but he had no intention of returning," Emily insisted.

"He booked passage on a ship bound for Boston."

"He never came."

"No, because Aurelia lied and wrote him Leonora had died of a fever."

266

"What if she did? Leonora wasn't his daughter. She was Clyde's daughter."

"How do you know? The only way to determine parentage with certainty is by DNA testing, and they didn't do that then."

Emily shrank into her chair. "Go away!"

"Not until you've heard me out."

"I won't listen." Emily put her hands over her ears.

Raising her voice, so Emily couldn't help but hear, Kathryn said, "Aurelia told you Clyde's version of what happened that night, but she knew from Cutter's letters there was another side to the story. In fairness to him, she gave you the letters, along with the ring, leaving you to decide who to believe."

"There was never any question in my mind that Clyde told the truth."

"How can you be sure?"

"I just can."

"What if you're wrong about Jared Cutter's being the killer, just as you may have been wrong about Gordon?" She hadn't intended to bring up Gordon, but Emily's stubborn refusal to budge, combined with her own growing doubts that Gordon had murdered Diana, made her push back harder.

"What's Gordon got to do with it?" Emily glared at her, but Kathryn caught a flicker of fear in her eyes. Almost as if the old woman had begun to wonder if she'd made a mistake shooting him.

"What I said—you could've been wrong about both of them."

Emily's eyes blazed and her face and the bare patches on her scalp turned red with rage. "I wasn't wrong. It was the husband both times."

"You have no proof. The murderer could have just as well have been the lover. Both times."

"The lover both times?" Emily repeated in a strangled voice. "Do you realize what you've just said?"

Horrified, Kathryn clamped a hand over her mouth. "I didn't mean—"

"Oh yes, you did. And you—you—" Emily pushed herself up from the chair. Grabbing the cane hooked to the arm, she held it aloft as she advanced on Kathryn. After a few steps, she stopped and clawed

267

at her chest. The cane crashed to the floor. A look of terror came over Emily's face. The next instant she toppled to the floor like a scarecrow knocked from its perch by a strong wind.

Kathryn rushed to Emily's side. *Oh, dear God, what had she done!*

Chapter 59

Kathryn shut the door of the Farley house and went into the living room. She sank onto the couch, weighted down with guilt for having caused Emily's stroke. Two days had passed since then. She'd just come from another visit to the hospital, where Emily lay in a coma, surrounded by a changing guard of family and friends.

If only she hadn't rushed over to Emily's when she was fired up with anger. She should have waited until she was in a calmer mood, and had a chance to think things over. Then, she might have realized she'd have to tread very carefully when she confronted Emily, or better yet, not confront her at all.

Emily had spent part of her life believing she was a Judd. To learn that her grandmother, Leonora, was the illegitimate child of Clyde Barker and Marguerite Cutter must have been a blow. A blow softened by Aurelia's telling her that her great-grandfather wasn't a murderer, but the victim of his lover's husband's jealous rage. Emily had made her peace with this. Now in her nineties, she didn't need to be told that something she'd accepted as truth for a long time might be otherwise.

Kathryn also wished she hadn't challenged Emily's conviction that the husband had been the killer both times. That had really set the old woman off. Still, she couldn't help wondering if she were right. She'd tried hard to deny her suspicions about Earl, but they had finally pushed to the fore.

I warned you about him, she imagined her grandmother saying. *But did you listen? No! You went right ahead and got involved with*

*a man who most likely murdered his previous lover. And who will
kill you, too, if you don't watch out!*

Kathryn shivered and hugged herself. Had she made a terrible
mistake by falling for Earl? Was she really in danger from him? From
where she sat, she could see the break in the woods that marked the
beginning of Gordon's road. Diana had traveled that road the night
of the killings, and now Kathryn tried to picture her journey. She
saw Diana, infuriated by the blare of rock music, storming into the
woods to confront Brian a second time, and getting shot. That was
one version. But Cheryl wasn't certain she'd heard any music that
night, and according to Joey Babcock, Brian wasn't armed.

Someone else could have taken Garth's gun to the mill ruins, and
that person could have been Earl. He went there to patch things up
with Diana after their "spat." But they had another fight and he shot
her. Panicking, he dropped the gun and fled to the Stag to establish
an alibi. The men at the bar didn't realize he wasn't there the whole
time, because of the strong resemblance between him and his brother
Wayne. And they were hammered, besides. Then, when Brandy called
Hank about her missing son, Earl joined in the search and pretended
to be shocked by what they found.

It all made sense except for one thing: Brian. While she could
almost imagine Earl shooting Diana in a jealous rage—Millie had
cautioned her about his jealousy, and since they'd become lovers,
she'd caught glimpses of it—she couldn't imagine him killing Brian.
Earl just didn't strike her as a person who'd shoot an innocent boy,
even though the boy had witnessed him committing a crime. She ran
through the scenario with Earl as Diana's killer several times, but
each time, she balked when it came to his shooting Brian.

Garth, however, was mean enough to shoot both of them. Or
maybe Emily was right, and Gordon had shot Diana and Brian. Yet
much as she'd disliked Gordon, she had trouble picturing that big,
lazy man exerting himself to such an extent. True, he'd gone after
Emily. But that had been on the spur of the moment, whereas killing
his wife would have required planning. Gordon would have had to
go to Garth's, steal the gun, and find his way into the woods. And
without Diana's second will, there was no evidence she was planning

to leave him.

Then again, Joey Babcock could have been lying about Brian not being armed, and Cheryl could have arrived on the scene too late to hear the music. She'd come full circle.

Caught up in these different scenarios, Kathryn lost track of time. When she finally forced herself to take a break from the constant replay, she knew from the difference in the light that morning had given way to afternoon. Yet she remained sitting there, captive audience to another round of replays.

"Star?"

Her heart stopped. *Speak of the devil.* But was he really a devil? Or was she the evil one to suspect him? She felt a stab of guilt as sharp as if he'd caught her with another man. And said the first thing that came into her head: "How'd you get here?"

"In my truck, same as always." He looked at her wonderingly, as well he might after such a stupid question. "You must have been pretty distracted not to have heard me. Don't blame you. Em collapsing like that's been a big shock to all of us."

"Yes," Kathryn said, glad of the excuse. "Have you seen her since I was there this morning? Is there any change?"

"I just got back from the hospital, and there's no change."

"Too bad. At least her family's there in case she regains consciousness."

He nodded, studied her a moment, then said, "Speaking of family, Dad's got something he wants to show us this afternoon."

"*Now?*" She stared at him with surprise.

"Yup. He was going to put it off when he found out about Em's stroke, but he's changed his mind."

"What's he want us to see?"

He cocked his head, a glint of mischief in his blue eyes. "It's a surprise."

In spite of herself, she fell into the game. "Oh, c'mon. Give me a hint."

"It's something I think you're really gonna like." He grinned broadly, then with sudden boyish uncertainty, added, "At least I hope you will."

Against her better judgment, she followed him out the door like a child entranced by the Pied Piper.

Chapter 60

"Where are we going?" Kathryn asked, as Roy herded them across the road, away from the family compound.

"Didn't Earl tell you it's supposed to be a surprise?" Roy looked at her with the same mischievous glint that had been in Earl's eyes. They both had the joker gene, and where once Earl's jokiness had annoyed her, now she found it endearing.

"Can't you at least give me a hint?"

"Nope. Afraid I'd give it away if I did." Roy winked at her. Kathryn smiled back. As they passed the white house, Kathryn saw Millie's face at the window. She glanced away and when she looked back, Millie was gone.

"Is it here?" Kathryn asked when Earl's trailer came into view. With a shake of his head, Roy steered them into the woods. Here, the ground sloped upward almost as steeply as it did at the ledges on the other side of the road, but trees rather than rocky outcrops predominated.

The two men plunged into the forest. *Where* were they taking her? Without realizing it, she began to lag behind. Earl and Roy passed out of sight then a few minutes later, Earl came jogging toward her. "Hey, slowpoke, get moving. Be dark soon."

"Maybe we should wait until tomorrow."

"No. Dad wants to do this now. The going's kind of rough, so I'll give you a hand like I did to the cemetery."

"Is that what's up here—another cemetery?" she asked, as he took her by the arm.

"Nope."

"What then?"

"Be patient." He helped her up the hill to where Roy was waiting for them. They continued to ascend through trees and brush until Roy finally stopped. "Well, Kathryn, what do you think of this spot?"

She hesitated, uncertain how to respond. They were in the midst of dense forest with nothing in sight. "It's . . . nice," she said finally, cautiously.

"Glad you like it, 'cuz I'm giving this piece of land to Earl. It's yours also, for as long as you two stay together. Consider it my Christmas present to you both. Was gonna wait till then to show you. But I got to thinking, what the hell, show 'em now. That way, Earl can start clearing the land before the snow flies."

His Christmas present to them. So that's what this was about. Her mind whirled. When it stopped spinning, she realized they were staring at her like they expected something. Where were her manners? When someone gave you a present, you were supposed to thank them.

"Thank you. Thank you very much," she said, hoping she sounded sincere.

Roy smiled and nodded. "The Farley house is gonna be sold eventually, and I don't think you'll like living with my boy in the trailer for very long."

True. So why did she suddenly feel trapped? As if she were being railroaded into something she wasn't sure she wanted. Not now, when fear and suspicion had invaded the exquisite cocoon of love in which she'd wrapped herself for the past couple of weeks.

"Even if you're only here on weekends," Roy continued, "you don't wanna be tripping over each other, or tromping across the road every time you want a shower. You need a place of your own. I'm giving you the land to build it on. You'll have privacy up here and a fine view once you cut down some of these trees. Have to build a road, too, bring up power lines, drill a well."

"Right." Earl paced the area excitedly. His father joining him, they discussed where the house would go, which way it would face, and other details. Kathryn watched, amazed. Obviously, they saw clearly what she could barely perceive: a house with lighted windows and a curl of smoke rising from the chimney that Roy, a mason by trade, would build, piling stone upon stone with his strong hands. They saw a vista of rounded fields and forested slopes shading into purple mountains under a blue, cloudless sky that Earl would open up with his heavy equipment. They took pleasure in this view and in the sight of the house with its promise of warmth and comfort within.

She wished she could share their vision. But she couldn't. Not while her mind remained stuck in a different part of the woods where two people had died under mysterious circumstances. And if she expressed her doubts, would she become a hateful creature like Diana?

A hateful creature that must be destroyed?

Chapter 61

Kathryn lugged the stack of Sunday newspapers into the house. She'd just come from another guilt-ridden vigil by Emily's hospital bedside, and hoped to unwind with the papers. The pile of cookbooks on the kitchen counter reminded her of something else she needed to do.

In a rash moment, she had offered to bring a homemade apple pie for tonight's dinner with Earl's family. She'd never baked a pie before, so she got a bunch of cookbooks from the library. A glance at the various recipes told her there were different ways of making both the crust and the filling. Unable to make up her mind, she bought the ingredients for the different kinds. All that remained was to pick a recipe and make the pie. She decided to postpone the chore and took the newspapers outside.

The sun had come out and the temperature was edging into the fifties. She settled in a lounge chair and was soon engrossed in the arts section of *The Boston Globe.* It was quiet at first, but after a while she became aware of noise up the hill. The noise of heavy equipment Earl was using to clear the land his father had given him. Given *them.* He'd been at it almost a week now, starting the day after Roy showed them the land. He went to the site after he finished his regular jobs, working like a demon until it was too dark to see. Now that it was the weekend he was putting in entire days there, rising at first light and returning after sundown. She'd tried to get him to stop pushing himself so hard, but he wouldn't listen, just said he wanted to get as much done before the snow came.

Even at a distance, the noise was deafening at times. If it was bad here, it must be even worse further up the hill. She didn't envy his parents and other family members living across the road from it, or Millie just below. Millie must know Earl was clearing the land so he could build a house for Kathryn and him, as he'd done for her. And she suspected Millie might not be pleased. They'd barely spoken since Fred and Marsha's anniversary party. Millie always seemed too busy to talk when Kathryn saw her at the post office. The few times they'd run into each other at the hospital, other people were around and a private conversation wasn't possible.

What had been a rumble ratcheted up to a roar, then died down again, only to be replaced by a sound closer at hand. The ringing phone. She ran inside.

"Kathryn," Alan said, "I just got off the Pike and—"

She was so startled she nearly dropped the handset. "What're you doing here?"

"I've got to talk to you. I know you probably don't want me coming to the house, but is there someplace we could meet?"

"No. It's over between us, Alan. How many times do I have to tell you?"

"I know that, but I still care about you. And right now I'm concerned for your safety. Very concerned. I wouldn't have driven all this way if it weren't important."

"Alan—"

"Please."

She hesitated a long moment before giving in. "All right. I can meet you at the Lion's Den Pub in Stockbridge in a half hour."

"Thank you!"

*****

On this Sunday a few weeks before Christmas, Main Street in Stockbridge was filled with people. They poked into shops and galleries, reemerging to join the flow of pedestrians. Every available parking spot in front of the Red Lion Inn was taken, but Kathryn was able to find a place just around the corner on Elm Street. She was glad of the crowd because she could easily lose herself in it, passing unnoticed by anyone she knew. Not that she expected to run into someone from New Nottingham in this chi-chi town.

She hurried under the red awning and down the stairs into the pub. Alan sat at a round table in a far corner. He rose as she approached, his brown eyes serious behind horned-rimmed glasses. His face wore its customary city pallor, but in weekend clothes—jeans and a down vest over a flannel shirt—he almost blended in with the locals. He looked thinner than when she'd last seen him, and the streak of white running through his dark hair seemed to have grown. Perhaps it was only her imagination.

"Thanks for coming. I've ordered a beer. Would you like anything?" he asked with an air of tentativeness that tugged her back to their first meeting. Then, the bar had been crowded and noisy, while this one was empty except for a much older couple quietly poring over the menu.

"I'll have a beer also."

Alan motioned for her to sit facing him and even pulled out a chair for her. She hesitated, wondering if it would be better to take his place, where she could see whoever came in, but decided in favor of giving the other customers her back.

After the bartender had brought their drinks, Alan cleared his throat and said, "I won't keep you long, and I need to get back to the city myself, so I'll get to the point. How much do you know about Earl Barker?"

"What do you mean?"

"Do you know he had a lover, and that she was killed?"

"Yes."

"What were the circumstances of her death?"

"She went into the woods to confront a local teenager, because she didn't like him playing loud music there. He had a gun and shot her. Then he turned the gun on himself."

"That's one version, but if you read the newspaper stories about the shootings and the police report, which I was able to obtain, you'll see there are questions about what really happened. Here, have a look." He gave her a manila envelope.

Her hands trembled as she removed a sheaf of papers. They were copies of articles about the murder/suicide from *The New York Times*, *The Boston Globe*, and *The Berkshire Eagle*, as well as the police report. A name had been highlighted in yellow on several pages: Earl Barker.

She shoved the papers back at him. "I don't need to look at these. I already know all about it."

"Including the fact that the boy's friend claimed they didn't steal the gun, that when he left, the alleged shooter was unarmed?"

"Yes!"

"What does that suggest to you?"

"Well, obviously, that someone else could have brought the gun to the scene."

"Right. And that someone could have been Earl Barker."

"That's what you'd like me to believe, isn't it? Well, what if I don't?"

"Don't or won't? Think about it, Kathryn. He was her lover, and according to what I've heard they had a stormy relationship."

"So? He had an alibi."

"Uh-huh. Drinking with his buddies at that bar."

Hillbillies protect their own. They've got a code so strict that . . .

"Stop it! Why are you doing this?"

"I care about you, Kathryn, and I'd hate to see anything happen to you."

"It won't."

"Are you sure?"

"Why wouldn't I be?"

"Because I've heard things . . . I'm not the only one who's concerned about you. Your friends here are worried, too."

"Who have you been talking to?"

"Friends of yours."

She leaned forward, thrusting her face at him. "Who, dammit!"

Startled, he leaned away. "I've never seen you like this before."

"Like what?"

"Angry and defensive. As if you're afraid to face the truth."

Like Emily, Kathryn realized with a jolt. She was behaving just like Emily when she'd confronted Emily about the letters. She couldn't help it. Alan's words struck at the core of her fear and suspicion. And beyond, with his mention that friends of hers here were worried about her. That really frightened her, but she didn't want him to know. In a calmer voice, she said, "I'd just like to know who these concerned friends are."

"I'd rather not say."

"Why?"

"Because I promised this . . . uh . . . person our conversation would be strictly confidential."

"Oh, c'mon. This isn't about a client of yours, but someone who's been making accusations against Earl."

Alan frowned and bit his lip. "All right, if you must know . . . it was his ex-wife."

Kathryn could hardly believe her ears. "Millie called you!"

"Yes, she thought I should know his jealousy has reached the point where she's worried about you."

"When did she call?"

"A few days ago. I wrestled with whether to contact you. Decided that before I did anything, I should look into the shootings. What I found, combined with what his ex-wife told me, convinced me I needed to speak with you in person."

"Why didn't Millie tell me this to my face?"

"You'll have to ask her. I've said what I came to say, and it hasn't been easy. I knew you'd think I was trying to win you back by raising suspicions about your lover. I do want you back. But your welfare is more important to me than anything else. If you've made a mistake by getting involved with Earl Barker, I hope you won't be too stubborn to admit it and move on. It really *is* better to be safe than sorry, Kathryn." He held her gaze for a long moment then said, "And there I rest my case." He stood, reached for the manila envelope and held it out to her. "You're sure you don't want this?"

"Yes."

He put the envelope back in his briefcase and placed some bills on the table. "Take care of yourself."

"You, too."

He turned to go, but almost immediately turned back. Removing a small brightly wrapped package from his briefcase, he tossed it on the table and left in a hurry.

For a brief moment, she was tempted to follow him and admit she *was* worried about what might happen between her and Earl. She understood now why Marguerite had been reluctant to leave her husband for Clyde. Jared Cutter had represented wealth, social position, and most important of all, security. Clyde, on the other hand, was a wild card with nothing sure about him except his passion for her. She understood also why even a free and apparently fearless spirit like Diana had held onto the familiar cushion of Gordon instead of casting her lot with wild card Earl. Still, she resisted the urge to run after Alan.

Her attention returned to the package. What did it contain? Might as well open it and see. Inside was a picture frame made by gluing four popsicle sticks together. It was decorated with glitter and sequins, interspersed with globs of dried, white glue, clearly the work of a child's hands. Inside the frame, Sophie stared back at her: a lost lamb with her thick blonde curls, wide, staring blue eyes, and wistful smile. Kathryn felt an awful pang. Poor Sophie: abandoned by her mother, and now by another fickle adult.

Tears came into her eyes. For Sophie, for herself? She wiped them away and glanced quickly around, wondering if anyone had observed the little drama between her and Alan. The elderly couple had left, and the bartender's attention was focused, not on her, but on something in the farthest of three windows before her. The windows were curtained with a sheer white material that let in light, but also allowed anyone outside to peer in. When she stared at the third window, she caught a blur of motion, as if someone had been doing just that. The face—if that's what it was—disappeared, and she was alone with the bartender in a room that began to feel oppressive.

Intent on Alan and what he had to say, she'd paid little heed to her surroundings. Now that she did, she was aware of the stale air, the low ceiling with exposed pipes that seemed to press down on her, and most of all, the redness of everything. Red ceiling. Red walls. Worn red-flowered carpet. Red bar. It wasn't a bright red, but the faded red of Earl's truck, Diana's study, and Millie's tomato soup. Red: the color of love but also of madness and bloody death. Her throat went dry and she had trouble breathing.

She fled the pub, and once outside, gulped in the chill, fresh air. A glance at her watch told her it was three p.m. It would take at least a half hour to get back to New Nottingham. She had two hours to make a perfect pie and have it ready by five-thirty when she and Earl were due for dinner at his parents. She wasn't sure that was enough time. Not if she made a mistake and had to start over again. There was a small market on Elm Street. Maybe she should buy a pie to have on hand for "insurance." Luck was on her side: she spotted a few, obviously homemade pies for sale by the counter.

Leaving the market with an apple pie, she noticed a tall, lanky figure hurrying up the street. He wore jeans, a black tee shirt, and a gray wool cap. "Pete?" she called after him. He didn't stop or turn around, but darted into an alley out of view. It probably wasn't Pete, but someone who resembled him. After all, what would Pete be doing in Stockbridge on a Sunday afternoon?

Chapter 62

"You were awfully quiet tonight at dinner," Earl said.

So he'd noticed. She had tried to join in the conversation about the land and the un-built house, but obviously she hadn't succeeded. Not while her mind was consumed by doubts and fears.

She'd arrived home to find him already there. He was so worn out he'd decided to quit early. "Thought you'd be in the kitchen, putting finishing touches on the pie," he said.

"I got cold feet and bought one."

"Doesn't look store-bought," he commented when she showed it to him.

"It's not. I heard about this woman who bakes pies and sells them from her house."

"Oh? Who's that?"

"Um . . . Mi—Mandy—Mandy Russell." In her haste to come up with a name, she gave him a mangled version of Millie and Brandy Russo. She was a terrible liar and held her breath, waiting for him to call her on it.

He frowned a moment, then said, "Never heard of her. But you're a funny one, going out and buying a pie instead of making one yourself. It doesn't have to be perfect. My folks would be happy with anything you baked. They like you, Star."

But would they still like her if they knew she'd met with her old boyfriend? Would he? "Just don't do anything to make him jealous," Millie had said. And now she had. If Earl had been mad when he suspected her of wearing Alan's ring, he'd be even madder if he found out she'd actually seen Alan. And if he became seriously angry, what would he do? What did Millie know that she didn't?

Those questions had rattled around in her brain during dinner with his parents. Until she had answers, she couldn't rest easy. Right now, he was looking at her, as if he expected an explanation for her silence. "Guess I'm just tired," she said. "Working myself up into a state over a silly pie."

"Sure, that's all?"

"What else could there be?"

"I don't know. I thought maybe . . ."

"What?" she asked, half dreading his answer.

"You're not so keen on the house and land deal, on our having a place of our own." His blue eyes bore into her.

"I am, but . . ." She looked away.

"What?" He grabbed her by the chin, forcing her to look at him. *Oh god, how can I ever bring myself to tell him the truth?* "I don't like the idea of you driving yourself so hard," she said finally, hating herself for the lie.

"I'll be okay," he said in a more relaxed tone. "I may be over forty, but that doesn't mean I don't have plenty of steam left." His hand traveled from her chin, down to her breasts, caressing them.

She could feel herself yielding, but on the verge of surrender she pulled back. "If you're getting up early again, maybe we should go to bed."

"Sounds like a plan." He rose and led her upstairs. In the bedroom he started undressing her, but she stopped him. "I need to use the bathroom."

He plopped down on the bed and grinned. "I'll be waiting."

She stayed in the bathroom longer than necessary. When she came out, he was fast asleep. She gazed at him with a mixture of regret and relief. Regret because they would not make love tonight, relief for the same reason. If she wasn't sure about staying with him, maybe she better start weaning herself from him physically and emotionally. It wouldn't be easy. She'd felt wedded to him from the moment they first made love. Had it been like this for Millie? For Diana? Diana whom he might have . . . No! She wouldn't think about that now. She glanced at the dresser, where a wistful

Marguerite stared back at her, almost as if she understood Kathryn's turmoil.

Her gaze returned to the man lying before her, wearing nothing but his boxer shorts. His jeans and shirt lay in a crumpled pile near the foot of the bed. She picked up the shirt and draped it over a nearby chair, but as she grabbed the jeans, loose change fell from a pocket and clinked to the floor. He stirred. She stopped dead in her tracks, holding her breath lest he awaken. When he lay still again, she put the jeans on the chair with the shirt, and the loose change on the dresser top, where he would be sure to find it. Glancing back at him, her eyes settled on his legs. Even with his body in repose, she was aware of the knots of muscle in his calves and thighs. There was a bruise on his left thigh just above the knee. Bluish in the center, it was pale yellow around the rim, a wan winter sun forcing its way through the clouds. She wondered briefly when this injury had occurred.

Her gaze traveled down to his feet. He had removed his boots, but his socks were still on. She noticed that one was black, the other brown. In his hurry to get off to the work this morning, he probably hadn't noticed. Or he had and didn't care. She doubted Millie with her passion for order would have let him out the door with mismatched socks. She would have made sure his socks were arranged in neatly folded matching pairs, would have been dismayed to find him thus. Yet to her just then, the discovery of mismatched socks made Earl seem human and ordinary in a way that was comforting and endearing, as if a man who wore mismatched socks couldn't also be a murderer. As if one thing canceled out the other. Which was ridiculous.

Still . . .

She pulled off the socks and studied his bare feet. They were large and callused from years of rubbing against hard leather boots, with splayed toes and ragged-edged toenails that could use a trimming. Work feet joined to work legs.

She examined his upper body. Alan's chest was covered with a layer of dark hair, dense as a sweater, but Earl's had only a sprinkling of reddish brown hair that rippled with the rise and fall of his breath. His arms and shoulders contained more knotted muscles, and coiled on one of the knots was the snake tattoo, now as familiar and benign to her as a blemish on her own body. Once she'd thought the tattoo hideous. Odd how her perception of this and other things about him had changed.

Naked except for his boxer shorts, he looked vulnerable. The fact that he was sleeping so soundly gave her a certain power over him. She could do anything she wanted: tickle his toes, cut off his hair like Delilah did to Samson . . . or slip away and go someplace where he'd never find her?

But she couldn't leave him like this. She covered him with the extra blanket that was folded at the foot of the bed, pulling the soft end up around his chin. She felt tender toward this man who looked so innocent and peaceful. She slipped under the covers beside him, nestling her cheek in the fine hairs on his chest, rocked by his rhythmic breathing, soothed by his slow, steady heartbeat, as when he'd carried her down the hill from the family graveyard, away from the rattler and harm.

Then to her surprise, his arm curled protectively around her. *He was awake, dammit!* She glanced at his face and saw that his mouth was curved in a smile. His eyes were shut tight, though. Maybe he was still asleep. Maybe her waking dream had become his unconscious one. To test this theory, she removed his arm and rolled away from him. When nothing happened, she felt a keen, double-edged disappointment—at herself for not moving more than a few inches away while she had the chance, but also at him for not pursuing her even this short distance, even in sleep.

Chapter 63

When Kathryn awoke the next morning, sunlight streamed in and Earl was long gone. Gone to do his regular job, then to work clearing the land where they were supposed to live happily ever after. Last night she'd considered leaving, but in the end she couldn't tear herself away. How could he be a murderer, this man who wore mismatched socks, who knew her innermost secrets, and aroused her deepest passion? Yet she knew he still could have killed Diana. While that possibility existed, she could never feel safe with him. How to replace possibility with near certainty—one way or the other?

The answer was Millie. She had to find out why Millie now believed she was in danger. She called Millie at the post office only to be told by a woman who was filling in for her that Millie's father was seriously ill, and she'd gone to New York State to be with her parents. The woman didn't know when Millie would return. Kathryn decided not to ask for a number where Millie could be reached. This wasn't the time to approach her with questions about Earl. She'd just have to wait. Still, she would have given anything to know what Millie knew that she didn't.

She went out on the patio and tried to relax, but for once, the peacefulness of the scene failed to calm her. The day stretched before her, a gaping hole she needed to fill. She drove into Great Barrington for her usual vigil by Emily's hospital bed. Then she had lunch at a café in town, and made use of its Wi-Fi to check her e-mail and search the Internet for the same newspaper stories about the shootings she'd refused to take from Alan yesterday. She skimmed a couple of articles without finding anything conclusive. The police report might have been more helpful. She regretted refusing Alan's packet of information, but it was too late now. Finally, when the clink of glasses and clatter of tableware told her the tables were being set for dinner, she shut down her computer and left.

She'd no sooner entered the house than she sensed something was wrong. It was the same feeling she'd had when she returned to find the stuffed snake on the staircase. But if someone had indeed been here and left something nasty behind, it wasn't immediately obvious. At least not in the living room or the kitchen. She went into the dining room and there on the table lay two pictures. She stopped in her tracks, heart pounding. She had to force herself to take a closer look.

One was a copy of the photo Suzy had taken of Earl feeding her a piece of cake at the anniversary party. Except that now pointy ears sprouted from her head, a long snout replaced her open mouth, and she had a bushy tail. The word "VIXEN?!" was written in large block letters at the top of the photo and repeated on the top of the second picture. It showed her with Alan at the Lion's Den. Again, she appeared in the guise of a fox, but there was also a message written with the same black marker pen used for the drawings:

"Give you a chance to explain before I show my boy. Meet me at the ruins of the old mill at four. Roy."

Her throat seized. She swallowed hard. The grotesque images reminded her of Diana's defaced wedding picture. Had Roy been responsible for that, too? If she still had the wedding picture, she could have compared them, but it had disappeared from the attic with Gordon. A more important question was how Roy had gotten the photo of her and Alan. Could he have followed her to Stockbridge or just happened to be there, seen her go into the Lion's Den, and become suspicious? Neither scenario seemed likely. Yet someone had taken the photo. She remembered the blurred face in the window, and afterward on the side street, the glimpse of a teenager.

Pete? He'd been her friend in the beginning, but how did he feel about her now that she was involved with his father? Every time she'd been around him lately, he seemed ill at ease, hardly speaking to her, barely meeting her eyes, always finding an excuse to leave as soon as possible. He might resent her being with Earl, because didn't most kids of divorced parents secretly wish their mom and dad would get back together? Pete could have hoped Millie and Earl would reunite after Diana's death, but then she'd come along and wrecked that dream. If he was angry at her, he must have been angry at Diana also. Enough to . . .? Impossible. He'd been ten when she was killed.

She needed to talk to him, have the conversation they probably should have had when she and Earl first got together. She tried his home in case he was back from school. The machine picked up, so she left a message.

She could only guess why Pete had gone to his grandfather instead of Earl with the photo. Maybe he was afraid his dad would be angry at him for spying on her. But then again, Roy could have put Pete up to the spying. Roy knew Earl was worried she might still be in contact with her old boyfriend. Perhaps he wanted to see whether there was any truth to it. And now that it appeared to be so, Roy was clearly mad at her. He wouldn't have called her "vixen," his nickname for Diana, if he weren't. But not so mad that he wasn't willing to hear her side of the story. Something Earl might be incapable of. At the anniversary party, Millie had said it was like Earl to shoot first and ask questions later. Roy, however, had asked her directly where the ring had come from. He'd wanted them to patch things up. Had been on her side then. Maybe he would be again, if he believed her reason for meeting Alan. He had, after all, written "vixen" with a question mark. Perhaps it was a good thing he wanted to meet with her.

But why the mill ruins? She supposed it was because there could be other family members at his house, while at hers, Earl was likely to show up. Then too, Roy might have ruled out meeting at a public place on the off chance someone would eavesdrop. The ruins, on the other hand, were far enough out of the way to give them complete privacy. And Roy probably knew she'd been there. Still, she wasn't confident she could find the spot as readily as she had with Alan. Well, she'd just have to do her best.

Kathryn checked her watch. It was already after four. Surely, Roy would wait, but not forever. She shoved her feet into hiking boots, grabbed the daypack with a flashlight, headed out the door, and then stopped.

Omigod! She'd left the incriminating photos on the dining room table. She rushed back inside, took a last look at them and shuddered. The images drawn in thick black marker pen were so ugly. Again, she thought of Diana's defaced wedding picture and also of the marred inscription on Marguerite's original gravestone. An intense hatred had produced those defilements and now these. She could almost see the clenched fist holding the pen to make the drawings.

But she was letting her imagination run away with her. Roy didn't hate her; he just wanted to clear the air. Quickly stuffing the photos under the cushion of a dining room chair, she flew from the house.

Chapter 64

Kathryn sprinted to the break in the trees that marked the beginning of Gordon's road. She climbed over fallen trees and pushed back brush until the way cleared, and she followed a leaf-strewn path, pock-marked by hunters' boots. Descending the slope, she crossed the rocky stream bed and scrambled up the other side.

She stopped a moment to catch her breath then forged ahead. At this time of year, the light would be gone soon, and she didn't want to be alone in the woods at night. Dark clouds were rolling in from the west. In the gathering gloom, everything looked different. Even with the flashlight she'd brought, she'd have trouble finding her way home. But why worry about that? She could return with Roy.

Through an opening in the trees, she caught a glimpse of the early rising moon. Ordinarily the sight would have heartened her. Not tonight. It was neither a thin, lovely crescent nor a big, bright full moon, but something in between. Gibbous. An ugly name for an ugly, misshapen moon. The visible part stuck out like a woman's pregnant belly. Like Sis's belly before Garth shot himself and she lost her child.

She had to reach the ruins, do her explaining to Roy, and get out fast. To her enormous relief, she spotted the dried up stream bed and plunged down, heedless of the loose stones that made her slip, slide, and nearly fall. Ahead she heard the brook burbling into Leech Swamp. Almost there!

In the rapidly fading light, the swamp seemed eerier than she remembered. The brown hillocks became burial mounds, the dead tree trunks, ghosts rising from the thin layer of ice that now covered the water. Not a place to linger, even if she hadn't been in such a rush. She escaped into the shelter of the forest, glad she was headed to where a living person waited, instead of a specter.

Picturesque in the daylight, the ruins were forbidding in the dimness. As if some monster lurked within those dark, moss-covered piles of stone. And where was Roy? She'd expected to find him waiting in front of the twin pillars. Had he given up and gone home? "Roy?" she called. No answer. Had she come for nothing? Would she ever find her way back? She should have left something to mark the path. Roy *had* to be here; he couldn't have abandoned her. "Roy?" she called again. Still no answer. She wanted to cry with sheer frustration.

A light suddenly flicked on in the maze of roofless underground storerooms to one side of the pillars. Thank god!

*****

Earl put down the chain saw. His back ached and it was getting dark. Time to quit. The work was addictive, though. He'd just cut down one more bush, one more pine tree, then he'd stop.

He hefted the saw and began, its dull whine reaching him through his ear protectors. He welcomed the noise and exertion because they kept his mind off Kathryn. He hoped that if he gave her a lot of loving, built her a house, and made a baby with her, he could hold her fast. Yet already he felt her slipping away.

The bush fell to the ground. One down, one to go. Maybe he should stop while he was ahead, while he still had the energy to get down the hill, shower and change, have dinner and make love to Kathryn. Last night he hadn't and that bothered him. Maybe she was right to worry he was driving himself too hard. If he didn't have the strength to give her what he thought she wanted at the end of the day, he was in trouble.

The physical connection was important to him, too. Had been ever since that afternoon on the patio when she called him *kane* and touched the snake tattoo on his arm. Then, he'd felt the first, faint stirring of an emotion he sensed could grow into love. Having been burned once, he'd tried his damnedest to keep away from the fire. But it had caught up with him the day he snatched her from harm's way and carried her down the hill from the cemetery. He felt a tenderness toward her he'd never experienced with any other woman. Not with Mill. They'd been too young and too hot for each other. Not with Diana either. Their passion had a ferociousness that was nothing like the aching sweetness of his love for Kathryn. The mere thought of losing that sweetness drove him wild.

Glancing upward, he saw the rising moon. It wasn't a full moon or a crescent, but some phase in between. He couldn't remember the name. Didn't matter. What mattered was how it looked: the side that was visible, beautiful and rounded, the way Kathryn's belly would look when she was carrying their child.

He wished he was holding her in his arms now instead of this frigging chain saw. But they needed a place of their own, and if he didn't get the land cleared, they wouldn't have it.

Earl walked over to the pine he'd decided to take down. The tree loomed above him, taller than it had appeared from a distance, its shadow adding to the growing darkness. He better put on his headlamp before he began cutting. Its band didn't fit comfortably around his head while he wore ear protectors and protective glasses. He tossed both aside and turned on the light. Now the tree trunk was clearly visible.

The saw roared to life. Without his ear protectors, the noise was deafening. The saw felt heavier, too, probably because he was tired. Heavier and more difficult to control, almost as if it had a mind of its own.

He wrestled the saw to the tree trunk and started cutting. Suddenly the blade hit a knot, bounced back, and smashed into the tree again. A shard of wood flew into his face. Earl closed his eyes and dropped the saw. It sputtered to the ground and shut off. He felt a searing pain near his left eye. When he tried to open it, blood blinded him. His fingers fumbled in the sticky mess, searching for the injury. The chunk of wood had created a gash dangerously close to his eye. His vision remained intact, though. Thank heaven for that! He couldn't afford to wind up blinded like Garth, or his great-great-uncle, Clyde. Clyde who'd regained consciousness only to find himself sightless, his lover dead and gone. Earl shivered. He needed to get back to

293

Kathryn and reassure himself that she was all right, that *they* were all right.

Stanching the blood with his handkerchief, he hoisted the chain saw onto his shoulder, and started downhill. He hadn't gone far when he stumbled on a rock, lost his balance and fell, landing facedown. Dirt and pine needles ground into his wound. It stung like hell. With difficulty, he raised his head and saw a pinprick of light winking low on the horizon. The evening star. His Star summoning him down from the mountain top.

Earl wanted to cry with joy when he saw the light in the trailer. She must have come to wait for him. He ran the last few yards and threw open the door—not to Kathryn but a worried Pete.

"What's up, son?"

"I—what happened, Dad?"

"Had a little accident. I'll just—" He started toward the sink, but Pete caught him by the arm. "I gotta talk to you—now!"

Chapter 65

"So you're here after all, Roy," Kathryn called. "C'mon up and we can talk." No answer. The light flicked off abruptly. She squinted into the gloom. What was going on? Was he teasing her like Earl at the boat ramp when he'd switched his lighter on and off? They both had the joker gene. "Quit playing games and show yourself."

Silence. Moonlight filtering through the trees provided scant illumination— not enough to locate Roy in the dark recesses of the labyrinth. She got out her flashlight and trained it downward. Suddenly it went out. She jiggled the flashlight, trying to get it to work. Nothing. Damn!

Kathryn scowled into the murky, sunken rooms. And saw Roy's light! On, off, on again, as if he were winking at her. She still couldn't see him, but the light was now directed at the steps leading down into the storerooms. He wanted her to come to him. "All right, have it your way," she groused, mentally cursing herself for a fool. This was crazy.

She started cautiously down the steps, one hand pressed against the cold, mossy stone wall beside them to steady herself, following the trail of light. When she was almost to the bottom, it suddenly went out, she missed a step, and tumbled to the ground.

She flung her arms out to break her fall, glad she landed on a pile of leaves rather than a hard surface. Still, she was annoyed that Roy had chosen that moment to extinguish his light. But maybe it wasn't intentional, maybe his flashlight was dead, too. She was relieved when it came on again. It flashed at her from the opening of a nearby room, vanished, and then flashed a second time. Again, he seemed to be signaling to her. He certainly wasn't making this easy.

Levering herself up, she groped toward the light. Her feet crunched on leaves, weeds swiped at her legs and rocks got in her way. A beating of wings erupted overhead. A bird disturbed from its nest? More likely departing bats. She flinched at the thought of an inky black creature flying at her. She was tempted to flee then and there. Instead, she followed Roy's flashlight deeper and deeper into the maze. "Hey, Roy," she protested, "can't you stay in one place?"

Silence. The light went out, and came back on. She chased it into another room. And found it abandoned on the ground.

The next instant, everything went black. Scratchy wool enveloped her from behind. A scream caught in her throat. Panic ripped through her. A rope was wound and cinched around her forearms. Hands spun her like a top until, dizzy and nauseous, she crashed into a wall.

"Roy, what . . .?" she groaned.

"Not Roy," a woman's voice rasped.

Millie! A deep chill shot through Kathryn. "What're you doing here? Where's Roy?"

"He couldn't make it, doesn't even know you're here."

Kathryn's heart pitched against her rib cage. *Dear God.* She'd walked straight into a trap. Millie had gotten Pete to spy on her and take the photo. Then Millie had written the note and made the drawings, portraying Kathryn as a fox so she'd think Roy was responsible. Millie had probably defaced Diana's wedding picture, too. And lured her into the woods and . . .

"You killed Diana."

"She was a filthy, home-wrecking bitch!"

"And Brian."

"Didn't mean to," Millie said with a twinge of regret. "But if I let him live, I'd have spent the rest of my life in jail. Can you imagine what that would do? My boys need me. The whole community needs me. Without me, the village would fall apart. But nobody was going to miss Brian."

Kathryn was about to point out that Brandy still grieved for her son, but stopped. She'd only anger Millie more. Best to agree with her. "That's right, you're a helper."

Millie was silent a moment then she laughed. "Want a last look at your old friend? Okay, I'll cut slits. Better hold still. Don't want to hurt you . . . just yet."

Just yet. Fear gripped Kathryn like a vise. A sharp object slashed the blanket. She shut her eyes tight, sucking in her breath as it grazed her eyebrow.

"There! Did it with only a teeny nick," Millie said. "You can open your eyes."

Millie had gotten her flashlight back. It cast weird shadows up into her face. Kathryn recoiled. The perky, former cheerleader was now a demon with lank hair, hollow eyes and bared teeth.

"Earl belongs with me!" Millie cried. "Always has. Always will. With you outta the way, he'll come back to me." She brandished her weapon—a hunting knife with a long, curved, serrated blade.

Kathryn swallowed hard. She was helpless. Unless . . . She bowed her head, feigning defeat. Then, summoning all her strength, she barreled into Millie with such force that Millie fell backward. Carried forward by her own momentum, Kathryn landed on top of her. Millie grunted and twisted violently, trying to dislodge her. Kathryn struggled against the rope holding the blanket around her. During her fall, it had hiked up. She tore off the makeshift hood.

A ray of moonlight glinted on the blade of the knife. It lay on the ground, just out of reach. She grabbed at it but missed. She tried again, muscles strained to the limit, heedless of the roiling motion beneath her. Motion that left her flat on the ground, as Millie slithered out. Kathryn's fingers were about to close on the knife when the sharp heel of a boot stomped on them. Yelping with pain, she sank her teeth into Millie's leg.

"Ahhh!" Millie shrieked. Snatching the knife, she jumped aside. But she'd be back for the kill. Kathryn glanced wildly around. Light from Millie's fallen flashlight revealed a pile of debris in a corner of the room. She hurled herself at it, even as Millie lunged. Kathryn spotted rocks and threw them at Millie. Her supply exhausted, she yanked a large tree branch from the rubble and, just in time, used it to fend off Millie's knife thrusts. Millie was relentless. She found an opening and stabbed Kathryn's leg. A searing pain, so intense Kathryn almost dropped the branch. Recovering, she whacked the knife from Millie's hand, as Millie thrust again.

Millie retrieved it and was about to launch another assault when an angry voice made them both freeze.

Chapter 66

"What the hell's going on?!" Earl stood before them, a cyclops with the single eye of his headlamp blazing in the middle of his forehead. A cyclops with a shotgun. Intent on the struggle with Millie, Kathryn hadn't heard him coming. Neither apparently had Millie. She turned slowly toward him.

"Drop the knife, Mill!"

"No! She's been cheating on you and deserves to be punished. Gotta photo to prove it."

"I've seen that photo and I know how you got it. Pete told me everything. The knife, Mill!" He pointed the shotgun at her.

Millie didn't move.

"Shoot it outta your hand if you don't."

"You wouldn't dare."

Earl fired a warning shot. "Now!"

Millie let the hand with the knife fall to her side. The next instant, she spun around and hurled it at Kathryn. It was a wild throw: the knife whizzed past Kathryn, landing in the rubble behind her. With one swift blow, Earl knocked Millie down and hurried to Kathryn.

"Omigod! You're hurt," he cried when he saw the blood gushing from her leg.

"But you—what happened to you?" Up close, she could see his face was caked with blood, dirt, and pine needles.

"Never mind. Gonna take care of your wound, then I'll get you outta here." He put down the shotgun, while he tore off his shirt, made a tourniquet and tied it tightly around her leg. "If you're able to walk, you can lean on me. Otherwise—"

"Stay right where you are," Millie ordered.

Earl whipped around to face her, barricading Kathryn with his body. She craned her neck around him. His headlamp illuminated Millie, feet planted apart, aiming the shotgun at them.

"Give me that." Earl held out a hand.

"No!" Millie shrieked, backing away.

Earl strode toward her. "Give me the gun, Mill."

"Shoot you dead before I do!"

Kathryn's heart stopped. Millie was just crazy enough to kill the man she loved. Yet Earl went right on walking toward her retreating figure. Advance, retreat, advance, retreat. As if they were locked in a dance. A dance that would end with the blast of a shotgun.

She had to distract Millie long enough for Earl to seize the upper hand. If she threw rocks or the knife at Millie —No. Earl was in the line of fire. Only one thing to do. She was the person Millie wanted to kill.

Adrenaline surged through her, overriding the pain in her leg. Her heart pumped furiously. Assuming a runner's crouch, she counted to three and took off with a yell.

Millie whirled toward her and fired. Too late, too high. Kathryn scrambled into the shadows, skidded to a stop, and turned.

Two figures, ghostly in the moonlight. A struggle, caught in awful strobe-like flashes from Earl's headlamp.

His hands on the barrel, forcing it skyward.

Her booted foot kicking him in the shins.

Grunting.

Millie wrenching the gun downward.

Slamming her knee into his groin.

An animal-like howl.

No!

The light dimmed. Clouds swarmed across the moon like giant rats. Darkness except for the headlamp. Twisted in the struggle, it now pointed away from the battling figures. Kathryn groped toward them, desperate to do something.

BOOM! The noise shattered her eardrums. Its force lifted her from the ground. She landed on her feet, heart in overdrive. Who was shot? Earl?

A moan, then a deep sigh. The rats abandoned the moon. Earl knelt beside Millie, cradling her in his arms. A wound blossomed on her chest like a large, bright crimson flower. He stroked her hair, murmured words of comfort. *Oh, dear God!* Kathryn took a step toward them, but stopped.

She would not—could not—intrude on the dying woman and the man she'd never stopped loving.

Chapter 67

Kathryn eased into a lounge chair on the patio. Hard to believe only a little more than two months ago, she'd rested here after driving from Boston and unpacking. So much had happened in that short period. Now, in early January she wore a down coat and a hat against the cold. She shifted in the chair, careful not to jar the stab wound in her leg. It was starting to heal, but it would probably leave a scar. The nightmares and flashbacks were another matter; she didn't expect them to go away anytime soon.

The revelation that Millie had shot Diana and Brian and tried to kill Kathryn before dying violently had sent shock waves through the village. Having watched his mother become crazed with jealousy, Pete was taking her death especially hard. Earl had moved back into the white house to be with him, though Earl was badly shaken himself.

She was badly shaken, too. Millie had put up such a good front she'd never dreamed Millie had killed Diana and Brian, or that she was in danger. Only in hindsight did she realize there'd been hints of trouble: the damaged mail at the post office after her visit to the boat ramp with Earl; Norm St. Clair comparing Millie to a hummingbird—pretty on the outside but downright nasty when defending its territory; Millie's "friendly" advice to steer clear of Earl, and finally, her approaching Alan with her fears for Kathryn instead of Kathryn herself.

Another big reason Kathryn had never suspected Millie was that Millie didn't belong in the story that had become so compelling to her: the romantic triangle involving Marguerite, Clyde and Jared Cutter, and later Diana, Earl, and Gordon. One woman and two men. But that wasn't the only kind of love triangle; there was also the triangle with two women and one man. That was Millie's story. Kathryn's mother's, too. Unlike Millie, Kathryn's mother had turned her anger inward. Still, her mother and Millie had something important in common: they'd never stopped loving their men.

Without realizing it, she'd also been involved in a two-women-one-man love triangle. And now that her rival was gone, what lay ahead? She didn't know. So much seemed broken. She wasn't sure what—if anything—could be mended.

The noise of a vehicle on the driveway interrupted these thoughts. Earl's red truck came into view. Her very first sight of that truck had filled her with unease. Then, she hadn't known the driver or his business. Now, she was uneasy for a different reason.

Earl sprang from the cab and strode to the patio. "Mind if I join you?" He gave her a teasing look, but she heard the uncertainty in his voice.

"No," she told him, though she shared his hesitancy.

"They're predicting a big storm in a few days. I'll be exchanging my bulldozer for a plow," he said, settling into a lounge chair beside her.

"That's what you do in the winter?" She was relieved he'd started with the weather.

"Uh-huh. Besides helping clear the town roads, I've got several private customers whose driveways I plow."

"You're not working up at the house site anymore."

It was a statement rather than a question. Nevertheless, he nodded quickly and looked away. They fell silent, gazing at the pond, still and serene with a glaze of ice. "I wish you weren't leaving," he said after a few moments.

So much for small talk. But then she'd suspected this was coming. "I told my boss I'd return to work after the first of the year. That was always the plan." *God, she hoped she was doing the right thing.* "And I'll be back on weekends." She did her best to sound upbeat, but he wasn't fooled.

"Will you?" His eyes searched her face. "I wouldn't be surprised if you never came back."

"Don't." She raised a hand to silence him.

He waved it away, his expression somber. "Hear me out. I've said it before, but I gotta say it again. Most of this is my fault, and I'm truly sorry. I should've realized what Mill was up to and put a stop to it."

"I was wrong about her, too. Everybody was."

"Yes, but I'd already been through something similar with Mill. She spied on Diana and me and badmouthed each of us to the other. Diana laughed at Mill, but I took her seriously when she insisted Diana would tire of me and return to Gordon. Because in my heart of hearts I didn't believe I deserved her. I was just this hillbilly and she was way above me."

"Like Marguerite was to Clyde?"

"Yup. I did things that made Diana mad and drove us apart. You'd think I'd have learned my lesson. But when Mill started in on you, I'm ashamed to admit I started doubting you. It never occurred to me that Mill had shot Diana and would try to kill you. If Pete hadn't come to the trailer that night . . ."

"Thank heaven for Pete!"

"For Amore, also." He referred to the cat's leap onto the dining room chair, which had dislodged the cushion, revealing the photographs and the note from "Roy" asking her to meet him at the ruins.

"Those were lucky breaks," she agreed. "But like you, I didn't believe Millie was capable of violence. On the contrary, she almost had me—" She broke off, unwilling to finish the sentence.

He must have guessed what she was about to say. "Did you think I'd killed Diana and was going to kill you?"

Her heart thudded. He'd asked the one question she'd hoped to avoid.

His eyes bore into her. "Please. I've got to know."

It was her turn to look away. Then, forcing herself to meet his gaze, she said, "There were times I did."

His fist bounced off the wooden arm of his chair. "I thought so! But I needed to hear it from you. And now that I have . . ." Shaking his head, he rose and paced, his expression so tormented it hurt to look at him.

"I'm sorry."

"*You're* sorry?" He stopped and looked at her incredulously. "I'm the one who should apologize for not trusting you more and letting my goddamn jealousy get the better of me."

"I should've trusted you more, too."

"Maybe," he said with the ghost of a smile. "So where does that leave us?"

Where indeed? She stared into space, her mind a blank. Then, gradually the events of the past two months took shape. She'd lived a dark fairytale with Millie as a murderous shadow villain and two other villains, Garth and Gordon, who were simply mean. An old woman figured in the tale, too. Sometimes Emily seemed like a wicked witch; other times, a good but misguided one. There was also a flawed prince. But if Earl was flawed, so was she: a reluctant princess who'd shed her cloak of aloofness when she'd fallen for him, only to give way to fear and suspicion. And now, what was she going to do? Withdraw in the face of obstacles that in her worst moments appeared insurmountable?

Her eyes focused on the pond. The trees cast long shadows across its icy surface, but the woods no longer frightened her as they once had. She'd looked death in the face and survived. She felt stronger, braver, less likely to succumb to her grandmother's gloom-and-doom, and more determined than ever to embrace life and love like Aunt Kit.

She rose and stood beside Earl. "I don't know what the future holds, but I hope we can work things out."

"You do?" Again, he looked at her incredulously.

"Yes, Kane." She stroked the snake tattoo on his arm. "What about you?"

"Yeah," he said in his husky, crooner's voice.

His kiss was long and tender, a reminder that while grudges ran deep in these hills, so did love.

About the Author

An award-winning author of books about American history and biographies, Leslie Wheeler has written three Miranda Lewis "living history" mysteries: *Murder at Plimoth Plantation*, *Murder at Gettysburg*, and *Murder at Spouters Point*. Her mystery short stories have appeared in various anthologies including *Day of the Dark, Stories of Eclipse*, and those published by Level Best Books, where she was a co-editor/co-publisher for six years. A member of Mystery Writers of America, and Sisters in Crime, she is Speakers Bureau Coordinator for the New England Chapter of SinC. Leslie divides her time between Cambridge, Massachusetts, and the Berkshires, where she does much of her writing in a house overlooking a pond.

CPSIA information can be obtained
at www.ICGtesting.com
Printed in the USA
LVOW10s2203200218

567343LV00001B/20/P